JULIE ELLIS

A *Sacred Obligation*

HarperCollins*Publishers*

HarperCollins*Publishers*
77–85 Fulham Palace Road,
Hammersmith, London W6 8JB

www.fireandwater.com

This paperback edition 2001

1 3 5 7 9 8 6 4 2

First published in Great Britain by
HarperCollins*Publishers* 2000

ISBN 0 00 651347 6

Set in Sabon

Printed and bound in Great Britain by
Omnia Books Limited, Glasgow

For my longtime dear friends,
Florence and Ed Fink – with whom
I share cherished memories

Chapter One

The midafternoon April air – this spring of 1970 – was crisp and refreshing. The trees about Manhattan's Columbia campus offered vibrant evidence that spring was arriving. The ever-simmering student unrest, which at intervals erupted into overheated demonstrations, seemed in abeyance today. With her usual swiftness, first-year journalism student Diane Phillips left the campus behind her and strode south on Broadway. Her last class of the day had been exhilarating, had pushed aside for the moment her painful awareness of the date.

Her charcoal pea jacket was buttoned at the throat and enlivened by a bright plaid scarf. Masses of near-black hair tumbled to her shoulders, framed her lovely, expressive face. Her eyes the same glorious blue as the Mediterranean.

Usually Diane exuded an appealing zest for living, and was able to thrust aside the knowledge that she was the child of a Holocaust survivor – and so inexorably tainted. But today was the anniversary of a tragedy that Mom called the worst day of her life, more difficult to accept than the Holocaust years.

Diane debated between walking to her West 84th Street apartment or boarding a bus as usual. Walk, her mind ordered. She was conscious of a tightness in her throat, a knot between her shoulder blades. Each year she dreaded this day. Twenty years ago today – when she was two – her father died in an act of violence. The police – and his father, stepmother and half-sisters – labelled it suicide. His father had said that Kevin was depressed about his marriage.

Each year at the anniversary of his death, Diane's mother

railed at this deception: '*We had a wonderful marriage. Your father would never kill himself. He was murdered – and his murderer walks around free!*' A conviction that forever haunted her.

For a little while – married to Dad – Mom had been happy. For a little while she'd even been able to shed her guilt that she and Uncle Erich had survived the war while the rest of the family had been killed. How ironic that Dad had lived through World War Two – his plane shot down over occupied France – only to come home to die at twenty-eight. He'd been rescued and hidden by the same French family who'd hidden Mom and Uncle Erich when their parents went off to fight with the Resistance and to die a year later. Mom was fourteen, Uncle Erich eleven when France was invaded by the Nazis.

A warm and dedicated teacher, Mom couldn't bring herself to go into her classroom when she was plagued by anguished memories. She'd sit in her room and mourn as though Dad had died yesterday. Usually so gentle and compassionate, this morning Uncle Erich had struggled to hide his impatience with Mom.

'Your father's been dead for twenty years!' he told Diane. 'When is your mother going to let go of her grief? We lost our grandparents, uncles and aunts, cousins to the concentration camps, our parents to Nazi troops in France. She survived that.' His lean face reflected fresh pain, his eyes a perennial sadness. 'Life must go on for the living.'

Now, at the corner of 104th Street and Broadway Diane paused before a dazzling display of golden daffodils that seemed to defy any expression of despair. Mom loved daffodils.

'*Dad and I planted over a hundred daffodil bulbs in the front yard of our little house in Eden when I realized I was pregnant.*' Eden was the small Georgia town where they'd lived after the war. '*I wanted daffodils to be the first flowers you saw.*'

Why couldn't she have some memory of her father? She felt so cheated. He and Mom had shared a storybook love. Beth – who adored watching old movies on TV – said it sounded like 'a forties Hollywood movie with Cary Grant and Irene Dunne.'

Beth – whose mother had spent three years in Bergen-Belsen – had been her best friend since third grade. Right away she and Beth knew that – deep inside – they were different from the others in their class. Each had a mother who was a Holocaust survivor. She remembered even now the day she'd first seen the blue numbers that would remain for ever on Mrs Bertonelli's arm – her number in the camp. But Beth was lucky. Her father's family – second generation Italian-American – was warm and loving. So often Diane wished she was part of a big family like Beth's, especially on holidays. She had only Mom and Uncle Erich. Her father's family – down in Eden, Georgia – wanted no part of her or Mom.

Diane quickened her pace. She'd be arriving home twenty minutes later than usual. She knew Mom was a worrier – like Beth's mother. A hangover, she and Beth understood, from the war years when any moment could bring death. That was why she always tried not to give Mom cause for anxiety.

She doubted that today Mom would notice that she was late. Mom would sit in her bedroom with the blinds closed and turn the pages of the album with photos of the three of them. Dad and Mom, and herself as a baby. They'd had such a little while together. Over and over again Mom would gaze at each snapshot, as though willing those years back once more.

Mom clung to a fantasy that one day – once *she* had her degree in journalism – they'd go together to Eden and track down Dad's murderer.

'*There was no proper police inquiry, though your grandfather had money and influence. We'll go down there and we'll find proof that Kevin was murdered. I'll have no peace until that happens.*'

Diane slowed down at the approach to Cake Masters. Should she pick up three of those cinnamon Danish that Mom liked? Yes. They'd have them, warmed up to delicious stickiness, with coffee before bedtime – a little thing but it might cheer Mom a bit.

The daffodils cradled in one arm, a hand clutching the bakery bag, she turned west on 84th Street, then slowed her steps. What was happening here? She stared at the trio of police cars parked at an angle to block the traffic. She felt an odd sense of unease while she watched the pedestrian gawkers being pushed back by police officers. In front of her apartment building.

Alarm surged through her as she started to hurry. Then, through a gap among the avid spectators, she spied her uncle, ashen-faced and dazed as he talked with a man who appeared to be a detective. She saw the outline of a body lying beneath a dark covering on the sidewalk. She froze in terror. The bunch of daffodils and the bag of Danish fell from her nerveless fingers. With savage strength she pushed her way through the crowd.

'Uncle Erich!' Her voice was shrill. 'Uncle Erich!'

'Oh God, Diane!' He moved towards her in a protective gesture. His eyes swept mutely to the windows of their seventh-floor apartment. Her own eyes followed. One window – in her mother's bedroom – was open as far as possible. 'I went down to buy a quart of milk . . . She seemed all right . . .'

'Oh, Mom!' Diane made a move towards the body on the sidewalk, but her uncle pulled her back.

'Diane, no –'

'Why did I decide to walk? Why didn't I take the bus the way I always do? I would have been here with Mom! She needed me – and I wasn't here!'

Diane moved through the next two days in a haze of unreality, vaguely conscious of what was happening around her, her uncle and Beth always at her side while she tried to cope with her mother's death. A group of her mother's colleagues, several students, Uncle Erich's two close friends – Hans and Joseph – attended the funeral services. Mom had allowed herself no close friends. To be close, to love, was to be in danger of losing.

Only Uncle Erich, Beth and Diane accompanied the body to the cemetery. At the apartment after the funeral Beth's mother and sister took charge of the flow of friends who arrived, served platters of food. In the midst of her grief Diane was conscious of gratitude for Mrs Bertonelli and Fran's efforts.

There was no family – only Uncle Erich and herself. Mom had survived the Holocaust; why hadn't she been able to survive Dad's death? But she knew the answer: Mom couldn't handle the unspoken accusations by his family that Dad's marriage had pushed him into deep depression.

Diane was indignant when, two days after her mother's death, Beth – and then Uncle Erich – reminded her that she must pick up the threads of her life, return for the final five weeks of school.

'Diane, you can't throw away this year of school.' She saw the anxious glance Uncle Erich exchanged with Beth. *How could they talk to her about school when Mom was dead?* And now anger intruded on grief. Did Mom love her so little that she could desert her this way?

'You know how your mom felt about your education.' Beth's determinedly realistic voice brought Diane back to the moment. 'She was so proud that you were going to be a journalist. Don't let her down, Di.'

'Next week,' Diane hedged. To Mom to have a profession was important. It was security in a world without family. 'We have to sit shivah.' The Jewish ritual of mourning.

'You'll go back tomorrow,' Erich said with rare forcefulness. 'That's what your mother would want. God will forgive you for not sitting shivah.'

Knowing sleep would be elusive, Diane said an early good night and went into her bedroom. She reached into a dresser drawer for a fresh nightgown, saw a small white envelope with her mother's tight, neat handwriting that lay atop a pile of nightgowns. She stood immobile, her heart pounding, while she read the words on the front: 'For Diane, my precious baby'.

She ripped it open and withdrew a single white sheet. The paper fluttering between her fingers, she read the few lines written there. A poignant apology for taking her life and a plea that

Diane read the journals hidden in her bedroom closet. 'Read, then destroy them, my darling. Try to understand.'

Trembling, Diane sat at the edge of her bed and reread these words, the last she would ever have from her mom. She trailed her fingers over the writing, as though to caress her mother one final time. She knew about the journals her mother had kept throughout those wartime years in the French farmhouse. Only now was Mom willing to share them.

Fighting for calm Diane went to her mother's room. She walked inside, flipped on a lamp – hearing in the background Uncle Erich in a phone conversation with Hans about the state of the stock market. For an instant she was angry, closed the door against the sound of his voice. But she understood – he was fighting to deal with his grief. Mom always said the stock market was a game with Uncle Erich. His salary as a research chemist allowed only a minor investment, but he enjoyed the diversion. His life consisted of work, the hours with Mom and her, and his two friends who had survived Buchenwald. At forty Uncle Erich – like his friends – seemed twenty years older.

With a sense of unreality, she opened the closet door and reached to the top shelf, as her mother had instructed. She brought down a cluster of notebooks, the kind she recalled using in elementary school. Five of them, she counted as she settled down to read. Each dated. She was holding the most important years of her mother's life in her hands, she thought with fresh anguish.

Most of what she read in the first four books she'd heard from Mom and Uncle Erich. About how their parents had moved from Frankfurt to Paris right after their marriage because their father was eager to study at the Sorbonne. They remained in France, prospered through the years. Mom's father became a teacher, her mother managed a bookstore.

Mom remembered frequent visits to grandparents, aunts and uncles and cousins in Frankfurt. In turn, the Frankfurt family visited them in Paris. Then Hitler came to power and there were no more visits.

'*Mama and Papa urged their parents – and the aunts and uncles and cousins – to leave Frankfurt. Over and over they pleaded with them to leave. But the others refused to believe that Hitler would stay in power. This insanity would pass. And then it was too late – they couldn't leave. They died – every one of them – in the camps.*'

Diane's brain was seared by what her mother had told her about Hitler's invasion of France. Students were given gas masks at school, had frequent air-raid drills – taking refuge in the school basement. Food was scarce. In June 1940 – when Paris was near deserted – German bombers flew over the city. In the middle of the night residents ran to shelters. But there were no bombs. In the morning Parisians began to flee the city. '*Mama said, "Where can we go?"*' Diane remembered her mother saying.

The Germans marched into the city with no opposition. Those who ran away began to come back. There were attacks on German soldiers – and hostages were taken and killed or sent to labour camps.

For French Jews the situation was ominous. They were ordered to use only the last car in the métro, to go shopping only on certain days, when nothing was left. They were not allowed to go to the movies, were required to register their radios. In the métro, posters with violent anti-Semitic slogans were displayed. Everybody knew it was a matter of time before all Jews would be rounded up and shipped to German camps.

Diane remembered her mother's vivid description of how, in the middle of the night, she and Uncle Erich had fled with their parents to the farm where they had gone every summer at vacation time – only hours before Nazi troops began a roundup of Jews. They took a minimum of clothing, but books so that Sophie and Erich could secretly continue their schooling. The owner of the farm was a Resistance leader. '*Not until then did we understand Papa was a member of the Resistance.*'

So often in her growing up years she'd felt guilt at leading such a comfortable life in comparison to the nightmare existence of Mom and Uncle Erich during the war. Mom always stressed they had not suffered the horrors of the concentration camps that Uncle Erich's friends and Beth's mother had endured. But they'd lived in constant terror, never knowing when they might be betrayed by a nearby villager, periodically forced to hide for days in a secret cellar beneath the farmhouse. And after only a few days at the farm they'd said goodbye to their parents – never to see them again. Like many French Resistance fighters their parents died at the hands of the Nazi invaders. Another Resistance member had managed to get word to them.

Diane skimmed the notebooks dealing with the years on the French farm, where her mother had met and grown to love her father. Lingering only over the brief segment that told of her mother and father's marriage by a local judge.

Tonight we took our vows before the judge who'd been part of the rescue team when Kevin's plane was shot down. By day he is a judge, faithful to the Pétain government. By night he is part of the Underground. The marriage is legal. Kevin and I are husband and wife. I never thought I could be so happy in the midst of such horror.

Now Diane opened the last of the notebooks, the one that dealt with the brief years in Eden, Georgia. The traumatic years. Mom's in-laws, newspaper owners, made a public pretence of welcoming her, but, in truth, she was resented. Not only had Kevin taken a foreign bride, but she was Jewish. His father and stepmother made it clear they felt he had disgraced the family.

'I was never welcome in their home. We were seldom invited there. Lloyd Masters would phone and order Dad to come to the house to discuss some business about the newspaper – and Dad would have to join the family at dinner. They were furious when your father told them you'd be raised in your mother's

8

faith. You were Lloyd Masters' only grandchild – and he never held you in his arms. He seldom saw you.'

Diane closed her eyes. In the stillness of the small, neat bedroom she could hear her mother's voice again: *'Kevin was a warm, loving man – everything his father was not. He was completely his mother's child.'*

Diane knew that her father's mother died when he was a baby. His maternal grandmother, whom he had adored, died when he was seven. At the vulnerable age of eight he was shipped off to boarding school, as were his four younger half-sisters when they reached that age. He'd endured a lonely childhood with little family life. Back from the war, he'd wanted no part of the business side of the family newspaper empire.

'Dad wanted to be a journalist,' Mom repeated at frequent intervals. Had that prodded *her* in the same direction? *'He had a journalism degree from the University of Georgia – but his father insisted he be groomed to take over the business in the years ahead. He was the only son – the heir presumptive.'* Diane remembered the contempt in her mother's voice.

Dad's father declared that 'Journalists are a dime a dozen. I can hire all I want. You'll learn to run the business.'

Diane returned to the last of the journals, read through tear-blurred eyes. Mom was so grateful for Dad's efforts to trace what had happened to her Frankfurt family after the war. He'd contacted detectives there, and they'd come up with conclusive proof that the entire family had died in the camps. Only she and Erich had survived. She said Dad had saved her sanity, had been wonderful to Erich.

I'm so happy!

Sophie wrote a few days before tragedy invaded her life again.

Kevin agrees with me. We both love Eden, but this is not a place for us to live. Not a place to raise our precious baby. He's going to tell his father that we're moving to New York

9

City. Kevin's sure he'll be able to find a job on a newspaper up there.

Her mother wrote of the anguished days and nights following her father's death. She wrote how she'd discovered her father-in-law and his attorney were plotting to have her committed to a mental institution.

They're saying I've become unhinged because of Kevin's death. They're going to commit me as mentally unbalanced. They're a powerful, important family. They can do this. I'm leaving tonight with Diane – when no one will be around to stop me. Erich will take care of us.

Diane read the few final entries, which dealt with the painful year before her mother pulled her life together. Then at Erich's insistence she began to study for a degree in education. She would become a teacher. 'My life is on course again. For my precious baby this is important.' But even as a little girl, Diane realized they weren't like other families. It wasn't just that Mom and Uncle Erich had survived the Holocaust. Her father had been murdered.

Cold and trembling, Diane read the last lines scrawled across an otherwise untouched page, dated the twentieth anniversary of Kevin Masters' death.

For your father and me, my darling, make the world know he didn't kill himself. I wasn't a bad wife who drove him to suicide. Find out the truth so we may both rest in peace.

Diane sat motionless, staring at the journal without seeing. Her mind in torment. Mom had truly meant for the two of them to go back to Eden once she had her journalism degree. It had not been just the fantasy that she herself and Uncle Erich had believed. In Mom's mind a journalist – even a fledgeling one – would know how to ask questions, find answers. She heard her mother's voice again, talking with awe about Marguerite Higgins of the *New York Herald Tribune*. Marguerite Higgins and Sergeant Peter Furst of *Stars and Stripes* liberated Dachau, Mom had read somewhere – and that gave special cachet to journalism.

Dad's father was responsible for Mom's death. As much as if he'd pushed her out that window himself. *He* killed Mom. To please Uncle Erich she'd finish this school year. Then she was going down to Eden, Georgia. She must dig up evidence that would make the police reopen the case.

For Mom she must do this.

Chapter Two

The evening was unseasonably sultry for early June. Diane sat in the charming but modest living room of the apartment she had known most of her life – tense but determined not to waver in her just-voiced decision to leave shortly for Eden, Georgia. Despite the air-conditioned coolness invading the room, Erich's face was flushed. Perspiration glistened on his forehead.

'Diane, are you out of your mind?' He stared at her in disbelief. 'What makes you think you can go down there and solve a murder that happened twenty years ago?'

'Nobody's ever tried to solve it.' She struggled for an appearance of calm. 'They accepted the suicide story. Nobody would believe it was murder. But I'll –'

'You'll make a fool of yourself,' he interrupted agitatedly. 'You're a twenty-two-year-old kid who's –'

'Uncle Erich, this is something I have to do!'

'You're not a lawyer. You're not a detective. What can you do?' A pulse pounded in his forehead.

'I have to go down there and try to dig up proof that my father was murdered. Haven't reporters solved murders the police pushed aside years earlier? *It happens*.'

'Your mother wouldn't want you to wreck your life this way!'

'Mom asked me to do this. How can I not try? It was Mom's last wish.'

'Your mother wanted you to stay in school and have a profession! We're not like other people. When I'm gone you'll be alone in the world.' He was terrified at her putting so many miles between them. He and Mom had never truly recovered from that last goodbye to their parents, who had never returned.

She was conscious of a blend of compassion and impatience. Would the Holocaust never be put to rest? Like Uncle Erich himself said, 'Life must go on.'

Erich closed his eyes for a moment, then continued, 'We have no way of knowing if your father's death was murder or suicide.'

'Uncle Erich!' Diane stared at him in shock. 'You never had doubts before when Mom talked about it.'

'What else could I do, knowing the way she felt? I don't know what happened that night. Suicide seems unlikely, but how are we to know what goes on in somebody else's head? Your mother couldn't accept a suicide verdict – she couldn't live with that. I don't know what happened that night. We'll never know, Di.'

'We'll know!' Her eyes were ablaze. Uncle Erich was saying that to dissuade her from going down there. 'I'm coming to it with a fresh approach.' She tried to sound matter-of-fact. 'Nobody'll know who I am. I'm Diane Phillips, not Diane Masters.' As though to reject the Masters family, her mother had resumed her maiden name. Her uncle had legally adopted her so that she, too, would be have the name Phillips on legal records. 'I'll dig.'

'You'll find nothing!' A vein pounded at Erich's temple. 'The police wrote it off as a suicide, closed the case.'

'The police did nothing.' She could hear her mother's anguished voice in much repeated accusations: '*Why didn't the police listen to me? Why didn't they ask questions? Kevin was murdered by someone who mistook him in the dark for his father. His father had dangerous enemies. Why else did he always travel with an armed bodyguard? Why did he keep a loaded gun in a desk drawer in the library, another in his bedside table? He knew there were people who wanted him dead.*' But she knew why the police covered up the murder. That was what Lloyd Masters ordered. Because in some fashion to unmask the murderer would open up ugly secrets.

'I'll follow up any lead, no matter how tiny,' Diane pursued. 'I'll come up with answers.'

'You'll come back to school in September.' Erich was grim. 'You can't mess up your education. Your mother wouldn't want that.'

'I'll take a year off.' She'd take off as long as was necessary. 'I'll have money to live on for a year. And enough to see me through the final year at Columbia.' Mom had left a substantial bank account in trust for her. 'I'll find a job down there . . .' Maybe on the *Eden Herald*.

'You're being foolhardy.' But she saw the glint of defeat in his eyes. He knew she couldn't be dissuaded. *This was a sacred obligation. Mom's last wish. How could she not at least try to prove Mom right*? Erich allowed himself a lengthy sigh. 'When do you plan on leaving?'

'I have plane tickets for the day after tomorrow.' She felt a flicker of relief. No more battling.

'I'll arrange to take the day off and –' he began. Uncle Erich *never* took time off from his job.

'You don't need to do that,' Diane said gently. 'Beth will be able to take the morning off and go with me to the airport. She's piled up vacation time.'

'You be careful. Remember, the Masters family probably still runs that town. You'll hit one dead end after another.' He paused. 'You can't have any memory of Eden. You were just past two when your mother brought you here.'

'I only know what Mom told me.' She fought back tears. 'I'll try for a job on either the *Eden Herald* or the *Eden Evening News*. Nobody will know I'm Kevin Masters' daughter. I'll be a dropout from Columbia School of Journalism, impatient to get into the newspaper field. Uncle Erich, it's something I have to do!'

Diane was too tense to sit in the waiting area while she and Beth watched for the boarding announcement for her flight. They stood at the perimeter, managed an aura of isolation from the milling crowd. Always vivacious, Beth spoke with an almost hysterical gaiety now.

'If I thought I'd have a job on the newspaper when I came back, I'd go down with you.' For the past three months – after seven months on a low-paid job on a so-called glamour magazine – Beth had been an associate editor on the *West Side Guardian*, a newly established weekly magazine of what was called 'the giveaway variety'. An English major, she'd elected to go right out into the job market after earning her BA at Hunter along with Diane. 'Also, I'd be nervous about leaving town right now – when Jack is just beginning to talk serious.'

'Beth, I didn't expect you to go with me.' Diane tried for a smile. They'd always been so close – closer than many sisters. She knew, too, that Mrs Bertonelli was terrified when Beth was away from the city. All these years later Mrs Bertonelli still remembered the day she and her sister were separated from their parents by Nazis at the camp. She and her sister never saw their parents again. Any overnight separation from Beth was traumatic for her mother. 'Mom and Aunt Millie live in a different world now. But part of them still lives in Bergen-Belsen,' Beth had explained to Diane.

Now she said, 'I hate to see you going down there alone.'

'It'll be fine. And how could you leave Jack?'

To appease her mother, Beth had gone out on a blind date with Jack Coleman, who'd be a first-year law student in September. They'd clicked, Beth proclaimed, as though they'd been custom designed for each other.

'Look, I want to know everything that happens down there,' Beth ordered. 'It's kind of an adventure. I don't mean that you're going down there for fun,' she added hastily. 'But we've led such insulated lives.'

Much of the time they almost convinced themselves they were like others in their age group. They studied the same subjects in school, loved the same music, the same movies, wore the same clothes. Yet deep in their subconscious they felt chained to the past. Would they never be free?

'I was born in Eden.' Diane forced herself back to the moment. 'Of course, I don't remember the place – but Mom made it come almost alive for me.' The way she'd made Dad seem alive. 'Every once in a while she'd go to that newsstand in Times Square where you can buy out-of-town newspapers and pick up a copy of the *Eden Herald* or the *Eden Evening News*. Once she showed me a photo of Dad's father and, another time, a photo of two of his sisters at some country club gathering. I felt so weird. There they were – my grandfather and my aunts – but I'd never seen them – except when I was a baby, too young to remember them.' She suppressed a shudder. 'Arriving in Eden will be like walking into a town full of ghosts.'

Diane's flight was announced for boarding. She exchanged a warm embrace with Beth and said a shaky goodbye.

'I'll call you at your hotel tonight.' Beth giggled. 'My phone bill is going to jump up into the stratosphere now. But Tom promises me a raise soon.' After graduation, to her parents' consternation, she'd moved from the family apartment into a studio in the West 80s, close to the Phillipses' apartment. Her older sister, Fran, hadn't left home until her wedding day. 'You've got the brochure from the Chamber of Commerce?' she asked in sudden anxiety.

'I've got it.'

Throughout the flight to Atlanta Diane gazed out the window and fought against panic. She knew her uncle was right: she had no training, no real knowledge of how to handle the task she'd laid out for herself. In a moment of exasperation last night Uncle Erich said she was behaving like the heroine in a bad TV movie.

Her mother's voice invaded her mind: '*Dad had gone over to the family house to talk to his father. His stepmother and sisters were away on a spring vacation. The servants were off for the night. Lloyd Masters claims he walked into the library – along with his lawyer – and found Dad on the floor, a revolver beside him.*' The gun his father kept in a desk drawer in the library. Dad's fingerprints were on the gun. '*But it couldn't have been that way*,' Mom had insisted.

It had unnerved her when Uncle Erich said he didn't know

if Mom was right in her suspicions. Yet instinct told her Mom had not concocted a fantasy about Dad's death because she couldn't bear the thought that he had killed himself. Dad and she were happy, they were preparing to leave for New York and a new life. Why make plans if he was on the verge of despair? *He hadn't killed himself.*

As the plane approached its destination Diane found herself caught up in the view below, a mosaic of sprawling suburban houses set amidst brilliant displays of flowers, of stretches of lush green pine forests and terracotta clay. At bustling Hartsfield Airport, Diane changed for the small commuter plane that would take her to Eden. So small it seemed a toy, she thought with faint unease. The plane was barely aloft before the pilot was preparing for landing.

Mom said that twenty years ago there had been only a primitive airport in Eden. But in twenty years the town had mushroomed in size, with a population of over thirty thousand, double what it had been when Mom lived here. Still, the airport remained extremely small.

Along with the other passengers Diane emerged from the commuter plane, walked through the air-conditioned reception area into the outdoor heat. She climbed into a waiting taxi and gave the driver the name of the hotel where she had made a reservation. A wave of turgid air enveloped her as the cab pulled away from the kerb.

'We *got* air-conditionin',' the driver conceded when she made a hopeful enquiry, 'but the boss don't allow us to use it. If we do, the cab starts stallin' in traffic.'

The airport was four miles from downtown Eden. Modest frame houses lined both sides of the road. Diane was conscious of a pleasing openness, of a landscape that was dotted by young trees. This was a recently developed area, not the farmland Mom remembered.

Diane's heart began to pound as the taxi approached Main Street, which her mother had described in sharp detail. Today there was a seedy air about the business section, though here and there she spied a smart-looking shop. The movie theatre Mom had talked about was boarded up, its years-old posters torn and dirty. The town had changed in twenty years. The Main Street Mom remembered had been replaced.

In the distance a tall, imposing structure rose into view, seeming incongruous in a town of only thirty thousand. Diane leaned forward curiously, guessing at its height in a town where the norm appeared to be two or three storeys. Sixteen floors?

'What is that tall white building?' she asked the driver.

'That's the Masters Building,' the driver told her with possess-ive pride, and she recoiled as though he had slapped her. 'Mr Masters spent a fortune puttin' it up.' He whistled expressively. 'It's the national headquarters for his newspaper chain. He owns a string of newspapers all around the South, but he lives right here in Eden. He don't think he's too good to stay in a town this size.'

'It's impressive.' Diane struggled to sound casual. The build-ing was meant to be a monument to himself, she surmised in distaste. Mom said all Lloyd Masters and his wife cared about was public appearance. '*He considers himself a philanthropist. He only gives when it adds lustre to his name. And his wife is no better.*'

Sooner or later Diane knew she'd come face to face with Dad's father, his stepmother and sisters. It would be rough to hide her feelings, but she could do that. Nobody here in Eden must know she was born Diane Masters.

'That's the Ashley House right ahead,' the driver told her, gesturing towards what appeared to be a four-storey colon-naded, white-stucco mansion that bore a strong resemblance to Tara in the movie of *Gone With the Wind*. 'It's the newest and best hotel here in town.' He glanced at her in his rear-view mirror. 'You plan on stayin' long?'

'If I can get a job.' She was faintly self-conscious now. But weren't people flocking to the South these days in search of a less pressured lifestyle?

'A great-lookin' gal like you won't have no trouble landin' a job. Business is good here in Eden.'

The driver carried her luggage into the elegant air-conditioned lobby, wished her well, managed a final, approving glance at her small, slim figure. A smiling bellhop, exuding Southern politeness, picked up her two valises and escorted her to the registration desk. This isn't real, she thought dizzily. She felt as though she was playing a role in a movie.

A few minutes later, alone in her comfortably furnished room, she sat motionless at the edge of the bed and ordered herself to focus on immediate needs. First, she must find an apartment. Start looking immediately. To job-hunt she'd need a permanent address and a telephone. She needed a job to cover her being here.

She could hear her mother's voice again. '*People are so polite and nice. Living is slow and easy. We would have loved living in Eden except for your grandfather.*' Mom had felt no love for the other members of the family either, Diane remembered; they'd shown only hostility to her. Except for Dad's youngest sister, Gerry. Mom said Gerry was sweet and friendly.

In a burst of restlessness – and a sudden realization that she was hungry – Diane decided to leave the unpacking for later and go into town to find a place to have a late lunch. Out in the street again she felt the heaviness of the summer heat. Nobody walked fast, she noted, heading south to the business district.

She stopped short before a small, inviting restaurant that belied the shabbiness of surrounding shops. Her heart pounding, she read the name splashed across the broad window: The Bird Cage. Mom had talked about coming here with Dad and her for early dinners. '*You were such a good baby – we could go anywhere with you.*'

Captured by a sense of *déjà vu*, she walked into the restaurant, sparsely populated at this off-hour, but Diane surmised that earlier it would have been crowded. She smiled in appreciation of the blast of air conditioning that greeted her and glanced about the room. The cages of exotic birds that Mom had talked about were gone. Only one bird cage, inhabited by a pair of golden canaries, hung from the ceiling. But the atmosphere was warm and charming.

A friendly waitress came over to her table, took her order. She gazed at the grossly overweight, middle-aged, henna-haired woman who sat at the cash register, and tried to envision her twenty years younger. Had she been here when Mom and Dad came in for dinner? Was there a special table that Mom and Dad considered theirs?

Waiting to be served – feeling a poignant closeness to her mother – she reached across to a neighbouring table for a newspaper that had been abandoned. The *Eden Herald*. Lloyd Masters' name, of course, was on the masthead as publisher. Her grandfather. The uncrowned Emperor of Eden. She was conscious of a ferocious desire to dethrone the Emperor.

'He's an evil man underneath that façade of benevolence. But one day somebody will break through that façade, and all the corruption and filth will pour out for the whole world to see. And I'll be so happy, Diane!'

Diane pulled herself out of recall, turned to the real estate section of the *Herald* and studied the listing of available furnished apartments. They were few, but the rents quoted were low compared to those in New York. Determined to be realistic, she dug into her purse and pulled out a pen. Better to start to look right now for a place to live.

Recalling segments of the brochure mailed to her by an aggressive Chamber of Commerce, she suspected that of the four apartments listed, three were located in outlying areas. One was within walking distance of the downtown area – on Maple Street. Without a car – she didn't even have a driver's licence – she needed to be close to where she would be working. A faint apprehension brushed her. She would be able to find a job, wouldn't she? It wasn't just for the money, she needed that cover for her presence here.

The waitress brought a western omelette and an over-sized glass of iced tea to Diane's table. She ate with pleasure, ravenous after having barely touched her tray aboard the New York-to-Atlanta flight. With the last fragment of the omelette demolished, the last sliver of toast devoured, she sipped at her iced tea and plotted her afternoon. She'd ask directions to the available apartment, go over to see it.

The cashier provided her with the required directions.

'Oh, you'll like Miz Roberts. We all call her Miss Elvira. She's a real fine lady. Folks who move in with her are always happy there. Tell her Stella at The Bird Cage said "hello".'

Diane followed the cashier's instructions. Three blocks south, then turn left. That must be where Courthouse Square used to be. From the diagram supplied by the Chamber of Commerce she gathered it was now the site of a cluster of 'modern civic buildings'. Mom had loved Courthouse Square.

'It was such a lovely square. This regal red-brick courthouse sat in the middle of a square block, surrounded by lawns and circles of flowers. And all around were benches where mothers and nursemaids came to sit with their kids. Though Dad said there were nowhere near as many nursemaids as there had been before World War Two. He said times were changing in the South – no matter how people declared they weren't. The days of three-dollar-a-week nursemaids were gone for ever.'

Diane inspected what had been Courthouse Square with an air of reproach. In her mind she visualized the days when she had played here with other toddlers while Mom and a cluster of mothers watched from benches. She wished she could remember those days – when Dad had been alive. Now a group of impersonal, white-brick buildings covered most of the area. Walkways were lined with narrow borders of sun-tortured grass.

She followed the route to 'Miss Elvira's', approached a pleasant white clapboard house of generous dimensions, a wide porch stretching across the front. A small side porch suggested that this wing of the house had been divided into an apartment. The foundation of the house was flanked by glorious masses of blue hydrangeas.

The moment Miss Elvira opened the door and invited her

into the house, Diane knew she would like this small, elegant woman who welcomed her with such graciousness. Her hair was almost white, her face lightly lined – only the drooping jawline and her neck betrayed her age. She was probably in her early seventies but still beautiful.

'Isn't this weather just awful?' Miss Elvira apologized when Diane explained that she'd just arrived from New York and was looking for a place to live. 'You come right into the living room. The air conditioner in there works real well.'

Diane learned that Miss Elvira had been born in this house, and had lived here with her husband until his death a dozen years earlier. Her son and daughter and their families lived in Atlanta now.

'On my mother's side we were among the first settlers in Eden. My father was born in New York.' Her smile was whimsical. 'Born a Yankee but raised here in Eden. But enough of all this talk. Let me show you the little apartment I have for rent.'

The apartment was tiny but charming: a small living room, tiny bedroom and a walk-in closet that had become a kitchenette. The furniture was eclectic yet pleasing. And the rent, Diane remembered, was low by New York standards.

'I don't keep the air conditioner running since no one's living here at the moment,' Miss Elvira explained. 'But it's most comfortable in the whole apartment when it's on.'

'When can I move in?' Diane asked.

'Oh, honey, just any time you like.' Miss Elvira was radiant. Diane surmised that the income was welcome.

'Tomorrow morning?'

'That'll be just fine. Now let's go into my living room and I'll write you out a receipt for the first month's rent. And while I'm doing that, you can glance through the album showing the house the way it used to be in its heyday, when my mother and father were alive.'

Miss Elvira talked with the vivacity of a young girl while she brought out her receipt book and Diane viewed the snapshots of the house in earlier days.

'How did you decide to come down to Eden to live?' Miss Elvira asked with candid curiosity.

'Oh, I had this yearning to live in a small Southern town – you know, away from the pressures of New York. I took out a map of Georgia, closed my eyes, put my finger down on the map. It settled on Eden, so here I am.' Diane fought for an air of levity to match her fabrication. 'Tomorrow I move in, then I start job hunting.'

'Secretary?' Miss Elvira asked. 'Or something in the retail field?'

'I have one year of journalism school behind me, in addition to my BA – so I thought maybe I could land on a newspaper here in town. I understand you have a morning and an evening paper.' She sounded like a raving idiot, Diane scolded herself.

'The headquarters for the Masters newspaper chain is here in Eden. You must have noticed the Masters building. You can see it from just anywhere in town.'

'I saw it,' Diane said politely, gearing herself to hear an accolade to Lloyd Masters.

'Folks here in town are proud that Mr Masters makes this his base of operations, as he calls it. He's done so much for Eden. He and his wife are on every philanthropic committee in town. Two years ago the Baptist church needed a new roof after a tornado hit town – he provided for it. He built the Kevin Masters Memorial Hospital –'

Diane felt herself go rigid in shock. Mom must have known from reading this in the Eden newspapers, but she'd never mentioned it.

'The hospital was named for his son, who died tragically at an early age.' *Did everybody in Eden believe Dad killed himself? That Mom had been a bad wife?*

'My daughter, Laura –' Miss Elvira continued, 'she and her husband live in Atlanta now, like my son, Don, and his wife – went to school with Kevin from kindergarten through third grade. It's a fine hospital.'

'I gather Mr Masters is very highly regarded in Eden.' Diane managed a deferential smile.

'Oh, yes.' For an instant – so fleeting Diane asked herself if she was mistaken – Miss Elvira's voice seemed edged with sarcasm. 'Folks here in town do so admire Lloyd and Maureen Masters.' Again a glint of irony in her voice, Diane interpreted. Miss Elvira repeated local sentiment without sharing it. 'But let's talk about you, sugar. Were you born and raised in New York?'

'Yes, I was,' Diane told her. This was not the time to say she had been born right here in Eden. 'But my father was born in the South. In South Carolina,' she fabricated.

They talked briefly about Diane's interest in journalism, then Diane rose to leave.

'Sugar, you take yourself right over to the phone company and order phone service,' Miss Elvira urged. 'Though until you get it, you feel free to use my phone number. You'll need that for your job hunting. And most of the time I'll be here to answer it. If I'm going to be out, I'll give you the key and you come right in to answer. You can hear the phone ringing plain as day.' Her smile was apologetic. 'I can't believe the day has come when right here in Eden folks bother to lock their front doors. But that's part of our expanding population, I suppose.'

'Is the phone company nearby?' Diane asked.

'Just five short blocks away,' Miss Elvira told her, and supplied directions.

Recoiling from the torpid heat of the afternoon when she was outdoors again, Diane abandoned her customary quick pace for the more leisurely Southern one. What a hot, sticky day! Her cotton summer dress clung damply to her back. Perspiration edged her forehead, trickled down her slender neck.

With the matter of the phone installation arranged she headed back for the hotel. She'd shower and change into something fresh, have an early dinner in the hotel dining room. By then it would be late enough to call Uncle Erich. He'd be home from the lab.

Approaching the hotel, she noted the evening papers were on sale at the neighbourhood candy store. She stopped to pick up a copy of the *Evening News*, anticipating the pleasure of walking into the comfort of the air-conditioned hotel.

Forty minutes later – coddled by the blessed presence of air conditioning – she headed for the hotel dining room. The dining room was charming and serene, lightly populated at this early hour. Diane brushed aside a surge of self-consciousness at dining alone. One older woman sat at a corner table and appeared to be engulfed in a paperback book while she waited to be served. The only other diners were two middle-aged men talking heatedly about how hard Jimmy Carter was campaigning for the gubernatorial elections in November.

'I don't care about the hundreds of speeches he's made and how many hands he's shaked,' one was blustering. 'He'll never beat Carl Sanders. All the newspapers are supporting Sanders – he's got all the endorsements. Lloyd Masters himself has gone out to campaign for him.'

'I'm putting my money on Jimmy Carter,' the other man said, his smile defiant. 'We need a man with his ethics and his humanity in the Governor's Mansion.'

The town had changed a lot in twenty years, Diane told herself. But Lloyd Masters still ruled.

Uncle Erich would be arriving home in a few minutes, she surmised after a glance at her watch. Poor Uncle Erich. The apartment would seem so empty to him tonight. He'd cook his dinner, then settle down to watch the evening news on television. Later he'd read. Or maybe he'd meet one of his friends. On a hot night like this he might decide to go to the air-conditioned cafeteria for coffee.

Dinner was excellent, the service gracious, and Diane found herself relaxing. Maybe that was a good omen. That's what Beth would say.

Upstairs in her room she tried to put through a call to her uncle. The line was busy. One of 'the boys', as he called his friends, must have phoned. They knew he would be alone tonight. She'd try again in ten minutes. Now she reached for the *Evening News*.

She scanned the inside pages, paused at the Society section. A name leapt out at her. 'Mrs Lloyd Masters and her daughter, Mrs Hugh Jamison, are co-chairing the dinner dance to benefit the Eden Children's Fund.' Dad's stepmother and his sister. All at once she felt almost overwhelmed by the realization that she was here in the same town as her grandfather, aunts, probably cousins whose names she didn't even know. But they wanted no part of her, she reminded herself with brutal candor. Yet she was conscious of a yearning to see them – not to talk with them – just to *see* them. But at the same time the prospect was intimidating.

Fresh doubts welled in her. Was Uncle Erich right? Was she out to do the impossible? To solve a murder that happened twenty years ago? But how could she rest until she'd proved Mom was right about Dad's death? *Murder – not suicide.*

Chapter Three

Despite her conviction that she would fall asleep the moment she put aside the book she'd been reading, Diane found sleep elusive. The first grey streaks of dawn were creeping through the drapes when she at last succumbed.

She awoke with an instant realization that she was in a strange bed, in a strange room. She lay immobile for a few moments, her mind digesting this situation. Now she began to chart the day's activities. First on the agenda – check out of the hotel and move into the apartment, get settled in; shop at the small A&P she'd spotted in town.

She rose with a sense of urgency, showered, prepared for the day. Though air conditioning provided a pleasant temperature here, she suspected another scorcher would greet her when she left the hotel. She repacked what little she had removed from her luggage last night, went down to the hotel dining room for breakfast. The last big splurge. After this, she was on a tight budget – unemployed. She meant to touch the money left her by her mother as little as possible.

She fought against an urge to abandon her day's schedule to rush to the local library and dissect the pages of the *Herald* and the *Evening News* for the month of April 1950. But that must wait. First she must establish herself as a resident of Eden, Georgia. A working resident.

An hour later she was hanging clothes in the generous-size closet in the bedroom of her new apartment. The phone would be installed in four days, but she was mindful of Miss Elvira's offer that the house phone was at her disposal until then.

By noon she had stashed away the last of the groceries she had lugged home from the A&P – with a vow to buy a shopping cart for future ventures. Now she sat at the tiny bistro-style wrought-iron table in the corner of the living room and alternated between bites of grilled cheese sandwich and swigs of orange juice. She'd picked up a copy of the morning's *Herald* to check on job openings, but a quick perusal had revealed nothing that warranted pursuit. The Sunday papers would have listings. That was only three days away. She must focus on finding a job.

All at once her heart was pounding. She knew what she would do this afternoon. It was a long walk to the Masters Building, but she was going over there, locate the employment office, and apply for a job on either the *Herald* or the *Evening News*. Why not? She had a year of journalism school behind her. She wanted to spend her life working on a newspaper. Nobody would know she was Lloyd Masters' granddaughter.

She was relieved to discover a town bus passed right by the Masters Building. Disembarking at her destination, she stood on the sidewalk for a few moments and gazed up at the monument her grandfather had erected to himself. Sixteen storeys of white brick, glass, and concrete rose into the sky, proclaiming itself the centre of power in Eden.

She walked with unwise swiftness to the entrance, strode inside, sought for the directory. The employment office was on the twelfth floor. Involuntarily her eyes settled on the offices of Lloyd Masters. The penthouse, of course. She walked to the bank of elevators, where a handful of people waited.

Today she was conscious of the melodic softness of Southern voices – an air everywhere of 'all's right with the world'. The Southern atmosphere was most seductive. But what was life truly like here, beneath all the charm and graciousness?

In the employment office she was given an application form to fill out. Sitting at the desk provided for this, she fought against stifling self-consciousness. This was the *employment office*; Lloyd Masters would never grace this area with his presence. Yet when an older, tall, silver-haired man strode through the door, she tensed – until she heard him addressed by an unfamiliar name.

The woman who interviewed her was unimpressed by her credentials.

'How's your typing speed?' she asked Diane.

'Sixty words a minute.'

'You might want to fill out an application for a secretarial position. That pops up every now and then.'

'All right.' Diane managed a casual smile. So she would never be considered for an opening as a reporter. All the reporters – except for those working on the Society section – were men, she guessed in silent rage. The *Herald* and the *Evening News* lived in pre-war times. They hadn't learnt that women were not second-class citizens.

The following day Diane answered four ads, was interviewed, and politely rejected for each opening. Instinct told her that here in Eden job applicants without Southern accents were regarded with either curiosity or suspicion. At her final job interview – for a position as saleswoman at a women's specialty shop – the store manager suggested she might do better in Atlanta.

'Atlanta's much more cosmopolitan,' he explained. 'Here in Eden we're kind of partial to our own.'

Subdued, fighting discouragement, Diane walked home in the sultry afternoon heat. Miss Elvira waved from her porch as Diane approached, heading for the side entrance to her own small apartment.

'What an awful day to be walking,' she called. 'Come and have a glass of lemonade with me.' She turned now to pay the yard man, who'd been weeding for her. 'Next time, Arnie, you come later in the day when the sun's down. The flowers won't mind.'

'The weatherman says the heatwave will probably break in another twenty-four hours,' Diane said. 'We'll all be glad for that.'

'Come inside where it's cool.' Miss Elvira reached for the door. 'How's the job hunting?'

'Not too good. At the newspaper office yesterday they told me to fill out an application for a secretarial position – one *might* come along. Today I had four turn-downs.'

'Something will come up,' Miss Elvira soothed, beckoning Diane to follow her into the kitchen. 'You've only been looking a couple of days.'

At Miss Elvira's prodding Diane sat at a maple table in the sunny, charming breakfast nook. They talked over ice-cold lemonade and chocolate chip cookies.

'Would you believe, I've just learned to bake in the last few years? It's so hard to get domestic help these days. I'm grateful to have a woman come to clean once a week. My late husband, John, would be shocked at the changes in Eden in the last twelve years.'

'You miss the old days?' Diane was sympathetic.

'Oh, things had to change.' Diane was startled by Miss Elvira's emphatic reply. 'John and I knew it was coming. We couldn't send our coloured boys off to fight in a war and not expect changes. We had some rough times after the Supreme Court ruling on racial integration, but I think we've handled it well here in Eden. No thanks to our newspapers,' she said caustically.

'The *Herald* and the *Evening News* fought against integration?' Anger against her grandfather – always on tap – flared in Diane.

'Oh, I know there was a lot of pressure on them,' Miss Elvira conceded. 'The White Citizens' Council members would have cut off most of their advertising if they didn't go along with public sentiment. And public sentiment was against integration. The Masters family – they own the Masters newspaper chain – are revered in this town. They built the day-care centre for working mothers. Lloyd Masters offered to match funds voted by the Town Council for the new library that's under construction now.' She paused, her smile enigmatic. 'It's going to be beautiful. It's to be called the Lloyd Masters Library.'

'How generous of him.' Diane struggled to make the perfunctory response.

'I told you how the Masters' only son died very young, very tragically?' Miss Elvira's face reflected a genuine compassion.

'Yes,' Diane's reply was barely audible, but Miss Elvira seemed caught up in nostalgic recall.

'I was so fond of him and his wife. And they had an adorable little girl.'

'You knew them?' All at once Diane was trembling.

'Oh yes. They lived right across the street.'

'*I loved our little house on Maple Street.*' Her mother's voice filtered across Diane's mind. How could she have forgotten that they'd lived on Maple Street?

'They were so much in love they brought tears to my eyes sometimes,' Miss Elvira continued. 'They had a beautiful marriage. And that house was charming in those days. Now it's rundown, like much of the area. Folks keep telling me I should sell and buy out in the suburbs, but I was born in this house. I inherited it when my parents died. John and I came back here to live thirty-five years ago. I feel close to him here. I know some of the folks in town consider me eccentric, and something of a rebel, despite my age.' Amusement brightened her eyes. 'But that's the way I like it.'

Diane fought to appear casual. *Mom and Dad – and she – had lived in the house just across the way*. 'I gather this is quite a conservative town.'

'That's putting it mildly' Miss Elvira chuckled. 'If you have any liberal leanings, you keep them to yourself in Eden. But it's still a lovely town. You'll see for yourself once you settle in and begin to meet people. And the best way to do that,' she said vigorously, 'is to join a church.'

Diane smiled. 'I'm Jewish.'

'Then join the synagogue. We have two in Eden. I know you'll be welcomed.'

Diane remembered her uncle talking about the abundance of synagogues in New York City. 'But many Jewish people don't belong to a synagogue,' he'd said. 'A lot of us carry our synagogue in our hearts.'

'I have to find myself a job before I do any joining.' Diane reached for another cookie. 'These are so delicious . . .'

Later Diane stood on Miss Elvira's front porch for a few moments before going to her own apartment. That sadly rundown little house – redeemed only by the pair of towering magnolias at one side – was where Mom and Dad had lived? *She* had lived there. Mom had talked about the hundred daffodil bulbs she and Dad had planted. Did they still bloom gloriously in the spring? Except for the ugliness with his family, Mom and Dad had been so happy there.

Fate had brought her to Miss Elvira's. Each time she looked at that little house across the street, she would feel a closeness to Mom and Dad.

On Sunday morning Diane walked to the Main Street newspaper store to pick up the *Sunday Herald*. En route she was conscious of the throngs of neatly dressed residents walking or emerging from cars to approach the downtown churches. Especially on Sundays, she suspected, Eden wore this air of quiet relaxation.

Back home, with pen in hand, she sat down with the Help Wanted section, made notes. A number of jobs would have required ownership of a car. The bus system here was limited. Still, she told herself with forced optimism, there were four openings that she should be able to fill.

The day seemed endless. At intervals she crossed to her living-room window that looked out on the small, care-hungry house across the street. She had lived there with Mom and Dad. For Mom that had been such a happy place for a little while. Why did Mom and Dad have so little time together?

Mom didn't talk often about the war years. She'd stashed them away in a locked room in her mind except for those bittersweet bursts of recall. Sometimes, Diane mused, she felt herself a silent spectator to events that happened before she was born. Like the scene Mom recreated for her of that night when Dad brought his plane, the tail already in flames, down into the night-dark field a quarter-mile from the farmhouse where she and Uncle Erich hid from Nazi troops.

'It was a bitter cold night, with the snow covering the ground, weighing down the few trees around the house. All at once we saw the fire in the sky. Pierre knew instantly what it was . . .'

'The Germans have brought down a plane!' Pierre was instantly on his feet. 'Two Americans were to parachute here tonight. We've been on alert for them all evening!'

Pierre and Erich hurried out for the truck, drove towards the plane. Marie put up pots of hot water, ordered Sophie to bring out the first-aid kit kept handy for any injured arrivals. The farmhouse was a way station for Resistance people in trouble.

Sophie and Marie waited anxiously for the truck to return, grateful that the snow would cover the car tracks when Nazi soldiers were sure to come searching the neighborhood for any survivors. They stifled the cries that welled in their throats when they saw the plane explode into flames.

'Sophie, go into the cellar,' Marie ordered. 'Soldiers are sure to have seen the plane. They'll be searching every house for miles around. Take the bandages and medication down with you. If Pierre and Erich were able to bring anyone from the plane, you'll have to care for him down below . . .' She was already lifting the faded scrap of rug that concealed the trapdoor. 'If anyone asks, I'll say I'm boiling water to wash clothes. No time for this during the day.'

'The car's coming!' Sophie ran to open the kitchen door.

Moments later Pierre and Erich helped a dazed young man in an American Air Force uniform into the room.

'Take him below,' Pierre ordered. 'You go downstairs too, Erich. In twenty or thirty minutes some of their damned motorcycles will be pulling up before the house.'

With a speed learned in earlier encounters Sophie and Erich helped the young Air Force officer down the shaky stairs that led to the hideaway. Sophie treated the small cut across his forehead while Erich told her what happened.

'We just managed to pull him out before the plane exploded. There was no way we could rescue any of the others.' Erich was pale, shaken from the experience – heady for a fifteen-year-old.

'They'll think everybody died in the fire.' Sophie struggled for calm. 'They might not even come.'

Each time they heard the roar of German motorcycles, she and Erich felt discovery hovering over their shoulders. They, along with Pierre and Marie, would be shipped off to the camps if they were found with an Allied soldier.

Almost from the first night, Mom said, she knew that the young flier hidden in the cellar was to be important in her life.

Kevin made life worth living. We dreamt of the day when the war would be over and we could live in freedom. Together.

How strange, Diane thought, to be living here in this town where she had been born – where Dad was born. But now Dad was gone – and Mom was gone. And she had a mission to accomplish.

On Monday morning Diane sat with a mug of coffee and debated about which job offering to pursue first. She was both repelled by and drawn to a job as receptionist/typist at the Kevin Masters Memorial Hospital. How would she feel to walk five days a week into a building dedicated to her father's memory, built by the grandfather she hated? Yet part of Dad lived in that memorial.

She arrived at the hospital office to find two other applicants ahead of her. All at once she knew she wanted *this* job. Instinct told her that here she would learn much about Lloyd Masters. All of it no doubt flattering, she conceded. Yet – as with Miss Elvira – there might be some here who knew the real Lloyd Masters.

Waiting for her turn to be interviewed, Diane was conscious that all the faces she saw in this department were white. Like at the newspaper office, she suddenly realized. Both offices reflected what Uncle Erich called the white Anglo-Saxon look. Yet Miss Elvira had said, with pride, that the schools here in Eden were integrated: 'I know a lot of folks down here consider it a fate worse than death, but we have to face reality. Integration is the law – and a necessary one. I'm proud we've integrated our schools.'

Eventually, Diane was summoned into the private office of the business office manager of the hospital. Almost immediately she relaxed. A pleasant-faced woman in her late forties, with a warm smile and lively eyes, Gladys Lowe had worked at Kevin Masters Memorial since it opened.

'I started out here as receptionist/typist,' she told Diane. 'That was sixteen years ago. It's not an easy job for all it sounds routine. When we get swamped, you'll find yourself stuck at the typewriter until nine or ten o'clock some nights. If you think you have to leave at 5 p.m. sharp every day, this isn't for you.'

'I don't worry about hours,' Diane said. 'I held on to a part-time job all through college. I'm comfortable with long hours.'

'Where're you from?' This wasn't wariness, Diane realized, but genuine interest.

'I was born and raised in New York City. But I got to the point – after my mother died recently – where I realized I want to live somewhere where the pace is a little slower. My father came from the South. He used to talk about the easy-going life down here. He loved it.'

'It's not always so easy-going,' Gladys warned good-humouredly, 'though I admit we put on a good show. Now you say your typing is about 60 words a minute?'

'Actually, it's more than that. But if I take a test, I'll probably slow down to 60.'

'No test. Just type up these two pages for me. Use the IBM over there in the corner. Paper is in the left-hand drawer.'

Diane took the two pages the business manager extended and crossed to the typewriter. She inserted a sheet of paper, began to type.

'Gladys, my love, I have to talk to you about this patient

we're about to discharge . . .' A slim, dark-haired, dark-eyed young man in his mid-twenties – a resident judging from the stethoscope protruding from a pocket of his white jacket – strode into the office. 'I know you'll point him in the right direction –'

'Another one with no health insurance,' Gladys supplied, 'and no place to go for convalescence. That's for the social worker, Dr Hendricks,' she drawled.

'But you're so much smarter, Gladys. Come on, help old Cliff with this one . . .'

'Meaning the social worker is giving you the brush,' she interpreted. 'All right, sit down, cry on Mother's shoulder.'

Diane focused on the typing, yet was conscious of the furtive, interested glances Dr Cliff Hendricks was beaming in her direction. He contrived to appear laid-back, yet she sensed an appealing intensity in him. No! How could she be thinking this way? She was here on a mission. No place in her life for frivolous thoughts.

'All right, all right,' Diane heard Gladys Lowe interrupt Cliff's monologue. 'There's a group in town that has special funds for cases like this. I'll buzz somebody I know. Now scat, I have work to do.'

'Gladys, you're the love of my life.' Cliff leant over to kiss her on the cheek. 'See you . . .'

Diane turned from the typewriter to intercept a covert glance in her direction before he rushed through the door.

'Isn't he a doll?' Gladys said. 'He has all the young nurses in a tizzy. If they ever try to draft him, I'll personally demonstrate against the war in Vietnam.'

'I have the typing done.' Diane was oddly disconcerted.

'That was fast.' Gladys reached out a hand.

Diane stood beside the desk while Gladys scanned the typed pages.

'Good,' she approved after a moment. 'Dora leaves the end of this week. Would you be free to start next Monday?'

* * *

Diane left the hospital and walked with no real direction. She'd been in Eden just six days, and she had an apartment and a job. That was satisfying. But now she faced her real objective in coming here: the need to prove her father had not killed himself but had been murdered.

All right. Take the first step right now. The present Eden Public Library was located in the downtown area. Rerunning Miss Elvira's directions in her mind, Diane headed for the library. Her heart was pounding. In realistic moments she admitted she'd taken on an awesome project.

Nobody knew why she was here or who she was. She was on the track of a murder that happened twenty years ago. Still, she must be careful. She wanted no roadblocks set up. Her grandfather could be a dangerous enemy.

The library was a red-brick building set on a grassy acre alongside a muddy river, at low ebb this time of year. While the grass was neatly cut and the flowerbeds well tended, the building wore an air of disrepair. A pair of broken windows had been faced with cardboard. Windowframes and the wide entrance doors cried out for paint. But then this would soon be abandoned for the new Lloyd Masters Library.

She walked slowly up the path to the entrance. Had Dad come to this library for books when he was a boy? No, not likely. Mom said he'd been sent to boarding school when he was eight. Summers he'd been at camp.

Inside the library she noted the large area to her left was devoted to newspapers and magazines. This was where she would acquire back issues of the *Herald* and the *Evening News* on microfilm. The files here would go back twenty years, wouldn't they? She would hate to have to go to the newspaper offices to ask for back editions.

She hesitated at the desk where enquiries were to be made. Don't be obvious about the year she meant to search.

'Would you have the April 1949 issues of the *Herald*?' she asked the small, stocky woman who glanced up.

'Yes, we have them on microfilm.' The woman reached for

a form. 'Just fill this out, please.' She extended the form to Diane.

'Thank you.' Diane managed a wisp of a smile. Did the librarian seem curious about her wanting these? *No*, she was over-reacting.

The requested microfilm in hand, Diane settled herself at one of the microfilm machines at a rear table in the area, threaded the reel and prepared to read. Feeling herself wrapped in unreality she scanned the front page. The NATO alliance was signed at the State Department. Communist general Chu-Theh began to mass one million troops on the north bank of the Gantze. Public support for Senator Joseph McCarthy was soaring as he saw Communists in every corner – though fellow Republican Margaret Chase Smith disseminated her anti-McCarthy 'Declaration of Conscience', signed by herself and five other liberal Republicans.

Diane ran the film through much of the first issue, finally arriving at the Society section. Her eyes focused on a large photograph of three women.

'Mrs Maureen Masters, wife of local philanthropist Lloyd Masters, and two daughters opened this year's Easter Egg Hunt.'

An icy coldness crept over Diane as she read the article, then inspected the faces in the photograph. *Dad's stepmother and two of his sisters*. Maureen Masters was a pretty woman at that time, though an austere air detracted from that prettiness. Diane recalled that her father's four half-sisters, Alison, Peggy, Linda and Geraldine, were younger than he. Her mind computed ages. At this time Alison – not in the photograph – would have been twenty-two, Peggy twenty-one, Linda nineteen. Geraldine, his baby sister, also not in the photograph, would have been seventeen.

By then, Diane remembered, Alison had become a recluse. At sixteen she had been the victim of a gang rape. '*Poor little Alison*,' Mom had commiserated. '*She never emerges from her private little apartment in the family house. She sees nobody except her father*.'

All at once Diane felt an urgent need to escape from the library. She rewound the reel of film – her hands sweaty despite the comfortable air conditioning in the library – and returned it to the librarian. Her mind in chaos, she hurried out into the late morning heat, fleeing the images of her step-grandmother and two aunts. She hated them, she told herself in silent rage. She hated the whole Masters family. *They* lived – but Mom's family had died in the Holocaust.

For the first time since her arrival, Diane felt a deluge of home-sickness, compounded by what she tried to convince herself was an irrational sense of foreboding. Why had she left the library without asking to view the microfilm that was truly important to her? Tomorrow she would go back there, and she would read the April 1950 issues of the *Eden Herald*. Nobody would question her reasons. Nobody cared.

Despite her determination not to run up a big phone bill, she waited impatiently for the time she expected Beth would arrive home, reached her on the second try.

'Guess what,' she said with a specious display of high spirits. 'I've got a job already.'

'Di, that's great! What'll you be doing?'

'Nothing wildly exciting.' She sighed. 'Receptionist/typist at the local hospital.'

'Hey, that has possibilities,' Beth jested. 'All those young residents floating around.'

For an instant Diane remembered Cliff Hendricks, who'd seemed so warm and friendly. 'Stop talking like a Jewish mother.' Diane tried for matching lightness. 'But I bombed out on the newspaper. They're living back at the turn of the century. The only woman on the staff does the Society section.'

'You said you're forty-five miles from Atlanta,' Beth pointed out. 'I know it's a long commute, but they must have several newspapers there.'

'Beth, I want to live and work in Eden. It's a beautiful town, and everybody is so nice.' But – like Lloyd Masters – did they wear pretty façades that hid ugly realities?

'Di, hold on. I hear Jack at the door . . .'

'It's OK, I'll call you Sunday morning,' Diane said. 'I just wanted to let you know I had a job.'

'Are you all right?' All at once Beth sounded anxious.

'I'm fine,' Diane lied. 'I'll talk to you on Sunday.'

Diane put down the phone. She wasn't fine at all. She felt frighteningly alone. She fought against an urge to call her uncle, to hear a familiar caring voice. But Uncle Erich would try to talk her into coming home – and she mustn't do that.

She gazed about the small, charming living room that tonight seemed oddly menacing. Should she have waited a while – six months, perhaps – before coming down here? No! Too much time had been gone past already. Tomorrow she'd be at the library again.

Chapter Four

The Eden Library opened at 10 a.m. At ten past, Diane approached the librarian in the periodicals and newspapers division. All at once self-conscious because she sensed the librarian's curiosity at her return appearance, she asked for the 13 April 1950 edition of the *Atlanta Constitution*, then – as though an afterthought – added the *Herald* and the *Evening News* of the same date. Should she drop a hint about working on a doctoral thesis? No, say nothing.

She waited with a tense smile until the librarian returned with the three reels of microfilm, then headed with them for the rear table in the thus far deserted periodicals area. She was grateful for the solitude. Not that anyone could guess why she was here. Still, she made a point of running the reel of the *Atlanta Constitution* first, lest her interest in Eden at that period arouse curiosity. She raced through the film, seeing nothing, conscious of the absurd pounding of her heart.

Then with trembling hands she removed the *Constitution* reel and replaced it with the *Herald*. Her eyes scanned the front page of the 13 April issue, then focused on the small black-bordered paragraph on the lower right-hand corner:

Eden grieves with publisher Lloyd Masters and his family in the tragic death of his son Kevin, age 28. Long suffering from severe depression, Kevin Masters took his life at the family house early yesterday evening. Funeral services will be announced shortly.

41

She stared in disbelief That was all? In her mind she heard her mother's voice: '*There was no investigation. No police report. Nothing! How could people who knew Kevin and me – knew how happy we were – believe he suffered from depression?*' Didn't anyone in this town ask questions?

She forced herself to scan every page of the issue with the unrealistic hope of finding more about her father's death. But there was nothing further, nor in the following day's edition. Then in the 16 April paper she found a spare report of the funeral and a brief biography, listing the schools and college Kevin had attended. No mention of his wife and child. Was that to be interpreted as a silent reproach for his wife, who had presumably driven him to suicide?

Diane sat motionless, staring at the film without seeing. She was aware that others were arriving in the reading room, also intent on research. She read the obituary again, noted the cemetery where her father was buried, probably the only cemetery in town. She needed to go there, she told herself with sudden urgency.

She returned to her apartment, dug out the brochure from the Chamber of Commerce, sought for directions to the cemetery. The city bus would take her there. She left her apartment and hurried out to the bus stop.

Stepping down from the bus, the only passenger leaving at this destination, Diane saw Eden Cemetery just across the road. At the office she acquired a copy of the layout of the large, sprawling place. The air was fragrant with the scent of roses and honeysuckle, the bushes rising to impressive height at the perimeter of the area. She walked over the well-tended paths, careful to follow the guide.

Just ahead, she told herself at last with a blend of anticipation and anguish. She came to a halt at the entrance to an indicated small plot that offered a final resting place for three. But only two lay there: her father and her paternal grandmother. She read the words etched on the two headstones – 'Claire Masters, 1901–1924, beloved wife and mother'; and on the other, 'Kevin

Masters, 1922–1950, beloved son'. No mention of his roles as husband and father.

Dad's father had remarried exactly one year after his mother's death, and their house had become a cold and lonely place for a sad little boy.

Diane sat on the Georgia granite bench provided in the plot that obviously received perpetual care. Her family, she thought with an agonizing sense of loss. Tears welled in her eyes, spilled over unacknowledged. The third resting place in this tiny plot would never be used, she guessed. Lloyd Masters had begun a new life with his second wife and four daughters.

Her mind charged backwards through the years. She remembered the theory her mother had often repeated.

'Somebody meant to kill Lloyd Masters and mistook Kevin for him in the dark. Oh, for all the way people idolized him in Eden, he'd collected enemies through the years. With his string of newspapers he'd trod on a lot of toes. He kept a gun in the night table beside his bed and another in the desk in the library. His chauffeur always carried a holstered gun. Your father said there'd been lawsuits, ugly threats.'

All right, work on Mom's theory that the murderer had mistaken Dad for his father. What she must do now was to read back through the years, latch on to somebody who hated Lloyd Masters enough to kill him. Someone carrying a grudge – perhaps for years – and vowing vengeance.

Look for lawsuits filed against Lloyd Masters and his newspaper chain. Beth's boyfriend, Jack, was going into law school, she recalled in sudden excitement. If she came up with a lawsuit, couldn't he track down the facts through legal records? Now she had a direction to follow.

On Monday Diane began her job at Kevin Masters Memorial. Her research would be limited now to the one midweek evening the library was open, and long hours on Saturdays. The office was small and the staff congenial, consisting of the bookkeeper, Norma, and a file clerk in addition to Gladys and herself. Gladys

Lowe was an efficient yet pleasant boss. Diane soon realized that Gladys adored all the young residents who streamed through the hospital – but Cliff Hendricks held a special place in her heart.

'That Cliff is something,' she told Diane with an indulgent smile when he'd popped into the office with a gift for her, a box of cookies made especially for her by his mother. 'And he comes from good stock.' Diane was conscious of Gladys's covert speculation. But Cliff flirted with all the women in the hospital, she told herself, not just with her. 'His parents live in Atlanta – which is one of the reasons Cliff accepted a residency at a small hospital like this. To be near them.' Gladys chuckled. 'For the rare weekends he can make his escape.'

Diane, too was busy. She arrived at the office each morning a few minutes before nine. Gladys was already there by then. Norma, and Deedee, the file clerk, always rushed in about five or six minutes late. Usually the office closed for the day at 5.30.

The evenings – except for Wednesdays when the library was open – would be the worst, Diane quickly realized. And Sundays, she warned herself, when the long, empty hours of her second Sunday in Eden dragged interminably. She was frustrated, too, by the task before her. She was convinced that somewhere in the files of old Eden newspapers lay the fragile clue that would lead her to the truth about her father's death – but there were so many years to search!

At the end of her second week on the job Cliff asked her out for dinner and a movie.

'I can't pull another double shift this week,' he said firmly. 'I'll go on strike. Dinner and a movie OK tomorrow night? *Easy Rider* is playing at the Bijou. It got great reviews. And I promise *not* to fall asleep.'

'OK,' Diane said, astonishing herself. She couldn't afford any diversion. But Cliff was warm and amusing – and she was so lonely after office hours.

She spent Saturday morning and much of the afternoon at the library, poring over old editions of the Eden newspapers. She'd heard one of the librarians whisper to another that she must be researching for a novel with a Southern background. Let them believe that.

Earlier than she'd planned – though her eyes were already strained from the hours of reading – she left the library and hurried home through the hot, sticky afternoon. This was no big deal, she exhorted herself, she was just going out for dinner and a movie with a resident at the hospital. There was no room in her life for a serious relationship.

She remembered the conversation she'd had a couple of days ago with Norma, the thirtyish, recently married bookkeeper.

'Those poor guys really break their butts,' Norma had told her. 'They have no lives outside the hospital. What girl wants to go out with somebody who half the time has to break their date to fill in at the hospital – or falls asleep the first time they sit down for more than ten minutes? They have no room in their schedules for girlfriend or wife – and the girls here in town find that out fast enough.'

Had Norma meant that as a warning to her? Going out with Cliff was just to relieve her loneliness. She hadn't realized how lonely she'd be in a strange town where she knew nobody. At odd moments she ached to be back home among familiar places, familiar faces. She missed Uncle Erich so much, missed Beth, grieved for her mother. The phone calls home were what kept her from packing up and running back to New York.

The Bijou was right in town, she remembered as she emerged from her second shower of the day. Would they be walking or did Cliff have a car? Wear something cool and casual. She changed her dress three times before she settled on a flower-sprigged challis minidress – rejecting the two midis she'd bought in an unwary moment. Even staid Uncle Erich disliked the new midi length.

Cliff said he'd pick her up at 5.30 – so they'd have time for a leisurely dinner and be able to catch the early evening show at the Bijou. He was on duty at 7 a.m. Sunday morning – 'No late nights for the likes of me.' But he was philosophical about his hours at the hospital: the thirty-six-hour shifts. Gladys said he was one of the brightest residents who'd ever come into Kevin Masters Memorial.

Cliff arrived twenty minutes late and full of apologies.

'By now you know the routine at the hospital.' His smile was simultaneously wry and ingratiating. 'Residents aren't supposed to have social lives. But we can still make the early show at the Bijou if we settle for dinner at the China Gardens. They're fast there. You like Chinese?' he asked in sudden anxiety while they walked to his car at the kerb – which he'd just described as about five years from antique status.

'I love Chinese.' Also, Chinese was inexpensive, and residents were low on the pay scale.

'My mother and dad claim that one of the things they like best about Atlanta is that the city's loaded with ethnic restaurants. Every Saturday night – unless I can get home – they eat out "in a different country", Mom says.'

Diane learnt now that, like herself, Cliff was an only child.

'They waited ten years for me, and they've spoilt the hell out of me,' he admitted good-humouredly. 'Putting me through med school was a rough deal for them. They refused to allow me to take out loans. "We don't want you coming out of school with loans on your back," they both insisted.'

'My mother died in April,' Diane whispered in sudden desolation. 'My father died when I was two.'

'That's tough,' he said gently.

'That's one of the reasons I cut out of New York and came down here.' Why was she talking this way? 'You know – change of scenery.'

'It'll take a while,' he sympathized. 'How do you like working at the hospital?'

'It's OK.' She was grateful to have the conversation rechannelled. 'I was hoping for a job on one of the newspapers. I have a year of journalism school behind me. But no luck there. Maybe I should have stayed at school and earned my degree.'

'You could go back to school down here.' He hesitated. 'It's a long commute to Atlanta.'

'For now I'll let it ride.' So he'd consider her unambitious. 'How do you like the hospital?'

'It's great. Oh sure, I cuss every now and then at the crazy hours we work.' He grinned. 'I like the hospital, and I like living in Eden. I'd love to be able to do research in a town like this, in paediatrics, but that's unlikely. The research hospitals are all in good-sized cities.'

'My uncle in New York – my only relative now – is a research chemist. Sometimes he keeps insane hours, but he loves the work.'

'It's important to like what you do.' All at once Cliff was serious. 'I'd hate like hell to be stuck in a job that held no real interest for me. My dad should have gone into politics. He's so bright and clear-thinking. It amazes me sometimes how he's been able to compromise. You know, running his business when he's one of those rare guys who should be running a town or state or even the country. I know we've had a Catholic president,' he drawled, 'but I'm not sure the country is ready for a Jewish president.'

So he was Jewish, Diane noted.

'Anyhow, Dad married and went to work in his father-in-law's store and eventually took it over. Now he runs a shop at a mall in Buckhead – that's a great Atlanta suburb. He made a comfortable life for his family.' Cliff was swinging the car off the road now. 'There's the China Gardens.'

Few diners had arrived this early. Diane and Cliff were led to a cozy corner table. The background music was low and sweet, the décor charming, the waiters eager to please. Cliff made a ceremony of their ordering. It was clear that he was here often. With one of the pretty nurses at the hospital? Diane asked herself; then self-consciously dismissed this.

'My roommate and I celebrate small victories here,' Cliff confided. 'We bring only special people to the China Gardens.'

'I may work in the business office, but I don't have Gladys's pull.' Her eyes were alight with laughter.

'I knew the minute I saw you – the day you were applying

47

for the job, I gather – that I wanted to know you better.' He made it seem a flirtatious comment, but his eyes were serious. *She wasn't ready for that.*

The waiter arrived with their soup, and banter was abandoned. In the course of dinner, with cautious checks on the time, Cliff regaled her with humorous hospital stories.

'A resident's social life is the pits.' He sighed mockingly while he waited for her to break open her fortune cookie. 'Dinner and a movie is a major occasion.' He was silent while she read the words on the slip of paper pulled from the fortune cookie. 'Well, what does the soothsayer have to say?'

Her throat had tightened as she read the message. Now she read it aloud. '"You face a rough mission, but you've just met someone who'll be very important in your life."'

'I'll help you with the mission if you'll let me be very important in your life.' His smile was ingratiating. 'Deal?'

'What does yours say?' she dodged.

'Let's have a look.' He broke open the cookie, pulled out the scrap of paper. '"You're warm, impetuous, romantic. Expect an exciting arrival in your life soon." You know, this guy is damn good!'

Diane was grateful that the office was making unexpectedly heavy demands on her time. Work helped to alleviate the recurrent bouts of homesickness. Her sleep was haunted by nightmares. At intervals – always casual – Cliff would take her out to dinner and to a movie. They never moved past a light goodnight kiss. She told herself that Cliff understood she wasn't ready for anything more. Yet on occasions when Cliff, exhausted from long hours on duty, fell asleep at the movie, his head slipping towards her shoulder, she was startled by the unexpected arousal this evoked in her.

At every opportunity she was at the library, reading back issues of newspapers. At moments she was ready to concede that the task was hopeless, but each time she reached out for fresh strength. Somewhere in Lloyd Masters' past, before Dad's death, there was an enemy who wished him dead, plotted his murder. Beth promised that if she could come up with a name, Jack would follow up the lawsuit. She clung to this promise.

Aware of Lloyd Masters' position in the state – in the whole South – she was extending her reading to the Atlanta newspapers. A seemingly endless project, she warned herself in despairing periods.

'You're like one of the staff now,' the older of the librarians joshed when she arrived on Saturday morning in August with her usual request for back issues of the *Atlanta Constitution*, the *Herald* and the *Evening News*.

'You're all so very nice.' Diane was polite but uncommunicative.

But she was learning much about the Masters family, was recognizing their faces from newspaper photographs, as she compulsively devoured each day's *Herald*. Lloyd Masters was involved with many local groups, his wife, Maureen, active among the various charities. She knew that Dad's sister Peggy was now Mrs Luke Cranston and the mother of two daughters. Her first cousins. Linda was Mrs Hugh Jamison and the mother of a son and a daughter. His sister Gerry was Mrs Clark Watson and had no children.

'Oh, how nice to see you back from St Simon's, Mrs Masters!' Diane, waiting for the microfilm she'd requested, froze in shock as the head librarian greeted a newcomer. 'We're all so thrilled with the progress being made at the new library.'

She'd known that in time she would come face to face with members of Dad's family. But she hadn't expected it to happen this way – without warning.

'Yes, it's coming along well.' Maureen Masters was slim and tall, her ash-blonde hair perfectly coiffed, her face made up with an artistry that almost masked the fact that she was in her late sixties. Her bearing that of a woman who held herself above the crowd.

Such arrogance, Diane thought in distaste, forcing her gaze away, her heart pounding, her throat tight. Fighting for poise.

'*Maureen Masters shipped Dad away to boarding school when he was eight,*' she heard her mother's voice in scathing condemnation. '*She sent her own daughters away at that age. What kind of a woman would do that?*'

The head librarian and Maureen Masters were in discussion now about a special project for the local children. *Her* project, Diane gathered.

'You know how shy Gerry is,' Mrs Masters was saying in a voice that dripped Southern charm, 'but I persuaded her to take on the Saturday morning story-telling sessions. She'll drop you a note about that when she returns from Paris.'

Diane sighed with shaky relief when the other librarian on duty emerged from the rear area with the microfilm. She was impatient to be out of sight of her step-grandmother. She hurried to her usual table and ordered herself to focus on the morning's reading.

Why was she trembling this way because she'd just encountered Maureen Masters? In the months ahead she was sure to come face to face with her grandfather, her aunts, her cousins. She wasn't expecting – didn't *want* – recognition. She was here to prove that Dad had not committed suicide, that he and Mom had shared a beautiful marriage. To let all of Eden know that.

Earlier than she'd planned, Diane left the library and headed for home. She was too shaken by the near encounter with Maureen Masters to concentrate on her morning's reading. And now the towering doubts that had threatened at intervals assaulted her again. Was she being naïve to believe she could track down Dad's murderer, as Uncle Erich insisted? Even Beth had tried to convince her she was tilting at windmills.

How many years of newspapers must she read to find that one lead to Dad's murderer? But she'd only been searching for a few weeks. She'd known it wouldn't be easy.

She approached the house almost simultaneously with Miss Elvira, arriving from the opposite direction.

'Good morning, Diane.' Miss Elvira sighed. 'Do you think

we'll ever see a break in this heat wave? They say it's setting records.'

'There's talk of rain tonight. That'll bring some relief.'

'Come inside and have a lemonade with me,' Miss Elvira invited. 'I know, you have a million things to do on your weekend off, but relax with me for a bit. This heat is so enervating.'

The two settled themselves in the living room with tall, ice-islanded glasses of lemonade.

'Let's stop this "Miss Elvira" thing. Please, I'm Elvira from now on,' Diane's landlady ordered ingratiatingly. 'Have you been reading that series in the *Herald* about their objection to the Supreme Court ruling on conscientious objector status? I'm just furious about it.'

'I don't agree with any of its editorial stands,' Diane admitted.

'I just wish we had another newspaper in town. One not controlled by Lloyd Masters.' Elvira paused, forced a smile. 'Of course, it's only natural for a newspaper to take a stand its publisher considers right. But it would be nice for this town to hear both sides of a question without having to turn to the *Atlanta Constitution* or the *Journal*.'

Diane contrived a show of interest in Elvira's report of a battle between Lloyd Masters and the Board of Education a few years earlier on desegregation.

'Oh, they might not have liked the need to speed up integration in our schools, but the Board of Ed recognized that it was the law.'

'A newspaper can't control everything in a town.' But even as Diane said this, her mind was charging ahead on another course. She was wasting her time looking for leads in Lloyd Masters' newspapers. He'd kill stories of any suits against him – why hadn't she realized that? But the Atlanta newspapers – which she made a pretense of reading – would publish news of the Lloyd Masters empire on their business pages. Scrap the reading of the *Herald* and the *Evening News*. Concentrate on the *Atlanta Constitution* and the *Journal*. Go back twenty-five years. Somewhere in those pages she'd find a lead to someone out for vengeance against Lloyd Masters.

Did Lloyd Masters suspect who murdered Dad? Had he been silent to avoid bringing out an ugly earlier incident that would reflect badly on himself? Mom had said all he cared about was the image he'd built up through the years. Nothing must be allowed to diminish that. Even though it meant allowing his son's murderer to go unpunished.

But that was what she meant to change.

Chapter Five

At intervals through the day – while she did the routine Saturday chores – the arrogant image of Maureen Masters seeped into Diane's mind. Uncle Erich always worried about Mom's never-ceasing rage at the Masters family, but she was infected by that same rage. She could hear her uncle's voice now: 'Why waste yourself on such anger? It costs you too much, Sophie. In time people get what's coming to them.'

She could put her own anger to sleep once she'd fulfilled her purpose in coming here. She would pursue it for as long as was required. She owed that to Mom.

Moving about the tiny apartment this afternoon she was painfully conscious of being alone in a strange town – far from the two people in this world who were closest to her. Ever conscious of the presence of her despised grandfather.

Tonight she'd be seeing Cliff, she remembered, and was grateful. Cliff had been given tickets to a summer theatre production of *On The Town* – and they'd have dinner before the performance.

In a spurt of restlessness she glanced at the small mantel clock. Call Beth. They alternated phoning each other on Sunday mornings, but she needed to talk to Beth *now*. Beth would probably be home. Jack had gone to Cleveland to visit his family for ten days. Eagerly she dialled Beth's number.

'Hello?' Beth's voice brought her a glorious burst of closeness.

'I know it isn't Sunday morning,' Diane said with an effort at levity, 'but this is still an economy time to call and I needed to hear your voice.'

'I needed to hear yours, too. Jack's only been gone three days, but I miss him already. Can you imagine how I'd feel if he was drafted?'

'He won't be drafted.' Of course, graduate students had lost their deferment status, but Jack had a punctured eardrum. Diane remembered that Cliff said his number was low; he wasn't apt to be called. 'Look for something good on TV or dig up a good suspense novel. Jack will be back in a week.' What did Beth see in Jack that was so fascinating? Sure, he was awfully good-looking and he wouldn't be headed for Columbia Law School if he wasn't bright. Yet instinct told her that all Jack cared about was what was good for Jack. 'Or phone him out there.'

'I don't think his family knows about me.' Beth paused. 'He might be upset if I called. Anyhow, he'll be back next Sunday. What about you and Cliff?'

'We're going out to dinner tonight and then to a summer theatre performance of *On The Town*. It's all just casual,' she insisted. 'He's fun to be with – we enjoy the same movies, the same kind of restaurants. This is his first weekend off in months. We're going out tonight, and in the morning he's driving to Atlanta to spend the day with his parents.'

'Jack says he's giving notice on his job when he comes back.' Caution crept into Beth's voice. 'He'll work until school opens, though.'

'I thought he needed the job to handle his living expenses.' A part-time job once classes began, Diane recalled. He had student loans to augment what his parents were able to contribute towards law school tuition.

'He's giving up his apartment and moving in with me when he comes back from Cleveland. Mom's having a fit, but it seemed the practical thing to do,' Beth said – as though expecting an argument from her, Diane thought. 'He may take a Saturday job, but everybody says the first year of law school is a bitch. Jack's so ambitious, he wants to come out at the top of his class. That's important if he's to make it into a major law firm. But God, is Mom carrying on! Dad just looks grim.

This is 1970 – when are they going to understand that gals and guys live together without a marriage licence?'

Off the phone, Diane considered Beth's words. 'Lots of women help their guys through graduate school.' True, Diane conceded. Jack talked eloquently about the future that lay ahead for him and Beth: 'Hell, when you get connected right, the money flows. Two years out of law school we'll be looking for a house in Westchester, buying a classy car.'

The heat of the day diminished as the sun went down, giving way to ominous clouds. Diane turned off the air conditioner, opened the windows. The air was fresh and sweet. The scent of honeysuckle and roses blended with that of just-mown grass. From Elvira's kitchen came the succulent aromas of a well-spiced pot roast.

Why not call Cliff and invite him to have dinner here in the apartment rather than their eating out? It wouldn't have to be something special. Why should Cliff, on a resident's salary, always be paying?

Her mind catalogued the contents of her refrigerator, the kitchen cabinets. Spaghetti with a heavy sauce made from scratch, salad, and she always kept a garlic bread in the freezer. Yes!

She dialled Cliff's apartment, waited, hearing a steady ring at the other end. He was stuck at the hospital, she guessed in disappointment. It was understood that he was always subject to elongated hours. Then as she was about to hang up, his voice came to her.

'Hendricks' Happy Haven.'

'Hi.' All at once she felt self-conscious at calling him.

'Hi.' A warm, special 'hi', she thought. He wouldn't take this suggestion the wrong way, would he?

She hesitated, needing space before inviting him to dinner. 'Have you heard anything new about Bob Evans?' Bob was a resident at the hospital who'd gone through med school with Cliff and had just had a nervous collapse. 'I thought I saw him on the paediatrics floor today.'

'No, he's still under treatment in the psychiatric division. They don't know if he'll be allowed to resume his residency. It's tough, falling apart the way he did after making it through med school and into his second year residency. But it's happened to others.'

'It looks as though it's going to storm like mad any minute now. I thought maybe you'd settle for spaghetti and a salad at my place – then we can head for the theatre.'

'Sounds great. What shall I bring?' An ingratiating ebullience in his voice now.

'Just yourself. There'll be nothing fancy,' she warned. 'Spaghetti, salad and garlic bread.'

'I'll bring a bottle of wine,' he began.

'No wine. You'll be driving.'

'Yes, ma'am. I'll be there in about forty minutes. OK?'

'Fine.' She'd have to rush – but she could manage. 'See you then.'

Moments later the rain began to come down, in trickles at first, then in torrents. Now, with Cliff's anticipated arrival, it seemed to Diane that the apartment radiated a pleasant coziness. The rain pounding on the windowsills seemed friendly rather than intimidating.

The table was set, salad ready, water boiling for the spaghetti when Cliff arrived – sodden despite the shortness of the run from car to door.

'I feel like a drowned pup.' He extended a bakery box. 'I hope this stayed dry at least.'

'Dessert.' Her smile effervescent, she opened the box, inspected its contents. 'Ooh!' Two luscious, chocolate-dipped cannoli lay before her. 'Take off your jacket and put it over the back of the chair to dry.' She hurried into the tiny kitchenette, all at once attacked by misgivings. Had she made a mistake inviting Cliff for dinner? She'd seen the ardour in his eyes and was unnerved by her own arousal. But they would have to hurry through dinner to get to the theatre in time. *Nothing was going to happen.*

She dropped the spaghetti into the boiling water, stirred the tomato sauce, then popped the garlic bread into the oven. Cliff disposed of his wet jacket, crossed to fiddle with the radio. The voices of Peter, Paul and Mary singing 'Blowing in the Wind' filtered into the room. Cliff smiled in approval. For a poignant instant Diane's eyes met his. Of course, he would love Peter, Paul and Mary – as she did.

'We could start with salad,' she said, all at once uneasy. 'The spaghetti will be OK without my company.' She tried for a flippant air. 'Thank God for timers.'

'I'll bring it out.' He headed for the refrigerator. 'Sit. You've been labouring over a hot stove.'

'Sure, for all of twenty minutes. We're doomed to bottled dressing. My cookbook library is limited.'

Cliff was keeping the conversation on a light level. Yet she was conscious of unexpected arousal – clearly reflected in him. *There was no place in her life for this.* She was relieved when dinner was over and, both huddled under an umbrella, they were dashing to the car.

The Saturday night crowd responded enthusiastically to the performance. With something akin to reluctance the audience strolled from the small playhouse after several curtain calls.

'Oh, it was fun!' Diane was caught up in the mood of the evening. 'I don't know when I've enjoyed anything so much.'

'Why don't we go back to my place for coffee?' Cliff coaxed spontaneously. 'When Brad's tense, he cooks.' Brad was Cliff's roommate. 'He came off a back-to-back tour this morning, made a great pizza before he collapsed. A rainy night like this just yells for pizza.'

'Sounds wonderful . . .' So Brad was there in the apartment.

Cliff opened the umbrella, held it over the two of them, one arm about Diane's waist, as they hurried to the car.

'The rain's never going to stop,' Diane predicted as they settled themselves in the darkness.

'The heat wave's broken. The temperature must have dropped

30 degrees in the last two hours.' He was solicitous as he turned to her. 'Are you cold?'

'I'm fine.' She felt herself afloat in euphoria, reluctant to abandon this mood.

'The apartment's probably a mess. Brad's sister came down one weekend and declared us the worst slobs in the western world.'

'I won't look.'

When Brad didn't respond to the doorbell, Cliff fished for his key.

'He's probably still asleep. Brad would sleep through a bombing . . .'

Cliff thrust open the door and gestured her inside with a flourish. Books were stacked around the small living-room floor in untidy piles. A plate that had once housed pizza sat on the coffee table, a fork fallen unheeded to the floor.

'I'll put two slices of pizza in the oven.' Cliff started towards the kitchen. He paused midway, attracted by a sheet of paper dangling from a lampshade. 'I don't believe it! It's a note from Brad. "It's 7.22 p.m. and they're dragging me back on duty,"' he read. '"Why didn't I go to the theatre with you and Di?"'

'Poor Brad,' Diane sympathized. 'Aren't you glad you couldn't be reached?'

'They reach me often enough.' Cliff flinched in recall. 'Oh, I forgot to tell you about Brad's latest shtick.' He opened the refrigerator, pulled out the pizza, cut two wedges and transferred them to the oven. 'He bought a coffee grinder and beans so we can have what he calls "the real thing". I'll grind the beans while our pizza is heating up.' He, too, was conscious that they were alone in the apartment.

They'd been alone before, she reminded herself. For dinner this evening. For a cold soda after dinner and a movie on several occasions. They'd exchanged experimental, light, good night kisses. But this evening was different, Diane thought – uneasy yet expectant, her emotions in turmoil. Brad was at the hospital, he'd gone on duty after 7 p.m., he'd be away until morning.

'Cover up your ears,' Cliff warned and an instant later the shriek of the coffee grinder rent the air.

'I'll get the mugs.' Diane spied a pair on the dish drainer. 'And spoons.'

'It feels so good to have you here this way.' He reached out to pull her to him. Her heart was pounding. She wanted him to hold her like this. 'I've thought about it so many times.'

'Cliff, we – we shouldn't . . .'

She closed her eyes as his mouth came down to meet hers. Slowly, as if of their own volition, her hands reached up to rest at his shoulders. She'd never reacted this way to anyone before, she thought in a corner of her mind while their mouths fused in mutual hunger. She'd had casual romantic interludes through the high school and college years, but nothing serious. Beth teased her about saving herself for her wedding night: 'You've got a forties attitude in the seventies!'

'Di . . .' Cliff's voice was deep with excitement, his eyes questioning.

'We shouldn't . . .' But she'd die if he accepted that.

'No reason to stop us. We're both unattached. I've known since almost the first moment I saw you that I wanted you to be for ever a part of my life.'

Her hand in his, they walked into the darkness of the bedroom he shared with Brad. While they clung together beside one single bed, their mouths seeking to assuage a long hunger, Cliff contrived to push aside the bedspread, turn down the sheet. With infinite tenderness he helped her out of her dress. She abandoned herself to the tumultuous emotions that surged in her while his hands released the hook of her bra, then captured the lush spill of her breasts.

As though in a trance she heard her own murmurs of pleasure as his hands moved about her and her own explored. At this moment the rest of the world was forgotten. Nothing mattered except sharing this tumultuous experience . . .

*   *   *

Afterwards she lay naked in the curve of his arms and listened while Cliff talked about their future. Suddenly her whole life was changed. This was unreal but wonderful.

'Once I'm out of my residency, we'll know where we'll live. But it won't be my choice alone,' he insisted. 'Husbands and wives should share major decisions. I love Eden,' he acknowledged, 'but it's unlikely I'll be able to pursue a research career in a town this small.'

'Wherever you decide will be right for us. As long as we're together, it'll be a beautiful place.' Mom would have liked Cliff so much. Mom would be happy for her.

'It'll be a long wait.' Cliff was apologetic, wistful. She understood they'd have to wait for him to be out of his residency before marrying. From hospital gossip she knew how marriages dissolved during med school and hospital residencies. 'I still have another two years after this one.' He hesitated. 'I don't think we should tell my parents yet. They're so wrapped up in my finishing my residency – I wouldn't want them to worry about my messing up.' Because a wife could be a dangerous distraction, Diane interpreted. They both had obligations. But by the time Cliff finished his residency, she'd have tracked down Dad's murderer.

'Our secret,' Diane promised, conscious that Cliff was awaiting her response. Later she'd tell Uncle Erich about Cliff. He'd be pleased, wouldn't he? Or would he be shocked that this was happening so soon after they'd lost Mom? 'We'll go on as we've been doing, seeing each other when we can.' Only now there was this new dimension to their relationship. But this didn't mean she'd let up on her determination to nail Dad's murderer. Nothing must interfere with that.

Shortly past 2 a.m. Diane insisted that Cliff drive her home. Brad would be arriving in a few hours – and she shied from having Elvira realize she'd spent a night away from her apartment.

'Besides,' she reminded him, 'you're leaving around eight o'clock to go to your parents.'

'I'll be jealous of every hour we're apart.' He pulled her close again. 'Oh God, the years ahead are going to be rough. I want to tell the whole world that you belong to me. No –' he corrected himself – 'that we belong to each other.'

Early in September the *Herald* carried a front-page story about the enlargement of the day care centre in town. At lunchtime, in line at the hospital cafeteria with Norma, Diana heard two nurses ahead of them discussing the announcement.

'Wow, does this town need more day care,' one said exuberantly. 'My sister's been on the list for a year. With day care she can go back to work.'

'I don't understand all these women rushing back to work,' the other grumbled. 'They've got it made, staying home with the kids.'

'You're living twenty years ago,' the first scolded. 'Women want more out of life these days than waxing floors and changing diapers. Haven't you read Betty Friedan?'

'If I wasn't working, Joe and I wouldn't be able to meet our mortgage payments,' Norma confided while she and Diane reached for salad plates. 'It's not that I love coming to work every day – I love the pay cheque on Friday afternoons.'

Not until she and Diane were seated at a corner table flooded with sunlight did Norma bring up the subject of the day care centre again.

'Joe and I want to have a kid in a couple of years.' Her face was suffused with tenderness. 'When we feel we can afford for me to stay home for a year or two. Then I'll be damn eager for a day care centre. But you know, it's funny . . .' Her smile was whimsical. 'I mean, how Lloyd Masters is putting up the money for the expansion of the centre. My mother said she could never understand how he and his wife sent all their kids off to boarding school by the time they were out of third grade. Except for the oldest daughter,' she amended. 'Alison's health was delicate, they say. He may be the greatest guy in the world to most of this town, but that was a bitchy thing to do to those little kids.'

'They probably hated it.' Diane fought to keep her voice even. Not everybody in Eden belonged to the Masters fan club. Elvira had given her the first hint of that. 'What about his daughters?' Diane tried to appear casually curious. 'Are their children in boarding school?'

'Gerry hasn't any,' Norma said. 'Peggy has two girls – one nine and one twelve. Linda has a boy of nine and a girl who's only five.' *Her cousins.* 'None of them has been sent off to boarding school. And it's not for lack of money. Both husbands are in the company, in major positions.' Norma chuckled. 'Maybe to Lloyd Masters day care centres are the less affluent families' boarding schools.'

Two evenings later, for the first time, Diane saw a photograph of Gerry, Mrs Clark Watson, on the society page of the *Evening News.* Her mother had referred to her as being shy, Diane remembered. The photo accompanied an article about the Saturday morning story-telling sessions at the library.

Her throat tightening, Diane studied the photograph of her youngest aunt. Linda and Peggy were mirror images of their mother, but not Gerry. And then with an unnerving suddenness, she realized whom Gerry Masters Watson resembled. The same features that had been etched on her memory from snapshots of her father looked back at her. And all at once her mother's voice filtered into her mind: *'It's always made me so happy, Di, that you're the image of your father.'*

But nobody in Eden would recognize that she was the image also of her youngest aunt on the Masters side. Would they?

Chapter Six

Diane felt herself engulfed in constant emotional conflict. She revelled in the love she shared with Cliff – but was it derailing her from what she had come to Eden to accomplish? She was frustrated that her newspaper reading, relentlessly pursued, was revealing nothing of value. She mustn't lose sight of her reason for being here. And she could never quite thrust aside a sense of guilt because she wasn't being honest with Cliff.

How would he feel if he knew what had brought her to Eden? Would he – like Uncle Erich – think that she was being ridiculously childish to believe that she could right a terrible wrong? Would he think her stupid and neurotic? Or a vindictive bitch? She couldn't bear that.

She realized there was gossip around the hospital about Cliff and herself. He sought to spend every free moment with her – though a resident had little of that. But she, too, cherished every moment they had together. Was there space in her life for Cliff and her mission?

Norma invited Diane and Cliff – along with several couples – to a Sunday afternoon barbecue in late September.

'There's no way of knowing if Cliff will be able to make it,' Diane reminded Norma.

'Hey, I've been working at Masters Memorial for four years – I know the score, sugar. If both of you can come, great. If he can't make it, you come alone. I'm not one of the high-and-mighty social set that lines up guests like in Noah's ark.' She giggled. 'I'm not one of the Masters women, who do everything by the book.'

Before eight o'clock on Sunday morning, while Diane lingered in bed, Cliff called.

'Did I wake you, honey?' He was apologetic.

'No, but what are you doing up so early?' He'd been on duty till midnight, then had come to the apartment to spend an hour with her before she'd shipped him off to catch some sleep. While she realized how eager Cliff was to stay over in her apartment, she'd set a curfew for them. She knew it was absurd in this day and age, yet didn't want to advertise that she was sleeping with him.

'I just got a wake-up call from the hospital,' he said, and stifled a yawn. 'I have to rush over to fill in for a no-show. I won't be able to make the barbecue.'

'Oh, Cliff, you need a day off.'

'Once I'm out of my residency,' he warned, chuckling, 'you won't be able to wake me on a weekend morning before noon. Unless you want to get your little butt paddled.'

'I'll throw out the alarm clock.'

'I love you.'

'I love you, too.'

'Gotta run now. I'll buzz you when I get off duty.'

Diane felt self-conscious at arriving at Norma's alone. The other guests were already there. The men gathered around the barbecue pit Joe had built. The women – all strangers to her except for Norma – greeted her with the warm Southern cordiality she admired. In a corner of her mind she recalled that Norma had told her Gail's husband was a chaser: 'I only put up with him because Gail and I have been close friends since kindergarten.' From a transistor radio sitting on the umbrella-shaded dining table came the voice of a newscaster reporting on the game between the New York Mets and the Chicago Cubs.

'I'll wait until Joe's ready to throw the burgers on the grill before I bring out the cold stuff,' Norma said. 'Pull up a chair and sit down. It's too hot to move an inch. I told Joe we ought to cook outdoors and eat inside in the air conditioning. But you know men. Such creatures of habit. A barbecue means eating outside.'

At a commercial break in the radio broadcast Gail's husband ambled over to join the women for the moment. Norma was right, Diane thought, uncomfortable beneath his blatant scrutiny. He was a chaser.

'You chicks going to do your patriotic duty and vote in November?' he asked with masculine condescension.

'I never vote,' Norma admitted, shocking Diane. 'Nor does Joe. Because I vote Democrat and he votes Republican. We'd just cancel each other out.'

'You look familiar.' Gail squinted at Diane while her husband rejoined the men. 'Do you work in one of the shops out at the mall?'

'No, I'm at the hospital office with Norma,' Diane explained. 'You may have seen me there.'

'I never go there.' Gail frowned in frustration. 'You remind me of somebody . . .'

'People are always telling me I look like somebody they know,' Diane said in sudden unease. 'I have one of those faces.'

'Joe says she looks like a movie star,' Norma said. 'Thank God, I'm not the jealous type.'

'I know who she looks like.' Gail snapped her fingers in triumph. 'You could pass for Gerry Watson's kid sister – or daughter,' she amended while Diane froze. 'She's OK – I can't stand the other Masters girls. Nor their bitchy mother.'

'Don't let other folks in town hear you say that,' another of the wives chided. 'That's a dangerous club to belong to.'

Diane struggled for composure. She'd never expected anyone to notice the resemblance between her and her father's youngest sister. Yet what did it mean? There were always lookalikes that bore no family relationship. She was Diane Phillips. Nobody would connect her with the Masters family.

As the weeks passed, Diane felt herself drowning in despair. She'd gone through twenty-four years of Atlanta newspapers thus far without finding one item dealing with any kind of suit against the Masters newspaper chain. Then on a Saturday morning at the Eden Public Library – on the point of conceding she needed a fresh approach – she spied a brief article in a January 1949 edition of the *Constitution* that sent her hopes soaring.

Churning with excitement, she leant forward to refocus the microfilm on the screen. Here was the article she'd been seeking all these months! 'Lloyd Masters and His Newspaper Empire Are the Subject of a Million-Dollar Libel Suit by Texan Roger Ames.' Ames had been an unsuccessful candidate for the House of Representatives. He blamed his defeat on slanderous attacks by Lloyd Masters' local newspapers. 'Never in the history of Texas politics has such a false and scurrilous campaign been waged against a candidate for public office,' he was reported as saying. His teenage son had made threats against Lloyd Masters' life.

Diane reached into her purse for change, dropped it in the slot, waited for the printout.

Radiant, every nerve in her body tingling with elation, she rushed back to her apartment. At last a breakthrough! She was impatient to talk to Beth, to give her facts Jack could follow up for her. On Wednesday evening she'd go back and read later editions of the *Constitution*. There would surely be follow-up news on the suit.

Should she tell Cliff what had brought her to Eden? No, her mind cautioned. Wait until she had something conclusive.

At the apartment she dialled Beth's number, waited through endless rings. Beth wasn't home. Of course not. She would be doing the weekend chores.

At noon Diane forced herself to sit down to lunch and when she'd finished her sandwich and coffee, she reached again for the phone. On the third ring Beth picked up.

'Oh, Beth, I've been dying to talk to you!' She gave an eloquent sigh of relief.

'What's up?'

In a flood of words Diane reported on what she had discovered.

'Beth, tell Jack. He said he'd help. You know, dig into court records.'

'I'll ask him to get right on it. But he's going crazy with school work right now. It might take him time to track down the information.'

'Beth, push him.'

'Di, this happened twenty-one years ago.' Beth sounded troubled. 'How do you know you'll be able to track down this guy?'

'I'll find him.' Even if it meant hiring a private detective – and she guessed how expensive that could be. Somehow, she would find him.

'Di, he might not be the one –'

'It's the only lead I have. I have to run with it.'

Each evening she expected a phone call from Beth, but no call came through until their usual Sunday morning exchange of calls a week later.

'Jack says he'll dig into the court records for info about the suit any day now,' Beth soothed. 'He's just going nuts with class work. Be patient.'

Diane continued her search through the pages of the *Constitution*. The suit had been filed – there must be follow-up. Still, lawsuits had a way of being postponed for months, even years. She ploughed ahead doggedly. Why couldn't Jack take off a couple of hours to look for information for her? He had information at his fingertips, if he'd only look for it.

She'd been startled when Cliff suggested taking her home with him for Thanksgiving dinner. She was eager to meet his parents, yet fearful that they'd worry that Cliff would give his career second place in his life now. And always she asked herself if she had a right to love Cliff when she had a sacred obligation to her mother. Shouldn't that take precedence over anything else? Yet how could she deny her love?

Cliff wanted so badly to introduce her to his parents – even though they both knew the barriers that stood between them at this point.

'We'll be casual about it, sugar. You're a New York girl alone down here; you work with Gladys at the hospital. That makes you a family friend. Besides, I already told Mom I was bringing you.'

Beth heard the phone ringing as she slid the key into the apartment door. It wasn't Jack – he was holed up in the library working on a paper for school. Probably Mom, she decided, rushing to pick up before the phone stopped ringing. Gearing herself up for a series of fresh reproaches. To Mom it was as though she was walking around with a sign on her chest saying, 'Yeah, I'm living with a guy and I'm not married.' Hell, they had co-ed dorms at a lot of colleges these days – and nobody asked who slept in what room.

'Hello.'

'How are you, Beth?' Erich's voice came over the phone.

'I'm fine, Uncle Erich.' He'd been 'Uncle Erich' to her since she was nine. 'How're you doing?'

'I worry about Di,' he admitted. 'I was hoping she'd come home for Thanksgiving. Now she says something about being able to take a week off between Christmas and New Year. I just wanted to ask you to encourage her to come home then. It bothers me that she's out of school. One more year and she'd have her master's.'

'She mentioned something to me, too, about coming,' Beth comforted. 'I'll tell her we need to see her.'

They talked another few moments, and Erich said goodbye. Poor guy, Beth commiserated, all alone in the apartment. Should she have asked him to have Thanksgiving dinner with the family? He and Mom were very *sympatico*. No, he was cooking dinner for his friends.

Jack was flying home to Cleveland for the long weekend. His parents had sent him a round-trip ticket. She wished Jack wasn't so reluctant to tell his parents about her. Mom was making cracks about that.

Now she focused on what to make for dinner. She kept telling Jack two could eat as cheaply as one if you planned meals right, but it wasn't working out quite like that. So they'd have pasta again tonight. When Jack was a lawyer with fancy clients, they'd eat out twice a week at the best restaurants.

Within the next three days – in the tradition of Southern hospitality – Diane was invited to Thanksgiving dinner by Gladys, Norma, and Elvira. Without indicating where she would be, she graciously explained that she was 'all set for Thanksgiving'. She suspected that Gladys knew of her destination and was pleased.

She dreaded Thanksgiving day – her first Thanksgiving without Mom. It had always been such a special time for them. Mom would invite what Uncle Erich good-humouredly called their 'strays' to be with them: his friends Hans and Joseph plus Mom's unattached friends from school. These were their family for the day.

Dinner preparations were a team effort – the three of them crowding together in the kitchen on assigned tasks. As a little girl she'd been so proud to be part of what Mom had called 'our cooking team'. She could close her eyes and feel the warmth and conviviality that permeated the apartment on Thanksgiving day, even before their guests arrived.

Tantalizing aromas filled the kitchen, floated out into the other rooms: the turkey roasting in the oven, the yams popped in at the proper time. A deep-dish pumpkin pie sat on the counter, waiting its turn.

But this Thanksgiving Mom wasn't with them – and she was a thousand miles from home. Uncle Erich would prepare Thanksgiving dinner for just himself and his two friends.

On Thursday morning at 10.30, the air crisp and cold, Diane and Cliff left Eden for the drive to the Atlanta suburb of

Buckhead where his parents lived. Earlier, when she'd called Uncle Erich to wish him a happy Thanksgiving, she'd listened with strained patience to his urging that she return home and resume her schooling.

Now his voice ticker-taped across her mind: 'Di, what are you accomplishing down there? Better you should be back here and in school. That's what your mother really wanted for you.'

What Mom wanted was for her to nail Dad's killer. Why was Jack stalling this way? If there was a suit, wouldn't it be somewhere in the court records? Couldn't he take some time out to try to find it?

'I'll give you a guided tour of Atlanta after we've checked in with Mom and Dad.' Cliff broke into her introspection.

'That'll be fun.' She managed a smile, but her eyes were sombre.

'Hey, what are you so uptight about? You're going to meet my parents – it's not a trip to the guillotine.'

'They're going to know about us, Cliff.' The way he looked at her sometimes was a dead giveaway.

He was silent for a moment. 'Shall we tell them we plan on getting married when I finish my residency?' he asked gently, yet she suspected he was reluctant to do this. He didn't want to do anything that might cause them to worry. 'Will that make you feel better?'

'Not yet,' she hedged. 'Give them time to get to know me.'

'OK. I'll take you home with me for the first night of Hanukkah –' He lifted one hand from the wheel, crossed two fingers – 'Provided I don't get stuck with an extra shift. "And then at New Year I'll admit we're serious about each other."'

'Let's just get through Thanksgiving.' She laughed shakily.

'Mom and Dad will love you,' Cliff promised. 'They always wanted a daughter. They were stuck with just me.'

Diane fought against panic, natural enough when she was going to meet her prospective in-laws, she rationalized – but they didn't know that yet.

Cliff turned off the highway. Now they were driving through

lush, rolling countryside. Tall Georgia pines dotted the stretches of hills, then valleys – the winding roads lined with beautiful homes.

'Mom and Dad moved here nine years ago,' Cliff explained, 'when they began to worry about the sharp rise in crime in the city. That was when Dad moved his store to a shopping mall out here.'

Cliff slowed down and pointed to a house on their right, a well-maintained weather-shingled colonial cape that sat on the top level of a terraced acre. 'Mom and Dad's pride and joy. After me,' he derided affectionately.

'It's lovely,' Diane said, impressed yet nervous about the imminent encounter.

'Relax,' Cliff coaxed, turning into the driveway. 'Nobody's going to chop off your head. Though Mom may talk you to death about her son, the doctor.'

They saw the front door flung open as they approached the entrance. Cliff's father came forward to greet them – a slender man, not quite as tall as his son, with salt-and-pepper hair and Cliff's brown eyes. He exchanged a warm embrace with Cliff, then turned to Diane.

'We're always happy to meet Cliff's friends,' he said, extending a hand to Diane. A gentle, almost courtly man, Diane thought, relaxing.

'It's so nice of you to have me, Mr Hendricks.'

'Come inside and get warm.' He led Diane into the small, cozy foyer. 'Millie,' he called down the hall. 'They're here!'

'I'm coming, Bob . . .' A contralto voice exuding enthusiasm filtered down the hall, followed by its owner. Blonde, blue-eyed Mildred Hendricks was a small, vivacious woman who carried a fair amount of excess weight with a regal air. 'Oh, Cliff, you look so tired,' she crooned, holding her arms out to her son. 'They work you too hard at the hospital!'

'Today I'm goofing off. Mom, this is Diane Phillips. I've warned her, she won't get away from the dinner table without gaining two pounds.'

'We're so happy you could be with us.' Mrs Hendricks leaned forward to kiss Diane lightly on one cheek. 'I love to cook – and the more at the table the better. But come, let's sit down in the living room and be comfortable. I have coffee up. And cinnamon buns warming in the oven.'

Diane tensed in anguish, thrown back to that awful afternoon when she'd brought cinnamon Danish home.

'What time will we be sitting down to dinner?' Cliff asked as the four of them moved into the spacious living room, furnished with well-crafted traditional-style reproductions such as Diane's mother had loved. Birch logs were aglow in the brick-faced fireplace. 'I promised Di that somewhere along the line I'd show her a little of Atlanta. All she's seen is Hartsfield when she had to change planes.'

'Around half-past two. Is that all right with you?' Mrs Hendricks radiated a touching warmth.

'Great,' Cliff approved, exchanging a glance with Diane.

'Before you drive her into town, show Diane Lenox Square and Phipps Plaza. They're our two marvellous indoor shopping malls, across the road from each other,' she told Diane, then stopped short. 'Oh dear, all the shops will be closed today.'

'Show her our new Memorial Arts Center,' Bob Hendricks suggested. 'I know, the *New York Times* called it "a more sophisticated Soviet Palace of Culture", but we're very proud of it. And show her Peachtree Center. This town is really booming, Diane. Delegations from all over the country are coming here to study the city's growth.'

His parents were clearly proud of their city, Diane thought as they plied Cliff with suggestions for a sightseeing tour. And she sensed a nervousness in them that she was more to Cliff than 'a friend from the hospital'. Their whole world revolved around Cliff and his medical career.

Then Mrs Hendricks went out to the kitchen to bring in coffee and cinnamon buns, rejecting help from the others. Cliff's father talked sombrely about the soaring crime rate in Atlanta and the growing drug problem.

'We had no drug problem at all until this summer. But last summer thousands of kids swarmed into Atlanta from all over the country. They created a kind of hippie heaven in a segment of Piedmont Park. Most were good kids, but there was an unsavoury group among them. All of a sudden we had a drug culture.'

'We have good kids here in Atlanta.' Smiling confidently Mrs Hendricks walked into the living room with a tray. Cliff and his father jumped up to help. 'You two sit down,' she ordered and turned to Diane. 'My two men forget that women have abandoned the "helpless flower" attitude.'

'Mom, you've never been the "helpless flower" type,' Cliff derided, exuding love for her. 'As soon as I was in school full time, Mom was in the store helping out. And she's never stopped.'

'Oh, I wanted to keep an eye on my man,' she drawled. It was clear, Diane thought, that Cliff's parents shared a beautiful marriage. Like Mom and Dad had shared so briefly. 'Now dig into the buns while they're hot.'

'How do you like living in Eden?' Cliff's father asked Diane.

'Oh, I love it.' She struggled for lightness, trying to brush away painful memories. 'It's a whole new experience for me.'

'I was afraid at first Cliff would be bored out of his mind,' Mrs Hendricks confessed. 'I mean, after living in Atlanta. Of course, we soon realized all he had time for was the hospital. He was determined to be a doctor from eleven years old, and Cliff has a one-track mind.'

Diane intercepted a fleeting, anxious glance between Cliff's parents. They were worried she might bring chaos into Cliff's hectic existence. They knew there was no room in his life for marriage. She and Cliff knew that. How could they make Cliff's parents understand they were satisfied to share what they could manage until he had finished his residency? That what they shared wouldn't interfere with his career?

'OK, let's take off,' Cliff decided when they'd demolished the cinnamon buns and drained their coffee cups. 'We'll be back well before the turkey goes on the table.'

'They're so sweet,' Diane told Cliff in the privacy of the car as they headed for Lenox Square, the first stop of their tour. 'They love you so much.' The way Mom had loved her – and Dad, when he was alive.

'They'll love you, too, when they get to know you.'

'Cliff, we mustn't do anything to hurt them.'

'Never,' Cliff vowed. 'They'll be so happy when I've finished my residency, and we tell them we're getting married. We have no family other than distant cousins, and they have this awful fear of leaving me alone in the world.'

For an instant Diane saw Uncle Erich's anxious face, his voice. '*Di, when I'm gone you'll be all alone in the world.*'

'They'll be out of their minds with joy when they know they're getting a daughter-in-law,' Cliff said.

'But not until you've finished your residency.'

They could survive the two and a half years before this happened. And in the course of those two and a half years she must accomplish what she had come down here to do. In an odd fashion, she thought tenderly, Mom had brought Cliff and her together. Because of Mom she was here in Eden.

When was she going to be honest with Cliff, tell him why she was here? It unnerved her to hear Cliff talk about Lloyd Masters with such respect. Next week, new equipment he was giving to the hospital would be arriving. There was to be some dedication ceremony. How could she tell Cliff she hated this man who was her grandfather? That she lived for the day she could unmask him as a liar and an hypocrite? As a man who could let his son's murderer go free to protect his own image?

'You're awfully quiet.' Cliff's gently teasing voice dispelled her introspection. 'Did Mom and Dad scare you that much?'

'Cliff, I love them. They're beautiful people.'

'Remember that. If you ever get mad at me, you'll think twice about dumping me and losing them.'

Cliff showed her Lenox Square and Phipps Plaza, then headed into downtown Atlanta to the impressive Peachtree Center. They paused in admiration before the ultramodern twenty-one-storey Regency Hyatt House, with its enclosed garden roofed with glass domes.

'It's one of the largest hotels in the South. The grand ballroom can accommodate three thousand guests.' Cliff's hand was at her elbow, urging her on.

While the Atlanta Museum was closed, Cliff told her that within its walls were such tourist-favoured sights as Eli Whitney's original cotton-gin and mementoes of *Gone with the Wind* author Margaret Mitchell. He drove through Grant Park and pointed out the Cyclorama – a dramatic depiction of the Battle of Atlanta in the Civil War.

'Oh, you have to see the antique merry-go-round here in the park. It's one of ninety remaining in the country. It was built by a man who brought skilled wood carvers over from Germany to carve the animals. It's a lost art now.' Cliff smiled wryly.

From Grant Park Cliff drove to Underground Atlanta – one of Atlanta's new attractions. Here old buildings beneath the viaducts had been restored, stripped of paint to reveal the names of shops of the 1870s and 1880s – saloons, banks, packing house, a variety of stores. Added to the old were clusters of bright new shops and restaurants, all eager for tourist dollars.

'We'll come some time other than a holiday,' Cliff promised. 'The place really swings, Restaurants, cabarets, boutiques, even a theatre.'

By the time they returned to the house, Diane and Cliff breathed in savoury aromas with candid appreciation.

'You're right on time,' Bob Hendricks greeted them. 'Dinner will be on the table in ten minutes.'

Over dinner Mrs Hendricks coaxed Diane to talk about her own background.

'Cliff told us you were from out of state. I realized right away that you weren't from the South,' she said with genuine interest.

Haltingly Diane told Cliff's parents about her mother's recent death without saying this was self-inflicted – and they didn't pry, were warmly sympathetic. With some odd compulsion she told them about her father's death when she was two, and how her parents had met in hiding in Nazi-occupied France. She talked about her grandparents who'd died as Resistance fighters.

'I spent three years in uniform during World War Two.' All at once Cliff's father was caught up in painful recall. 'I was with the American troops that liberated Buchenwald. It was one of the largest concentration camps in Germany – on a small hill a few miles outside Weimar. What I saw there is etched on my brain.' The atmosphere in the dining room was electric as he continued. 'The smell of death was everywhere. Men and boys in rags, children with haunted eyes, ribs showing through their paper-thin shirts. Rows of naked bodies piled up like so much cordwood.'

'I remember, all these years later, hearing Edward R. Murrow report on radio about his visit to Buchenwald,' Mrs Hendricks added. 'I think half of the country cried when they heard him.'

'My uncle's two closest friends were in Buchenwald.' Diane's voice was a tortured whisper. Cliff's father might have seen them in that hellhole.

'For months I had nightmares about those first hours at Buchenwald. Life goes on – but you remember.' Bob Hendricks forced himself back to the present. 'But enough of bad memories. Let's remember the good things today. We're alive and well. The world is at peace. Relatively,' he amended. 'We won't think about Vietnam on Thanksgiving Day.'

'It's time to bring out dessert.' Mildred rose to her feet. 'Diane, you'll help me bring out the pies? Pumpkin pie in honour of tradition, chocolate pecan pie because that's Cliff's favourite.'

'Don't let her talk your ear off about "her son the doctor,"' Cliff called after Diane. 'To Mom I'm the next Louis Pasteur.'

Chapter Seven

When Diane walked into the hospital grounds on Monday morning, she realized instantly that this was the day the new equipment was to arrive. A platform had been erected before the hospital entrance. Here the Hospital Board would officially accept the Masters family gift. According to the *Herald* and the *Evening News* this was a gift not just from Lloyd Masters but from the entire Masters family.

'Rumour is that the old man is about ready to shove one of his sons-in-law into the State Legislature,' Elvira had mentioned yesterday with caustic humour. 'He figures he can do that.'

A few early spectators had already arrived, were taking up choice positions. A crew from the local TV station was setting up cameras. More cars than usual sat on the parking area.

Inside the hospital the atmosphere was electric. The receptionist inspected her reflection in a large make-up mirror that rose from an open desk drawer. Volunteers were arranging flowers in the spacious reception area. A trio of porters were zealously polishing woodwork and brass. Diane hurried down the long hall to the business office. As she'd expected, Gladys was already on duty, debating aloud about where to place a vase of red roses.

'It'll be a madhouse in another thirty minutes,' Gladys predicted. 'Every resident, every nurse is going to make sure to be here when that new machine arrives. It'll give Masters Memorial big city status.' She was radiant with pride.

Diane told herself this was just another day on the job. She sat at her desk, switched on her typewriter. She wouldn't be going out there to watch the ceremonies. Somebody had to stay on duty in the office. She didn't *want* to watch the ceremonies. From the newspaper accounts she gathered that the entire Masters family would be on the platform. Except, she reminded herself grimly, for Lloyd Masters' oldest grandchild – herself.

She'd stay here in the office. She wouldn't have to see any of them. Her throat tightened as she considered this. The din of voices outside now told her the ceremony would be well attended. Gladys expected the guests would make a tour of the hospital facilities after the ceremony. Please God, don't let them come in here.

'They'll bypass the business office, of course,' Gladys surmised, wistfully ignorant of the turmoil within herself, Diane realized.

'Shouldn't we all go out and participate?' Norma exchanged a hopeful glance with Deedee.

'You all go out. I'll mind the store,' Diane offered.

Gladys smiled in agreement. 'I don't think much is going to be happening here. OK, let's go.'

Diane sat before her typewriter and tried to focus on the work at hand. She could hear voices outside, though their words were – for the most part – unintelligible at this distance. Then there was a huge uproar. Lloyd Masters was arriving, she surmised. Her grandfather – her only living grandparent – was to give the opening speech.

She wouldn't allow herself to go to a window, to be a spectator even at a distance. She stared without seeing at the pile of bills to be logged. She was here in the hospital dedicated to her father's memory. *His* father was taking his place on the platform outside. If Dad could know what his family had done to Mom and to her, how furious he would be. He'd be furious that his father was allowing his murderer to go free.

All the residents, the nurses, the aides that weren't absolutely required to be at their stations, were cheering Lloyd Masters for his magnificent gift to the hospital. She'd spied Brad charging down the hall ten minutes ago, eager to be part of the ceremony.

Where was Cliff? He'd been scheduled to come on duty at 7 a.m.

At last the noise outside died down. Gladys returned with Norma and Deedee.

'It was a beautiful ceremony,' Gladys told Diane, who forced herself to appear impressed. 'Mr Masters is such an elegant gentleman. Such a compassionate man.' Gladys didn't know the real Lloyd Masters. 'For years he's come into the hospital in the evenings – on his way home after a long day at the newspaper – and he goes up to paediatrics to give stuffed animals to little kids he knows are having a rough time. He never talks about that, but the nurses on that floor are just worshipful towards him.'

'Did you see that fur coat his wife was wearing?' Deedee was awed. 'Somebody said it was sable.'

'I don't wear fur.' Reproof in Norma's voice. 'Fur belongs on the animals who were born with it.'

'My mom says the Masters are kind of like our royal family,' Deedee said with awe.

'Deedee, we live in a democracy,' Norma shot back. 'We don't need royalty.'

'OK, let's settle down,' Gladys ordered. 'Party time is over.'

Still, it was difficult for Diane to thrust from her mind the knowledge that her grandfather was at this moment making a ceremonial tour of the hospital premises. She glanced at her watch at regular intervals. It was getting close to lunchtime. She didn't want to bump into the Masters entourage on her way up to the cafeteria.

'Ready to go to lunch, Di?' Norma was reaching into a desk drawer for her purse. 'Let's beat the mob today.'

'Sure. I'm starving.' Suppose she did bump into them? Nobody knew she was Kevin Masters' daughter. Suppose they came face to face and she blurted out the truth? What would happen?

Then the Chief of Staff pushed open the door to their office, stood aside for another man to enter – tall, silver-haired, expen-

79

sively dressed, immaculately groomed. Diane's heart began to pound. Even before Gladys rushed forward in effusive greeting, Diane knew this was Lloyd Masters. But she must be silent. This was not the moment to confront him. She struggled to hold back the recriminations that threatened to erupt.

'I just wanted to stop by and say hello on this special day,' he said with a courtly smile. 'You know, Gladys, you and your staff are an important part of this hospital.'

'Thank you, Mr Masters.' Gladys beamed.

'You're all doing a great job.' He glanced swiftly from Norma to Deedee to Diane – yet Diane sensed he didn't see them. 'Keep it up.'

'Our moment of glory,' Norma drawled when Masters was gone, and Gladys frowned in reproach; Diane fighting for composure. 'Come on, Di. Let's go to lunch.'

For the rest of the day and into the evening Diane was haunted by the image of her grandfather. He came across with the charisma of a fine British character actor, she thought grimly. Elegant, charming, compassionate. But she wasn't alone in thinking another man existed behind that façade. Elvira saw through him. So did Norma.

Cliff phoned as she washed her few dinner dishes.

'I'll be here for ever. Too late even to stop by for an hour.' He sounded wistful.

'Come even if it's late,' she encouraged. 'We haven't had any time together since Thanksgiving.'

'God, it seems so long.'

'I know. But it won't be like this for ever.' Why did she so often feel these surges of guilt? She wasn't failing Mom by loving Cliff.

Diane put down the phone, went out to the kitchen for more coffee. It was absurd to be sleepy at this hour of the evening. She needed to learn to relax – then she'd sleep better at night. But she was so frustrated that Jack was doing nothing to follow up her lead about Roger Ames.

Her *Atlanta Constitution* reading was almost up to date, but not one more word had she seen about the suit. If the suit hadn't come to trial before Dad was murdered, did that mean Ames wasn't a real suspect? The possibility that she could be on the wrong track was unnerving. What other lead did she have?

She settled down with another cup of coffee, flipped on the TV, neither of which did anything to combat her drowsiness. All right, take a nap here on the sofa. Cliff had a key to the apartment – he could let himself in. She drifted off, awoke with a start at the insistent ring of the phone, went to respond. Knowing it would be Cliff.

'Hello?'

'Di, I won't get out of here before morning.' He sounded exhausted. 'I'm sorry, sugar.'

'I understand. We'll talk tomorrow night.' She glanced at the clock. It was 3.10 a.m. No wonder so few residents dared to marry.

Lloyd Masters sat with smug satisfaction at the head of the table in his decorator-designer Regency dining room, surrounded by three of his daughters and their husbands as a maid served coffee in Sèvres china. He gazed for an instant at his wife at the foot of the table. Maureen looked bored, as usual, he thought with momentary annoyance. Still, she played her role well. To the public she was the charming, caring wife of one of the South's leading citizens. At home she was bored. *When* she was home. She was talking about yet another trip to Europe.

'Everybody's raving about the dedication services at the hospital yesterday,' Linda reported, then frowned. 'I don't know why the *Atlanta Constitution* didn't do a story about it.'

Her husband, Hugh, chuckled. 'Do you expect the *Constitution* to say anything laudatory about the family that runs the Eden newspapers? They've been our mortal enemy ever since we fought so hard against segregation in our public schools.'

Lloyd smothered a grunt of distaste. The 'family' didn't run the Eden newspaper chain. *He* did. The sons-in-law stood in for the son who should have been at his side. The best of his children were long lost to him.

'Mayor Randall's making noises about his son Peter running for the State Legislature,' Clark said casually. Lloyd understood this was a dig at his own inaction. 'He's a bleeding heart liberal!'

'Pete won't run,' Lloyd predicted, his tone ominous. 'Bill Randall owes me.' Most of the politicians in this town owed him. He hesitated a moment. 'We'll talk about your running, Clark, when the time looks ripe to me.' That was putting Linda's nose out of joint. She wanted Hugh to run for the Legislature. He needed Hugh in the business – in the role he designated. And Luke had developed into a sharp attorney. For all Peggy's unsubtle hints about Luke's capabilities as CEO, let them both understand Luke stayed where he was.

They were all so conscious that next month he'd be celebrating his seventieth birthday. All of them waiting greedily for him to announce his retirement. Preparing to fight for control of his empire. *Fuck them.* He had only contempt for that retirement shit. He'd be running his newspaper chain twenty years from now.

Why did he have to lose Kevin that way? For Kevin – his war hero son – he would have been willing to share his empire. If Kevin had lived, he might have had grandsons to carry on. Linda and Hugh's boy, at nine, wrote poetry.

'Let's break this up.' He pushed back his chair. It wasn't productive to dwell on depressing memories. 'Let's go into the library for some business talk.' Maureen would take the girls upstairs to show them the clothes she'd shopped for on her last weekend trip in New York. That way she didn't have to listen to their chatter.

Later, when the others had left and Maureen had retired to her own suite for the night, he'd pick up a few of the stuffed animals sent to him regularly from F.A.O. Schwarz in New York and go over to the children's ward at the hospital. He envisioned the stillness, the air of other-world serenity that invaded the hospital late at night. There he could push aside times best forgotten. A half-hour there and he'd feel a hell of a lot better.

On Wednesday Diane grabbed a fast dinner at the hospital cafeteria with Cliff, on a break. After dinner she headed for the library. She asked for her usual allotment of microfilm and headed for her favourite machine. She was grateful that there were so few people here in the reading room. It would be embarrassing to have someone see her with her eyes closing as she tried to read. And she was ever fearful that there would be some very small, important article that she would miss.

Ten minutes into her reading Roger Ames' name leapt up at her. She tensed in excitement. Slowly she read the article, reread it in soaring disappointment. The case of Roger Ames vs. Lloyd Masters and Masters Newspapers Inc. had been settled out of court. No details. She returned the reel of microfilm to the periodicals desk and headed home.

Her mind was racing. This didn't mean Roger Ames wasn't a suspect. He may have been forced to settle out of court. Lloyd Masters may have held something over his head that he couldn't fight. All right, she needed to find out where Roger Ames was the night her father was murdered. Hire a private detective. That would put a serious dent in the money Mom had left her – but she mustn't overlook a possible suspect.

She couldn't go on keeping this from Cliff. Tonight, when he came round she'd tell him what had brought her to Eden. And she'd call Beth, who felt so guilty that Jack wasn't being helpful. How would she go about hiring a private detective? Ask Beth to go over to Grand Central; they had phone directories of every large city there. Tell Beth to look up Private Investigators in the Dallas phone book. Take it from there.

At the apartment she put up coffee, checked the refrigerator for sandwich makings. Cliff's dinner had been both swift and light – he'd be hungry by the time he got here. Now call Beth.

'Hello?' Beth's voice reached across the miles with welcomed warmth.

Diane filled Beth in on what she had discovered at the library, and what she plotted as her next move.

'Honey, private detectives are expensive as hell! And you're working on such a gamble.'

'I have the money. Mom would want me to use it for this. My salary pays all my living expenses.'

'I hate to see you hurt, Di. Oh, wait a sec, will you? There's a delivery boy at the door . . .'

Moments later Beth returned to the phone.

'Jack will be home from a late class any minute now, and I'm having a rotten period – I don't feel like cooking. *Voilà*, Chinese.'

'I'll let you go.' All at once Diane's head was reeling. She was icy cold. Her eyes sought out the small calendar on the telephone table – to confirm her sudden suspicion. 'Enjoy the Chinese.' She managed to sound casual.

Off the phone she sat immobile, struggling to accept what her mind – and the calendar – had just thrust upon her. Beth was having a rotten period, but *she* was over two weeks late. That never happened. But they'd always been so careful. Hadn't they?

She and Cliff wanted a family, yes – but not now, when Cliff had over two years of residency ahead of him. Not before she'd accomplished what she'd come down here to do. They figured he'd finish his residency and then they'd be married. He'd line up a research position, and a couple of years later they'd start their family. Now wasn't the time.

While she sat searching her mind for answers, she heard Cliff's light touch on the doorbell. He only used his key late at night. She hurried to respond.

'I smelled the coffee outside,' he said, reaching for her. 'There's something so sexy about coffee when you're tired and hungry.'

'I figured you'd be starving after that light dinner.' She forced herself into flip conversation. 'I've got cold chicken in the fridge. Ask me sweetly, and it's all yours.'

Not until Cliff had eaten and moved to the sofa with coffee mug in hand did Diane allow herself to talk seriously to him.

'Cliff, I think you'd better put down your mug and listen to what I have to say . . .'

The unevenness of her tone put him on alert. 'Di, what's wrong?'

'I think I'm pregnant.'

For an instant his face was luminous. This was the ultimate affirmation of their love. Then he flinched. 'Oh God!'

'I just became suspicious this evening. I guess I haven't been watching the calendar. I've been so sleepy, and I haven't felt like eating breakfast . . .'

'We'll work this out.' He reached to pull her close, his eyes betraying his shock. 'Three years from now we'd be ecstatic, but –'

'Cliff, I'm so sorry –'

'Sugar, it was a joint effort.' He tried for a touch of humour as he cradled her in his arms. 'But we're not sure. Before we start to worry, let's make sure you're pregnant. I'll put a rush on the lab. We'll know tomorrow night.'

She'd go along with the pregnancy test, Diane thought, but there was no doubt in her mind it would be positive.

Diane lay sleepless far into the night. At intervals her hands closed in protectively about her still-flat belly, as though to comfort the tiny embryo that grew within her. Her baby – hers and Cliff's. But how could she saddle Cliff with a wife and child when he was so overburdened? What kind of marriage could they have? Cliff would come to hate her. His parents would be devastated.

Early the following afternoon Cliff called her on her office phone.

'You were right,' he told her gently. 'I should be out of here about eight tonight – with a little luck. We'll talk about how to handle it.'

'See you then . . .'

Diane put down the phone. Her heart was pounding. Cliff would know some doctor who could take care of her, she told herself. Abortion wasn't a dirty word any more. Of course, in Georgia abortion was illegal except to protect the life or health of the woman, or in the case of rape. But under the new New York State law, abortions on demand were legal. New York City was now called the abortion capital of the country. In the last few months, she'd read somewhere, over 100,000 legal abortions had been performed there. They were done by good doctors under proper conditions.

She winced, recalling a magazine article she'd read. In one New York hospital the staff took patients in four shifts, starting at 7.30 a.m. Doctors did D and Cs simultaneously in three operating rooms. But that was a public hospital. Thank God, she could afford one of the private hospitals.

But she didn't want an abortion. *She wanted this baby*. She felt an incredible surge of tenderness, of love for this tiny seed within her. Her arms ached to hold this baby that would be so loved. But that was unrealistic. This was the wrong time.

Abortion was what Cliff meant when he said, 'We'll talk about how to handle it.' They both understood that. Abortions weren't wrong; women had a right to control their bodies. She wouldn't want Cliff to marry her because he felt he *had* to. They were young – they'd have children later. This would be a safe abortion under proper conditions.

But how could she know if she'd ever be pregnant again? This could be the one time. So many women pray for a child, and for them it never happens.

It was almost ten o'clock before Cliff called to say he was on his way. Feeling as though she were moving in a nightmare, Diane put up coffee, prepared a sandwich for him. If they married now, her mind taunted recurrently, he'd come to hate her. He couldn't take on the responsibility of a wife and child with the insane hours he worked at the hospital – and on his small salary.

She heard a car pull up at the kerb, ran to the door to wait for Cliff. He was trying so hard to appear cool, but she felt his distress, which matched her own.

'Sorry to be so late. But then how often am I on time?'

Cliff closed the door behind them, drew her close. 'Like I said, the test was positive. But I spoke to one of the doctors – you know, asking for information for "a friend". He gave me the name of a doctor in Atlanta. I figured we'd do better out of town.' He paused, feeling her grow tense in his arms. 'Di, if you don't want to do this, we don't have to. We can get married and –'

'No, we can't.' She was firm. But in a dark corner of her mind she was plotting another course, devious and scary. 'Bad timing. Later we'll have our kids. Sit down, I'll bring you coffee and a sandwich.'

After he had eaten and was fighting yawns, Diane geared herself to tell him her latest decision – what she could tell him of it. It would be best for both of them. The only right way to go. She owed this to Mom.

'You know I'm supposed to take a week off from work between Christmas and New Year. I'll ask Gladys if I can take next week instead.' She must carry this off – for both their sakes. 'I'll go up to New York and have it done there, where it's legal. No problems.' She tried to sound convincing, yet she saw anxiety in Cliff's eyes.

'I want to be with you –'

'It's nothing serious,' she reminded. 'You don't need to be with me. Beth will go with me. Several hospitals in New York specialize in abortions.' She frowned involuntarily; that was such a painful word. 'I won't go to one of those places where patients are in and out in a few hours. I'll go in one day and come out the next. I'll stay in the hospital overnight. The magazines have been full of reports about how well they're being handled. Cliff, I'll be fine,' she insisted because he seemed so upset.

'I'll dig up the money.'

'You don't need to do that. I have money in the bank. Cliff, we'll survive this.' But she didn't want to think about the years ahead.

Tonight there was a special intensity to their lovemaking. Only she knew it was to be their last time together. She had wrestled all through the agonizing night with the problem that faced her. Now she accepted the answer. There was no room in Cliff's life for a wife and baby – but she desperately wanted this child.

She'd lost Mom. Only she and Uncle Erich now survived from their family. Her daughter or son would carry on the line that had been almost obliterated in the Holocaust. She could go home to Uncle Erich. He would understand.

She tried to block from her mind the image of a life that didn't include Cliff. But that wasn't meant to be. The timing was all wrong.

Chapter Eight

On Friday morning, exhausted from lack of sleep, Diane went into the office with the knowledge that her life was about to move on to a traumatic new track. She tried to thrust off guilt that she was not being honest with Gladys. But she forced herself to say what must be said quickly, before Norma and Deedee arrived.

'If it's important to you to take off next week rather than wait, I think we can handle it,' Gladys agreed amiably. Later Gladys would learn that she wouldn't be back. Monday, Diane reminded herself. Gladys would have a week to replace her.

As Diane began her day's work, part of her mind dealt with the mundane details of her departure. At lunchtime she'd go over to the telephone company to have the service discontinued. The electric was supplied by Elvira. She'd offer to pay next month's rent on the apartment since she was leaving with no real notice. Also at lunchtime, she'd pick up her airline ticket. A one-way ticket. Cliff insisted he'd drive her to Hartsfield in the morning, that she was not to take the commuter plane from Eden, but with his weird work schedule there was a chance he wouldn't be able to make it. She prayed he wouldn't. It would be easier to say goodbye on the phone. He wouldn't know then that she wasn't coming back to Eden, that what they'd shared was over for ever. Not until he received her letter on Monday morning. Gladys would receive her formal resignation from her job then, too.

Cliff would be so upset, so hurt – but there was no other

course for them. The timing for them was all wrong, Diane told herself yet again.

Around three o'clock she glanced up from her typewriter to see Cliff charging into the room. Instantly her heart was pounding. He paused to talk with Gladys, then made a casual detour to her desk.

'I may get stuck till all hours,' he whispered. 'But I'll pick you up in the morning for the drive to Hartsfield.'

'No,' she said, her throat tight with anguish. 'You'll be too groggy to drive if you're on duty till late. Sleep, Cliff . . .' She tried for a smile. This was the last time she would see him. What little time they'd had together must last her for a lifetime.

'I love you . . .' His mouth formed the words, lest the others hear. 'Take care of yourself, you hear?'

'I love you, too,' she whispered. 'And I'll be fine.'

The day dragged in painful slowness where normally the hours sped past. Each time the office door opened, she tensed – aching to see Cliff once again and yet fearful of this. At the end of the day she accepted the good-natured sallies of the other three women about 'people who dash off for midwinter vacations'.

In Elvira's charming living room – stammering in her unease, remembering her first meeting here – Diane explained to Elvira that instead of going home for the week's vacation she'd planned, she was returning for good.

'It was kind of a rush decision,' she apologized. 'You've been so lovely to me; I feel awful doing this to you. Of course, I'll pay next month's rent –'

'No need for that, Diane,' Elvira said. 'By the first of the month I'll have another tenant. But I'll miss you, that's for sure.'

Early this morning Diane had phoned Beth to tell her she was coming home – and why. Now Beth's words filtered across her mind: 'You're taking on an awful load, honey. Maybe Cliff's right – maybe you should consider an abortion.'

But she knew she must have their baby. She had grown up in the shadow of the Holocaust, with the knowledge that she and Mom and Uncle Erich were not like other people. 'When I'm gone, you'll be alone in the world,' Uncle Erich had warned. But with her baby she wouldn't be alone. If she married Cliff, she might lose him in the stress of their lives these next two and a half years. She might wreck his career. She couldn't bear that. But she couldn't give up their baby.

Again, she slept little, her mind in chaos. She was making the right move, she reiterated. For the three of them – Cliff, the baby, and herself. She had a goal in life – marriage would get in the way of that sacred obligation. She mustn't allow that to happen. She'd gone off course. She was back on track again.

Now she was uneasy that she had not told Uncle Erich that this was not just a visit. He'd seemed so happy that she was coming home 'for nine days'. He had to be at the lab much of tomorrow, but Beth would meet her at the airport.

In the morning – on Elvira's phone with her own now out of service – Diane called for a taxi. Elvira kissed her goodbye, urging her to keep in touch. At the Eden airport Diane bought a ticket for her flight to Atlanta, waited for the boarding announcement. Between flights at Hartsfield she mailed the letter to Gladys and the one to Cliff – written last night with such anguish. Cliff wouldn't be able to trace her. He didn't know the address of the apartment in New York and the phone had always been unlisted. Cliff didn't even know Beth's last name. She'd disappear from his world. She tried not to visualize a world without Cliff.

She was grateful to have a window seat on the flight from Atlanta to New York. She could stare out the window at the clouds, and no one would see the tears that relentlessly filled her eyes. Those few months with Cliff had been so precious. He would be so hurt, so bewildered, when he received her letter on Monday morning. Then he would be furious that she could treat him this way – and eventually he would hate her.

Beth was waiting for her at La Guardia. Diane was conscious of relief at seeing Beth's familiar face. She reached for Beth in gratitude.

'It's so wonderful to see you! But I feel so guilty, taking you away from work.'

'Hey, I wasn't going to let you schlep luggage all the way to the taxi station.' Beth clucked in reproach. 'Little mother.'

'I'm about seven weeks pregnant – I can carry luggage.'

Together they walked outdoors to the taxi station, pleased that there was a short wait.

In the cab Diane leant back, fighting off a wave of tiredness.

'Tell me what's happening with the paper,' she ordered. Beth was so enthusiastic about her job.

Not until they arrived at the apartment did Beth bring up the subject of the baby again.

'You still haven't told Uncle Erich?'

'How could I tell him over the phone? When he comes home from the lab, I'll tell him.' It was an intimidating prospect. And what would she do if he wanted no part of her now? She had money to live on for a while, but she needed Uncle Erich's approval, his emotional support.

'I thought we could all have dinner together tonight,' Beth began apologetically, 'but Jack's made plans for us to have dinner down in the Village with a friend from law school and his girlfriend.' Her smile was wry. 'The girlfriend's father is a judge. Jack thought it might be a good connection one day.'

'You'll be seeing plenty of me from now on.' The cheerful air Diane had managed to exude since her arrival began to ebb away. 'Did you get over to the Grand Central phone directories?'

'Yeah, I have a list from the Dallas Classified. But Jack says you'll be buying a pig in a poke. An expensive pig.'

'I'll do a lot of investigating before I hire anybody.' Diane tried to sound optimistic.

'Suppose this Roger Ames guy was nowhere near Eden when your father was killed?'

'Then I'll have to look for another path. I'm not giving up on this. I have to find answers. My life will be raising the baby and discovering who murdered Dad. I know I'll never love any man but Cliff. There'll be no more romantic involvements in my life. I know what I have to do.'

'Let me help you unpack.' Beth rose to her feet. 'And I'll clear out before Uncle Erich arrives. I figure you'd rather be alone.'

'I dread telling him, Beth. He'll be so upset.' Diane winced in anticipation. 'He'll be happy to see me back in New York, but how will he feel about the baby?'

'He loves you very much,' Beth reminded her, but Diane sensed her apprehension. 'Now let's put away your gear . . .'

Erich arrived only minutes after Beth left the apartment, joyous at Diane's return.

'This apartment has been empty without you.' He embraced her with tender warmth. 'It's wonderful to see you.'

'Uncle Erich, there's this man I wrote you about –'

'Roger Ames,' he picked up dismissively. 'It's a wild shot.'

'I mean to follow it up.' She braced herself for what must be said. 'But that isn't what brought me home. I was so lonely down there – and scared.' She hesitated, prodded herself to continue. 'I met someone.' He looked so startled, she thought. 'A resident at the hospital. You'd like him so much – under normal circumstances. He took me to meet his parents. We were going to tell them at Hanukkah – as I was going to tell you – that we were serious about each other. But then – then things got out of hand.' She managed a poignant smile. 'I'm pregnant.'

'He doesn't want to marry you?' Erich's voice soared in rage. 'What kind of a man is he? I don't understand the way young people live today! All this sleeping around! I don't understand the new morals!'

'It's not the time for us to marry.' Diane struggled for calm. 'He has another two and a half years as a resident before he can go out into practice. You can't imagine what medical residents go through – the insane hours they work, the terrible pressures. There's no space in a resident's life for marriage or for a baby. He thinks I've come home for a legal abortion. I'll let him believe I'm having it.' Her voice broke. 'Monday he'll get my letter saying that I won't be coming back to Eden – that it's all over between us. But, Uncle Erich, I want to have the baby.' Her eyes implored him to understand. Then a chill darted through her as she realized the depth of his shock. 'If you don't want me to stay here, I'll –'

'Of course, you'll stay!' All at once his face was suffused with love. 'You'll have the baby. Together we'll raise her – or him. It's wonderful, Di. Don't you see? *Our family lives.*'

On Monday evening Cliff came home from the hospital after another thirty-six hour shift. He was anxious at not hearing from Diane. He'd expected her to call when she arrived in New York. Belatedly he realized he had no address – no phone number – for her in New York. She'd said she could handle everything without her uncle knowing. She'd work out some story about spending a couple of days with Beth. Had she gone immediately to the hospital? Had something gone wrong?

Reaching for his key, he heard the radio blaring inside. Brad was off duty. He unlocked the door and walked into the living room. Brad was on the floor, doing push-ups.

'Hey, I don't want to see that,' Cliff scolded. 'I'm so bushed I can't even walk straight.'

'I figure I need to get in shape if I'm going to last through my residency.' But Brad was abandoning his efforts. 'I baked when I got off duty. A great Black Forest cake.' He sighed. 'I ate half of it – that's why the push-ups. It's in the fridge.'

'Any mail – other than bills?' Cliff dropped into the lounge chair, lifted his aching feet to the foot stool.

'A letter for you.' Brad reached for an envelope on the coffee table. 'Here . . .'

Cliff took the envelope and recognized Diane's large, up-slanted scrawl, turned it over: no return address. Why hadn't she just phoned? He ripped open the envelope, pulled out the small sheet of notepaper.

He stared in disbelief at the brief message. She wasn't coming back to Eden after the abortion. She was remaining in New York.

It was over with them – it had been a mistake from the beginning, she wrote. It was time for them to go their separate ways.

'I don't believe it.' He was ashen. 'She can't mean this!' He reached for the envelope again. No return address.

'What's happened?' Brad demanded.

'It's from Diane. She's not coming back to Eden. I don't even have a forwarding address or a phone number!'

'You two have a brawl before she left?' Brad was solicitous.

'No!' Cliff hesitated. 'Not exactly. Diane's pregnant. She said she'd go up to New York for an abortion. She wouldn't even let me pay for it. Oh God, Brad, I let her down. We never said anything to anybody, but we were going to get married as soon as I finished my residency. I was taking her home to my parents next week, to tell them we were serious. She was going to call her uncle and tell him. She didn't want to have an abortion,' he said in sudden realization. 'But she didn't tell me that! I told her we could get married –'

'While you're still in your residency?' Brad scoffed. 'Di's a bright little gal – she knew what that would do to you. She remembers how Ralph's wife walked out on him because she couldn't take living his crazy life.' Ralph was a third-year resident with a wife and baby. 'Look, it's rough, but it's not a disaster.'

'To me it's a disaster.' Why had he been so blind? Why hadn't he seen she hadn't wanted an abortion? And now – because she was having it – she wanted no part of him. 'I meant to build my life around Di. We were so right together.'

'Look, you'd have been crazy to tie yourself down to a wife and child at this stage. Be practical, Cliff. Play the scene, and we've got it made. Five years out of here we'll be living like royalty. You know the score. With Medicare and Medicaid paying the bills, can't you visualize the loot that'll be pouring in? You announce you accept Medicare and Medicaid patients, and you have a line at the door from 9 a.m. to 9 p.m.'

'I don't worry about being the richest doctor in the country.' Cliff shook his head in disbelief. How had he allowed himself to lose Diane? 'You should know by now,' he picked up, 'that I really want to go into research.'

'Bullshit,' Brad dismissed this. 'You're going to ignore the gravy train that's out there waiting for us?'

'Did you read that article in *Fortune* last January?' Half-heartedly Cliff allowed himself to be derailed.

'You shoved it down my throat,' Brad recalled. 'All the sad statistics about how hard it is to find medical care these days – even for those who don't live in poor city neighbourhoods or rural areas. All the doctors who insist on working nine-to-five five-day weeks,' he drawled. 'God forbid anybody should get sick over a weekend.'

'I can't even get in touch with Di.' Cliff reached for her letter again. 'I have no address – no phone number. How can she write us off just like that?'

'You'll get over it,' Brad soothed. 'Think ahead. Almost every doctor in the country thinks Medicare is the greatest thing on earth.'

'I don't like what a lot of doctors are doing with Medicare and Medicaid,' Cliff said bluntly. 'They order too many unnecessary tests, procedures that aren't necessary. Damn it, Brad, you see it every day in the hospital.'

'They're protecting themselves against malpractice suits.' Brad's smile was smug. 'So who's to stop them? You'll change your viewpoint in about three years. When you see all the Mercedes and Jaguars floating around with MD licence plates.'

'I didn't go into medicine to be among the richest men in the country.' Cliff was grim. 'I'll talk to Gladys in the morning,' he said with a glint of hope. 'Maybe she has Di's New York address.'

Diane tried fiercely to accept this new life she had plotted for herself. She knew that Cliff would try to find her, but he couldn't, she comforted herself. He had no address, no phone number.

She was grateful for her uncle's acceptance, his tenderness, his pleasure at having her home – and his joyous anticipation of a grandniece or grandnephew. Beth's married sister, Fran, guided her into the care of an obstetrician. When the new semester began at the Columbia School of Journalism, she would resume her studies – taking a light load in deference to her pregnancy. But Cliff was missing from her life, and that was painful.

Uncle Erich had taken on the task of vetting private investigators and Diane was waiting now for him to choose one on her behalf. She knew he had little faith in what this effort would accomplish, yet comprehended her need to pursue this. She told herself he was right in not rushing ahead with the first name on the list, even while she fretted at the delay.

By late January – preparing for the beginning of the school term – she was resorting to the use of pins to fasten the waists of skirts and slacks. Beth insisted they go shopping for maternity clothes the following Saturday.

'We'll shop in the morning, then have lunch at the Charleston Gardens,' Beth decreed. 'I'll pick you up at 9.30. We'll be at Altman's when the store opens.' She sighed. 'You should hear the dirty cracks I'm getting from Mom. Either I should marry Jack right away, or "toss the bastard out of your life". She's the one who threw me at him. "A bright Jewish boy going to law school,"' she mimicked. 'It kills her that I'm helping him through law school. She can't understand that it's for both of us.'

'She means well.' Diane forced a smile. But she understood Mrs Bertonelli's anxieties. 'I wish Uncle Erich would settle on a private investigator. I want to see some action.'

'You said he seems set on this latest one,' Beth reminded her.

'He's going to give him the go-ahead, I think,' Diane conceded. 'I wish he wouldn't set a time limit. I know, I have to put a cap on how much to spend. Uncle Erich's so sweet – he wants to pay for the investigator, but I insisted he would come out of the money Mom left me.'

'Di, don't pin too much hope on this.'

'I realize it's a long shot.' She hesitated. 'I hate to lose touch with Eden. Could I order a subscription to the *Herald* in your name?' She knew it was irrational, but if she read about Eden she'd feel closer to Cliff. 'To be delivered to you?'

'Honey, you know you can.'

'I'll have to go back to Eden. Not for a while, of course. But the answers I need are hidden somewhere in that town. I don't care if it takes the rest of my life, Beth. I'm going to track down my father's murderer.'

The private investigator in Dallas took on her case. He'd be clear any day, he reported, to give full attention to locating Roger Ames, whom he knew by name. 'Ames has been involved in local politics for years now. He's had a lot of support but a bad press from one of the local papers.' Lloyd Masters' newspaper.

In the meantime, Diane devoured each edition of the *Herald*, even while she told herself it was absurd to expect some nugget of information to appear there. She was unnerved by her uncle's reaction when a photograph of her father's youngest sister, Gerry, appeared on the society page of the *Herald*.

'My God, Di, she's the image of Kevin!' Then he turned to her. 'The image of you.'

'Some woman at a party mentioned it,' Diane admitted. 'Nobody else noticed . . .' Certainly not Lloyd Masters, she remembered, though had he really seen her in that brief encounter?

She was tense with excitement when the private investigator wrote that he was now checking on Roger Ames' whereabouts the night Kevin Masters died: 'Remember, it was twenty years ago, it may take some time.' But Uncle Erich had given him a set number of days – at fees that had shocked both her uncle and herself. But if he needed more time, she thought recklessly, then he would have it.

Often these evenings – because Erich was dedicated to long hours at his lab – Beth came to the apartment to have dinner with her. Jack had late classes this semester. Tonight the two women were in the kitchen preparing dinner, which would be re-heated later for Erich, when the phone rang.

'Miss Phillips?' an unfamiliar male voice asked when Diane answered

'Yes . . .' Instinctively she knew it was the Dallas private investigator, even before he identified himself. 'You have a report for us?'

'It's not what you'd like,' he apologized. 'We've verified Roger Ames' whereabouts on the night of 12 April 1950. He was at the bedside of his wife in a Dallas hospital. Their son, too, was there. Mrs Rogers suffered a massive heart attack that morning.'

'Thank you . . .' Diane struggled for poise while he completed his report.

'What is it?' Beth asked anxiously when Diane, pale and shaken, put down the phone.

'Roger Ames couldn't have killed Dad. He was in Dallas that night. No doubt about that.'

'Honey, the odds are so heavy against you. Your mother wouldn't want you to drive yourself crazy with this.' Beth's eyes pleaded for Diane to listen to her. 'You're –'

'I know what Mom expected of me,' Diane broke in. *'For your father and me, my darling, make the world know he didn't kill himself. Find out the truth so we may both rest in peace.'* 'You hear all the time about murders that go unsolved for twenty or thirty years. There are special squads of detectives who work on these old cases. We talked about it in a class I took.'

'Maybe your father just walked in on a robbery, and the guy was cornered and shot him. That happens, Di. And what chance would you have to track him down?'

'If he murdered once, he'd murder again.' Diane's mind was in high gear now. 'He got away with it. He wouldn't change his way of life because he killed a man.' In sudden excitement her eyes focused on the headline of a tabloid Beth had left on

99

the telephone table: 'Serial Killer Attacks Again.' 'Beth, maybe – just maybe Dad was killed by a serial killer.'

'Di, you're off the wall!'

'No, I'm just following another route. I have to find out about other murders in Eden. I'd be surprised if there were very many and if I can find some link between other murders and Dad's, I'll have a lead! Serial murderers try again and again – till they're caught.'

'Put this to rest for a while,' Beth cajoled. 'Work at it again after the baby is born.'

'I can't go back to Eden. Not for three years.' Not until Cliff finished his residency and left town. 'But I can look for murders before and after Dad died; search for a link.'

'How can you do that up here? Be realistic.'

'Microfilm of old newspapers,' Diane explained, 'in the New York Public Library files. Or in the microfilm files at Butler, up at Columbia.'

'They won't have copies of the *Eden Herald*,' Beth protested. 'A small town like that?'

'No. But they'll have copies of the *Atlanta Constitution*. Eden's close enough to Atlanta for a murder in town to be reported there. I'll track this down. I won't screw up on school, but if there are links between other murders and Dad's I'm going to discover them.'

Chapter Nine

Cliff accepted the mug of strong black coffee Brad thrust at him, sipped with distaste. All he wanted at this moment was to fall in bed and sleep for twelve hours.

'You know I wouldn't ask you to cover for me if it wasn't urgent,' Brad said, hovering anxiously beside him. 'You can still catch a few hours' sleep. Look, I'll go in, stay for the first two hours – then you take over.'

'I'm bushed,' Cliff reiterated. 'I need more than five hours' sleep to function responsibly.'

'It's the four-to-twelve in the emergency room. What's going to happen in those hours? This isn't New York City. Tina wants me to be at that dinner. Her mother's hysterical because some character backed out at the last minute. They need an extra man.'

'Why do you have to be the "extra man"?'

'I'm thinking of asking Tina to marry me.' His grin was triumphant. 'She's not going to turn me down. God, she can't get enough!'

Cliff tensed. 'You're talking about getting married, after all the shit you threw at me about how no resident in his right mind tries that scene?' It would be a long time before he could think about Diane without reviling himself.

'We won't get married for at least a year. So don't start looking for another apartment-sharer. But I need to know Tina's going to be there for me. The last year of my residency I'll be able to handle being married – when I know what'll be waiting out there for me. Tina's old man is worth millions. The family has the kind of friends that make great patients. You know, they don't care what anything costs. The more tests, the more procedures, the happier they are.'

'And they have million-dollar health insurance policies.'

'OK, I can stay at the hospital just until six o'clock. Then I have to come home to dress. Cliff, cover for me. Just from six to midnight.'

'OK.' Cliff yawned, almost upsetting his mug of coffee. 'But you better call me a little after five to make sure I can get vertical. And call back every ten minutes,' he warned, 'until you know I'm fully conscious.'

In the French provincial-style master bedroom of the Watson house – a scaled-down version of the Masterses' mansion a quarter-mile down the road – Gerry Watson heard the heavy footsteps of her husband moving along the upstairs hall. Her hands trembled as, seated at her dressing table, she lifted an earring to one ear. Why was she bothering with jewellery when Clark was in such a foul mood?

The doorknob was turning. The door swung wide. Tall, broad-shouldered, handsome when not consumed with rage, Clark stalked into the room.

'You little bitch,' he said through clenched teeth. 'How dare you give Dora the day off!'

'She came in with a terrible cold.' Gerry braced herself against her dressing table. 'And you know how you carry on about germs.'

'I wanted to bring Francis Melton home for dinner. One of those casual, last-minute invitations – to show him how well orchestrated I am. But no!' He moved towards her. 'You let Dora go home. Thank God, I called you before I invited him!'

'You would have been upset if you saw how sick she was,' Gerry stammered. 'But I have a roast in the oven. We'll have dinner –'

'I don't want your bloody dinner!' His face was flushed with anger. 'I wanted to be able to tell the old man we had Melton here for dinner. It would make me look good! You know he's stalling on putting me forward for the State Legislature!' He towered threateningly over her.

'Clark, don't hit me,' she pleaded, but already his fist rushed out to land a blow on her chin. 'Not on the face, please –'

'You ask for it!' he yelled. 'You provoke me!'

She closed her eyes, tried not to scream out, because that only made him more furious. Then she felt an excruciating pain as he twisted her arm behind her, a pain so piercing that she was momentarily faint and would have fallen if he hadn't caught her.

'What now?' he demanded. 'You're such a rotten faker!'

'My arm,' she moaned. 'I think it's broken.'

All at once the room was blanketed in silence.

'You weren't looking where you were going,' he fabricated. 'You fell down the stairs again. Get your coat,' he ordered after a moment's cogitation. 'I'll call Dr Ross to meet us at the hospital.'

With the stoicism acquired through the years Gerry went into the walk-in closet that held her designer wardrobe. She pulled down the mink coat that had been Clark's tenth wedding anniversary gift, draped it with her good arm awkwardly about her shoulders.

As usually happened on these occasions, and despite her pain, she was conscious of a defiant rebellion. Why had Mother sent her back to Clark that first time, before they'd been married a year? Mother and Dad didn't want to hear that her husband beat her. Didn't they believe her? She remembered what Kevin had said in a distraught moment long years ago: 'Mother and Dad believe what it pleases them to believe.'

Between boarding school and camp she'd seen so little of Kevin, though she adored him. She was only eleven when he'd gone to fight in World War Two, but she'd cried herself to sleep when she'd heard he'd enlisted. She'd cried when he was reported missing in action. Though she knew she mustn't admit it, she'd loved Kevin's beautiful young wife and then their darling baby. So sad that Kevin died that way. Sometimes she wondered what happened to Sophie and their little girl. Mother said Sophie had just packed up and left after the funeral, leaving no trace behind her.

'Gerry!' Clark's voice – harsh with exasperation – intruded on her introspection. 'For God's sake, move it!'

'I'm coming . . .' She adjusted her coat again with her uninjured arm. 'Let's go,' she said quietly, dreading the wise glint she sometimes saw in the attending staff at the hospital emergency room.

At Masters Memorial the emergency room had been fairly tranquil this evening. Then the staff was alerted by Dr Ross that a patient of his was coming in for treatment. 'She fell. Her husband thinks she may have broken her arm.'

'It's Gerry Watson,' the head nurse told Cliff, now standing in for Brad. 'The Old Man's youngest daughter. We roll out the red carpet for this one.'

Despite his awareness of the deference shown the Masters family at Masters Memorial, Cliff was astonished at the obsequiousness that permeated the emergency room when Clark Watson solicitously helped his wife into a treatment room. Cliff and the head nurse, along with the prestigious Dr Ross, went into action.

'I keep telling Gerry to wear glasses, or be fitted for contacts,' Clark Watson said, holding the hand of her uninjured arm. 'But you know women.' His smile, aimed at the three men in the room, bypassed the head nurse and the pair of student nurses who'd joined the group – mainly, Cliff thought, because Gerry Watson was the Old Man's daughter.

An X-ray proved the arm was fractured. The bone was set, with her husband sharply demanding painkillers even before this procedure was begun. Gerry dismissed the suggestion that she remain overnight in the VIP suite.

'I'd rather go home,' she said softly. She turned to her husband. 'Please, Clark . . .'

Cliff watched Gerry Watson, flanked by her husband and Dr

Ross, leave the emergency room to head for the sedate black Mercedes her husband drove. She seemed so vulnerable, somehow touching. She reminded him of Diane, he realized all at once. The same dark hair and glorious blue eye, the same delicate features.

'We haven't had that star attraction in here for about six months,' the head nurse said. 'She's accident-prone, you know.'

'Accident?' Cliff challenged, only now admitting the suspicions that had run across his mind. 'Did you see that bruise on her chin?'

'Don't even think about it,' the head nurse warned. 'In this hospital that would be treason. The Old Man wouldn't like it one bit.'

And he doubted, Cliff thought compassionately, that Gerry Watson had liked it at all. Wouldn't it bother the 'Old Man' – as this whole town affectionately referred to Lloyd Masters – that his daughter was being physically abused by her husband?

For the rest of the shift he was haunted by Gerry Watson's face. So like Diane's.

How could he know for sure that Diane was all right? She had the abortion in a hospital, under legal conditions, but, God, he'd like to *know*! He'd spent an entire evening on the telephone, calling every Phillips in the Manhattan phone directory, after spending unconscionable time copying the numbers at the Atlanta library.

This was all wrong, he'd told himself endless times. How could he reach her, talk to her? All he knew was that she lived in Manhattan, on the Upper West Side, 'a brisk twenty-five-minute walk from the Columbia campus.' Maybe he ought to go up to New York the next time he had a few days off, walk around the area, ask questions. But damn it, he didn't even have a snapshot of Diane.

The late afternoon was grey and cold, with a hint of snow in the air. Diane waited for a bus on the corner of Broadway and analysed her feelings about this first day of school. It felt good, she admitted, to be back in the old grind. Yet it seemed as though years had passed rather than months since her last day on campus.

She'd thought she'd feel self-conscious at being pregnant and in class – and she was showing now – but nobody seemed to think it was odd that a graduate student was pregnant. The baby wasn't due until late July. The last days of classes were in late May; she could handle school with no sweat. Yet at unwary moments between classes her thoughts travelled to Eden. How was Cliff? Was he hurting because of her – or had hurt turned to anger? She'd made it clear in her letter that she would have the abortion. He couldn't know about the baby.

The bus pulled to a stop. She climbed aboard. She'd go to Zabars and pick up a barbecued chicken for dinner, she decided. Uncle Erich wouldn't be home from the lab yet for another two hours.

The phone was ringing as she unlocked the apartment door. All these weeks later she was still tense each time the phone rang – fearful that, in some unexpected fashion – Cliff had tracked her down. Part of her hoping he had.

She picked up the phone. 'Hello?'

'Hi.' It was Beth. 'Just checking to see if you were home. I'll run over with a batch of the *Herald*s that just arrived.' The newspaper shipped in weekly batches. 'I'll be there in five minutes.'

'I'll put up coffee,' Diane said.

Beth arrived with the pile of newspapers plus yet another knitted sweater for the baby.

'Your mother thinks I'm expecting triplets.' Diane's smile was affectionate. 'Thank her for me.' Now she turned eagerly to the newspapers.

'Read. I'll check on the coffee.' Beth headed for the kitchen.

Diane settled herself on the sofa, newspapers spread across the coffee table. She'd skim them now, read more carefully later. Entering the small world of Eden again, she was conscious of wistful regret that she couldn't write to Elvira or Gladys or

Norma. In her few months in Eden they'd become important in her life. They must think her such a kook for running off that way.

She always read with a sense of expectancy that some important item would leap out from the pages. Now she skimmed the society column that dealt with comings and goings of the socially prominent. Gerry Watson was leaving for a cruise in the Mediterranean. Hadn't she been in Paris several months ago? An earlier edition of the *Herald* had reported that Maureen Masters was at The Breakers in Palm Beach for a month's stay. Elvira had said the Masters women were the local jet-setters, Diane remembered.

While not reported on the society pages, it was widely known in Eden that Lloyd Masters travelled constantly between his various newspapers. Lloyd and Maureen Masters might make frequent public appearances in Eden that portrayed them as a devoted couple, but Diane suspected theirs was not a perfect marriage. A devoted wife wouldn't run off so often on solitary vacations.

Then excitement soared in Diane. Her eyes clung to the page before her. Representing the residents on staff at Masters Memorial, Cliff had written an article – on order, she surmised – about the near-miracles the recently donated equipment was accomplishing at the hospital, about its importance to the community. She hesitated, then with infinite care, ripped out the article to savour again – and again, she suspected. Cliff was so bright, so dedicated to his profession, so compassionate. And so convinced, she thought in rebellion, that Lloyd Masters was God's special gift to the town of Eden.

Beth returned to the living room with mugs of coffee. Diane reported on the two points of interest thus far in the *Eden Herald*.

'The newspaper, *my* newspaper,' Beth emphasized with a giggle, 'is giving me some freedom on an article for the next week's edition. You may get a wild call tonight for emergency aid.'

'I'm all yours.'

'Jack thinks I'm nuts to stay with the paper. He says I could be pulling down a bigger salary if I just went after an "administrative assistant" job.' She sighed. 'I can't make him understand I love what I'm doing. I mean, I could love it once Tom understands I'm capable of more than the little he's been throwing at me so far.'

'You can live on what you're earning – that's what counts.' Jack was hungry for more small luxuries in their lives, Diane thought grimly, to be supplied by Beth's salary. 'And you're building a career.'

'I'll never be a Marguerite Higgins. God, how you talked about her all through high school,' Beth drawled.

'My career plans have taken a shift.' Without realizing it, Diane moved a hand to the faint rise of her stomach. 'I can't go traipsing around the world and raise a daughter.'

'Hey, you could be spoiling for trouble thinking like that. Suppose the little one in there is a son?'

'I'll love him just as much,' Diane said. 'But I just know this is a daughter.'

'Drink your coffee before it gets cold, Little Mother. I have to go home and throw together dinner for Jack and me. Then I zero in on this article. It's got to be good – even if I'm writing for a giveaway weekly.' The *West Side Guardian* was distributed free – the advertising was calculated to cover costs and show a profit.

Always Diane read the *Herald* with hopes of latching on to a report of murder in Eden, though the place remained frustratingly murder-free. Each week she spent hours in the microfilm room at Butler Library, reading back issues of the *Atlanta Constitution*, fretting that she had no access to back issues of the Eden newspapers. And to her astonishment she realized how much she missed Eden. She confessed this to Beth on a glorious spring Sunday afternoon as they strolled along the promenade that flanked the Hudson River on the Upper West Side.

'Mom used to tell me how she and Dad loved living in Eden – except, of course, for his father's trying to dictate their lives. She liked the slow Southern pace, the friendliness everywhere, the air of serenity.' She paused, laughed. 'All right, I sound like the Eden Chamber of Commerce. I know that underneath all that lovely serenity there's the usual amount of ugliness.'

'I'd miss New York.' Beth squinted in thought. 'The theatre, the ballet, the museums, the great department stores.'

'Eden's forty minutes away from Atlanta – you have all that there,' Diane countered. 'And how many times a year do you get to the theatre and the ballet and the museums?'

'So not too often, but it's there when I want it. Of course, on my budget these days, who can afford anything but the museums?' Beth sighed elaborately. 'Thank God, they're still free.'

'You know what I think would be an exciting lifestyle?' For the first time Diane gave voice to what had been fermenting in her brain for weeks. 'To live in Eden and run a newspaper. Not a daily – a weekly giveaway like your *West Side Guardian*.' There was a messianic glow in her eyes now. 'Our tiny weekly confronting the *Herald* and the *Evening News*. The two of us taking on Lloyd Masters, fighting against the evil his newspapers dump on the town.'

'Two little Davids fighting the giant Goliath,' Beth flipped. 'Honey, that's a fairy tale.'

'Don't say that. One of these days somebody will come along with the strength to unmask Lloyd Masters. And I pray that it will be me.'

'Cool it, Di.' All at once Beth seemed unnerved. 'Don't let yourself become obsessed by him. You don't need that kind of rage.'

And in a corner of her mind Diane remembered her uncle saying something quite similar to her mother.

The last few weeks of the school term were physically difficult for Diane. She was sleeping poorly. She chafed at not being able to put in the hours before a microfilm machine that she had managed earlier in her pregnancy. She rebelled against her constant tiredness.

Always she thought about Cliff. How was he? Was he seeing someone else? But that didn't concern her. He was out of her life. She'd chosen the path her life was to take. No room in that life for Cliff. No room in his hundred-hour working week for her and their child.

On a steamy mid-July night Diane went into labour. Along with Erich she was watching the late TV news when the first pain rocked her into alertness. Not until the newscast was over did she tell her uncle.

'I'll call the doctor –' Striving to hide his anxiety, he rose to his feet.

'Not yet. Take a nap,' she encouraged. 'I'll wake you when it's time to go to the hospital. And I'll call Beth.' She'd promised Beth she'd call at the first sign of labour. Beth and Uncle Erich would be at the hospital with her.

Sooner than she'd anticipated, the baby signalled her – or his – impatience. She phoned her doctor between pains that startled her with their intensity. Arriving at the hospital with Erich, she spied Beth emerging from a taxi just ahead of their own.

'OK, let's get this show on the road.' Beth was flippant, but her embrace was warm and anxious.

'We're both ready –' Diane stopped short, caught in another surge of insistent pain. 'Wow,' she said breathlessly when it was over. 'That was a real yell for action!'

Immediately, the receiving nurse deciding there was no time for paperwork at this point, Diane was propelled into a wheel-chair and taken to the maternity floor, with Erich and Beth in attendance. While Diane was wheeled off to a labour room, Erich and Beth settled themselves in the waiting area.

In her bed in the labour room – between bouts of pain, and doctors and nurses intruding at short intervals – Diane thought about Cliff. He ought to be here with her, she told herself in momentary rebellion. This was his child, too, that was fighting to come into the world. Through the wall between her labour room and the next she could hear the consoling, encouraging voice of a soon-to-be-father. She wanted Cliff here with her.

Then, imprisoned by the increasingly frequent pains, she abandoned thinking. Five hours after her arrival her labour was over. In a haze she heard the obstetrician tell her she had delivered a daughter. She managed a shaky smile of approval. She'd known that all along.

Later a nurse brought her the small bundle that was Sophie Jennifer Phillips, the name to be listed on her birth certificate. Holding her daughter in her arms, Diane marvelled at the miracle of birth. Her daughter. Her precious child. Raptly she examined the tiny red face. Jennie was the image of Cliff, she realized with a start, then felt suffused with tenderness. Part of Cliff would always be with her.

Finally Erich and Beth were standing beside her bed. Uncle Erich looked so shaken, she thought. He'd been terrified for her.

'The family lives,' he whispered with touching pride.

'She's gorgeous,' Beth said. 'In a few years you'll be chasing boys away from your door. Oh God, wait till Mom sees her. All I'll be hearing: "When are you and Jack getting married? When do I have another grandchild to spoil?" And of course,' Beth said gently, 'she'll insist on being a surrogate grandmother to Jennie.'

Diane thought about Cliff's father and mother – what wonderful and proud grandparents they would be. If the timing was right. And she was conscious of a deep sadness that Jennie would never know loving grandparents. She would never know a father's love. But those around Jennie would make up for that, Diane vowed.

And Jennie would grow up with no feeling of being different because of the Holocaust. She'd be a normal little girl with no hang-ups, no fears. Mom had never guessed how many nights she'd lain awake – a terrified little girl, fearing that what happened in Germany could happen here; that they could be taken off to concentration camps, perhaps to die terrible deaths. Mom and Uncle Erich never suspected what their stories about the Holocaust planted in her mind.

Beth announced she was taking a week's leave from the newspaper to be with Diane and Jennie during their first days at home. Despite Diane's insistence that it wasn't necessary, Uncle Erich was up with her each night for Jennie's 2 a.m. feeding. He was there with the 6 a.m. bottle. She was amazed at the way he handled Jennie – with a skill and a gentleness that touched her. And then she remembered that he'd been the stand-in father for her since she was two.

'Uncle Erich, you're spoiling me,' she protested at intervals.

'I want to make sure you build up your strength again for school,' he said with mock gruffness. 'Don't forget you start evening classes in September.'

Life in the Phillips apartment revolved around Jennie. Any faint sound from her crib brought instant attendance. For Diane and Erich an incredible happiness had entered their lives. These first weeks the outside world seemed not to exist for them. Their world was Jennie.

Diane's evening classes started. Erich baby-sat and when he was stuck at the office, Beth took over.

Diane was impatient to resume her research via microfilm files of the *Atlanta Constitution*. She knew that both her uncle and Beth had thought Jennie's arrival would be a distraction. But it was important for Jennie, too, that Dad's murderer be brought to justice.

It became a ritual for either Erich or Beth to stay with Jennie each Saturday afternoon while Diane went to the microfilm room at Butler Library to read.

On this balmy October afternoon Beth was to pick her up at the microfilm room so the two of them could go out for an early dinner. Jack was holed up in the law library – 'until they throw me out.'

'You need some diversion – more than just the baby and school and the library,' Erich had insisted. 'Go with Beth for dinner at Tip Toe Inn. My treat.' Everything was Uncle Erich's treat, Diane thought lovingly. He wouldn't allow her to spend a cent of her own money.

In the microfilm room Diane rewound the roll of film on the spindle, removed it, positioned the next roll on the spindle. She glanced at her watch. Beth would be here any minute. But run this roll.

It was so frustrating to find nothing after all these months, she admitted, scanning the pages of the newspaper. Was Uncle Erich right when he said that a murder in Eden was not important enough to be reported in the *Constitution*? And while she considered this for the hundredth reluctant time, she spotted a small item that commanded attention: 'SUSPECT SOUGHT IN EDEN MURDER'.

Her heart pounding, she read the few lines allotted to the account. A forty-eight-year-old black woman had been viciously stabbed to death. The police had no leads. And then Diane's eyes were riveted to the last line: 'Annie Williams had been a domestic for the past eleven years in the home of newspaper magnate Lloyd Masters.' *That was a link.* She didn't know just how, but there *was* a connection between this murder and her father's, she told herself recklessly.

'Hi.' A whispered greeting in deference to the setting.

'Read this . . .' Diane began excitedly.

Without sitting down Beth read the item. She seemed startled, then wary.

Diane rewound the film, impatient at the need for this when her mind was in such chaos.

In tacit agreement Diane and Beth said nothing about what was ricocheting in their minds until they were out of the library and striding across the Columbia campus in the direction of Broadway.

'Beth, this is what I've been searching for all this time. This is a link to what could be a serial murder!'

'Di, don't jump too fast,' Beth cautioned. 'It's just another murder –'

'Annie Williams worked for Lloyd Masters,' Diane broke in. 'Don't you see? That's two murders that touch the Masters family. It –'

'It doesn't mean there was a connection. She was stabbed to death – not shot,' Beth pointed out. 'It happened in her own house. It could be a coincidence that she worked for Lloyd Masters. There's no real pattern established.'

'I have a gut feeling that I'm on to something important. This woman was murdered in 1957. I want to read further – see what the police come up with. So far they say they have no leads. Maybe it wasn't solved. I know it happened seven years after my father was killed, but serial murders happen that way. I have to find out what happened with this murder, whether it was ever solved.'

'Don't you have enough on your plate with Jennie and school?' Beth challenged. 'Put all this behind you now.'

'No. This is the first real lead I've discovered. I won't stop now!'

Chapter Ten

Diane contrived to squeeze in two or three hours each week when she could devour back issues of Atlanta newspapers, despite the demands of caring for Jennie and of her Columbia classes. Fighting impatience at the slowness of her efforts and the pain of continual frustration, she scanned the newspaper columns in search of a follow-up to the 1957 murder in Eden.

Thanksgiving approached. Diane felt herself awash in poignantly sweet memories of the previous Thanksgiving, when Cliff had taken her home with him for the holiday dinner. Would he be with his parents this Thanksgiving or on duty at the hospital? Did he remember last year this time? Guilt blended with pain in her. She was depriving Jennie of her father's love – her grandparents' love. But Cliff had wanted her to have an abortion. He hadn't been prepared to take on marriage and fatherhood.

She remembered other Thanksgivings, when her mother had been alive. Despite an aura of festivity, she'd always recognized that for her mother and uncle the day evoked anguished memories of those who would have been at the table except for the Nazi horror. Their family had been almost obliterated. It was a knowledge that never allowed them real peace.

Beth's mother had invited Uncle Erich and her and, of course, darling Jennie to share her family's Thanksgiving dinner. Uncle Erich thanked her but pointed out that it was a tradition for his two close friends to come to the Phillips apartment on this holiday. 'And for Jennie's first Thanksgiving we should be at home,' he'd confided to Diane.

Diane was grateful for Uncle Erich's help in the kitchen on Thanksgiving morning. It helped to block out memories of last Thanksgiving with Cliff and his parents. Jennie was asleep in her crib, and in three hours Hans and Joseph would arrive. Later in the day Beth would drop in. The day would pass.

'I remember my first Thanksgiving in this country,' Erich reminisced while he coaxed stuffing into the turkey cavity. 'In some miraculous fashion your father had managed to get your mother and me over to New York – at a time when GI brides and even some troops were still awaiting passage after VE Day. We stayed in a hotel and had Thanksgiving dinner in a fabulous restaurant. Longchamps,' he recalled. 'Sophie and I were so impressed with this special American holiday.'

'You didn't spend much time in Eden, did you?' She knew this, of course, yet she wanted to hear about it again.

'Just some brief school vacations. Your father used his saved-up army back pay to get me into a special school that was to prepare me for college entrance. I made it into City College; worked part time during the school years, full time during summer vacations. Kevin and Sophie sent me money that helped me survive.'

'You never met Dad's family.' It was a statement rather than a question.

'They wanted no part of me. Except his kid sister. She came to dinner a couple of times while I was there during a winter break from school. Gerry, I think her name was. She adored you.'

'We'd better put the turkey in the oven. It'll need four hours.'

Erich chuckled. 'Send plenty home with Hans and Joseph or we'll be eating turkey for the next five days.'

Though Jennie was just five months old in December and hardly old enough to comprehend, Erich insisted she be at the table each evening of Hanukkah while he lit the candles in the meno-rah – the candelabra designed to hold eight candles.

'Let Jennie know who she is,' he said with pride on the first of the eight-day holiday.

Even though Jennie couldn't understand, Erich explained to her that Hanukkah was the Jewish Feast of Lights, commemorating – after three embattled years – the Jewish victory in 165 BC against the Syrian tyrant Antiochus.

'The celebration was held in the temple of Jerusalem, where they found only one cruse of oil to light their holy lamps. And miraculously the oil lasted for eight days,' Erich told Jennie – uncomprehending but listening avidly to her much-loved great-uncle. 'Each evening of Hanukkah an additional candle is lighted, until the menorah holds eight candles.'

With the approach of New Year's Eve Beth made an effort to include Diane in her own celebration.

'We're having just a small party. Tom and Rita from the newspaper, three of Jack's friends from law school, and the couple next door. You know Uncle Erich will be happy to babysit Jennie.' Erich was devoted to watching New Year's Eve at Times Square via television. To her uncle, Diane knew, the arrival of each new year was a kind of victory that he was alive and free. He had never totally banished the years of hiding from the Nazi menace from his memory. 'Di, it'll be fun,' Beth coaxed.

'Stop trying to fix me up with one of Jack's friends,' Diane scolded.

She dreaded the holidays. It was a reminder that she would never spend a New Year's Eve with Cliff. They'd had only a few months together, yet it seemed she'd known him for ever. At errant moments she dallied with the tumultuous thought of writing to him, telling him they had a wonderful daughter, even sending him photographs of Jennie. But each time her mind rebuked her for this. Neither of them was free for a life with the other.

Diane's routine in the new year of 1972 followed the pattern of the previous year. Each Saturday afternoon she took her place before a microfilm machine and read through copies of old Atlanta newspapers, ever perplexed that she discovered no follow-through on the 1957 murder in Eden. Endlessly she reminded herself that a murder trial could be postponed for many months – if there was to be a trial.

'I don't understand it,' she confessed to Beth after returning to the apartment one Saturday afternoon in March after a session at the library. 'How can there not be some further report on the murder? I've covered almost a year now – not only in the *Constitution*, in the *Atlanta Journal* as well. But then I didn't expect this to be easy,' she said abruptly before Beth could reply. 'I'll keep reading.'

A reproachful wail from Diane's bedroom told them Jennie was awake.

'Ah, our precious doll decided nap time is over.' Beth – who'd been babysitting – leapt to her feet along with Diane. 'Thank God, she's not teething for a while.'

'She's such a happy baby when the teeth aren't pushing through.' How sad that at such a tender age she had to contend with pain, Diane commiserated. 'Oh, Uncle Erich's picking up another batch of snapshots on his way home from the lab. I'll have to start another album soon.'

Jennie was standing up in the crib, shaking the railing with exuberance, her face rosy from sleep.

'Did you have a good nap?' Diane crooned, reaching to lift Jennie from the crib.

It was unnerving sometimes, she thought, when Jennie gazed at her in that quizzical fashion, so like Cliff at special moments. Oh, he would adore Jennie. But his life would be totally disrupted if they were living under the same roof. Better this way than to be married to Cliff and watch their marriage disintegrate.

The two women returned to the living room. Diane deposited Jennie in the circular mesh playpen, littered with the soft toy animals that Erich constantly brought home for her. With Jennie happily diverted, Diane picked up her earlier thought. Now she confided the suspicion that had been gnawing at her for weeks.

'I have this crazy hunch that the 1957 murder in Eden was

never solved,' she told Beth. 'Like Dad's. If there were other murders after those two, there's a serial murderer operating in Eden.'

'It's a shaky theory, Di.' Beth was unconvinced.

'How can I find out if this woman's murder was ever solved without spending the next six months reading right up to the present?' A woman who'd worked for Lloyd Masters. 'This slowness is driving me up the wall!'

'It would have been followed up in the Eden newspapers,' Beth surmised, and Diane nodded in agreement. 'But to get the information would mean going down to Eden.'

'What about phoning the Eden district attorney's office?' Diane clutched at a fast solution. 'Not me,' she admitted, 'but you could call up – you know, as a reporter on your newspaper – and say you're doing an article on unsolved murders in various parts of the country. They couldn't refuse to tell you whether this murder was solved, or if it's still on the record as an unsolved case. Could they?'

'We won't know until Monday. Saturday afternoon isn't the time to phone the Eden district attorney's office. I'll phone from the newspaper,' Beth plotted. 'In case they get cagey and want to call me back to verify my story.'

On Monday afternoon, right after Diane had put Jennie in the crib for her nap, Beth called.

'What happened?' Diane demanded anxiously. 'Did they talk to you?'

'If you'll shut up, I'll tell you. They didn't like my calling. I talked to three people, all of them hostile. Then some woman in the DA's office contrived to phone me back – collect. You may be on to something. The murder remains on their "unsolved cases" list. But then again, this could be just a coincidence.'

'It's back to the microfilm room,' Diane sighed, yet she felt a first surge of triumph. She *was* on to something. 'I have to track down the next unsolved murder in Eden.'

'Honey, you're going out on a limb. Suppose there was another – and it was solved?'

'Maybe there was an unsolved murder *before* Dad's . . .' Diane jumped on a fresh track.

'Di, you're going in circles. You can't spent the rest of your life sitting before microfilm machines!'

'I'll go back ten years before Dad died,' Diane plotted, dismissing Beth's admonitions. 'If I unearth another unsolved murder in Eden, I'll have three to use for ammunition. Three unsolved murders would mean a serial killer was loose in Eden. Maybe then I can convince the police to go back and investigate Dad's death as a murder rather than a suicide.'

'The police would have to fight Lloyd Masters. They won't do that.'

'I'll find a way to ferret out the truth,' Diane said defiantly. 'If it comes down to a battle between my grandfather and me, I'll fight him every way I know how. I don't care how long it takes – how low and dirty I have to get. He ruined my father's life – and he killed my mother.'

Diane dreaded the month of April – the twenty-second anniversary of her father's murder and the second anniversary of her mother's death. How sad, she mourned yet again, that Mom could not be here to know Jennie. How sad that Jennie would never know her grandmother. Thank God for Jennie, she told herself again and again – and she knew that Erich, too, found solace in Jennie's presence.

In May Diane was joyous that her degree in journalism was almost within her grasp. She realized, of course, that she couldn't go out and look for a job in the newspaper field. Not yet. Jennie required her presence at home.

'I'll have the time to focus on freelance articles,' she told Beth, unease intruding on joy. The prospect was scary. That was the real world, not the classroom. 'Once school is out of the way,' she added with an effort at high spirits, 'I'll be a free woman.'

'You can try the *West Side Guardian*. They don't pay, but it'll be something to put on your resumé. You've spent your life on the West Side – you know what interests people here.

But face it, newspaper editors won't give a damn that you're graduating in the top two per cent of your class. It's what you produce that counts.'

'I know that.' Diane was startled by the sudden sharpness in her own voice. 'But if I can come up with some good articles, maybe your editor will consider them.'

'Honey, Tom will consider anything that comes in,' Beth said blithely. 'We have a lot of pages to fill – and nobody on staff except him, me, and Donna –' Their typist/receptionist – 'who also wants to be a reporter.'

The evening of graduation day Erich brought home a bottle of Dom Pérignon. Beth and Jack had been invited for a celebratory dinner. Diane's affection for Jack had not increased, but she knew Beth would be pleased if he was included in the small party. But Beth arrived alone.

'Jack has an interview with some judge about a summer law clerk job,' Beth explained. She frowned as Erich involuntarily lifted an eyebrow in doubt. 'The old boy asked him for dinner. I suppose that's a good sign. Where's my girlfriend?'

'Jennie's asleep. I figured a lot of fresh air on Riverside Drive this afternoon and she'd conk out early.'

'I'm starving. What do I smell in the kitchen?' Beth sniffed. 'Something with garlic,' she decided in approval.

'Would I serve you anything without garlic?' Diane headed for the kitchen. 'It's eye round roast.'

Over dinner Erich reminisced about his own college days in New York, his sister's years at Hunter – precious times in their lives. Diane knew that a love of and appreciation for education had been drilled into their heads by their father.

'This is a day that would so please your mother,' Erich told Diane, his voice husky with emotion. 'She was so eager to see you fulfil your father's dream. I know,' he added hastily. 'It'll be a while before you can get fully involved in the newspaper field. But with school out of the way you'll find time to freelance.'

Mom's dream, Diane reminded herself, was for the two of

them to go down to Eden to ferret out her father's murderer. Now she must do that alone.

Two days after graduation Diane was back in the microfilm room at Butler Library. Technically she was no longer eligible to use the library, but nobody questioned her right to be here.

Today, drowning in exasperation at her failure to locate yet another unsolved murder in Eden, she jumped three years in her reading schedule and requested the Atlanta *Constitution* for the month of April 1943. Annie Williams had been murdered seven years after Dad, she'd told herself, so why not try what happened seven years before? No reason to pinpoint this date, she admitted.

She settled down to the monotonous, tiring process of scanning page after page of old newspapers, always tense out of fear that she might miss some tiny but important item. And then – when she was on the point of calling it a day – she was startled into alertness by a brief article in the back pages of one day's newspaper: 'Eden Youth Brutally Murdered.'

Her heart pounding, she read the account of the sixteen-year-old high school senior who had been found murdered in his car on a near-deserted road on the outskirts of town. He'd been shot five times. No leads. 'Christopher Robson was an honors student, scheduled to graduate next month. Family and friends are devastated. Police have no leads in this brutal, senseless murder.'

Diane sought futilely for a follow-up on the Christopher Robson murder. She talked with Beth about calling the Eden district attorney's office again. Both rejected this. 'They'll blow me off,' Beth was convinced. But here was a second unsolved murder on the police records, Diane was convinced – and her father's murder made it three. Was Christopher Robson's murder connected in some way to Lloyd Masters?

A serial murderer could still be walking the streets of Eden. Diane felt herself at a roadblock. Where did she go from here?

* * *

Cliff and Brad carried their trays to a sunlit corner in the hospital cafeteria. Eden was in the midst of a July heatwave, but air conditioning made life bearable.

'You're a creep, you know,' Brad complained but without real rancour. 'Why do you have to go to New York on the weekend when Tina and I are getting married?' Early on Brad had talked about Cliff's being best man but they knew that was impractical. He could be called in for hospital duty ten minutes before the ceremony.

'You know why,' Cliff said calmly. 'I've got these interviews with that research team up in New York. One on Friday afternoon, another on Saturday morning. They're not going to change the date because you're getting married.'

'It's a whole year away. Why couldn't they interview in the fall?'

'Hey, I'm thrilled they're even willing to consider me.' Cliff's face reflected anticipation. 'I'm dying to be part of a research team like that.' And it was a chance to be in New York. Of course, it was ridiculous to think he'd be able to track down Diane over the weekend – but there was that one in a million chance that it could happen. All he knew was that she lived on the Upper West Side, that she'd talked about places like Zabar's, and Tip Toe Inn, and Shakespeare and Company.

'This whole research gig is a crock.' Brad grimaced. 'What kind of money will you be seeing?'

'It's what I want to do.' No use trying to make Brad understand. Still, he couldn't wash from his memory the way his father and mother had looked when he told them about this possible assignment in New York. Disappointed that he wouldn't be in Atlanta, yet trying to match his own excitement at being able to work with such important doctors and research people. It wasn't the kind of world any more where people were born, grew up, lived their lives in one place. People today were on the move.

'You could go into the group practice with me,' Brad reminded him. 'For some reason Tina's father thinks you're hot stuff,' he joshed. 'Probably because of that article you did for the *Herald*. Nothing like great PR to bring in patients. He'd talk to Cartwright – his great buddy – about bringing you into the group.'

'If the research team will have me, I'm theirs.' Only to himself would he admit the strong attraction of living in New York. He'd bungled the most important situation in his life. Even if he could track her down, there was little chance Diane would forgive him, yet he yearned to try to bring her back into his life.

'You won't even be at my bachelor party tomorrow night,' Brad scolded. 'But never mind, I'll drive you to Hartsfield in the morning.'

Cliff stifled a yawn. 'I'll probably sleep all the way into New York.' Unexpectedly he chuckled. 'Two and a half hours when nobody can call me. Nobody can beep me. That's a mini vacation.'

In the Phillips apartment Diane and Erich were at breakfast. Jennie sat at her feeding table – post-breakfast – and tried to deal with the crayons that had been part of her birthday loot last evening.

'Jennie loved the party,' Erich said with satisfaction. 'I think she understood it was for her.' Beth, her mother and sister had been affectionate guests at this first birthday party.

'Wait till she sees the beach at Fire Island,' Diane chuckled. 'The world's biggest sandpile.' Tom – Beth's boss at the *West Side Guardian* – was loaning them his cottage at Ocean Beach for the week of Beth's vacation. In about an hour Beth would pick them up in a cab for the ride to Penn Station.

'I'm going to miss you two,' Erich said tenderly. 'But it'll be great for both of you.'

'I'm so excited that Tom's going to run my article next week.' Diane glowed. No money, but it was a beginning.

'He should be paying you for it.' Erich frowned in reproach.

'The paper isn't making that kind of money yet,' Diane apologized for Tom. 'But he says if advertising picks up he'll be able to give me some paid assignments.'

'Tom's not afraid to be controversial,' Erich said thoughtfully, then grinned. 'Though God knows, you can be.'

'Did I tell you about that article on Governor Carter in Sunday's *Herald*?' Diane asked, fuming in recall. 'They implied that he'd misled the Georgia voters and won the election by subterfuge. They won't admit to his success in quelling racial disorders that used to be such a big problem in the state.'

'The *Eden Herald* and the *Eden Evening News* reflect Lloyd Masters' viewpoints,' Erich said with contempt. 'He still thinks we're going to win the war in Vietnam. He –'

'Mommie, Mommie!' Jennie's imperious summons interrupted them. 'Walk!' Ten days ago Jennie had taken her first steps. Now this was a glorious challenge. 'Walk!'

Forty minutes later – with Jennie clutched in her arms – Diane waited while Beth bought their tickets to Bay Shore, where they would take the ferry to Ocean Beach, Fire Island. With little pleasure Diane remembered that on Friday morning Jack – currently visiting his family in Cleveland – would join them at the cottage for the long weekend. He was jubilant about spending the month of August as a law clerk in some judge's office, though Beth said there'd be little money involved. But at least he'd stopped hounding Beth to leave the *Guardian* and look for what he called a 'job with some future'.

On the train Jennie was glued to the window, fascinated by passing sights. Diane and Beth talked sombrely about the burglary of the Democratic Party headquarters in the Watergate apartment complex in Washington last month – and the million-dollar civil suit filed by the Democratic Party against President Nixon's campaign staff. They discussed the Democratic Convention, held the previous week, in which Senator George McGovern was nominated for president and Senator Thomas Eagleton for vice-president. Diane railed against the *Herald* and the *Evening News*'s virulent attacks against McGovern and the Democratic party in general.

Inevitably the talk moved to Diane's exasperation at having no additional leads to a possible serial murderer in Eden. She could realistically point to only the murders of Chris Robson and Annie Williams. Kevin Masters' death was on the police records as suicide – and two unsolved murders would not be accepted as the work of a serial killer.

'I have to go back to Eden.' Only in Eden would she be able to find clues that would link Chris Robson's murder to Lloyd Masters. 'The odds are too strong against me the way I'm working. I know,' she halted Beth's rejoiner. 'I can't go back until Cliff's out of his residency. That happens next July. And that's when I mean to go down there. Sure, it's a gamble. Uncle Erich will be upset, but I have to do this for Mom.'

'Di, it's become an obsession with you,' Beth accused. 'It's not just finding your father's killer. You're harbouring this awful rage against Lloyd Masters. Don't let it eat you up. What happened to the Di I used to know, who always made me laugh?'

Diane's smile was wry. 'That was another world.'

Cliff emerged from the exquisitely cool offices where his second interview had been held and flinched at the heat that settled about him with murderous tenacity. On this torpid weekend the New York City streets seemed oddly deserted. Anyone who could had escaped to beach or country – or sought the comfort of air-conditioned apartment, movie house, or restaurant.

In a corner of his mind he told himself he should be euphoric. He knew he'd landed this research berth; he had clicked with both interviewers. The second one had made it clear official notification was just a formality. When he finished his residency in July of 1973, he would fly to New York to join the team being set up within the next few months.

For much of the afternoon, despite the heat, he walked up one side of Broadway and down the other. He wandered through the aisles of Zabar's, bought a paperback at Shakespeare and Company. He backtracked and had dinner at Tip Toe Inn – which Diane had talked about with affection.

Mom and Dad had liked Diane. His face softened in recall. But they'd worried, too, when he'd brought her home for Thanksgiving dinner, that he might complicate his life by marrying before he finished his residency.

When would he accept the fact that fate had destined them for separate paths?

Chapter Eleven

Waiting for the hospital elevator after thirty-six hours on duty, Cliff stifled a yawn. Rain pounded against the windows. It had been raining for two days now. The wind howled through the towering pines that edged the hospital grounds. Hadn't there been something on the news about a hurricane moving up from the Caribbean? He'd never thought of November as being hurricane weather.

He glanced at his watch. It was past 9 p.m., but Mom and Dad would still be awake when he arrived in Buckhead. It was Mom's birthday. He'd been so sure he'd make it home in time for dinner, but as so often happened, hospital demands had decreed otherwise. But damn it, he'd be there for a piece of birthday cake.

An elevator pulled to a stop. The door slid open. Cliff walked inside. The hospital night quiet was punctuated on the floor below by a shrill emergency call. Thank God it didn't involve him, he thought with a flicker of relief. He couldn't wait to get out of here tonight. He'd have birthday cake and a glass of wine with Mom and Dad, then fall into bed for twelve hours.

He hurried to the side exit, frowned at the deluge of rain that pummeled him as he ran to his car. Inside he shed his raincoat, started the car. He turned on the radio – something noisy to keep him awake on the drive to Buckhead. A moment later the Rolling Stones' 'Brown Sugar' rent the air.

He was relieved that there was little traffic on the road tonight. He'd make good time. He resisted the temptation to speed – he'd seen too many cases come into the hospital emergency room. But he congratulated himself at being able to be home for his mother's birthday at what his parents considered a respectable hour, though he knew the 'welcome' sign was out for him whenever he arrived.

He felt a rush of satisfaction when he saw the familiar Atlanta skyline rising ahead of him. Another twenty minutes and he'd be home.

Then all at once he was blinded by headlights coming directly at him. What the hell was that car doing in his lane? Charging head on! He swerved with all his strength – but it was too late. He was conscious of a loud impact, of shattering glass, of a horrible pain in his back. Then darkness closed in about him . . .

Diane settled herself in the living room to work on another prospective article for the *West Side Guardian* – in longhand rather than typing lest she awaken Jennie, asleep now in her cot. Erich was tied up at the lab for the evening. Beth had called to say she was coming over with the latest copies of the *Eden Herald*.

Diane tried to focus on the work at hand – to fend off another wave of discouragement because she was accomplishing so little in her search for her father's murderer. In truth, she admitted to herself, she was pushing away the weeks and months until she could go down to Eden.

She heard the elevator slide to a stop on their floor. Beth? She deposited her notepad on the coffee table, crossed to open the door. Beth was striding towards her.

'Hi.' Beth was tense, Diane thought. Another battle with Jack?

'Look, I want you to stay cool,' Beth ordered, handing over the newspapers. 'Cliff's been in an accident – but he's going to be all right –'

'Oh my God!' Her heart pounding, Diane scanned the front page of the top newspaper. Cliff had been involved in a head-on collision just outside of Atlanta. He'd suffered a fractured spine plus other injuries.

'I called the hospital in Atlanta,' Beth rushed to reassure her. 'He's off the critical list.'

Diane was assaulted by frightening images. 'A fractured spine, Beth! Will he be in a wheelchair?'

'He'll have a long convalescence.' As always in crises, Beth was matter-of-fact. 'But he's young – he'll come out of it as good as new –'

'I'm going down to Atlanta,' Diane said 'I have to see him! I have to know he's going to be all right!' She paused, her mind racing. 'I'll take Jennie with me –'

'Di, call the hospital yourself,' Beth urged. 'They'll tell you he's doing OK. He's off the critical list,' she repeated. 'You don't have to go to Atlanta to know that.' She paused. 'Unless you're thinking in terms of reconciliation . . .'

Diane froze. 'No,' she whispered. 'After what I did to him? Walking out that way? Beth, he hates me for hurting him like that.' *And the situation hadn't changed.* There was still no room in his life for a wife and child.

But please God, let him be all right.

'You can call the hospital every day,' Beth soothed. 'The information office gives out reports to anybody who calls. You'll be able to follow his progress. Di, he's going to be all right.'

'Let me read the *Herald* article.' Diane picked up the newspaper again, read slowly this time around. 'But how could it have happened? He's such a such a careful driver!'

'The other driver was drunk. There was nothing Cliff could have done to avoid the accident.'

'If he'd swung out of the way two seconds earlier, he might have avoided a bad smash-up! He was exhausted from a long shift at the hospital. Why do they work the residents those terrible hours?' Diane's voice was unnaturally shrill. 'It's a miracle there're not more bad accidents!'

'This will probably delay his finishing his residency,' Beth warned. Meaning, Diane understood in dismay that she would have to delay her return to Eden.

'Maybe not.' She couldn't think of that now. 'There'll be

more news in later editions of the *Herald*. We'll watch.' Her mind was in chaos. The hospital was responsible for Cliff's accident! If he hadn't been so exhausted, he could have avoided it. His reflexes had been slowed by all those hours on the hospital floor.

'Cliff's going to be OK,' Beth emphasized. 'Don't freak out over this.'

'I won't.' Diane managed a weak smile. 'I can't afford that luxury.'

Atlanta was being blanketed by a barrage of giant-sized snow-flakes that were beginning to settle. The sky promised much more of this. But Cliff, who loved snowy weather, was unaware of anything outside his hospital room. He lay immobile in his bed, his eyes staring at the ceiling without seeing. The words of the specialist who'd been brought in on his case ricocheted in his mind: 'With proper treatment and extensive physio-therapy you ought to be back on your feet in six to seven months. Consider yourself lucky, young man.'

He wouldn't be finishing his residency in July. The berth on the research team in New York was down the drain. He'd have to write and tell them.

'Come on, don't look so sombre!' The sultry voice of one of the young night-shift nurses broke his introspection. She was a tall blonde who managed to look sexy even in a sedate nurse's uniform.

'I'm bored,' he drawled, taking refuge behind a casual façade. 'They won't let me go to a disco tonight.'

'It's slow on the floor.' Her eyes told him she found him attractive – even flat on his back. 'I'll get us some coffee and you can tell me the story of your life.'

'Do you play chess?' he asked suddenly. *Diane played chess.*

'I'm willing to learn. Let me go see what I can dig up in the rec room. I'm Sylvia,' she said. 'In case you didn't know.'

He was curious about why she'd gone into nursing. She was different from other young nurses he'd known through his residency. He knew what Brad would say: 'She's one of those who come into the field intent on marrying a resident with a rich future ahead of him.' She'd be disappointed if she considered him a candidate, he thought wryly. He didn't see himself in a practice that brought in the big bucks. Research was the action he wanted. Damn, he loathed missing out on that deal in New York.

Diane tiptoed out of the bedroom she shared with Jennie and went into the kitchen to put up coffee. Her uncle and his two cronies were playing pinochle in the dining area. They were simultaneously arguing about who would win the nomination at the Democratic Convention in July, though it was five months away. It was their customary Friday evening game.

Sometimes Diane was impatient that Erich, Hans and Joseph seemed unable to put the Holocaust years behind them. She remembered three women she'd encountered at intervals in Eden, at a popular little restaurant. They were in their late fifties, and were all survivors of Auschwitz. Now, with reparation from the German Government, they lived comfortably in the serene South. They had contrived to put the past behind them.

That had never happened for Mom and Uncle Erich. Nor for Beth's mother. In odd ways the Holocaust had coloured her life and Beth's. And how did she know what ugly recall haunted the nights of those three women? Uncle Erich said the Holocaust left scars that never completely healed.

The phone rang, splintering the apartment quiet.

'I'll get it,' she called to her uncle. It was probably Beth. They talked every night about this time if they hadn't seen each other during the day. Sometimes Beth had word for her about the latest article she'd submitted for the *Guardian*. Finally, Tom was giving her definite assignments. He didn't pay much, but she felt more professional now.

Diane picked up the phone. 'Hello?'

'This is Uncle Erich's pinochle night, isn't it?' Beth asked.

'Yeah. Why?'

'Then he can watch Jennie for you. Come over to my pad. I need to talk to you.' Her voice was strident. Diane sensed she was distraught. 'Di, please come.'

'I'll be right over.'

Waiting to be buzzed in at Beth's building, Diane asked herself if Beth and Jack had had another of their wild battles. That was happening an awful lot in these last few weeks.

Emerging from the elevator on Beth's floor, she spied Beth waiting at the half-opened apartment door. Anxiety gripped her as she rushed forward. Beth's face was drained of colour, and she seemed dazed, shaken.

'Beth, what's happened?' They went into the apartment and closed the door behind them. 'Tell me, Beth.'

'That lying, dirty bastard Jack!' Beth shook her head in disbelief. 'He's moved out. He's marrying the daughter of that judge he clerked for last summer. He let me see him through law school – and then he takes a walk . . .' Her voice broke.

'Honey, I'm so sorry he's hurt you, but you're well rid of him,' Diane said softly, reaching to pull her close.

'I know you never liked him. That used to bother me. But I thought you just didn't understand him. Then a few weeks ago I got curious about all the evenings he was away from the apartment. I knew it was crazy, but I began to follow him. Last night I saw him meet this Wasp blonde. She drives a Jaguar. He kissed her and then slid behind the wheel of the car. When he came home last night, I pretended to be asleep. Then this afternoon I faced him with it. He said what we'd had was dead. He was moving on. He told me he was marrying the blonde.'

'You're not the first to help a man through grad school and then watch him walk off with somebody else.'

'I can't believe it! I just can't believe it!'

'Better now than five years later,' Diane soothed. 'You don't need Jack.'

'I feel so used. And so alone . . .'

'You're not alone. You've got me – you've got your family.'

'Oh God, can't you just hear Mom? You know how she's felt all along about Jack.'

'Your mother will be fine.' Diane's smile was tender. 'She carried on when she thought you were doing something that would hurt you. But she'll be supportive now.'

'Why did it take me so damn long to see what was happening?' Rage replaced anguish for the moment. 'The signs were there – I just didn't want to see them. Until they were so blatant I had to face them.'

'He's been spoiling for a break-up for weeks,' Diane said, remembering the battles. 'He wanted a confrontation. It was easier that way.' She sought for some mild diversion, 'Tomorrow is Saturday. Uncle Erich will be home by one o'clock. Let's go on a wild shopping spree.'

'Why do women always shop when they're upset?' But Beth managed a shaky smile. 'The way inflation's running wild maybe I ought to buy before prices go out of sight. Who's running sales this weekend? There's nothing like a great sale to lift my spirits.'

Diane knew that Beth was hurting. In a corner of her mind a plot was germinating. Maybe she could persuade Beth to go down to Eden with her. She'd feel so much better if Beth was there. Jennie adored Beth. And a change of scenery was what Beth needed.

First, of course, she must discover Cliff's schedule. He was out of the hospital. Cautious – anonymous – phone calls had informed her of this. Would he go back to Masters Memorial when he was on his feet again? How would the accident affect the term of his residency? She couldn't go back to Eden until he had left town.

'Di, stop fretting and ask questions,' Beth ordered when she confided her anxiety about the timing of her return to Eden.

'Whom do I ask?' Diane countered.

'Call Masters Memorial – or let me call. I'll give some story about having gone to med school with Cliff and trying to catch up with him. What could be wrong with that?'

'Call.' Diane struggled for calm. She glanced at her watch. 'It's twenty minutes to five. Ask for the business office. You'll probably get Gladys.'

Diane sat at the edge of her chair while Beth put through the call. She waited impatiently, finding no answers in Beth's brief replies after her initial explanation about trying to reach Cliff. Then Beth was off the phone.

'Well?' Diane demanded.

'She said Cliff is no longer associated with Masters Memorial. She told me about the accident and said that when he recovered completely he'd be on the staff at a hospital somewhere else in the state –'

'Why won't he finish his residency at Masters Memorial?' Diane broke in.

'Maybe it has something to do with follow-up medical. You know – physiotherapy. She wouldn't give me his address but would forward a letter if I write care of Masters Memorial.'

He was recovering, Diane told herself with a surge of relief. He was scheduled to resume his residency at another hospital. There was no reason now for her not to go back to Eden. She'd tell Uncle Erich early in May, she promised herself.

Not next month – not in April. Beth's mother had said once – and it had remained in her memory – that most people have one month in the year that they approach with dread and leave with relief, because in past years that month had been fraught with tragedy. For Mom it had always been April – and for her, too. She couldn't remember the April when her father died, but the April evening when she'd come home to find Mom had jumped to her death was for ever emblazoned on her brain. For Uncle Erich, too, April was the dreaded month.

Three days before the third anniversary of her mother's death, Diane received a late evening phone call from Beth.

'You know how I'm always bitching about mail and deliveries being screwed up in my building?' Beth's voice was electric.

'Yes . . .'

'A neighbour just brought me last week's *Herald*s that had been delivered to her. Di, come over and read what's happening down there!'

'Tell me, Beth!'

'Come over. I could be all wrong, but I think this is worth investigating.'

'I'll be there in five minutes.' Diane slammed down the phone, rose to her feet. Don't say anything yet to Uncle Erich, she cautioned herself. He wanted her to put this whole business behind her. She'd just say Beth asked her to come over to edit an article she had to turn in tomorrow morning.

Beth was at the door of her apartment when Diane emerged from the elevator in her building, her face flushed with excitement.

'There's been another murder in Eden! Some prominent doctor.'

'Who?' She knew many of the local doctors from her job at the hospital.

'Dr Desmond Taylor,' Beth said after a swift glance at the newspaper. 'Did you know him?'

'Just by sight.' Diane recalled him as an older internist with a jovial manner. 'Do they have any leads?' Diane followed Beth inside.

'Nothing.' Beth handed her a newspaper, the story of the murder emblazoned across the front page. 'His body was found near the river, his head bashed in. Not one clue so far.'

'Have the police connected it with Chris Robson's and Annie Williams's murders?' Diane probed.

'If they do, they don't say anything about it.' Beth hesitated. 'Look, they have no reason to connect any of them. The only similarity,' she reminded realistically, 'is that the other two were never solved and this one might follow suit.'

'But there must be a connection!' Diane churned with excitement. 'Annie Williams was a maid in the Masters house. I don't know what it is, but I have a gut feeling there's some link

136

between Chris Robson's murder and Lloyd Masters, and I mean to find out what it is. And what do you want to bet that Dr Desmond Taylor was the Masters family physician?'

'He was a prominent doctor, Di – he could very well have been the Masters family physician. That's not enough to –'

'It's enough to tell me that a serial murderer – his crimes spread out over a lot of years – may be operating in Eden. Probably for most of the time he appears a normal resident of the town – arouses no suspicions whatsoever. But then something clicks and he kills – always someone connected in some way we don't know yet with Lloyd Masters. And Beth, I promise you – we'll find out who he is!'

Chapter Twelve

Hungry for more information about the murder of Dr Desmond Taylor in Eden and frustrated that the next batch of *Herald*s wouldn't arrive for several days, Diane went to the New York Public Library to check out the current editions of the *Atlanta Constitution* and the *Journal*. The murder of a prominent Eden doctor might be reported in the Atlanta newspapers.

In the lofty-ceilinged first-floor periodicals rooms she waited at the counter for the requested newspapers to be brought to her. Her mind catalogued the facts at hand. The police listed her father's murder as suicide – but if Dr Taylor had been the Masters family physician, then, with Annie Williams, there were three murders with some as yet unexplained connection to the Masters family. *Enough to establish a definite link*. If this latest case was solved, would the police go back and investigate the deaths of Chris Robson and Annie Williams?

Was this a psychotic attempt to punish Lloyd Masters for some past injustice? The Masters newspapers were virulent in their attacks against politicians who didn't follow the Lloyd Masters line. The private investigator had cleared Roger Ames in Texas, but how many other politicians were seeking revenge?

'These are the latest we've received.' A library clerk approached the counter with a sheaf of newspapers.

'Thank you.' Diane reached to take them. 'I'm sure they'll be fine.'

Churning with anticipation, Diane settled herself in a comfortable armchair at a table near the rear, where spring sunlight poured through the tall windows. Nothing of the Eden murder appeared on the front page – but she shouldn't have expected that, she rebuked herself, and turned to the inside pages. Midway through the newspaper a small article leapt up at her: 'Prominent Eden Physician Victim of Brutal Murder.'

She read the brief report with disappointment: nothing more here than had been provided in the *Herald*. She leant back in her chair and debated about her next move. What about that newspaper store down at Times Square where Mom used to buy copies of the *Herald*? '*You wouldn't believe how many small-town newspapers they carry there, Di*.' Go there and look for a more current issue than the ones Beth received in weekly blocks.

She glanced at her watch. Beth had taken Jennie to the playground – she didn't have to be at the office until noon today. The Times Square newspaper store was a few minutes' walk from here. Go over there and check it out.

At the newspaper store her eyes swept over an incredible inventory of newspapers. She scanned the titles with soaring hope. *There!* The *Eden Herald*. The edition bought, she hurried from the store and out into the balmy late morning. Too impatient to wait, she paused on the sidewalk, scanned the pages. Then she spied her quarry – the report of Dr Taylor's funeral. She rushed through the customary background material, focused on the last few lines of the lengthy obituary.

'A friend for over thirty years, Lloyd Masters offered a warm and touching eulogy for the slain physician.' Here it was! Another link to Lloyd Masters. This was the fourth in a series of murders. She couldn't delay any longer. She must go down to Eden.

She'd tell Uncle Erich tonight, she plotted, folding up the newspaper and heading now for the uptown I R T subway. Beth would have to give Tom two or three weeks' notice – but she was beginning to hate the job, ever since Tom had turned down her article about the need for changes in the work habits of hospital residents. 'Hell, Di – that's too controversial. I'm chasing after the hospitals to run ads in the *Guardian*,' he'd said.

Diane hurried home. Beth and Jennie had arrived just minutes before. Beth was shucking away Jennie's coat.

'Mommie, Mommie!' Jennie held out her arms for hugs. 'We saw squirrels in the park.'

'Did you talk to them?' Diane asked, hoisting Jennie in her arms.

While she listened with avid interest to Jennie's chatter, Diane managed to convey to Beth that she had important news.

'Jennie, you haven't told Tiger about the squirrels you saw this morning,' Diane scolded gently, and Jennie went into her usual communication with her stuffed tiger.

Diane turned to Beth, explained her afternoon's venture.

'Lloyd Masters eulogized Dr Taylor at the funeral. They'd been friends for over thirty years. I have to go down to Eden and dig. I'm telling Uncle Erich tonight.' She flinched. 'Oh God, he's going to be upset – but I have to do this.'

'I'll wait till you're clear with Uncle Erich,' Beth said after a moment. 'Then I'll give Tom notice. And gear myself to hear Mom and Dad's carrying on.' She shuddered at the prospect. 'To them it'll be like I'm moving to Australia.'

Lloyd Masters sat behind the huge, leather-topped desk in his rotunda office and scowled at the sheaf of papers his son-in-law Luke had placed before him.

'Damn it, we're losing circulation in almost every area! For the fourth quarter in a row!' He stared accusingly at Luke.

'Lloyd, it's a fact of life today. Every newspaper's facing the same situation.' Luke's voice was conciliatory.

'Then we have to turn it around,' Lloyd told him. 'Go out on the road and see what's happening.' Peggy was pissed that Luke was out-of-town so much, he considered. But at least Luke kept his womanizing out there – away from Peggy. 'We've got to start cutting corners wherever we can. Tell Hugh I said to stop dragging his feet on negotiations for that paper plant. That's important to us.'

'I understand he's having a meeting out there the day after

tomorrow,' Luke reported. He paused a moment. 'Have you given any more thought to our expanding into cable TV? I can't keep those people dangling much longer.'

'I thought I made it clear.' Lloyd was brusque. 'I don't see us moving into cable TV. We're a newspaper chain.'

'I hear strong rumours that the Cox family is moving into that area.' A faint reproof in Luke's voice now. The Cox family owned the *Atlanta Constitution*.

'I don't give a shit what the Cox family does. We're in the newspaper game.' Hell, they were dragging him into the computer crap, the electronic equipment scene – that was enough.

'Joel's finishing up that tribute to Dr Taylor that you want him to run on Sunday. He was surprised that you asked him to see it yourself before it goes in.'

'Yes, I want to see it,' Lloyd snapped. 'Desmond Taylor was my friend since the day he set up practice here in town. He deserves the best send-off we can give him.'

'What a hell of a way to go.' Luke was sympathetic.

He ought to be, Lloyd thought drily. Des did the abortion on that little slut Luke knocked up last year.

'Take these figures.' Lloyd handed him the current circulation reports. 'They make me want to throw up. And talk to Hugh about the paper plant negotiations,' he repeated.

'Sure thing. We'll have a report for you in the next forty-eight hours.'

Lloyd sat immobile, staring into space when his son-in-law had left the office. Damn, Des's death put him in a rotten spot. How the hell was he going to deal with Alison now? Except for himself and her nurse, Des was the only person she allowed in her room. What if she got sick, needed medical attention?

Maureen, of course, was useless in this situation. After the first few months she'd given up trying to deal with Alison. All these years it had been his problem. His and Des's. Maureen claimed it just upset her to try to talk to Alison. Living under the same roof, she hadn't seen her oldest daughter in almost twenty years! Every time there was a problem Maureen took off on another trip with that woman friend of hers in Atlanta. Sometimes he wondered what went on between the two of them. No loss to him – he hadn't been in her bed since Gerry was a baby. She was as cold as a winter night in Siberia. She'd tolerated him. He'd learnt to find better outside of her bed.

Now his mind zeroed in on the emotional scene yesterday with Zoe Taylor. What did she expect him to do when the police told her they had no leads on Des's murder? The *Herald* and the *Evening News* couldn't do anything about that. The case would remain on the books – but the police would put it on ice.

On impulse he reached for his phone, buzzed his executive secretary.

'Carol, call the florist and have a dozen long-stemmed red roses sent to Zoe Taylor. Enclose a card – "I grieve with you. Love, Lloyd."'

Diane put an eye round roast in the oven, then focused on the evening routine with Jennie. While she was getting Jennie into her pajamas, she heard her uncle come into the apartment. He'd pop into the bedroom in a few minutes and sit down to tell Jennie her usual bedtime story.

'Something smells good.' Erich appeared in the doorway.

'A roast,' Diane told him.

'How's my little princess?' He crossed to Jennie, sprawled on her mother's bed.

'A story,' Jennie said imperiously. 'Want a story!'

'I think that can be arranged,' Erich said tenderly, sitting on the edge of the bed.

'I'll get on with dinner.' As always Diane was filled with pleasure at the tableau of her uncle and Jennie engrossed in their nightly story-telling session.

Tonight Jennie drifted off early. Erich went into the living room to listen to a TV newscast until Diane summoned him to the dining table. Moving about the kitchen, she could hear the news commentator reporting the latest on the American Indian sit-in at Wounded Knee, South Dakota.

Then dinner was ready. Diane called Erich to the table.

'Are you working on another article for the *Guardian*?' Erich asked, when they dawdled over coffee.

'I'm searching around for a subject.' Diane sighed. 'I was so disappointed – no,' she corrected herself, 'I was so angry when Tom turned down the hospital story.' Beth, too, was feeling hemmed in by Tom's new restrictions.

'I've been thinking, Di.' An undercurrent of excitement in Erich's voice captured her attention. 'Jennie will be two in July, old enough for you to leave her with a nursemaid and not worry.' Meaning, Diane understood, that if something wasn't right, Jennie would be old enough to communicate that to them. 'Then you'll be able to go out and try for a real newspaper job.'

'Uncle Erich, a nursemaid will be so expensive.' She wouldn't be here. She was going to Eden.

'I'm not pushing you,' he soothed, 'but we can afford it. The stock market's been kind to me. Think about it . . .'

'I will,' she promised. She'd tell him tomorrow night that she was going back to Eden, she hedged.

Erich went to his room for one of his financial magazines, his usual after-dinner reading matter, and returned with it to the living room. He sprawled in his favourite lounge chair, his feet on the footstool, his nightly routine except when he went with his friends to the chess house or they played pinochle here.

'Another cup of coffee?' Diane asked from the dining area, knowing the answer.

'That would be nice,' he said, smiling.

Diane brought him a second cup of coffee, returned to the kitchen to stack the dishes in the recently acquired dishwasher, then headed for the television set. It wouldn't disturb Uncle Erich if she watched TV for a while. But her mind kept darting back to the newspaper report of Dr Taylor's funeral. He'd been a friend of Lloyd Masters for over thirty years – and he'd been viciously murdered.

The TV programme did nothing to release her tension. How could anything divert her tonight, she taunted herself, when all her suspicions about a serial murderer in Eden were evolving into fact?

She glanced up at a faint grunt from Erich.

'You OK?' she asked. He looked pale. With warmer weather approaching he ought to get out into the sun instead of hiding himself away indoors so much. 'Uncle Erich –' She leant forward solicitously.

'Yeah, I'm fine,' he said. 'Some of this crazy market stuff . . .' He gestured disparagingly.

A few moments later he summoned her with an air of apology.

'Di, would you get me an Alka-Seltzer? I ate too much tonight. I've got a little indigestion.'

'Sure . . .' Di smiled and headed for the kitchen, where Erich kept his digestive aids.

But when she returned to the living room with the Alka-Seltzer, Erich lay slumped in the chair, eyes closed, face drained of colour. Her heart pounding, Diane rushed to his side.

'Uncle Erich!' Panic made her dizzy. He was unconscious. 'Uncle Erich –'

She knew every second counted. She darted to the phone, dialled 911, explained the situation and asked for an ambulance. Now she dialled Beth's number.

'Hello?'

'Beth, something's happened to Uncle Erich! I've called 911 –' Her voice was shrill with alarm.

'Hold on, Di. I'll be right there.'

The ambulance and Beth arrived simultaneously. But even before the intern on ambulance duty turned to her with compassion, she knew what he would say.

'I'm sorry. He suffered a massive heart attack. He's dead.'

Dazed and disbelieving that her uncle was gone, Diane allowed Beth and her family to propel her through the next traumatic forty-eight hours. Beth never left her side. Beth's mother and sister handled all the details of the funeral, took over Jennie's care.

'Jennie doesn't know what's happened,' Diane told Beth when the apartment was at last clear of all except Beth and Jennie and herself – and Jennie asleep in her cot. 'She loved Uncle Erich – she's going to miss him so much.'

'We all will. He was special.'

'Why?' Diane railed, as she had questioned her mother's death. 'He was forty-three years old! Why did this happen?'

'There are no answers. We'll have another cup of coffee and call it a night,' Beth said gently. 'Dad'll be here tomorrow morning at nine to go over Uncle Erich's papers with you.'

'What is it about this family?' Diane trailed Beth into kitchen, as though reluctant to be alone even for a few moments. 'My father murdered at twenty-eight, Mom dead at forty-four, and now Uncle Erich, long before his time. Will I be dead in a few years and Jennie alone in this world?' Her voice soared, close to hysteria.

'It won't be like that, Di.' Beth poured coffee into a pair of mugs now. 'The bad deals are behind you. For Jennie and yourself you have to be positive.'

'What are you putting in my coffee?' Diane accused.

'Something to make you sleep.' She handed Diane the mug. 'You have to get some rest, Di. You'll need a clear head to help Dad tomorrow.'

Despite the sedative in her coffee, Diane was awake before 7 a.m. The morning was cold and grey. Heat rattled in the radiators. She tossed aside the comforter and sat at the edge of the bed to gaze at her small daughter, still sound asleep in her cot. Already Jennie was asking for Uncle Erich. How could she make her understand he'd never be with them again?

With a numbing sense of unreality, Diane prepared for the morning. She left her bedroom and headed for the kitchen. Beth was stirring on the sofa. She'd chosen to sleep there rather than in Erich's bed – which Diane understood.

'You're awake early.' Beth pulled herself up into a sitting position.

'You, too,' Diane pointed out. 'I'll make us breakfast. Jennie will probably sleep for another hour.'

They were sitting at the table with second cups of coffee when Jennie's plaintive wail reached them.

'Mommie? Mommie!' More insistent now – almost fearful, Diane thought, and hurried to respond. In some way Jennie knew their lives had been disrupted.

At ten past nine Mr Bertonelli arrived.

'I brought fresh bagels,' he said with determined good spirits. 'We'll have them a little later.'

Diane forced herself to go with Mr Bertonelli into her uncle's bedroom. Ever practical, Erich had insisted that Diane know where his personal papers were kept: his bank books, his stock portfolio, his will.

'Everything's in here . . .' She pulled open the dresser top drawer and gestured for Mr Bertonelli to take out the contents.

While Beth took Jennie back into her bedroom for playtime, Diane and Mr Bertonelli settled themselves on the living-room sofa, the collection of bank books, stock certificates and a pair of manila envelopes deposited on the coffee table.

'Your uncle was a far-seeing man,' Mr Bertonelli said after a few moments. 'There'll be no need to file a will. Everything is in trust for you.' His eyes were unexpectedly curious. 'Are you aware of the extent of his finances?'

'No.' Diane's stare was blank. Was there a problem about money? She knew how expensive funerals could be. But she had Mom's money, she and Jennie would be all right for at least a year. 'I know he liked to play with the stock market. What he called his "little diversion".'

'He was a very astute operator,' Mr Bertonelli said, with obvious respect. 'Between his stocks and his bank accounts you'll have well over two hundred thousand dollars.'

Diane was astounded. Uncle Erich had given no indication of such affluence. Now she tried to focus on what Mr Bertonelli was explaining to her about how she would acquire the assets her uncle had left her – but at the same time her mind was seizing on her unexpectedly healthy financial situation. She knew what she would do now. She and Jennie, along with Beth, would leave for Eden as soon as Uncle Erich's affairs were in order. She would close up the apartment for an indefinite period. Now she was impatient to be alone with Beth – to present her daring blueprint for their return to Eden.

They lingered briefly over bagels and coffee, then Mr Bertonelli left for his office. Only now did Beth learn about Diane's inheritance.

'I don't believe it!' Beth seemed dazed. 'He lived so frugally.'

'He never forgot that it was a lack of money that kept his grandparents and aunts and uncles and cousins in Germany when there was still time to run. Money was security.' She'd known he had savings accounts. She hadn't known the extent of those accounts – nor of his stock portfolio, which Mom had laughingly called 'Erich's toys'.

'He wanted security for you and Jennie,' Beth said, tears welling in her eyes.

'I know what I'm doing with that money,' Diane said, almost defiant now. 'You and I are going to go to Eden and start up a weekly newspaper.'

'Di! That's a terrible gamble!' Beth was shocked.

'You've learned a lot working with Tom – and I've picked up points listening to both of you. Between us we know enough to get a small-town weekly into operation.'

'You could lose every cent!'

'We'll watch ourselves – keep a cap on expenses,' Diane plotted. 'Tom taught you a lot of angles.' She paused, excitement spiralling in her. 'We'll call it the *Eden Guardian*. Our own newspaper, Beth. We can pull this off.'

Chapter Thirteen

In her bedroom – leaning over to kiss Jennie goodnight – Diane
flinched at the verbal explosion that had just erupted in the
living room. Beth must have told her parents about their plans.
They'd invited the Bertonellis for dinner tonight so they could
break the news about their going down to Eden. She closed the
door softly behind her and hurried to back up Beth.

'I think you're both out of your minds!' Mr Bertonelli's voice
was unfamiliarly harsh. 'You're two kids – what do you know
about running a newspaper?'

'Dad, we're not kids.' Beth rejected this. Did you have to be
sixty before parents considered you adults? 'I've been working
on a newspaper for almost four years. Di has a journalism
degree –'

'We've thought this out carefully.' Diane jumped in. 'We
know the pitfalls. We can handle them.' She managed an air of
confidence.

'We won't be competing with the *New York Times*.' Beth
was fighting not to lose her cool, Diane sensed. 'We're talking
of a smaller version of the *West Side Guardian*. I've watched
Tom – I've seen his mistakes and his smart moves. We –'

'Erich would turn over in his grave if he knew about this.'
Mrs Bertonelli was shaken. Diane remembered her terror whenever Beth was out of the city. Separations were frightening. 'Di,
that money was supposed to be security for you and Jennie.'

'Erich's stocks are all blue chip. Let me take a chunk of the
savings account and buy more good stocks,' Mr Bertonelli said.
'You'll have a guaranteed income.'

'We won't be laying out a lot of money to set up the kind of newspaper we want to publish. It has a great potential. There's nothing like it in Eden. We'll have the field to ourselves.' Nobody would deter them, Diane told herself. 'We'll do local news, community activities . . .' And fight the *Herald* and the *Evening News* when they supported bad deals.

'We'll run an entertainment page, a restaurant page,' Beth rushed in. 'For towns like Eden eating out is a major diversion. We'll be performing a public service.' Beth was deliberately flip. 'In one month we'll have every restaurant in town advertising with us.'

'We'll be a low-budget business. The two of us are all the full-time staff we'll need.' How weird, Diane thought, to be fighting this way for their newspaper when she should be sitting *shivah* for Uncle Erich. But Uncle Erich would understand.

'You'll need to pay yourselves salaries.' Mr Bertonelli was grim. 'You can't live on air. There's office rent, utilities, printers. I have a client in the paper field. Right now there's a terrible shortage of newsprint. Prices are skyrocketing.'

'Rent's dirt cheap in Eden. We'll keep our salaries low.' Beth refused to be cowed.

'It could take three or four years before something like that shows a profit – you could run out of money,' Mr Bertonelli blustered.

'Dad, this is our chance to build up something from scratch,' Beth told him.

'A thousand miles from home,' her mother added.

'Aren't you always boasting about how you enjoy your job because you have only yourself to answer to?' Beth challenged her father. 'You're the boss.'

'Up to a point,' Mr Bertonelli hedged. 'I still have to answer to my clients.'

'But you have none of the corporate complaints that Mom's always moaning about.' Her mother had been an executive secretary for sixteen years.

'It's the field we both want to work in,' Diane said quietly. 'I'm sure we can pull it off.'

'What about your apartments?' Mrs Bertonelli asked after a heavy pause. 'Who gives up rent-stabilized apartments these days?'

Diane and Beth exchanged a relieved glance. Finally Beth's parents understood they were serious.

'We'll sublet,' Diane said. Subletting indicated they expected to return. That would appease Beth's parents for now. 'Furnished –'

'I'll take care of that.' Mrs Bertonelli frowned in thought. 'There's a young couple in my office who're dying to move out of their furnished studio. And I'll find somebody for your studio, Beth. You'll even make a little money since you're subletting furnished.'

And so it was decided. Seeking to be practical Diane and Beth settled on 1 July as their departure date. Beth's mother arranged for sublets for both apartments. 'For one year,' Mrs Bertonelli specified. Neither Diane nor Beth made any effort to contradict her, though they were committed to a long-time pursuit of the projected weekly.

Diane was astonished by the demands the preparations for the move to Eden made on her time – yet grateful to be so occupied because that meant fewer hours each day to be swamped by grief. At anguished intervals she sat down with Jennie to try to explain that 'Uncle Erich had to go away, darling.' A dozen times a day something about the apartment – his special coffee mug hanging in the kitchen, the way his favourite armchair bore the impression of his body, his cherished books that filled three tall bookcases – taunted her with the knowledge that he was for ever gone from their lives.

Beth gave Tom six weeks' notice. After his initial shock over their plans, he designated himself their 'business adviser'.

Diane realized that she would have to explain her sudden departure from Eden when, on her return, she encountered people she already knew there. She sat down with Beth to work out an explanation that would sound plausible.

'I'll say that my old boyfriend came back from Vietnam – we'd fought about his going, broke off.' Gladys would remember Cliff, she thought guiltily, but so be it. 'He came home, called me, we made up. I went back home and married him –'

'And right away got pregnant.' Beth nodded in approval.

'Then we realized it was a terrible mistake. We got divorced when Jennie was an infant,' Diane continued. 'He disappeared into the wild blue yonder. I went back to my maiden name, and Uncle Erich adopted Jennie so she could carry the same name.' The way *she* had become Diane Phillips. 'Beth, I hate lying this way!'

'You know a better scenario? It's workable.'

On Sunday, 1 July Diane, Jennie, and Beth boarded their flight to Atlanta. Diane had chosen this date so they would be able to celebrate Jennie's second birthday – a diversion if she was upset by the move – in their new home. Jennie was enthralled at the prospect of flying.

Diane's mind was in chaos. She was flooded by last-minute apprehensions. *Was* she out of her mind, as she was sure the Bertonellis believed? And she was trying to gear herself for the return to Eden – where for a little while she'd been so happy with Cliff.

Reading recent editions of the *Herald*, she'd learned that the police had come up with no leads in Dr Taylor's murder. She was impatient to go back and search for a link between the murders of Chris Robson, Annie Williams and Dr Taylor – and her father. She wasn't becoming obsessed, she told herself defensively. There *was* a connection.

Approaching Hartsfield Diane was conscious of almost over-whelming tension. In forty minutes they'd board the commuter flight for Eden. Twenty minutes later they would be there. A barrage of images assaulted her: the chance encounter with Maureen Masters at the library; Lloyd Masters' arrival in the hospital business office on the day the new equipment was officially installed; Elvira talking with barely veiled irony about him; Norma's candid assessment of him as a father.

No need to fear she'd run into Cliff. He hadn't been in Eden for months. He was finishing his residency in another town. She brushed aside the errant thoughts that crept into her mind at intervals. It was too late for Cliff and her to pick up the threads.

'Jennie, look at all the pretty flowers,' Beth cooed, bringing Diane back to the moment.

In Eden they'd go straight to the Ashley House, where she'd made reservations for them. Tomorrow morning they'd start the search for a place to live, plus an office for the newspaper. She felt an unexpected flicker of amusement. The word would spread around town fast that two women from New York were launching a weekly 'giveaway' newspaper. In Eden everything circulated fast.

Their plane came down on the runway. Diane and Beth were impatient to disembark, to be on the final brief lap to Eden. The terminal was glutted with vacation-bound travellers. Clutching Jennie in her arms, Diane followed Beth to the gate for their connecting flight.

'Mommie, I'm sleepy.' Jennie's eyes were drooping.

'We'll be at the hotel soon,' Diane soothed. 'You'll have a nice nap. Just another very short flight . . .'

Before the plane was aloft Jennie was asleep. Diane stared out the window without seeing. So many times she'd convinced herself – almost – that she had erased Cliff from her mind and heart. But memories washed over her. Her first encounter with Cliff, their first date, the first time they'd slept together.

So many nights she'd lain awake, remembering the precious months with him, his sweetness, his compassion. Their mutual passion. The tenderness of his hands on her, the feel of him beneath the touch of her hands. Those months must last for a lifetime.

'So that's Eden . . .' Beth's effervescent voice brought her back to the moment. 'I think we can handle it.'

Jennie awoke as the plane prepared to land.

'I'm hungry,' she announced matter-of-factly. 'Real hungry.'

'We'll go out for a late lunch as soon as we're settled in our hotel,' Diane promised.

'What's a hotel?' Jennie was on another of her question sessions.

'Where we're going to stay until we find ourselves an apartment,' Beth told her.

'Can I have ice cream?' Jennie asked hopefully.

'Since this is a very special occasion, yes,' Diane told her. 'After you've eaten your lunch.'

With a disconcerting sense of *déjà vu* Diane led the way to the taxi stand, instructed the driver to take them to the Ashley House. In a corner of her mind she realized that Beth was keeping Jennie engrossed in conversation to allow her to cope with the flood of emotions that inundated her. She was back in Eden – but Cliff wasn't here.

Within three days Diane and Beth had rented a two-bedroom apartment in the only garden apartment complex in Eden, and were shopping for furniture that was available for immediate delivery. On first sight Diane and Beth loved the white-brick apartments, surrounded by greenery and a lush array of summer flowers. A small, imaginative play area told them Jennie would have playmates here. They chose modest-priced but pleasing furniture, confining themselves to essentials. Diane bought a used car.

'Thank God you can drive,' Diane told Beth.

'You get a learner's permit immediately. I refuse to be the family chauffeur. But don't drive the way you walk,' Beth flipped. 'My mother says she always knows when it's you coming to the apartment from the elevator. You're the speed demon.'

'I haven't been exactly speedy in other areas.' Diane's faint smile was ironic.

'One project at a time at this point. We've got a newspaper to set up.'

'I need to learn more about Dr Taylor,' Diane said sombrely, 'and about Chris Robson. But right now we have to make this town understand that a weekly "giveaway" is about to be born.'

Fighting self-consciousness Diane called Norma to announce her return to Eden, explaining her sudden departure and her activities since that time – and her reason for being in Eden now.

'I know I should have been in touch,' she apologized, 'but life was so chaotic.'

'Oh, I'm dying to see you!' Norma bubbled. 'And Jennie!'

The tenderness in her voice reminded Diane that Norma and Joe had been holding off having a family because they needed her wages to pay off their mortgage. 'Wait till Gladys hears you're back in town. You know, she was harboring romantic ideas about you and Cliff Hendricks.' A guarded curiosity in her voice now.

'Cliff and I saw a lot of each other – I was so lonely and he was so sweet – but then Jason came back from Vietnam . . .' Her voice trailed off. She'd told Norma she was divorced. 'Anyhow, Beth and I decided to come down here and start up a "giveaway" weekly newspaper.'

'Lloyd Masters won't like that a bit.' Norma was blunt. 'About eight years ago some people came down here to publish a competing morning paper. He drove them out of business before the first year. Not that I mean to discourage you,' she said quickly. 'But you know Lloyd Masters runs this town.'

'We're no competition.' Diane struggled to sound optimistic. 'This is a local once-a-week community paper that's given away – there're a lot of them now around the country. We just have to struggle to bring our advertising to a point where we can pay our bills and show a reasonable profit.' She hadn't known about that other newspaper – but theirs would be *different*. And they had the finances to hang in there, she reminded herself defiantly.

'Joe says every now and then how he'd love to be in business for himself, not to have to answer to a creepy boss. But we're chicken. We like to know paycheques are coming in every week. Not everybody's cut out to be an entrepreneur. But I admire your guts.'

Within a week Diane, Jennie and Beth were able to move out of the hotel and into their apartment, though some of the furniture would not be delivered for yet another week. Now they focused on renting a small commercial space in town. They were delighted when they found a storefront right on Main Street – larger than they currently required but Diane was looking ahead to expansion. The rent fitted their budget. They were taken aback when the real estate broker made it clear he considered their venture a bad risk.

'I don't know if the owners will want to give you a lease,' he said dubiously. 'They're looking for a substantial business.'

'Call up Eden National,' Diane told him. The bank had been most impressed by the funds she'd transferred to her new account. And thank God, Eden rentals were a fraction of what they were in Manhattan. 'Call them,' she reiterated with a certain imperiousness she suspected would also impress him.

The broker phoned the bank, talked for a few moments, then broke into a broad smile.

'Thank you, Emmett. Yes, she's a client of ours.' He put down the phone. 'I'll draw up the lease and have it ready for you to sign tomorrow.'

After Diane and Beth had signed the lease the following morning, Beth took Jennie home to play with her new small friend Nicole, and Diane headed for the hospital for a brief visit with Norma and Gladys. She was sure Norma had announced her presence in town. Her heart pounding, her mind invaded by poignant recall, she crossed the hospital grounds.

She remembered her first moments in Gladys's office, when Cliff had charged in with a plea for help for a patient – and she'd known even then that he was drawn to her. She remembered her last day here, when she knew she must surreptitiously leave Eden behind her. Those few months – at first so lonely and alarming – had provided a heady happiness that would be for ever etched on her soul. But happiness came in small batches, she told herself, and always with a price tag.

'Diane!' Gladys jumped up from behind her desk at sight of her. 'Norma told me you were back in town.' The two women embraced. 'You look marvellous!'

'Where's Norma?' Diane asked.

'She took the morning off – she has a plumber coming to the house,' Gladys explained. 'She said something about your starting up a newspaper in town with a friend.' Gladys sighed. 'I was hoping you'd be interested in coming back to work with us.'

'We expect to bring out our first issue in six to eight weeks. It's just a little weekly that's given away.' Diane forced a smile. 'I'm hoping that maybe we can even coax an ad out of Masters Memorial.'

'Don't count on it. To some people in this town you'll be considered the enemy. But Norma says you have a little girl. Show me pictures!'

'Oh, sure.' Diane reached into her purse for her wallet. 'Jennie's almost twenty-one months,' she lied, lest Gladys start figuring, 'but she thinks she's ten.'

Diane hoped frantically – even while she feared this – that Gladys would bring Cliff into their conversation. She was sure he was now recovered, but she hungered for reassurance from Gladys. Had he finished his residency? Where was he living? Was he going into research, as he'd talked about with such fervour? Perhaps Gladys, intent on being diplomatic, was deliberately not mentioning Cliff, she told herself.

A few days later Diane and Beth quietly celebrated Jennie's second birthday. Diane fought off waves of guilt that she was making a point of pushing Jennie's public birthday off by three months so that there was no way anyone in Eden could count back and suspect that Cliff might be Jennie's father. She'd learnt by devious enquiry that entry into kindergarten required only a lease or deed to prove residency – no birth certificate.

Diane and Beth were astonished when the first local printing firm they approached refused to give them an estimate for printing their proposed newspaper, to be called the *Eden Guardian*.

'We got all the accounts we can handle now. Sorry.' Was the proprietor afraid of offending Lloyd Masters?

They discovered only one other printing house in town that was set up to handle their requirement. The owner's quote was shockingly high.

'Hey, paper prices are skyrocketing,' he pointed out. 'Of course, they won't stay that way. There's always this pattern of going up, then going down. You won't do any better,' he predicted.

Eventually they'd have to set up their own facilities, Diane surmised, but they weren't ready for that yet. They made a deal with Comstock Printing. Now they settled down to their next objective: setting up the first edition and pursuing advertising.

'Don't be so grossed out,' Diane scolded when Beth returned from her initial morning's selling venture. 'Didn't you tell me that Tom gave away free advertising for months? Go back and offer free ads – you know, "to introduce ourselves".'

Diane and Beth knew the importance of their first issue. It must deal with situations that were important to the community if they were to build a readership. And they must offer articles that would encourage advertising. Each night – with Jennie in bed for the night and a neighbouring teenager baby-sitting – they had dinner at a different restaurant. A full page in the first issue would report on their dining experiences around town.

Pumping Norma for information about the day care centre in town, Diane focused on a feature article dealing with the urgency for expanding this service in Eden. She knew there was a waiting list – useless for her to apply for a place for Jennie. She was relieved when Elise, the mother of Jennie's friend Nicole offered to take care of Jennie each week morning from eight until one. From then on Diane would have Jennie with her at their newly acquired office.

'Try to get Gerry Watson interested in the day care story,' Norma persuaded, then paused. 'No, maybe you'd better not. Her old man won't be happy that somebody's encroaching on his turf. I know you're a minuscule operation compared to his' she said, before Diane could break in, 'but he won't be pleased.'

Beth suggested they do a front-page tribute to Dr Taylor. Diane leapt at this. This was a chance to remind the town that here was an unsolved murder on the police records. On Wednesday evenings, she promised herself, she'd go to the library to start the search through back issues of the *Herald* for more data on the murder of Chris Robson.

With the office physically in working condition, their printer under contract, and a varied selection of free ads scheduled for the first issue, Diane and Beth concentrated on preparing their articles. They were confident that most of Eden was aware that the *Eden Guardian* was about to be launched. On this hot, steamy night Diane sat at their secondhand IBM and worked out the copy for their ad for boys to deliver the *Guardian*.

'Come look at this,' Diane ordered. 'I've cut it as short as possible.'

'Honey, the *Herald* doesn't charge *New York Times* rates,' Beth reminded, reading over Diane's shoulder. 'Unh-unh,' she reproached. 'We don't advertise for "boys" to deliver our papers. Teenagers,' she emphasized. 'And if girls want to deliver, why not?'

'Why not? I'll change it.'

Diane retyped the copy, pulled out the final draft to show to Beth. 'You don't suppose the *Herald* will refuse to run the ad?'

'They can't do that. It's not obscene or illegal. We'll go together tomorrow morning while Jennie's with Elise.' They were both relieved that Jennie looked forward each day to her mornings, plus lunch, with Elise and tiny Nicole. 'Unless you'd rather I go alone.'

'I'm not afraid to go into the *Herald* offices,' Diane shot back. 'I'm not afraid of Lloyd Masters.' Still, her heart pounded at the prospect of encountering him.

'Di, don't you feel strange sometimes?' Beth was troubled. 'I mean, living here in the same town with your grandfather and the rest of your father's family, and being "the enemy"?'

'Beth, it's not like with your family,' Diane reminded her impatiently. She remembered the warmth of Beth's parents, her grandparents, the aunts and uncles and cousins on her father's side; the *importance* to them of *family*. 'Dad's family never wanted any part of Mom and me.' But all at once she remembered the poignant moments in the Eden cemetery when she had sat on a granite bench beside her father's grave and that of her paternal grandmother. *They* were family. Like Uncle Erich.

In the morning Diane and Beth left Jennie with Elise and Nicole and drove downtown to the offices of the *Herald* before going to their own small office.

'Are we supposed to salaam when we enter the building?' Beth drawled, reaching for the door.

'I'll bet ninety per cent of the town does that mentally.'

They went to the classified department. At this hour they were the sole clients at the counter where advertising was accepted. Diane brought out the ad copy, handed it to the courteous clerk behind the counter. She and Beth watched, exchanging uneasy glances, while he perused the copy, then reread it.

'I'll be back with you in a few minutes,' he said tersely, and headed for a desk at the rear of the area. Here he reached for the telephone.

'What's the big problem?' Beth bridled.

'He has to clear it with his boss?' Diane lifted an eyebrow in derision, but her heart was thumping. By now the whole town knew about the *Eden Guardian*. Were they already stepping on Lloyd Masters' royal toes?

The clerk put the phone down. He walked back to the counter and handed the copy to Diane.

'I'm sorry. We can't run this.'

'Why not?' Diane challenged, her face hot. 'There's nothing obscene or illegal about this ad.' She was conscious that others behind the counter were eavesdropping on their conversation.

'We don't want to run it.' He tried to stare her down.

'Why not?'

'We don't need a reason. We won't run it.' Now he lowered his gaze and turned away.

'We'll put up notices in the high school,' Diane told Beth as they left. 'We'll put a sign in the office windows. We'll find our delivery crew.'

But Diane and Beth understood that open warfare had just been declared between the *Herald* and the *Evening News*, and the newly arrived *Eden Guardian*.

'What is it, Clark?' In his lush penthouse executive suite Lloyd Masters laid aside the contract he'd been studying with obvious annoyance at this interruption.

'You know that rag we hear is trying to set up operations in town?' Clark asked.

'What about it?' Sometimes he thought he'd give Clark the necessary push into politics just to get his most bothersome son-in-law out of his hair. 'Is a kitten going to bother a lion.'

'It's supposedly run by two women.' His contempt came through loud and clear. 'They had the gall to come into our classified and try to run an ad for help. Fred threw them out.'

'Clark, they don't bother me.' Lloyd gestured impatiently. 'They'll make their piddling attempt and fade away. It happens every few years.'

'I spoke to Zach Mason at the bank. He said one of the two women opened an account with a six-figure cheque. They're offering free ads. They've talked with Zoe Taylor about a front-page tribute to the old man. They're using the old community spirit approach –'

'Clark, talk with Luke about this,' Lloyd interrupted. Maybe they *should* step on this stupid operation. 'He handled that last deal here in town. Tell him I don't want them operating their sleazy rag in Eden. You two work it out.'

Chapter Fourteen

Luke sneaked a glance at his watch while Clark filled him in on their father-in-law's latest directive. Christ, Clark could be so damn long-winded.

'Cool it, Clark,' he broke in. 'I know what the Old Man wants. We give these two kooky New York women six months, and they'll be out of business. And if by chance they're not . . .' his smile was smug, 'then we'll know what to do.'

'Nothing out of line,' Clark stipulated nervously.

'Clark, we always do everything legal,' Luke drawled. Clark was scared that something might pop up to haunt him one day when he was running for the Legislature. 'You know how the Old Man feels about that. Everything above board.'

'We had some rough moments with that last team.' Clark's eyes were eloquent.

'They were three guys with heavy newspaper background and big money behind them. The way I hear it these are two young chicks out to play newspaper publishers. So we let them play a few months.'

'You said that eight years ago – and that got real nasty.'

'Look, I'm the legal department.' He frowned in annoyance. 'Didn't I kill that threatened suit? We were never in serious trouble.' He paused. 'Dig up whatever you can on these two. In case we need it.'

'Five years ago the Old Man hinted he'd be stepping down soon,' Clark grumbled. 'What's he waiting for?'

'He'll be sitting behind that desk until the medics take him away on a stretcher.' Luke shrugged this aside. 'Oh, while you're researching, find out who's printing their little rag.' Luke pushed back his chair and rose to his feet. 'I have an appointment in Atlanta . . .'

'I'll bring in a report,' Clark said tersely, turned and headed for the door.

The bastard couldn't stand being the lowest man on the totem pole, Luke thought with smug amusement. The last of the sons-in-law to come into the family. Would the Old Man ever push Clark into the State Legislature? Not if *he* could help it.

Diane and Beth spent long days – that dragged into the evenings – in preparing to launch the *Guardian*. Diane abandoned thoughts of library research on Wednesday evenings. Every waking moment, it seemed, was given over to details for the *Guardian*. They were publishers, reporters, editors, business managers – even staff photographers.

They talked at regular intervals with Tom, who advised them at critical moments. They were at first unnerved when their printer suddenly announced he wouldn't be able to bring out their first issue until mid-October – two weeks later than planned.

'Maybe we'll need that time,' Beth comforted Diane. 'Everything takes longer than we expect. But we've got our carriers set up, plenty of ads. Free,' she conceded, 'but Tom says it looks great when fifty per cent of the space is taken by ads.'

'I don't know why Mrs Taylor turned so cold.' Diane was worried. 'She was so sweet and co-operative until the last time we talked.'

Diane and Beth focused on the endless details of bringing out the first issue of the *Guardian*. They were increasingly pleased to have Elise and Ron Tucker as their neighbours. On a scorching Sunday afternoon the Tuckers invited the two women and Jennie for a cook-out. While Ron – who taught history in the Eden High School – presided over the grill, and Jennie and Nicole played in the Tuckers' sandbox, the three women relaxed in beach chairs and talked. Elise was intrigued by Diane and

Beth's determination to make Eden residents aware of the imminent addition of a weekly newspaper. They hand-delivered fliers, bought announcements on the local radio station, sent letters to churches, synagogues, local organizations, made many personal contacts.

It was on the Sunday of Labor Day weekend that Diane and Beth first realized that Ron Tucker was Jewish – and the Tuckers learned that Diane and Beth were Jewish.

'My father's Jewish by conversion,' Beth explained. 'He converted to make my mother happy.'

'I agreed that Nicole would be raised Jewish, to make Ron's parents, whom I adore, happy,' Elise confided. 'My parents were livid when I married Ron. They couldn't understand what I saw in him,' she reminisced, giggling. 'I mean, we're fourth generation Georgia Baptists. Most Southerners – except real ignoramuses – have a special kind of respect for Jews, my father has always said. You know, it's a Bible Belt thing – a reverence for the Old Testament. My family tolerates Ron, and they love Nicole, but we don't have the closeness we have with Ron's parents.'

'We've cornered the market here,' Diane joked. 'My father was Baptist, too – but even if he hadn't died, I would have been raised Jewish. Mom said he'd agreed to that right off.' And that had infuriated Lloyd Masters.

'I met Ron at college. It was kind of a thing back in the sixties for Christian college girls to date Jewish boys. You know, the rebellion scene. We didn't have the nerve to date black boys. And a lot of us discovered that Jewish boys were special. They were bright and considerate and fun to be with. Ron was the first boy I ever dated who cared about what I *thought*. He didn't think I was dead from the neck up.' She leaned forward to call to Ron, busy flipping hamburgers. 'You don't listen to this, you hear? I don't want you to get conceited.'

Elise told them that Ron's parents had sold their house in Alabama two years ago and moved here.

'His father's semi-retired,' Elise explained. 'He's an accountant. He said he wasn't ready to take up residence on the golf course so he handles a few clients. His mother keeps busy with volunteer work.' Elise sighed. 'I can't wait for Nicole to be in first grade. I'll cut out of the house so fast I'll break speed records. I have a degree in education and I'd like to put it to use, maybe start a day nursery.'

'Who wants the works on the burgers?' Ron demanded. 'And I mean, the works.'

Diane and Beth were ecstatic when the first issue of the *Guardian* brought in favourable comments. Still, they knew there would be a long chore ahead to convince local businesses to spend on advertising. Tenaciously they sought for stories of interest to local residents.

Early in December Diane and Beth argued about the advisability of running a year-end story about Dr Taylor's murder – still unsolved. They'd dropped the original story from the first edition when Zoe Taylor had ceased to be co-operative.

'We don't want to look as though we're harassing the police,' Beth warned. 'That'll turn off a lot of local people.'

'It's the fourth unsolved murder in the last thirty years on the police records,' Diane said stubbornly. 'OK, we won't mention that,' she capitulated. 'But when will we see some action in the Taylor murder case?'

'I think it's a bad idea,' Beth objected.

Instinct told Diane that Beth was right. But maybe – just maybe – the story would jog some memories. Maybe some people would begin to ask questions. 'Let's run with it.'

'OK, boss lady.' But Beth was unhappy.

The *Guardian* ran the story on the first Thursday in the new year.

The following morning the *Herald* ran a scathing renunciation: 'An upstart weekly tabloid in town dares to defile our fine police force.'

The *Guardian*'s very lightweight list of advertisers thinned out. When Diane encountered Gladys in the A&P, she was unfamiliarly cool.

'Hey, you're treading on toes,' Elise pointed out. 'Ron thinks you should do a follow-up, apologizing for throwing a bad light on the local fuzz. You know, you didn't mean it that way.'

'I won't do it.' Diane's colour was high. 'There's not just Dr Taylor's murder that's going unsolved. There've been two other murders in Eden in the last thirty years.' And the fourth she mustn't talk about – yet.

'Honey, except for the Chief of Police, the guys on the force now were in diapers thirty years ago,' Elise pointed out. 'Anyhow, you're just spinning your wheels trying to get action out of our police force. If it's not laid out for them, they don't do much digging.'

'Don't apologize exactly,' Ron suggested. 'Just say in an editorial you have such deep admiration for Dr Taylor that you find it difficult to see his murderer go unapprehended – and you hope some leads turn up that'll be productive.'

'Do it, Di,' Beth coaxed. 'We can't afford to lose advertisers.'

Diane sighed. 'OK, we'll do it.'

Now Diane and Beth collaborated on the day care article they'd been discussing for months. At the same time they were encouraging Elise to open up a small morning nursery programme for three-to-five-year-olds.

'Ron doesn't object, does he?' Beth challenged on a Sunday morning when the three women were sharing a late breakfast in the Tucker kitchen – the two little girls absorbed in play at their feet. 'I mean, he's not one of those guys who talk big about women's lib but don't want to see it in their house?'

'Sugar, you know Ron better than that,' Elise scolded her. 'He's all for it. I'm uneasy about setting-up costs. Of course, Mom and Dad keep insisting they'll help.' Ron's parents, Sally and Lou Tucker, were 'Mom and Dad'; her parents were 'Mother and Daddy'.

'Then go ahead with it,' Diane urged. 'We can tie in the

announcement with our article on the need for day care in town. Even if you don't open up for months, we can start plugging.'

'I'm talking about a three-and-a-half-hour playgroup,' Elise demurred.

'But you hope to develop it into a day care centre,' Diane pointed out in triumph. 'In time. What's available is so inadequate.'

They started at the sound of a car honking close by.

'That's Mom and Dad,' Elise said, her face lighting. 'Dad has this Sunday morning date with Nicole – they watch cartoons together. Mom says that at sixty-one Dad won't admit he loves cartoons. This makes it seem legitimate.'

'How's my littlest granddaughter?' A small, trim, prematurely white-haired man, Lou Tucker sauntered into the kitchen. He was followed by his wife, slim, dark-haired, easy-going. 'Hey, we've got a date.' He swooped Nicole up into his arms. 'And how about introducing me to your gorgeous little friend?'

In minutes he was settled before the television set with Nicole on one side and Jennie on the other, both little girls enthralled with his presence. In the kitchen Sally Tucker poured herself coffee and joined the three younger women at the breakfast table.

'I love that article you did last week about those volunteers who take dogs and cats into the nursing home for regular visits. Of course, we haven't had pets since Ron was three and we discovered he had an insane allergy to cats and dogs.' She hesitated. 'You haven't had any more problems with the *Herald*, have you?'

'We try to keep out of their way.' Diane managed a wry smile. That had been a vicious attack when they ran the tribute to Dr Taylor.

'I understand Gerry Watson brings armloads of flowers to the nursing home all spring and summer.' Sally turned to Elise. 'I hear she's taking over the Saturday morning storytelling sessions at the library again. She's so much better than Mimi Trent. The kids love her.'

'Maybe I'll take Nicole and Jennie next Saturday morning,' Elise said, turning to Diane for approval.'

Diane tensed. Mom had said Gerry was the only one in the family who had been nice to her. Why was she upset at the prospect of Jennie being in a storytelling group with her?

'Gerry Watson is the only woman in that family I like.' Sally grunted in distaste. 'Isn't there another daughter away some-where?' she asked in sudden recall.

'You mean Alison,' Elise said. 'She's not exactly away. She had a terrible experience when she was sixteen – a gang rape. Can you imagine something like that happening in Eden?'

'Is she in an institution?' Sally debated about accepting a Danish that Elise had just brought out from the oven, sighed and took it.

'Not an institution,' Elise explained. 'She just never leaves her room at the Masterses' house. She won't see anybody except her father and her nurse. People say he just worships her. He spends a fortune buying her the hand-painted antique kerosene lamps she loves. She sits for hours every day washing them. She won't allow electricity in her rooms – just those lamps and candlelight. I know,' she laughed. 'I'm gossiping again. My mother's cleaning woman is a cousin to a maid in their house – I get these little tidbits.'

'Somebody – I think it was your friend Norma –' Beth turned to Diane – 'suggested we ask Gerry Watson to do a gardening column for the paper. She's supposed to be wonderful with flowers.'

'I can't see Lloyd Masters' daughter writing a column for the *Guardian*,' Diane rejected wryly.

On Saturday morning Diane dressed Jennie for her trip to the storytelling session at the library. She'd ask Elise to drop her off at the office, she decided. Beth had driven down an hour ago to confront their printer about the last-minute deliveries that were giving them ulcers. By now Beth would be at the office to accept whatever ads might wander in off the street.

'Mommie, they're here!' Jennie said urgently as the doorbell rang.

'All right, we're ready.' She buttoned Jennie's coat, hurried to open the door.

'Hi. Let's get this show on the road,' Elise greeted them.

In a flurry of pleasurable anticipation the two women and two little girls settled themselves in the car.

'Why don't you come to the storytelling session, too?' Elise coaxed. 'Beth can handle the office on a Saturday morning. The kids are all so adorable.'

'Maybe I will go to the library with you,' Diane decided on impulse. In truth, Beth wasn't expecting her to come in until later. 'I've been dying to get over to do some research. This would be the perfect time.'

'Everybody talks about how great the new library is, but I kind of miss the old one.' Elise was wistful. 'It had such character.'

'I haven't been inside the new library,' Diane said. All these months since she'd returned to Eden, and she hadn't done one hour of research. It was time she got back on track.

'It's large and modern and well equipped,' Elise conceded, 'but it's impersonal. That won't matter to the kids, though.'

When they arrived at the library, they found the parking area already crowded.

'Remember,' Elise warned with mock sternness as they emerged from the car, 'I expect you girls to be good. You have to be quiet and not ask questions until a story is over.'

They arrived at the entrance at the same time as a small, dark-haired women in a beautifully tailored camel's-hair coat and slacks.

'Hi.' She smiled down at the two little girls. 'Are you here for the storytelling?'

'Yes!' chorused Jennie and Nicole.

All at once Diane was cold and trembling. She knew this was Gerry Watson – Dad's sister. She remembered Uncle Erich's reaction when he'd seen Gerry's photo in the *Herald*: '*My God, Di, she's the image of Kevin.*'

And though she'd told herself she hated the entire Masters family, she felt drawn to this fragilely slim woman with the vulnerable eyes. She was conscious of the light exchange between Gerry and Elise as they walked to the library. This was her aunt. Jennie's great-aunt.

Inside the library she glanced swiftly about until her eyes located her destination. While Elise led Jennie and Nicole towards the children's room, Diane hurried to the periodicals and newspapers desk. She thrust her mind into action. What had bothered her most in New York was her inability to read back issues of the *Herald*. She needed to find a link between Chris Robson and Lloyd Masters. Here was where she would find it.

'May I help you?' a pleasant young librarian asked. A librarian who hadn't been at the old library three years ago.

'I'd like the April 1943 issues of the *Eden Herald*, please.'

The librarian sounded doubtful. 'I don't know if our files go back that far. But I'll check it out.'

Why wouldn't they have it? The *Herald* went back to the late twenties. What was the local newspaper before the *Herald* started? Was it still around, along with the *Herald*, in 1943? Then she saw the librarian returning from the file room at the rear of the area, a small box of film in hand. She breathed a sigh of relief.

'We have it,' the librarian announced with pride.

Diane settled herself at a machine at the rear of the area. As always she was fearful – though she knew the possibility was almost non-existent – that someone at another of the machines would guess her reasons for being here. She swore under her breath when the film at first refused to attach itself to the take-up reel. Slowly, she exhorted herself. She'd threaded film a thousand times.

At last she was able to turn the wheel and read on the projector. The story should be on page one of an Eden newspaper, she reasoned – a murder would demand that. She sped through the first issue to check the front page of the next. Tension created a knot in the pit of her stomach as front page after front page offered nothing. And then, close to the end of the month's issues, she saw it: 'LOCAL TEENAGER MURDERED'.

The front-page article carried the high school yearbook photograph of Christopher Robson. He was described as a fine student, a member of the high school football team, and voted 'Most Handsome in the Class of '43'. He was the 'only child of Raymond and Anne Robson'. His father was a local pharmacist, his mother active in the Women's Auxiliary of the Baptist Church. 'Thus far the police have discovered no leads,' the article finished. Diane rewound the reel, returned to the desk to ask for additional film. Instinct warned her there would be no suspect tracked down. Conscious of the time – knowing the story hour would be just that – she rushed through the later editions. The police reported no leads.

Talk to Elvira about the case, she ordered herself. It would take for ever to keep reading month after month of microfilm.

Elvira would know if the case had been solved.

Chapter Fifteen

Beth listened sombrely while Diane reported on her research at the library.

'It's the same story,' Diane summed up in frustration. 'No leads so far.'

'Di, there's no connection here with Lloyd Masters,' Beth pointed out. 'You're spinning your wheels again.'

'I'm not ready to say that,' Diane countered. 'Was the murder ever solved? Elvira knows everything that's happened in this town since she was a little girl. I'm not going to spend time reading more microfilm. I'll ask her.' She glanced at her watch. 'I'll call her and see if I can drop by to talk to her this afternoon.'

While Beth involved Jennie in a lively discussion about the story hour, Diane phoned Elvira.

'I need to be filled in on some Eden history,' Diane confided to Elvira. 'May I drop by and pick your brain?'

'Any time, sugar,' Elvira said warmly.

'Now?'

'Come over and have tea with me. I'd love some company.'

Half an hour later Diane sat in Elvira's pleasant living room while they sipped Earl Grey tea and nibbled at cranberry muffins. Now Diane broached the subject paramount in her mind.

'I know it was thirty years ago – but do you remember when Chris Robson was murdered?'

Elvira closed her eyes for a moment in remembered anguish.

'Oh, it was an awful time in this town. Chris was the most popular boy in the high school. Half the girls in his class had a crush on him. His father suffered a massive stroke three days later. His mother had never worked a day in her life – she married right out of high school – but Anne had to go out to work to support herself and Ray.' She paused. 'It's supposed to be a secret, but a few people in this town know that after Ray's stroke Lloyd Masters sent a cheque to Anne Robson every month until Ray died. Every once in a while I'm amazed by Lloyd Masters. Most of the time the whole world hears about his philanthropies.'

'Was Chris the kind of kid to have been involved with bad characters?' Diane probed.

'Oh my, no!' Elvira shook her head with conviction. 'He was in Dorothy's class.' Dorothy was Elvira's oldest child. 'I have their class yearbook right here.' She rose to her feet, crossed to the antique breakfront that dominated the room and opened one of the doors to pull out a large, blue, leather-bound volume.

Diane waited while Elvira flipped through the yearbook, reminiscing at a page here and there.

'Here's Chris . . .' Elvira laid the book across the coffee table so that Diane could see the photos of the senior class of '43. 'I tell you, this whole town was upset for a long time.'

'Was the murderer ever found?' At last Diane asked the crucial question while her eyes scanned the array of young faces that stared from tiny photographs.

'The police came up with nothing,' Elvira said. 'I think even now Anne hopes that one day Chris's killer will be brought to justice.'

'It's so sad.'

All at once Diane's heart began to pound. On the page opposite the one that displayed Chris Robson's photograph she spied the face of a lovely young girl. Even before she read the name beneath the photograph, she knew this was Alison Masters. She bore a dramatic resemblance to her late half-brother and to her youngest sister. Alison Masters had been a member of the class of '43. A classmate of Chris Robson.

'Diane, why this interest in Chris?' Elvira was curious. 'I hope you don't plan on resurrecting that awful period,' she added in alarm. 'It would be devastating to Anne. She still keeps Chris's room exactly as it was the day he died.'

'But you said she still hopes that one day his killer would be found.'

'But don't you understand? That'll never happen. Why reopen wounds now?' Elvira sighed. 'That was a terrible year for this town. Chris Robson was murdered. A favourite young high school teacher was killed at Guadalcanal – and Alison Robson was gang-raped. Of course, her parents tried to keep it a secret, and my heart bled for them, but the word seeped out. She didn't graduate with her class. She became a total recluse. Diane, I don't know what kind of story you're thinking of running in the *Guardian* but, please, don't rake up old griefs.'

In April – a particularly beautiful month in Eden – Beth's mother and father came down for a week's visit. Beth and Diane were sure this trip was made in the hope of persuading them to give up the *Guardian* and return to New York.

'Mom and Dad will realize quick enough that we have no intention of leaving,' Beth told Diane while they waited at the airport for her parents to arrive.

'They're smart,' Diane said, though she dreaded what was certain to be an impassioned confrontation. 'They'll get the message.'

Diane and Beth overrode the Bertonellis' determination to stay at a hotel.

'No deal,' Diane insisted lovingly. She remembered how Beth's family had stood beside her when tragedy descended on her. 'You're staying with us.'

'You'll have my bedroom, and I'll sleep on the sofa,' Beth told them.

As Diane and Beth had expected, Tony and Irma Bertonelli tried in their first two days in Eden to convince the two that they should move back to New York. Then – acknowledging defeat – they relaxed their efforts and gave themselves up to enjoying their first encounter with Southern living.

Their second evening in town, Beth's parents were invited to dinner at Elise and Ron's apartment. Ron's parents – Sally and Lou Tucker – would be there, also. Jennie and Nicole were enthralled to be allowed to stay up for the grown-up dinner party.

'Oh Lord, are you spoiling these kids?' Ron joshed as the two older couples lavished attention and obvious affection on the two little girls. 'There'll be no living with them after this week.'

After dinner Elise took Jennie and Nicole off to Nicole's bedroom, to be put to bed for the evening. The atmosphere in the apartment was warm and loving, Diane thought as she brought second cups of coffee into the living room.

'After the crazy New York winter I can't believe the wonderful weather down here.' Irma was radiant. 'And I can't believe all the gorgeous dogwood trees in bloom everywhere.'

'We're very close to Atlanta, you know,' Ron explained. 'And Atlanta is known for its perfect weather – summers cooler than most Southern cities and winters so balmy our trees are always green.'

'Everybody hears how Atlanta is booming like mad,' Tony recalled.

'It's booming in crime, too,' Lou said ruefully. 'Thank God, that doesn't reach out to us.'

'The KKK has been pretty much in abeyance, hasn't it?' Tony asked.

'Oh, the KKK has gone into hiding,' Sally agreed. 'They know this is not their time.'

'For my father Atlanta was always associated with the Leo Frank trial,' Sally Tucker recalled. 'He couldn't understand how a man could be lynched for a crime he didn't commit because he happened to be a Northern Jew.'

'That was a bad time for the whole South,' Lou reminded. 'But times have changed.'

'To some extent.' Sally was tart. 'For all the assimilation we hear about, it exists only between 9 a.m. and 6 p.m. Outside of those hours, we see little assimilation. Oh, everybody's terribly polite, and we're all involved in the same civic activities.'

'The way I see it, we're Southerners who happen to be Jewish.' But Lou was clearly defensive.

'Oh, come on, Lou. Be realistic,' Sally scoffed. 'To most people we're outsiders. My family has been in Eden for four generations. You're first generation Georgia-born. But most of the time we socialize with other Jewish families. We even tend to live on the same blocks.'

'In a way that happens in New York,' Irma considered, and chuckled. 'Of course, there're so many of us. In New York we don't feel ourselves a minority.'

'But we had a Jewish mayor in Atlanta,' Ron pointed out.

'Who's now been replaced by the first black mayor in a major Southern city,' Elise picked up.

'Big cities and small towns in the South are two different ball games,' Lou said. 'In small towns most Jews are ever conscious that they're "different".' Unexpectedly he smiled. 'Of course, Sunday dinner usually includes chicken soup along with fried chicken and black-eyed peas and sweet potato pie. And in school we sang "Dixie" with the same enthusiasm as Georgia Baptists. No,' he concluded, 'we don't feel anti-Semitism as such in small Southern towns. Just an "after 6 p.m." social separation.'

'Of course, Ron and Elise managed to override that,' Sally said indulgently.

'I think Jewish kids grow up with some subconscious rules for themselves.' Ron squinted in thought. 'I mean, in school we always told ourselves we had to be the best. Jewish guys are never flashy dressers – because that's part of the stereotypical image. We don't look for fights – we want to be accepted.'

'And of course,' laughter lit Elise's eyes, 'Southern girls grow up hearing that Jewish boys make the best husbands. And Jewish Northerners come down to Emory and Georgia Tech in droves.'

'My roommate at college was from New York City,' Ron reminisced. 'He was absolutely fascinated by Southern Jewish girls. Southern girls – for all the talk about feminism – know how to flirt and make a guy feel important. Jewish girls as much as Christian girls. He married a classmate from Montgomery. When she made up her mind she wanted him, he didn't have a chance.'

'I don't know why it should matter whether we worship in church or synagogue or mosque or wherever,' Diane said softly. 'We're all members of the human race.'

'You dream of a perfect world,' Lou chided, but his eyes were sympathetic. 'I doubt that'll ever be.'

Too soon for Beth and Diane they were seeing Tony and Irma Bertonelli off for their return flight to New York.

'I'll come up in the fall,' Beth promised, kissing first her mother, then her father. 'And stop worrying about us. We're doing great.'

They weren't doing great, Diane acknowledged to herself. They'd not yet recovered from the loss of advertisers after the attack by the *Herald*. They were deeply overspent. But she refused to be upset. They'd known it would be rough to break even in the first year.

At regular intervals she was assaulted by frustration at being unable to bring out into the open – on the pages of the *Guardian* – her conviction that the unsolved murders in Eden were connected, the work of one killer who might strike again. It had to be a serial killer who'd murdered her father.

'You can't just plough in and open up old wounds,' Beth told her on a steamy Sunday afternoon in late May when they sat – imprisoned by the heat – in their air-conditioned living room and discussed this situation yet again. Elise and Ron had taken Nicole and Jennie to Lakeland Park to feed the ducks. 'And I don't want to guess what the *Herald* and the *Evening News* would pull on us if you did. You don't malign the police department in this town. We've learnt that.'

'*Why* is it always somebody connected in some fashion with the Masters family?' Diane demanded stubbornly. 'What does Lloyd Masters do to motivate this serial killer to rush into action?' Even she had to admit Lloyd Masters couldn't be the serial killer, though the possibility had prodded her into checking him out as a suspect.

'Di, it could just be coincidence,' Beth reiterated her usual comment.

'It's *not* coincidence. Lloyd Masters does something – maybe in his newspapers – and it's the catalyst that brings on murder. Why was my father murdered?'

'One of these days, out of the blue, the answer will come out. And –'

'It's thirty-one years since Chris Robson died. *When* is this answer going to pop up?'

'Sugar, right now let's focus on the *Guardian*. That's our major problem.'

Cliff allowed Brad to give him the full tour of the offices of his Druid Hills medical group. Thank God, he'd finished his residency – but he couldn't push aside an air of depression. The research job in New York was long gone. No replacement had materialized. He ought to be grateful that Brad's group was taking him in.

Their reception area, offices and examining rooms were expensively furnished, meant to impress their wealthy patients. Brad had insisted he go to his own tailor for several suits.

'Why?' he'd countered when Brad broached the subject. 'We're always hiding behind white jackets.'

'These are the dressing rooms.' Brad interrupted his introspection. 'On a rough day you can sneak in and take a nap.'

'Don't tell me,' Cliff drawled. 'You had an interior decorator do up the place.'

'Yeah,' Brad agreed. 'It's a tax write-off.' He grinned. 'It's a long way from the residency grind, huh? All those thirty-six-hour shifts.' He whistled in recall. 'Oh, the old boy told me he'd hired a new nurse to start this morning.' The 'old boy' was Roger Cartwright, the senior member of the group practice. 'Somebody you know.'

'Who?' Cliff asked curiously.

'Sylvia Lee.' Brad whistled. 'Sexy little package. She can entertain me in one of the dressing rooms any time she likes. She told the old boy she wanted an easier lifestyle than hospital duty.'

'Sylvia's not exactly the dedicated type.' Cliff's eyes went opaque. She'd made a blatant play for him at one point. He'd still been hurting after the break with Diane. He'd brushed her off. He'd been relieved when she'd been transferred to paediatrics – in the next building.

God, it was crazy how in the space of one evening his whole life had changed. Was it always that way, that you could look back and recognize the exact day – hour – where your life moved onto a different track? Why hadn't Diane said she didn't want to have an abortion? They would have married. Somehow, they would have managed.

He was conscious of a treacherous stirring low within him. There had been moments when he'd been close to locking away memory and going the whole route with Sylvia. She'd all but stretched out on empty hospital beds for him. But instinct had told him to stay clear of her.

He hadn't washed Diane from his mind yet. Even now there were nights when he lay sleepless, wishing he could hold Diane in his arms, remembering what it was like to love her. He'd made one wrong move – and it was over for them forever.

'OK, this is your office.' Brad pushed open a door and gestured extravagantly. 'Anything you want and you don't see, just buzz for Kathy. The old boy will summon you for a briefing sometime in the course of the morning. He's long-winded but sharp. He has serious income tax problems – which we're sure to inherit in time. Oh, Tina wants you to come to her dinner party Saturday. She always needs an extra man.'

In the course of the day Cliff caught several glimpses of Sylvia. They didn't come face to face until they were leaving the building at the same time.

'Welcome to the team,' Sylvia drawled. She had pulled her

white peasant blouse off the shoulders, which emphasized her high, full breasts, and her long peasant skirt fell seductively about her hips, hinting at never-ending legs. 'I was afraid it was going to be dull around here.' The inference that he was lighting up the scene for her.

'I'm looking forward to being part of the group,' He smiled, headed towards his eight-year-old Valiant – which Brad insisted ought to be soon replaced: 'Not part of the image the old boy likes.'

'Bye . . .' Sylvia's voice trailed after him in provocative invitation.

His hand on the door of the car, Cliff hesitated. He turned round. Sylvia stood where he had left her – as though waiting for him to return. 'Sexy little package' – Brad's words seemed to taunt him. He strolled back to her.

'Brad says there's a great new restaurant that opened up about a quarter-mile down the road. Would you like to give it a whirl?'

'I thought you'd never ask.' Her eyes glowed with promise. 'You lead in your car. I'll follow.'

Cliff told himself he was out of his mind to start up with Sylvia, yet he felt a rush of excitement as he drove towards the restaurant. At intervals he checked in his rear – view mirror. Sylvia was right behind him. He'd been living such a cloistered life, his body mocked. Wasn't it time he accepted that Diane was lost to him? He was young. He had needs.

Pulling into the parking area before the restaurant, he noted few patrons had arrived thus far. Involuntarily he remembered how he and Diane had sought to arrive at dining spots before the evening rush. They'd had so little time together – yet she'd become so important a part of his existence.

He emerged from his car, waited for Sylvia. The night was uncomfortably humid, heavy with the pungent scent of the honeysuckle that lined the road. Sylvia pulled up beside him, flung open her car door. Her long skirt had been hiked high on sun-kissed thighs. He cleared his throat, felt hot colour rise in his face. The little bitch knew what she was doing to him – and loved it.

The restaurant exuded an air of luxury – softly lit, fresh flowers on damask-covered tables, tapestry-upholstered armchairs. The tab was going to be high, Cliff surmised.

'This beats the hospital cafeteria.' There was a poignant quality in Sylvia's voice that was in sharp contrast to her customary flipness. 'But then we've both beat that rap.' Her smile was soft, unexpectedly appealing.

'Do you think you're going to like being part of private practice?' Cliff asked, as their dinner was served. He knew where his heart lay – and it wasn't in playing doctor to rich, society patients. But he ought to be grateful to have landed here, thanks to Brad. The economists all said the country was in the worst financial crisis since the Depression. 'It's going to be awfully quiet after the hospital.'

'I had enough craziness on hospital duty to last me the rest of my life.' He was conscious of a bare silken foot caressing his ankle. 'I'm making less money,' she conceded, 'but I'll have a life.'

'You have a point.' All at once he was anxious to be past the dinner scene. He knew Sylvia would invite him up to her place. All right, so he wasn't in love with her. She'd fill a need that had long gone unsatisfied.

'Let's skip dessert and coffee and head for my pad,' she murmured. 'I was sure you were special from the day I saw you flat on your back in the hospital. Show me I wasn't wrong.'

'You're reading my mind.' His eyes sought the waiter.

Tonight, he thought, he was seeing a sweetness and vulnerability that Sylvia had kept in hiding. This wasn't the sexy, smart-alecky nurse he'd known in the hospital. But instinct told him she'd be hot as a pistol in bed. After tonight, he suspected, his life would feel a little less empty.

Diane had hoped she and Beth could persuade Elise to go ahead and open her morning nursery group by September, when regular classes began, but Elise and Ron insisted it would have to remain on hold. Tonight the four of them were at dinner in a local restaurant popular for special occasions. They were celebrating Elise and Ron's fifth wedding anniversary – with Ron's parents babysitting Nicole and Jennie.

'It's August already,' Elise hedged when Diane brought up the subject yet again. Just last night they'd watched President Nixon announce on TV that he was resigning from office today. 'I know Dad is willing to sign a bank loan for us, but interest rates are so damn high! And everything costs so much. It's just too scary to take on a major project right now.'

'I'll loan you the money,' Diane offered. 'No interest.'

'We couldn't let you do that,' Ron said gently, his smile telegraphing gratitude at the offer. 'We'll wait till the situation is more stable.' He exchanged a sombre glance with Elise. 'It's just a passing thought – I mean, we said we wouldn't talk about it until we'd come to a decision. I've been offered a job in a private school in Atlanta that would begin in the second semester.'

'It pays a lot more than what he gets here in Eden. We're so tired of living from paycheque to paycheque.' But she wasn't happy at the prospect of a move, Diane guessed. 'Like most people, I suppose, we live one step from disaster.'

'We're not making any decision yet,' Ron emphasized. 'Just listening to what the Atlanta people have to say.'

'There's all that crime in Atlanta.' Elise was sombre. 'Nobody in their right mind goes to downtown Atlanta at night.'

'We wouldn't live in downtown Atlanta,' Ron pointed out.

'Unless we both worked, we couldn't afford the suburbs,' Elise reminded. 'And I won't be able to work until Nicole is in school full time.'

'I think you'd do well with a morning nursery school,' Beth encouraged.

'Mom and Dad think we ought to try to buy a house and use part of it for a nursery programme,' Ron said. 'But, again, interest rates are so bloody high. Even if we let Mom and Dad help us with the down payment, our monthly carrying charges would be out of sight.'

'I'll be the first client,' Diane said with a brilliant smile. 'Talk about it with your mother and dad.' The prospect of Elise and Ron moving to Atlanta was unnerving. Elise and Ron were their closest friends here in Eden. And Jennie would so miss Nicole.

'Hey, who wants to see *Murder on the Orient Express* next Saturday night?' Elise asked, making an effort to put her worries aside. 'Mom and Dad are available for baby-sitting.'

They arrived at Elise and Ron's apartment to find that Sally had fresh coffee ready to be served.

'I know it's muggy and uncomfortable outside,' she said blithely, 'but for most of the time we live in air conditioning.'

'You know Mom,' Lou chuckled, swatted his wife affectionately on the rump. 'You'd think she owned stock on the coffee exchange.'

'Tell me about dinner,' Sally ordered, heading for the kitchenette. 'Did the restaurant live up to its press?'

'It was great,' Elise called after her. 'Like the price tab.'

'Your mother and I were watching some financial whiz on TV,' Lou said, some of his earlier joviality ebbing away. 'Inflation's hit 10.3 percent. Unemployment keeps growing.'

'Every time I go grocery shopping, I see an increase in prices.' Elise was sombre. 'But nobody's seeing salaries going up.'

'Property owners scream any time there's talk of raising teachers' salaries – or any city employees,' Ron pointed out. 'They worry we're not providing good education – and in a way they're right. Our classrooms are all over-crowded; kids get shortchanged. And some of our best teachers are moving into private schools – for more money.'

'Don't talk to me about a raise in property taxes.' Sally came back into the living room with a tray of coffee mugs. 'I can't believe what we're paying on our little house. You'd think we were in a high-rent commercial district.

'That's because you bought just two years ago,' Elise pointed out. 'Old-timers pay a third of what you pay.'

'It's weird,' Sally grimaced. 'In this town everybody gossips about everything except property taxes. You ask casually what somebody's paying, and they charge off on to another subject.'

'My folks probably pay half of what you're paying,' Elise guessed. 'And they've got this big sprawling house on a full acre.' Diane remembered driving past the elegant colonial where Elise had grown up. The senior Tuckers lived in a modest two-bedroom ranch on a quarter-acre plot. 'But they bought thirty-five years ago.'

'That's so unfair!' Diane blazed. 'Can't you appeal?' Her gaze swung from Sally to Lou.

'We tried,' Lou told her. 'The tax office dropped it by twenty dollars.'

'There've been a lot of newcomers to Eden in the past few years.' Diane's mind was charging ahead. 'People are even commuting to Atlanta from here. Can't you all get together and fight this as a group?'

'It's not that easy,' Ron rejoined. 'Sure, Eden's a small town, but with even thirty thousand people, how do you know who's being suckered?'

'I think the *Guardian* ought to do something about this.' Diane exchanged an enthusiastic glance with Beth. 'Tax records have to be open to the public. Let's do some serious checking on figures. Maybe it's time for reassessing.'

'You'll be asking for trouble,' Ron warned. 'Half of the property in this town is owned by Lloyd Masters. You'll be bucking the *Herald* and the *Evening News*.'

'We'll have the facts to prove we're right.' She wasn't afraid to fight Lloyd Masters, Diane told herself defiantly. She welcomed the opportunity. 'Let's throw this whole situation before the town. Demand justice!'

Chapter Sixteen

Gerry sat at the exquisitely laid dinner table in the Masterses' dining room with a fixed smile. As usual she had tuned out of most of the table conversation. This evening's dinner was what her mother called 'the post-summer family reunion'. Her mother had spent September in London and Paris. Linda and Peggy – perennially tanned, their hair bleached to silver-blonde – had been in Bar Harbor until mid-September. Gerry had spent a week with Clark at the Hilton Head Inn on Sea Pines Plantation.

She'd loved the semi-tropical island off the shore of South Carolina, but she was always tense on the occasional brief vacations she shared with Clark. She was never sure how he would behave towards her. To her relief he'd spent the mornings on the golf course, cultivating contacts because he was on one of his periodic determinations to break away from the newspaper and move out on his own. Not that it would ever happen. Six months after their wedding she was sure Clark had married her because of her father's wealth, which he constantly hoped would spill over onto them.

She felt chilled in the heavy air conditioning of the house – the temperature designed for the comfort of men in summer-wool suits. Why did Mother insist the women wear dinner gowns at these family dinners? It was so pretentious. The men, of course, wore business suits. The children – Linda and Peggy's – were rarely included at family dinners. If she and Clark had kids, she thought wistfully, she would resent that.

'London was dreadful my first week there,' Maureen Masters said with distaste. 'Tourists all over the place. Next year I'll run over for the Paris couture shows at the end of July, come home, then fly back to London in mid-September when –'

'Maureen, I want you to start planning for our fiftieth wedding anniversary party in February,' Lloyd interrupted her monologue. 'At the Country Club, of course. Make it big and splashy. It just might coincide with the announcement that Clark will be running for the City Council.'

Gerry saw Clark's jaw drop in astonishment, saw the glint of malicious amusement in her father's eyes. Dad hadn't told Clark, she gathered. God knows, he'd been after Dad's political support long enough. But that should put Clark in a good mood for a while. It wasn't the State Legislature, but it was a move in that direction.

'I'm surprised you remember,' Maureen drawled sweetly. 'But yes, I think we should throw a bash that'll set this town on its ear. Not that it'll require much . . .' Maureen Masters' contempt for her home town was well-known to her family.

Gerry was impatient for dinner to be over. For weeks she'd been building herself up to approach her father about a job on the newspaper. After dinner the women would go into the living room for cappuccino – her mother's latest affectation – and the men into the library for coffee and cigars. She'd intercept Dad on his way to the library.

Linda and Peggy were off on to avid discussions about the anniversary dinner. The men exchanged bored glances. The maid and houseman came in to remove dishes, brought in dessert. Gerry and her mother dug with relish into the generous portions of Black Forest cake. Linda and Peggy sought out the kirsch-drenched cherries, ignored the cake and the whipped cream. Both were determined to remain fashion-model thin.

'I need to stretch my legs and relax with coffee and a good cigar.' Lloyd pushed back his chair, rose to his feet. The signal for the men to retire to the library.

Gerry laid a detaining arm on her father's as he strode into the hall.

'Dad, I need to talk to you . . .' Already her voice was strained.

'Now?' He paused reluctantly.

'It'll just take a minute.' There'd be no time later. 'I've been thinking about working – maybe at the newspaper.' Now she rushed ahead, intimidated by his grunt of impatience. 'I do have a degree in journalism, and I'm so bored with my life. I think –'

'Gerry, don't be selfish. How can you consider taking a job away from somebody who really needs it? Do some volunteer work, like your mother and sisters. The hospital always needs volunteers. Talk to your mother about it.' He gestured towards the living room, hurried away in the wake of his sons-in-law.

Gerry stood motionless, recoiling from this dismissal. She wouldn't set foot in the hospital unless it was urgent. How many of the staff accepted Clark's usual comment: 'my wife is accident prone'?

Dad never loved any of his children except Kevin and Alison. Mother tolerated them. Linda and Peggy could handle it. She couldn't. But in this family you didn't talk about going for help. Therapy was for the weak. Nobody in the Masters family was allowed to admit to weakness. That was why Alison lived in that third-floor prison and cut everybody except Dad out of her life.

Slowly Gerry walked towards the living room. The voices of the three women drifted out to her. To the town, she thought, they always presented the façade of the perfect family, though one that had suffered tragedies. Mother had taught them their public image. The men ruled, and the women sought satisfaction in high living.

She'd adored Kevin – even thought they were both always off at school or summer camp and they didn't see much of each other. She'd cried when he went off to fight in the war. She'd been so thrilled when he came home again. She'd loved Sophie, and then the baby.

Her face softened as she remembered occasions when she'd been home and had baby-sat for tiny Diane. Kevin and Sophie were so happy together. She could never believe he'd killed himself. She was so sad when Sophie ran off that way with the baby. Kevin and Sophie had showed her the only real love she'd ever known.

In the library the four men settled themselves on the facing pair of burgundy leather sofas. Lloyd recognized the tension that permeated the atmosphere. Luke and Hugh were pissed because he'd finally said he'd back Clark in a bid for the City Council. Two years on the Council and he'd push Clark for the Legislature – if Clark had handled himself well. The greedy bastards worried that he was making Clark top dog, spending money on campaigns that would do nothing for them. Screw them.

For a while the conversation revolved around the newspaper, then Lloyd took charge.

'Luke, you're sitting nearest my desk. Reach into the middle drawer and pull out that rag I stuffed there. The *Guardian*,' he grunted when Luke stared blankly at him.

'Sure . . .' Luke leapt into action while the other two exchanged wary glances.

'Those creeps are going after property reassessment,' Lloyd told them. 'You know there's a group in town who'll jump on the bandwagon with them. I want that series of articles they've planned derailed. Why the hell did you allow them to get this far?'

'They've been fairly harmless – until this.' Luke shifted in his seat. 'They're poorly financed –'

'Not true,' Lloyd shot back. 'I checked with their bank. *Take care of this*.' His eyes swept from one to another. Unexpectedly he chuckled. 'And do it all legally, you understand?'

Lloyd leant back and listened to the heated discussion of the three younger men. Then in a burst of impatience he rose to his feet.

'All right, follow through on this,' he said tersely. But he was pleased at their approach. They were sharp. 'I'll see you at the office tomorrow.'

They understood they were being dismissed. This was a familiar pattern. The others knew he wouldn't emerge from his library for good nights. When they'd gone he crossed to the bar and fixed himself a Scotch and soda. He sat down, sipped his drink, and waited for the sounds of farewells at the door. He heard the cars pull away. Maureen was going upstairs to her room. He wouldn't see her again tonight.

Now he crossed to his desk, reached into the bottom side drawer for the box of chocolates stashed away there earlier. He remembered that Desmond Taylor had said he shouldn't indulge Alison's cravings for sweets, but how could he not give her what brought her some minor pleasure? She was the sweetest part of his life.

In lieu of opening a morning nursery Elise had undertaken the day care of three pre-schoolers, including Jennie, for which Diane was grateful. Jennie loved the group. As she had done each morning since the project became a full-time deal, Diane lingered with Elise.

'Mommie, go,' Jennie ordered ebulliently. 'You don't have to stay with me like Betty's mommie.' Betty was still reluctant to part with her mother, though Elise was sure the situation would soon be solved.

'All right, darling.' Diane leant forward to kiss Jennie. 'I'll pop by to say hello at lunchtime.'

Now she joined Beth in the car for the drive to the office.

'What a relief that Jennie is happy with the group,' she told Beth. 'Elise is wonderful with the kids.'

'Elise would do great if she went into business full scale. Of course, there'll be expenses setting up. This way, with just the three kids and no public announcements, she won't have the Health Department barging in.'

'I think one of us should drive over to Atlanta within the next few days and solicit some advertising. "Freebies",' she stressed, because Beth had lifted an eyebrow in scepticism. 'I always remember what Tom said about half the space should be given over to ads, though I know, he meant *paid* ads . . .'

'I think the column about newcomers in town will arouse

interest,' Beth was striving to be cheerful, 'our version of the "welcome wagon".' The column would make its third appearance with the next issue.

'We should dig up somebody to set up a garden department.' This could bring in a hardware account. 'Somebody with a lot of knowledge and a pleasant writing style.'

'Maybe we should advertise. That's what Tom used to do.' Beth's smile was wry. 'Somebody who'll be glad to contribute without benefit of salary . . .'

They discussed the pros and cons of this until they arrived at the office.

'I'll run over to the printer's with that last page layout,' Beth began, then stooped to pick up the newspaper that lay at the office door. It was the morning edition of the *Eden Herald*, which they read religiously. While Diane unlocked the door, Beth focused on the front page.

'Good Lord!' She stared in disbelief at the lead story.

'What is it?' Diane demanded, then scanned the front page, also. 'Local Weekly Tabloid Violates Child Labor Laws.' The *Guardian* was the only weekly in town.

'We're not a tabloid!' Beth was indignant.

'We're not violating child labour laws.' Diane pulled the newspaper from Beth's hand, read the article as they walked into their store-front office. 'They're insane! Child labour laws are broken in New York City sweatshops, and in Third World countries.'

'I think we need a lawyer,' Beth said grimly. 'Don't we have grounds for a libel suit?'

'The *Herald* claims we have a twelve-year-old delivery boy who works until nine o'clock in the evening.' Diane focused on the newspaper's accusation. 'There's no law about the ages of delivery boys – and we don't have anybody under fourteen. And the papers are delivered in the afternoon. After school hours,' she emphasized. 'Not until nine at night.'

'Does the article mention a name?'

'Yeah. Chuck Johnson. He's fifteen! Remember, he came in

with working papers.' Chuck was a big, awkward redhead – over five foot nine and growing. We've got his working papers on file.' Diane paused. 'We can't jump into fighting this until we have plenty of ammunition.'

'We need a lawyer,' Beth repeated.

'First, let's get some facts together. There're no federal or state labour laws that apply to newspaper carriers. They're exempt.' They'd checked this out with Tom. And they paid their carriers exactly what the Masters newspapers paid.

'Dig out Chuck Johnson's address. I'm going over to have a talk with his mother.' How could Lloyd Masters be so petty as to attack them this way? No doubt in her mind that this had been instigated by her grandfather because of the *Guardian*'s campaign for property reassessment. In her mind she heard Ron's warning when she'd talked about fighting for this: 'You'll be asking for trouble. Half of the property in this town is owned by Lloyd Masters. You'll be bucking the *Herald* and the *Evening News*.'

'Here's Chuck's address . . .' Beth brought her back to the moment.

'All right. I'm going over there to confront his mother.' She doubted that Chuck's mother worked. He was a garrulous kid who talked about his mother's passion for the daytime soaps.

'What good will that do?' Beth was dubious. 'She'll just say the newspaper made a mistake.'

'We want a retraction from the *Herald*. I'll get a statement from Chuck's mother.' They had his working papers, even though they weren't necessary to deliver newspapers. 'And you're right. We'll need a lawyer.' Another expense, she thought in exasperation.

The area where Chuck lived was unfamiliar to Diane; a seedy section of Eden, she discovered. She slowed down to a crawl to watch for house numbers. There was the place: small, shabby, crying out for a paint job and windowpane replacements.

A delivery truck sat at the kerb. A man was pulling a dolly, on which there was a large box, up the path to the sagging stairs of the porch.

'Hey, take it easy with that,' the driver called out good-humouredly from behind the wheel of the truck. 'They want that TV in one piece.'

Her mind in high gear, Diane walked past the Johnson house, to allow the delivery to be made before she approached. Was that TV set a reward for setting up the *Guardian*? She and Beth had to knock that down fast. She wanted a written statement from Chuck Johnson's mother that the *Herald* had lied about his age.

Approaching Chuck's mother, Diane realized the drab, untidy, blowsy blonde in her forties was annoyed at her arrival. The new TV demanded all her attention.

'Whatever you're sellin', honey, I ain't buying.'

'I'm not selling, Mrs Johnson.' Diane struggled to appear ingratiating. 'I just want to straighten out a ridiculous mistake.' This whole thing was ridiculous! 'I'm Diane Phillips, co-publisher of the *Guardian*.' There, she'd captured Mrs Johnson's attention.

'I don't read it.' She stared warily at Diane. 'I got no time for reading.'

'Your son Chuck is one of our delivery boys. The *Herald* made an awful mistake in this morning's newspaper. They're trying to say he's twelve years old, and that we're breaking child labour laws by hiring him. But –'

'Sure, Chuck's twelve years old,' she interrupted, nervous now. She hadn't expected this confrontation. 'He's in the sixth grade at the elementary school. He got left back one year. He ain't dumb – he just don't like school. Like his old man.'

'Mrs Johnson, we have his working papers on file. They say he's fifteen.'

'No, Charlie's fifteen. Chuck musta lifted Charlie's workin' papers.' Her voice was unnaturally high. 'Look, I don't know nothin' about this.' She paused, her eyes defiant now. 'But Chuck's twelve, like I said.'

'You have two sons named Charlie?' Diane stared in disbelief.

'No, the first one's Charlie, the second one's Chuck. My old man – he wanted both boys named after him. That's the way we worked it out.' She smiled with an air of relief. 'You got somethin' to say, go talk to the folks at the *Herald*.'

'The *Herald* claims Chuck worked until nine o'clock at night,' Diane pursued. 'He picks up the newspaper at 3.15, right after school. By 5.30 he's made all his deliveries.'

'No, ma'am.' Mrs Johnson was emphatic. But her refusal to meet Diane's eyes told Diane the older woman was lying. 'Sometimes it's close to nine o'clock before that poor kid comes home. Look, I'm busy.' She was brusque now. 'Go on, get outta here.'

Trembling with rage, Diane strode out to the car. It was clear Chuck's mother would give them no statement – not with that large-screen TV as a payoff from the *Herald*. But not one of their delivery boys spent more than two hours on the job!

Now segments of the Child Labor Laws flashed across her mind. On school days children under sixteen weren't allowed to work before 7 a.m. or after 7 p.m. Chuck and his mother would both swear he worked until 9 p.m. on delivery day. Oh yes, the *Guardian* needed a good lawyer.

No matter that most people in town would read that article about their violating Child Labor Laws and laugh it off. Delivering newspapers was an American tradition – and it wasn't done after 7 p.m. How could a newspaper with the stature of the *Herald* stoop to something so stupid? This was a despicable effort, and she was ready for battle.

Chapter Seventeen

Driving back to the office, Diane charted a course of action in response to the *Herald* denunciation. They couldn't let this slur pass without a reply. This evening she'd ask Ron to recommend a lawyer – someone with realistic fees. Though the whole situation was absurd, they must clear the *Guardian's* name.

She parked close to the office, hurried to report to Beth. In a corner of her mind she reminded herself they'd need another delivery boy immediately. But that would be no problem. A lot of local teenagers were eager to earn a little extra money.

Beth was standing at their intake counter in conversation with a man, Diane noted as she approached the door. Somebody with a classified ad, she surmised. Their very low rates at least drew classifieds. And they *were* creating a core of approving readers, she reminded herself. Readers who understood the *Guardian* was trying to make a contribution to the town.

'Hi.' Beth glanced up at her approach, then turned to the man at the counter. Thirtyish, good-looking in a quiet way, Diane thought. 'This is my partner, Diane Phillips. Greg Lewis,' she introduced them.

'Hi.' Diane smiled, joined Beth behind the counter.

'Greg's from New York, too,' Beth told her.

'I thought I might get a plug in your "New Arrivals" column.' His smile was warm, ingratiating. 'I've just been in town three weeks. I'm opening up a law office with my old college roommate.'

'Sure, we'll run an item,' Beth told him. 'Just write up a paragraph of background information for us.'

'What brought you to Eden?' Diane asked. This wouldn't be an easy town for a newcomer, she thought sympathetically.

'My roommate comes from here. Calvin Cooper. Do you know him?' Greg's gaze shifted from Diane to Beth.

'We don't know many people in town,' Diane told him. 'Though we've been here over a year.'

'Cal and I were at NYU Law together,' Greg explained. 'We both went to work for the same corporate law firm – straight out of NYU.' He grimaced. 'Neither of us felt we were getting anywhere, and Cal kept talking about the easy lifestyle in the South. So we decided to cut out and set up down here. Cal's father is giving us space in his offices. He's a real estate agent.' Diane had vague recall of the Cooper Real Estate Agency. Hadn't Norma and Joe bought their house through them? 'And we can use his reception room and his receptionist. What could be better? If you know of any prospective clients, send them our way.'

Diane and Beth exchanged loaded glances.

'We might be clients,' Beth told him.

'Great.' He waited for them to elaborate.

'Come inside and let's talk.' Fresh anger soared in Diane. 'Just remember, this is a small town. Strange things happen here on occasion.'

'Who murdered whom?' Greg asked, chuckling. He stopped short as Diane winced. 'Did I say something wrong?'

'No,' Beth said quickly. 'It's just that a prominent doctor was murdered here in town last year – and it's never been solved. It's kind of a touchy point.'

'I'm not into criminal law, though it has fascinating aspects,' Greg conceded. 'But let's sit down and go over your problem.'

Diane sat behind her desk. Beth and Greg settled themselves in chairs across from her. As succinctly as possible Diane explained their situation, reported on her encounter with Chuck Johnson's mother.

'I know it sounds like small-town squabbling, but we can't

just sit back and ignore something so scurrilous. And I'm sure it all stems from our campaign to fight for property reassessment.' She paused. 'It's not our first bad scene with them.' She explained about the earlier encounter, when the *Herald* accused them of defiling the local police.

'You might want to cool that campaign for a while,' Greg said after a moment.

'We can't do that,' Diane was firm. 'There're people in town who're counting on us. They're being ripped off.'

'If the *Herald*'s after you, they're not going to stop with this,' Greg warned.

'They're not running us out of town.' Beth was emphatic. 'We like what we're doing here.'

'OK, let's be as diplomatic as possible,' he soothed, and squinted in thought. He was right, Diane told herself – they didn't want a knock-down-drag-out battle with the *Herald* at this point. It wasn't the right time. 'Would you be satisfied with a retraction from the *Herald*?' His eyes swung from Beth to Diane.

'Yes,' Diane said. 'If the *Herald* runs it on their front page,' she stipulated.

'All right, give me everything you have about this kid,' he ordered. 'I'll want a copy of his working papers. I'm not saying they'll go along with this,' he cautioned, 'but I don't think their lawyers want to drag this into court.' He chuckled. 'Even if their lawyers are on retainer.'

'About your fee –' Diane began.

'Run a splashy item for me in your "New Arrivals"! – let's call it a trade,' he said good-humouredly, and reached for a page from the notepad on Diane's desk. 'I'll give you some vital statistics.'

Three mornings later the *Herald* carried a brief retraction, indicating they'd been given false information.

'One tiny paragraph on the corner of the front page!' Diane blazed while she and Beth reread the item. 'And they don't say "We apologize"!'

'We'll blow it up and plaster it over our front page,' Beth pointed out. 'Greg got us a retraction.'

'Maybe we should have sued them for libel.' Diane churned with frustration.

'We can't afford a long-drawn-out suit.' Beth was practical. She knew how their capital was being depleted. 'Which a hundred to one – considering Lloyd Masters' power in this town – we'd lose. And our crusade for a reassessment of property taxes will have to go on hold,' she added pointedly.

'We're getting nowhere,' Diane fumed. 'We're afraid to tackle anything that might antagonize Lloyd Masters. We don't dare go after the police for not solving three murders.' Four including her father's. 'I came down here for one purpose, Beth – and nothing's happening!'

'You knew it wouldn't happen fast,' Beth chided, but her eyes reflected her sympathy.

'I don't see any clear road ahead. We're sure there's a serial murderer loose in this town, even though there're years between the killings. And we know that happens,' she said tiredly. 'We have a collection of tiny pieces that just won't fit together. There'll be *another* murder,' she predicted.

Would it be Lloyd Masters himself next time?

Cliff parked his leased Cadillac Coupé De Ville and left the area for the medical centre entrance. He was pleased their offices were in a beautifully laid-out suburban area rather than on a high floor in midtown Atlanta, with Muzak in the speed-demon elevators. But other aspects rankled – like being ordered to dump his old car and drive something 'more respectable'.

Sure, he ought to be thrilled to have been accepted into the medical group. Yet so much of the thinking of the other members riled him. Brad belonged with them – he didn't. He appreciated the kind of money he was seeing, but what had happened to ethics?

He reached for the door that led into the designer-furnished, carpeted reception room with a sense of reluctance. It wasn't for this that he'd gone through the tortuous years of training. If he hadn't been driving at the wrong time of the night, he wouldn't have had that rotten accident. He'd be in New York and working with a dedicated research team. By some lucky quirk of fate he might have run into Diane.

'Dr Cartwright said to send you right in to see him when you arrived,' Kathy reported, her tone foreboding. 'He's not in a good mood . . .'

'Thanks, Kathy.' He forced a smile. What did the old bastard want now?

Cliff was conscious of hostility the moment he walked into Dr Cartwright's palatial consultation room.

'Cliff, I thought you were a sharp doctor.' Cartwright's florid face was reproachful as he leant forward in his chair.

'Have I made a misdiagnosis?' All at once Cliff was anxious.

'No, nothing like that . . .' Cartwright dismissed this with a wave of a hand. 'But you're too slow on the tests, the special procedures.' He reached for a group of folders on his desk. 'You're doing just the very basic stuff here.'

Cliff scanned the names of the folders as Cartwright fanned them out before him.

'I saw nothing seriously wrong with any of them. No indications that any tests or special procedures were required.' Cliff stared blankly at the senior physician in the medical group.

'Oh, come off it, Cliff!' Cartwright grunted impatiently. 'You know we have to protect ourselves against malpractice suits. This is the way we do it.'

'I'm sorry, Roger –' Cliff cleared his throat in sudden unease. Roger Cartwright wanted more tests, more special procedures because he received a kickback on each one. Brad had brought this up his first day on the job. 'I didn't realize that.'

'Otherwise, you're doing a great job.' Cartwright nodded in approval. 'And I see you got yourself a decent car. Always remember, we have to keep up appearances.'

'I'll remember.' Cliff's smile was polite but enigmatic. God, he hated this shit! 'Anything else? I should go over some charts before my appointments.'

'Oh, my wife's giving a New Year's Eve bash. You're invited, along with the lady of your choice.' A lascivious glint in his eyes now.

'Thanks, Roger. It sounds like a great way to welcome in '75.'

Walking down to his own office, Cliff considered Cartwright's invitation. Did the old boy know he was seeing Sylvia outside the office? Was he annoyed that one of his associates was socializing with one of his nurses? No, he hadn't indicated that.

How the hell had he got involved with Sylvia, Cliff asked himself in exasperation. Of course, she was gorgeous and sexy – and surprisingly sweet at unexpected moments. And she was available and willing when the body made demands. And he was aware, too, that – as Brad pointed out – she was one of those nurses who considered marrying a doctor a top priority. He'd made it clear he had no such plan in mind.

It was four years ago this month that Diane had walked out of his life. He'd thrust her out, he told himself with recurrent rage. He'd been so damn dense – thinking only of his medical training. It was weird how sometimes he'd awake at night and remember holding Diane in his arms. Four years ago – yet at those times it seemed yesterday. He'd made a rotten move, and he'd pay for it for ever. But there were swatches of time with Sylvia when he could forget.

He settled down to his morning's appointments, fighting a wave of depression. Four years ago his life had seemed full of promise. One wrong turn, and everything went to hell.

He'd be happier in any research berth, but he couldn't afford to settle for a shitty salary at this point in his life. He'd piled up so much debt when he was laid up after the accident. Brad kept telling him a sharp lawyer would have got him a sensational settlement, but he'd had neither the time nor the patience to go into court.

'Dr Hendricks, Mrs Adams is here to see you.' Sylvia broke into his introspection, her smile brisk and professional. But there was nothing professional about the wink she shot at him. Only now did he remember that she was cooking dinner for him tonight. At her insistence. Usually they went out to some classy restaurant and then back to her place.

'Thank you, Sylvia . . .'

At one o'clock – his next appointment scheduled for two, with a patient who was always twenty minutes late – he went to lunch with Brad. The expensive, softly illuminated restaurant was another world from the hospital cafeteria they'd inhabited for years.

'You had a little meeting with Cartwright this morning,' Brad said when they'd ordered and the waiter had left their table.

'Do you have a video camera in his office?' Cliff tried for humour.

'I knew he was going to talk to you. Don't screw up, Cliff. I told you, the old boy has a piece of the action in the lab we use. He wants to keep the business humming. And it runs up our personal billing.'

'Damn it, Brad, that's plain thievery!'

'Look, it's courtesy of the government – if it's Medicare – or the insurance companies.' It bothered Cliff that Medicaid patients were not accepted by the group. 'We slaved for long enough, let's collect now.'

'What happened to ethics?' Cliff countered wryly.

'Hey, you're in the wrong century. I'm telling you, don't fuck up. We've got it made with Cartwright's group.'

'I need the money.' Cliff was candid. 'And don't worry, I know you went to a lot of trouble to bring me into the group. I won't screw up.'

Cliff was relieved when his last appointment was over for the day. He checked his watch. He was due at Sylvia's apartment in half an hour or so. He reached for the phone to call home.

'How are you, darling?' His mother's warm, vivacious voice conveyed a wealth of love.

'I'm OK.' Was he OK? 'I'm just checking with you at the end of the day.'

'Feel in the mood to come over for dinner tonight?' she asked. He went home once a week or so.

'Not tonight, Mom. I have a conference here. But I'll be over on Friday night.' Friday was 'dinner with Mom and Dad night'.

'Instead of business conferences better you should be having dinner with some bright, pretty little girl. And don't tell me, we're not supposed to call them "girls" today. After fourteen they're all "women".'

'Mom, stop trying to be a matchmaker,' he scolded. 'I've got career time to make up right now.' Mom had liked Diane so much. He and Diane had played it cool, but Mom had sensed there was something special between them.

'How's Dad? Did you convince him he's not to shovel snow out of the driveway?'

'How often do we have snow to shovel in Atlanta?' She chuckled. 'I think I convinced him I'm not ready to be a widow.'

En route to Sylvia's he stopped off to buy a bottle of white wine. It would help him to relax, he told himself as he slid behind the wheel of the car again. He was so damn tense all the time. He thought once he was out of the med school and residency rat race he'd stop feeling so uptight.

Money was rolling in – he'd soon be caught up financially. In truth, his financial situation was far better than he'd anticipated. Research might be soul-satisfying but the money was usually modest. He'd give up the medical centre arrangement in minutes for a decent research deal, but nothing had surfaced. Something his mother had said at dinner last Friday infiltrated his mind: 'You find out through the years that life is made up of a series of compromises.' But his mind and heart rebelled at the compromises he saw ahead of him.

Approaching Sylvia's apartment door, he sniffed the savoury aromas of a roast in the oven, spices he couldn't identify but found inviting. He'd been surprised when Sylvia suggested dinner at her place tonight instead of at one of the chic restaurants she relished. But at intervals an unexpected side of her emerged.

A few days ago he'd chastised her about her Old South background when she'd made an unthinking racist remark.

'Sugar, I come from Alabama, yes,' she'd drawled. 'But I was born Lichtenstein – not Lee.'

Only then had he learnt that she'd had to fight her way through nursing school, that she had lost track of her estranged married sister and brother: 'We think alike on nothing.'

He rang the doorbell, heard the chimes, and then she was pulling the door wide for him. She stood before him, slim yet curvaceous, provocative in a tight-fitting Mediterranean blue sweater that told him plainly that she wasn't wearing a bra, and slacks that clung to her narrow hips and long legs.

'I could set my watch by you,' she drawled. 'You're always so reliable.'

'That sounds dull.' He'd feel less uptight in a little while. Sylvia had a way of doing that for him.

'I'll give you a chance to disprove that.' She lifted her face to his but drew away in moments. 'Later. Nothing's going to ruin my roast. Put something on the record player while I go play chef.'

Cliff flipped through her collection of records, settled for an early Bob Dylan. The plaintive strains of 'I Threw It All Away' drifted into the small living room. He dropped into a chair, ordered himself to unwind. His mind traitorously resurrected his conversation this morning with Cartwright. If he believed Brad, then a hell of a lot of the medical profession was jumping on that same bandwagon. Not what he'd had in mind when he'd entered med school.

'Take off your jacket and get comfortable,' Sylvia called from the tiny kitchen. 'We're not dining at the Regency Hyatt.'

When he was becoming aware of hunger pangs, Sylvia ordered him to the table.

'Start on your shrimp cocktail,' she told him. 'I'll bring out the roast and salad.'

Despite her air of levity, Cliff was conscious on an underlying sombreness that revealed itself in her eyes. He was never quite sure what Sylvia was thinking. What was it Brad said about women? 'They're all ingratiating and loving before the wedding – but wow, do things change later!' Soon after his honeymoon Brad had begun to complain about the constraints of marriage.

'Is the roast too rare?' Sylvia asked solicitously when he lifted the first sliver of succulent eye round to his mouth.

'It's great.'

'My mother taught me two things.' She giggled reminiscently. 'How to make a roast and how to do the corners of a bed. Everything else I had to learn for myself.' Again, he felt a sense of anxiety in her.

'You're a good student.' Already his mind was roaming from food to bed.

They ate with relish, not rushing, yet both conscious of their ultimate destination.

'Do you want coffee now or later?' Sylvia asked as Cliff finished off a wedge of superb – bakery-bought, Sylvia said – pecan pie.

'Whenever . . .' He sensed a change in mood in her now.

'Let's go sit down . . .' She pushed back her chair and rose to her feet with the air of someone facing an unpleasant task.

'Sure.' He was puzzled.

Sylvia settled on one corner of the sofa. Cliff sat at the other. Waiting.

'Cliff, we have a kind of problem.' Her smile was apologetic. 'I thought we were always careful, but . . .' She paused, took a deep breath. 'I'm pregnant.'

Her words ricocheted in his brain. He was hearing Diane say that – four years ago this month. He was dizzy with shock.

'You're sure?' he asked automatically. He'd bungled that. Lost Diane.

'I'm sure, Cliff.' Her words were barely audible. 'I thought we were always careful,' she repeated, spread her hands in a gesture of bewilderment.

If he and Diane had married, they would have a three-year-old son or daughter, he thought in anguish. They'd be a family. But he'd lost Diane – and their child never had a chance. How had Diane phrased it? 'Our timing is way off.'

'Cliff, we'll have to take care of this quickly.' Sylvia's plaintive voice brought him back to the moment.

'We'll get married right away.' He wanted this child. Like Mom said, life was full of compromises. He and Sylvia would be a family. They'd make a life together with their child.

'Cliff, are you sure?' She was remembering his blunt statements about not wanting to be tied down to marriage; wanting to be free to pursue his career.

'I'm sure.'

'Cliff, it's going to be great for us . . .' She held out her arms to him. 'But don't let's wait till I'm showing.'

'We'll be married on New Year's Day,' he told her. Oh God, how was he going to prepare Mom and Dad for this? But they'd be happy . . . 'Start 1975 off with a bang.'

'Hey, watch your language.' She lifted her mouth to his. 'We'll have coffee later.'

Sylvia stood at the window and watched Cliff drive away in his leased Cadillac Coupé De Ville, experiencing a feeling of heady triumph. Everything had worked out as planned. Right away – before they'd sat down to eat – she'd got across the message she was anxious. He couldn't figure it out. It was an Academy Award performance.

They'd be married in five days. A few days later she'd discover she wasn't pregnant after all. *Whoops!* But what the hell, she'd be the wife of Dr Cliff Hendricks. Mission accomplished.

All the shitty years of nurse's training, the lousy hospital duty were paying off.

Chapter Eighteen

Diane lifted her eyes from the page of Jennie's latest Dr Seuss book, noted with approval that her small daughter was asleep. She laid aside the book, pulled the comforter over Jennie, switched off the lamp, and tiptoed from the room.

Beth looked up from the copy of the *Evening News* she was reading. Diane had scanned it earlier.

'Isn't this spread on the Masters golden wedding anniversary enough to make you throw up?' Photographs of the Country Club dinner – attended by fifty influential Georgia couples, from Atlanta and Columbus as well as Eden – were splashed across much of the page. 'Elise says the two of them haven't had a pleasant word for each other except in public for the past forty years.'

'My mother and father would have been married thirty-one years last month,' Diane said in wistful recall. She remembered Elvira's description of them. 'They were so much in love they brought tears to my eyes sometimes. They had a beautiful marriage.'

'I like your hair cut short that way.' Beth gazed at Diane in approval.

'It's easier to handle.' Beth knew why she'd cut it short: so that the resemblance between her and Gerry Watson would be less noticeable.

'I feel so guilty.' Diane sat in the lounge chair across from Beth. 'This is the second time this week I've allowed Greg to drag me off for the evening. It's not a date. We're going to a meeting of that new animal rights group.'

'So what would be wrong with a date?' Beth uttered an elaborate sigh. 'I wish some good-looking hunk would be making a pitch for me.'

'He's not making a pitch!'

'Sure he is. And what's wrong with that? This is 1975. You're an uncommitted woman.'

'I'm committed to other things.' Diane glanced at her watch. Greg wouldn't be here for forty minutes. 'How about a cup of hot apple cider?'

'You make it, I'll drink it. My feet are beat from chasing around Atlanta all day for ads.'

'You picked up two accounts.' Diane smiled in triumph as she walked to the kitchenette. 'OK – at "special rates",' she conceded. 'But those ads will look good in the paper.' They were close enough to Atlanta to attract some restaurant advertising.

'You're sure you'll manage if I run up to New York for nine days?'

'You're going.' Diane reached into the refrigerator, brought out the jug of cider. 'You promised your folks.' Without telling her mother, her father had pleaded with Beth to come for a visit: 'Mom needs to see you. To know you're all right.' 'You bought your airline tickets.'

'The *Guardian* bought my tickets. I'm not sure the company can afford it.'

'We knew we'd be in the red for a year or two.' Her usual response to Beth's attack of nerves about the way her capital kept diminishing. 'And we're doing better since the beginning of the year. We're becoming a habit with some readers.' She poured cider into a saucepan, lit the gas beneath it.

'Honey, don't you ever consider trying to contact Cliff?' Beth asked gently when Diane walked back into the living room. 'You know his parents live in Buckhead; you could call them –'

'Forget it.' Diane was startled at the sharpness of her voice. 'That's part of yesterday. Life moves on.'

'I see shadows in your eyes, all these years later.'

'Cliff must hate me for walking out that way.' But first he must have hurt – for a long time, she suspected.

'He'd forget about that once he held Jennie in his arms.'

'He's never to know about Jennie!' All at once Diane was trembling. She couldn't take a chance on his learning about Jennie. How could she know how he'd react? He might even fight for part-time custody. Jennie was a happy little girl. Her life mustn't be disturbed. And yet she harboured a ferocious longing to see Jennie surrounded by family; to experience what had been denied her. Cliff's mother and father would be such loving grandparents. 'You know what's wrong with you, Beth?' She struggled for an air of good-humoured mockery. 'You're such a romantic.'

'Maybe we ought to start running a "Personals" section.' Beth sighed with matching mockery. 'How else am I going to meet a guy in this town?'

'What about Greg?'

'Greg's got a thing for you. And don't tell me about his friend Cal. That guy's a creep.'

In April Greg asked Diane to go with him to see a performance by an experimental theatre group in Atlanta. A week later he took her to the Dogwood Festival, also in Atlanta. She was grateful that, in this age of casual sex, he kept their relationship on a light basis, expecting no more from her than a good night kiss, that occasionally threatened to erupt into something more.

But as the weeks passed, Diane was conscious of his eagerness to move their relationship on to a new level. He talked about how he meant to set down roots in Eden. He was candid about his political aspirations. And she was touched by the way he courted Jennie's affections.

'Greg's hungry for a ready-made family,' Beth said on a Friday evening when Diane waited for Greg to arrive. Tonight they were going to a local movie. 'Look how he fusses over Jennie.'

'Not this family.' Diane was faintly defiant. Last time they were out together he'd wanted her to go back to his apartment after the movie. She *never* went there. She didn't trust herself. 'I don't know why I keep going out with him.'

'Because he's charming and charismatic – and you're an unattached woman. He's serious, sweetie. He's got long-term ideas.'

'Oh, he talked to me on the phone this afternoon about our running an article by him on the need for the restructuring of our court system. What do you think?' Diane was ambivalent.

'Hey, even the *Herald* is on that bandwagon,' Beth reminded. 'Why not? So he wants to use the *Guardian* as a pulpit.'

'So many times I've wanted to talk to him about our serial murderer suspicions. He's a lawyer. He'd know angles we've never even dreamt about.'

'You know what he would say: "You can't go after suspects without evidence against them." All we've got are suspicions.'

'I'd never tell him that Lloyd Masters is my grandfather,' Diane admitted. 'I never even told Cliff. I wish we had the nerve to run a series on Eden's serial murders. That just might trigger someone who knows something into talking.'

'We'd have the whole police department on our heads. With the *Herald* and the *Evening News* blasting us for cheap tabloid reporting. Have you forgotten what happened when we ran the article on Dr Taylor?'

'*When?*' Diane lashed out impatiently. 'When can we take some action that'll bring out the ugly secrets hidden in this town?'

They both started at the sound of the doorbell. Diane hurried to the door.

'Hey, where's my special girlfriend?' Greg joshed, glancing about the living room. 'Couldn't she stay awake so I could kiss her goodnight?'

'Elise took the kids on a trip to the Atlanta zoo this afternoon,' Diane explained. 'After all that fresh spring air they were bushed. Jennie fell asleep before I could finish her nightly story.' He was so sweet with Jennie.

On the drive to the movie house Greg brought up the subject of his proposed article.

'I talked about it with Beth,' Diane said. 'We'd love to run it.'

'That's my girl.' He removed one hand from the wheel to reach for hers. 'I'd like to know you're my girl . . .'

'I'm not sure there's room in my life for anything beyond Jennie and the paper.' All at once she was trembling. Could Greg help her with the search that consumed her? Could he help her drive Cliff from her mind? 'I need some time, Greg . . .'

OK, take time,' he agreed, an undercurrent of confidence in his voice. 'I think Jennie's terrific – and a wife with her own newspaper is a definite asset for a man with political ambitions.' He grinned. They both knew, of course, that the *Guardian*'s influence in town was meagre. Thus far.

She ought to be honest with him. She hadn't been honest with Cliff – only in her love. She mustn't rush – but, yes, Greg could fit into the new life she imagined for herself. A father for Jennie, someone to help her with her real mission here in Eden.

Greg had parents in New York; two sisters. If she was Greg's wife, would they accept Jennie as Greg's child? A ready-made family for Jennie? Not right away, perhaps – but as time rolled on?

Cliff emerged from the shower, grabbed a towel. He wished to hell they weren't going to dinner at Cartwright's tonight. It would actually be business, he interpreted – as usual. After dinner the wives would go into the living room for coffee, and Cartwright would drag his associates into the library to talk about that deal he'd been touting for weeks, to set up a separate facility to deal exclusively with Medicaid patients. 'A health care mill with government subsidy,' Cartwright had labelled it.

Right now he himself was seeing more money each month than he'd ever anticipated.

'Cliff, get rolling!' Sylvia's voice filtered to him from the bedroom. 'You know Cartwright can't bear it if anybody's a minute late.'

'I'll be out in a few minutes.' Sylvia was sharp. She catered to Cartwright and the old boy loved it. He wished Sylvia would get off his back about their buying a house in Druid Hills. He wasn't ready to take on that kind of commitment. He knew what she was saying – how they were supposed to play the game as Cartwright saw it. In Cartwright's eyes she was the perfect doctor's wife. She learnt fast. But God, the way the bills came in every month! From Saks, Lord & Taylor, Rich's.

He'd acted like a jerk. Why hadn't he insisted on a pregnancy test? Diane had gone for a test. He'd been so shaken at the replay of that scene. He'd made such a God-awful mistake, driven Di right out of his life. That had been a wrong turn.

Had Sylvia really thought she was pregnant? He remembered Brad's earlier assessment of Sylvia – 'one of those chicks who goes into nursing with a vow to collect a doctor husband.' Then in a surge of guilt he pushed this suspicion from his mind. But face it, he had moved into a world where he was not comfortable.

Diane and Beth were enthralled when, early in June, Ron allowed himself to be persuaded to run for the empty City Council seat in October – where Clark Watson was considered the sure winner. The *Herald* and the *Evening News* were behind him.

'Ron's getting into the fight late,' Elise conceded while they explored the situation over a Sunday afternoon barbecue on the Tuckers' patio while Jennie and Nicole splashed happily in the tiny pool set up on a swatch of grass. 'Nobody expected a third party to put up a candidate. But they're so excited about pushing Ron for the seat.'

'I think it's a sensational idea.' Diane glowed. Ron was bright, compassionate, conscientious. She knew little about Clark Watson, except that he was Lloyd Masters' son-in-law, Gerry Watson's husband.

'Clark Watson's an obnoxious twit,' Elise said bluntly. 'I've heard him on the radio. He's just a puppet for his father-in-law. And I don't much care for his opposition.'

'I know we don't carry much weight, Ron, but the *Guardian* will be behind you all the way,' Diane promised.

'I'm not sure that's a good idea.' Ron's smile was lopsided.

'That won't cause any ripples at the Masters papers.' Elise dismissed his fears. 'They are sure Clark Watson's got this election sewn up.'

'Even Mom and Dad figure my chances are slight,' Ron admitted.

'They think that a Jewish candidate in Baptist territory hasn't a prayer. But Atlanta's had a Jewish mayor and now a black mayor. Let's face it,' Beth said ebulliently, 'the times they are a-changin'. Besides, Ron is one of the most popular teachers in this town. That's a lot going for him.'

'We'll at least make a statement.' Ron was sombre. 'Clark Watson – and his father-in-law's newspapers – are campaigning for a reduction in school taxes. They've never accepted integration; they're still crying, all these years later, that it was shoved down our throats. They want lower school taxes so that parents will have extra cash to send their kids to private schools.'

'We've got to get the black vote out.' Diane's mind was charging ahead. 'And the white voters who couldn't afford private schools even with taxes lowered. The way I hear it, Eden has some of the finest schools in the state. Let's fight to keep them that way.' Jennie would go to state schools.

'And the corruption in our town government is sickening. The waste is not to be believed!' Ron leant forward zealously. 'We can lower property taxes and still handle our school budget if our officials clean up their act.' He paused, his face suddenly dejected. 'I know, that's not likely to happen this year. But it *will* happen eventually.'

Dressing for an evening out – Jennie asleep in her new youth bed – Diane talked with Beth about Ron's campaign.

'I know the odds are against Ron's winning,' she agreed with Beth's judgement, 'but we can shake up this town. Like he said, why does the town have to have so many police cars? Half of our cops are tied down to office desks or manning radios or writing parking tickets.'

'Eden Motors belongs to Lloyd Masters and two of his sons-in-law, Hugh Jamison and Clark Watson,' Beth pointed out. 'So who profits when the township overbuys police cars from them? But we can't say that.'

'We can campaign for more economy in government. Damn it, Beth, I'm tired of thinking we can't say this and we can't say that! I'll ask Greg to write an article for us on cutting waste in town government. He can talk about the police cars without mentioning Eden Motors. The exposure does him good.'

'He'll turn you down on this one,' Beth prophesied. 'Everybody will know he's talking about Eden Motors and Lloyd Masters' connection with it. He'll be afraid to take on the *Herald* and the *Evening News*.'

'Greg's not like that. He got us a retraction from them, didn't he?'

'This is different, Di. You're putting him on the hot seat.' Tender laughter lit her eyes. 'Are you still playing the reluctant virgin?'

'I know – it's absurd. At my age – and in this age.' Diane forced a smile. 'We make love up to a point. Sometimes I don't want to stop, but something goes off in my head and I retreat. It's so sweet of him to understand.'

'It's not that he understands. He doesn't want to lose you. He's in pursuit of his ready-made family – for the time he feels he's ready to run for public office. And even the voice of a small newspaper like the *Guardian* is an asset for a struggling politician.'

Diane was startled. 'You make him sound so crass. I thought you liked Greg.'

'I do like him. With reservations.'

Why *did* she keep holding back with Greg? Always Cliff crept between them. Mom had never loved another man after Dad died. Would *she* ever be able to love someone besides Cliff?

'I'll talk to Greg about doing the article.' Diane dragged herself back to the moment. 'I'll tell him we'll do the leg work, get him figures. If a local lawyer – male – writes about it, it'll have more impact than if you or I do.'

But she was taken aback by Greg's response later when, in their favourite restaurant at the edge of town, she invited him to bring in an article about the police cars situation.

'Honey, I wish I could. But right now I'm all tied up with some tricky real estate closings. Maybe later, when things cool down.' His tone was conciliatory.

'Sure.' Diane smiled, hiding her disappointment. He wasn't that busy. He complained that he and Cal were not picking up more clients.

'It might be a wise idea to avoid confrontations with the *Herald* and the *Evening News*. It's one thing to support a different candidate, but everybody knows Masters is the major owner of Eden Motors.'

'I'm not afraid of Lloyd Masters!'

'Di, it's smart to know when to turn away from confrontations. You're acting on emotions. You don't like Lloyd Masters.'

Diane was startled. She hadn't realized her dislike was so obvious. Greg was always so calm and analytical, the attorney's mind always working for him.

'No, I don't like Lloyd Masters. And I'm not the only one in this town.'

'There're not enough of you to throw him off his throne. Masters has been a power in this town for too many years for that to happen.'

Home from her evening with Greg, Diane told Beth about his reaction to their airing the town's overbuying of police cars.

'Ron came over to talk about that,' Beth said seriously. 'He's still hot over the corruption in town, but he said he and Elise talked about it with his folks – and they pointed out he could find himself out of a job if he was linked to this. Lloyd Masters' son-in-law, Hugh Jamison, is head of the School Board. Like Greg said, we're not in a position to battle Eden Motors.'

Lloyd Masters was so powerful he could get away with anything in Eden, Diane fumed. Did he *know* who killed Dad? Mom had been convinced he did. Did he know who killed those others? Chris Robson, who was in Alison Masters' senior class. Annie Williams, who was a maid in his house. Dr Taylor, who had been his friend and physician for thirty years.

Was he being blackmailed into silence all these years?

Chapter Nineteen

The early August morning was already a scorcher, as Diane settled herself at her desk for what was sure to be a gruelling day. Their air conditioner had broken down yesterday afternoon. A repairman promised to come 'tomorrow or the next day'. Brushing perspiration-dampened hair from her forehead, she switched on the small fan Elise had loaned them this morning. The front door was propped open, doing little to alleviate the oppressive heat.

Their recently hired part-time typist, on her first job out of high school, had quit last night, leaving behind a rash of typing that Beth promised to tackle on her return from a conference with their printer. The perpetually petulant typist had been horrified when she saw the tax deductions on her first paycheque. 'I'm gettin' married next month. As soon as I get pregnant I'll be stayin' home anyway. I don't need this!'

Diane focused on copy-editing Ron's latest eloquent article about the mounting needs of the Eden school system. While public support was largely behind Clark Watson and his call for a reduction in property tax, the *Guardian* was receiving letters from more readers than they'd anticipated approving of Ron's stand.

It disturbed her that Greg continued to urge her not to lend the *Guardian*'s support to Ron. 'Sugar, it's a lost cause. You're not helping yourself.'

She glanced up as a woman hesitantly walked into the storefront. Gerry Watson, she recognized in astonishment, and rose to join her at the counter. The one member of Dad's family who had been nice to Mom. Diane knew from the society pages of the *Herald* that Linda and Peggy were in Newport for the races, their mother in the Greek Islands.

'Good morning.' Diane managed a cordial smile. 'It's a real hot one, isn't it?' Routine conversation to cover her inner chaos. What was Gerry Watson doing here?

'Mornings like this make me wish I'd gone to the shore or the mountains.' Gerry Watson seemed ill at ease but determined. 'I saw your ad for someone to do a gardening column for the newspaper . . .'

'We've been looking for someone for quite a while.' Could Lloyd Masters have sent his daughter to spy on them? No, that was absurd. 'It – it's an unpaid job.'

'That wouldn't bother me,' Gerry said quickly. Now she seemed to be searching for words. 'I have a degree in journalism, though I've never used it.' Like Dad, Diane thought in instant sympathy. 'And I have a lot of experience gardening. It's my favourite pastime. I thought that, perhaps, you'd give me a crack at it. I'd like to feel I'm doing something useful. I mean,' she stammered, 'may I submit a sample column?'

'Why, yes. We'd like that very much.'

'Oh, great!' Gerry glowed. 'I hope you'd let me write under a pseudonym? I'm Gerry Watson. My father's Lloyd Masters. My family would be upset if they discovered I was working for a competitor.' A glint of humour in her eyes now. 'But of course, you haven't hired me yet.'

'I'm Diane Phillips.' Gerry wouldn't remember that Mom's maiden name was Phillips. 'We'd love to see a sample column,' she said, all at once eager to put this vulnerable woman at ease. Norma had suggested they ask her to do a garden column, she recalled now. 'I've heard that you have a magic touch with flowers.'

'Thank you.' Gerry's face grew luminous with pleasure. 'I'll drop off a column tomorrow. Actually, it's in rough draft already.'

No, Gerry Watson wasn't here to spy for her father. Like Dad, she couldn't find a place in her father's empire as a journalist. All these years after college she was making a first attempt, Diane suspected. She remembered their brief encounter at the library. She'd felt strangely drawn to her father's youngest sister.

She sensed, too, that Gerry Watson was an unhappy woman. She'd heard pleasant things about Gerry from people here in Eden – nothing pleasant about Clark Watson. Still, everybody expected Clark to win that vacant seat on the City Council. But then the whole state, she gathered, had been strongly conservative since the 1964 presidential election, when historically Democratic Georgia had gone all out for Goldwater.

The following morning Gerry walked in to present her sample column. She seemed simultaneously elated and terrified.

'Why don't you sit down while I go over it right now?' Diane invited, though in truth she was backlogged with work.

'Thank you . . .' Faintly breathless, tense, Gerry sat in the chair before Diane's desk.

The column was excellent, Diane decided with relief. It would have been awful to have to reject it. 'It's too late for this week's edition, but we'll run it the following week. What name would you like to use?'

'I thought just "Gardening with Gina". If that's all right with you.' She hesitated. 'And nobody has to know that I'm Gina.'

'Nobody,' Diane agreed.

His eyes opaque, his smile impassive, Lloyd Masters leant back in his chair in his executive office while Clark paced back and forth. In a chair flanking his father-in-law's desk, Luke drew in a long breath that advertised his boredom. Luke figured that as the lawyer in the family, he should be the one running for public office, Lloyd understood. But Luke didn't have Clark's nerve; he was afraid to gamble.

'I thought we had this election sewn up,' Clark complained. 'Now we've got two groups scratching for votes. And you say we can't go after that shitty tabloid that's backing Ron Tucker.'

'They're small fry.' Lloyd shrugged with contempt. 'We go

after that rag, some folks might start feeling sorry for them. As for the other candidate – I have some chips to call in. Which I'll start doing tomorrow.' He pulled himself up in his chair. 'And tomorrow we bring out the Lloyd Masters Admiration Society in full force.' That brought both of them up sharp. 'I'm calling a special Board of Directors meeting for the day after tomorrow at Masters Memorial to announce that the Masters family – the *family* –' he emphasized – 'is joining together to establish a small but prestigious research department. Everybody knows my interest in our paediatrics service.' And the paediatrics department was damn loyal to him. They'd stood right behind him when that bitch of a nurse went after him – which was what he'd expected of them. 'We're hoping that our research department will come up with vaccines that will be helpful to children.'

'That's going to be expensive,' Luke began apprehensively. As always, worried that this might come out of Peggy's inheritance, Lloyd interpreted.

'I can afford it.' Lloyd was brusque. So he was seventy-five years old. He still had another fifteen years ahead to run his newspaper chain. 'I want people in town to know that the family – and that includes our candidate –' he nodded towards Clark – 'are concerned about health care. It'll add stature to Kevin Masters Memorial, give it more importance around the state. And Luke, tell Peggy to get together with Linda, now that they're finally back from their summer carousing, and give a couple of splashy campaign teas. The way the Kennedy women used to do.'

'The election's just five weeks away.' Clark was nervous. He'd been waiting for this deal for years. He was already planning a run for Congress, Lloyd knew. He figured on bypassing the State Legislature. It wouldn't hurt to have a son-in-law up there in the House to watch out for bills that were important to him.

'Stick with the campaigning,' Lloyd ordered. 'And be a little more careful about the women you're throwing into bed.' He ignored Clark's startled reaction, then his glare of injury. He didn't care how many women Clark screwed – just let him keep it under wraps in this town. 'Luke, tell Hugh to hold open three columns on the front page of the day after tomorrow's *Evening News* to report our latest philanthropy. Tell him to assign somebody to cover the Board of Directors meeting.'

No chance that Clark wouldn't be elected, Lloyd told himself – but it always paid to take super-precautions. He listened now while his two sons-in-law discussed this latest project. He waited a few minutes, then interrupted.

'Luke, get cracking. Clark, stay here. I want to talk to you about Gerry.'

They waited in silence until Luke had left the executive office, and closed the door behind him.

'What's the problem about Gerry?' Clark asked with an air of indulgence, but his eyes were wary.

'You two having marital problems?' Lloyd probed.

'No, Lloyd, where did you get that idea?' Clark bluffed, paused. 'You know Gerry – she's high-strung.'

'Is she developing a drinking problem?'

'God, no.' Clark appeared shocked, but Lloyd was unconvinced. Linda had hinted Gerry was hitting the bottle. 'Where did you get that idea?'

'She seemed a little on the high side at our dinner, night before last. It wouldn't look good for word to circulate that the candidate's wife was drinking too much.'

'Gerry's always a little hyper. But I'll keep an eye out,' Clark promised.

As usual, once dinner was over and Jennie in bed for the night, Diane prepared to read the *Evening News*. Beth was on a phone call with her mother, who was lecturing her about how she would never meet a prospective husband in a small town like Eden.

'Ma, I'm not concerned about getting married.' Beth was reiterating her usual response. 'Not yet, anyway,' she softened this. 'I'm twenty-seven years old – I'm building a career. Women today don't rush into marriage.'

Diane unfolded the *Evening News*, gaped at the front page centre headline: 'The Masters Family Brings Research Center to Kevin Masters Memorial Hospital.' Her heart pounding, she read the article, then read it a second time. How Cliff would love to be part of that! In her mind she heard him expounding again on the possibilities in paediatric research: 'We've developed vaccines for so many contagious children's diseases – but there are more out there to be conquered. It's just a matter of time when dedicated researchers will come up with new vaccines.'

'What are you looking so entranced about?' Beth's voice catapulted her back into the present.

'Read this . . .' Diane handed the newspaper to Beth. No need to explain what she meant by 'this'.

'Part of the campaign to put Clark Watson in office,' Beth commented while she read. 'That's expensive campaigning.'

'Masters can afford it.' Diane's mind was in chaos. She felt contempt for her grandfather's methods of operation, yet pleased that the hospital – her father's memorial – was to gain fresh stature with a research department. 'Cliff would be in heaven – to do research at Kevin Masters Memorial, right here in Eden.'

'Maybe somebody ought to pass the word along to him,' Beth said, overly casual. 'Didn't you say his parents live in Atlanta?'

Diane tensed. 'Beth, I can't call them.' She hesitated. 'It would be awful for me if he came back to Eden –'

'It might be great. You two had something special.'

'Don't jump on that bandwagon again. After what I put Cliff through, he hates me. And I can't take a chance on his knowing about Jennie.'

'He wouldn't have to know. People here in town think you were married and divorced. You pushed up Jennie's birthday so that there's no way he could know she's his daughter – unless you decide to tell him.'

'He won't ever know.' But she was torn apart inside. The research department would be hiring soon – and he had trained at this hospital. He was a natural to be part of the team.

'You could call his parents and say you knew him from the hospital – giving a phoney name – and you wanted to pass the word along to him about the new research department. And you'd find out, too, where he is.'

'His parents live in Buckhead. Elise has a Buckhead phone directory because she's always shopping at the Phipps Plaza mall there.'

'So go borrow it.'

'OK, I'll call Cliff's parents.' They wouldn't recognize her voice. She'd just met them that once – almost five years ago. How could she not pass this word along to Cliff, when it could mean so much to him? He wouldn't know about Jennie – Beth was right. They would never even meet.

She went to Elise's apartment, chatted briefly, brought the phone book home with her. She sat down by the phone, flipped through the pages of the directory.

'Is it still so humid out?' Beth returned to the living room with tall glasses of iced coffee.

'Awful. Thank God for air conditioning.' Then all at once her throat tightened. Her eyes had focused on a listing: 'Hendricks, Dr Clifford R.'

Cliff was in Buckhead! Excitement charged through her. She wouldn't talk to him, of course, *but she could hear his voice.* Just for a minute, then hang up. Her face luminous in expectancy, her hands trembling, she dialled his number. This was crazy, of course, but let her just hear his voice after all these years. It would be almost like seeing him.

She waited while the phone rang at the other end. It was evening, he'd be home, she surmised. Hang up quickly, she reminded herself. *Say nothing.* Then she was aware that the phone was being lifted off the hook. Her throat tightened as she waited to hear his voice. Of course she still loved him. She'd always love him.

'Hello?' A sultry feminine voice came over the line. *Had she dialled the wrong number*? 'Sylvia Hendricks here . . .'

Diane slammed down the receiver in shock. Cliff was married. Why was she so unprepared to discover this?

'What happened?' Beth put down her glass of iced coffee, her voice solicitous.

'I just talked to Cliff's wife . . .' Diane struggled for calm. 'They live in Buckhead.' From now on she'd avoid going to Atlanta. She might just happen to encounter him on the street. 'Forget about passing the word along. I don't want him to come back to Eden.'

For days Diane moved about in a state of numbness. Why should it come as such a shock to learn that Cliff was married? She had walked out on him almost five years ago. He was a warm, passionate man – he wanted a wife and family. It was like she'd always told herself: for Cliff and her the timing was all wrong. But the timing was right for him and a woman named Sylvia.

Chapter Twenty

Diane focused on promoting Ron these final weeks before the election, yet she fought against recurrent frustration. As Ron and Elise reminded her, if the *Guardian* revealed corruption involving Eden Motors, it could backfire for Ron. He could lose his job at the high school.

Along with most people in town, Diane and Beth were not surprised when Clark easily won his Council seat. Ron was philosophical.

'Hey, Masters was so anxious to guarantee Watson's election he came out – at the critical moment – with that research department for the hospital. I feel we helped bring that about.'

Diane noted no enthusiasm in Gerry for her husband's election. But Gerry was euphoric that her column was receiving much approval.

'We had a call from the Eden Garden Club,' Beth told Gerry when she arrived with her mid-November column. On this cloudy morning she wore dark glasses – 'a bad case of eyestrain,' she explained. 'They're dying to have you talk at their fund-raiser next month.'

'I can't do that!' Gerry was shaken. She turned from Beth to Diane. 'You know I can't.'

'Beth told them you wouldn't be available,' Diane soothed. 'But it shows that you're doing a great job. That vein of humour you weave into the column is terrific.'

'We'll have to work out a cover story for me. I do want to keep on with the column.' Gerry fidgeted nervously with her glasses.

Diane tensed in shock. Gerry wasn't suffering from eyestrain. Her left eye had been blackened. And Diane recalled Gerry's sprained wrist last month. Was Gerry Watson an abused wife? Diane felt sick as she considered this. All the family money, its social prestige – and Gerry's husband beat her?

'We'll play up the mystery angle,' Beth plotted confidently. 'It'll add a special touch.'

'Sure, it'll work out,' Diane comforted. It meant so much to Gerry to have this small success.

Moments after Gerry left the office, Beth pounced on Diane. 'Did you see that shiner? You remember the sprained wrist last month?'

'I suppose they could both have logical explanations.'

'I don't believe that. It explains her whole lack of self-confidence, that perpetual air of facing something traumatic.'

'I never associated abused wives with women in her position.' This was her father's youngest sister being battered. A sweet, bright, but frightened woman.

'Honey, it crosses all lines.' Beth sighed. 'But what can any-body do about it?'

'Why don't we run an article about abused women?' Diane challenged in sudden excitement. 'Stress the need in town for a shelter for them. People across the country are facing up to the problem.'

'If Gerry Watson is an abused wife, I doubt she'd ever run to a shelter for protection. But what about her family? Don't they see what's going on?'

'I'll bet the communication between Gerry and her family is non-existent. Her two sisters are always running off somewhere together. Their mother goes off alone. Beth, let's run an article on abused women, bring out a need for a shelter here in Eden.'

'How do we know there's a need?' Beth was ambivalent.

'I remember Cliff talking about women who came into the emergency department on Saturday nights or early Sunday mornings – always saying they'd fallen down a flight of stairs or walked into a door, the husbands standing by self-consciously. He said you just knew the husbands, or boyfriends, had been teed off about the outcome of a football or baseball or hockey game, swigged down a few beers and used the women as punching bags.'

'And like I said before, it's not just blue-collar wives,' Beth reminded. 'But somehow, I just never thought we'd see that here in Eden.'

'You see it everywhere,' Diane said tautly. 'I remember reading an article in some magazine last year. The first shelter was opened somewhere in England four years ago. People recognized the *need*. They've been set up all through the British Isles – and in some cities and towns here in the United States.'

'You think Eden is ready for that?' Beth was sceptical.

'Let's give it a run. Do some research first. Ask questions. Maybe run an opening article and ask for letters – anonymous so the women don't have to be afraid. But yes, let us know what's happening behind the pretty façade of this town.'

'We may run into hostility,' Beth warned. 'It's an ugly subject.'

'We're not running just society news and cooking and garden columns. We've pledged ourselves to provide community service. This is part of it.'

'Right. So some people will complain we're two hysterical women out to be sensational. So what?'

That evening – with Beth babysitting as usual – Diane went out with Greg for dinner at the new restaurant at the edge of town that was drawing well despite its fancy tabs. She'd offered once to split the cost. Women did that these days. But Greg had brushed this aside. She felt guilty that he always chose expensive restaurants, yet realized this was what Beth labelled 'one of his shticks.'

'That's a sharp outfit,' Greg approved, holding the car door open for her and simultaneously inspecting the smoky blue dress she wore beneath her usual black wool coat. She wore pantsuits to the office. On special occasions she brought out one of the two ageless Betsy Johnsons she'd bought in an extravagant moment after emerging from maternity clothes. 'It's sexy yet classy.'

When Greg drew to a stop at the traffic light at the Kevin Memorial corner, Diane focused involuntarily on the hospital. A montage of special moments there with Cliff charged across her mind. *Cliff was married.* She still felt a tremor of pain when she remembered the voice on the phone – 'Sylvia Hendricks here . . .'

By the time they arrived at the restaurant the parking area indicated a large crowd inside.

'I made a reservation,' Greg said with a smug smile.

The room was crowded, but they were seated immediately. Diane felt some of the tensions of the day ebbing away in the charming atmosphere of the restaurant – the lighting pleasingly soft, each damask-draped table provided with fresh flowers, the flatware and china elegant.

'The flowers are beautiful.' Diane leant forward to sniff the fragrant tea roses – hot house, she suspected, since this was mid-November. Still, Georgia gardens bloomed late.

'The restaurant's just become my latest client,' Greg told her with satisfaction while his gaze swept around the room with a proprietary air.

'Beth's been talking to them about advertising in the *Guardian*. But I guess we're just not important enough.'

A waiter arrived and they dispensed with personal conversation. When he left, Greg launched into a report of his latest real estate closing.

'This town's been damn lucky when you consider how many businesses have gone into bankruptcy this year throughout the country. They say we're pulling out of the recession – but President Ford's budget for next year entails a fifty-two-billion-dollar deficit. Still, Eden's doing all right.'

'For some people.' Diane jumped on to a favorite topic. 'I think it's terrible the way some homeowners are overtaxed.'

'Di, don't rock the boat.'

'What do you think about Jimmy Carter's chances in next year's election?'

'He's working like a dog already – but he'll never make it. Ford will be the Republican candidate, and he'll be a shoo-in. But why are we talking politics? You're looking particularly beautiful tonight.' His eyes made passionate love to her.

'Let's forget the movie tonight and go back to my apartment. When are you going to stop turning me away?'

'You've been so sweet. You're very special to me, Greg.' Startled, she was conscious of passion stirring within her. Could she, in Greg's arms, forget about Cliff?

'I'm not playing games, sugar.' Greg's voice was a caress. 'I'm a man of serious intent.' Beneath the joshing tone, he was clearly serious.

She hesitated, debating within. 'Let's forget about the movie,' she agreed.

'My apartment is a disaster area, but you won't mind,' he promised. And all at once she was jolted back through the years – hearing Cliff's voice the night they'd gone back to Cliff and Brad's apartment, expecting Brad to be there: 'The apartment's probably a mess . . .'

Diane ate the superb cuisine without tasting, her mind in chaos. She could have a real life with Greg. Jennie would have a father. Already Jennie was upset at unexpected moments because other kids talked about their daddies, and she had none. Only half-listening to Greg's commentary, Diane managed to make the required replies.

'Well, look who's just arrived.' His voice was electric. 'Two Masters sons-in-law and their wives. Where's the new Councilman and his wife?'

'I guess they don't travel in schools like fish.' Diane's smile was acerbic as her eyes swung to the arriving couples. She knew the four of them by sight, but she'd never been this close to Peggy and Linda. Both women were expensively dressed, carried themselves with an arrogance that to Diane was an immediate turn-off. So different from Gerry!

'The word's around that Clark Watson is already planning to run for Congress. The City Council is just a pit stop.' Greg's eyes were quizzical. 'How does a guy make that fast a jump?'

'You just said it. His father-in-law's Lloyd Masters.' Distaste was spoiling her appetite for the Crême Caramel au rhum their waiter had just placed before them. It was revolting to think Clark Watson might represent their district in Congress. 'He'll be running on his father-in-law's influence. But I promise you one thing,' she said in sudden defiance. 'The *Guardian* won't support him.'

'I think the *Herald* and the *Evening News* will buck that,' he joshed.

'Oh, we're off on a new campaign.' Diane forced her gaze away from the table across the room where the two couples had been seated. 'The *Guardian* is launching a series on the need in Eden for a shelter for abused women. We'll start off with –'

'Di, you don't want to do that! People in this town will resent the suggestion that such a thing exists here.'

'But it does exist, Greg.' She was startled by his reaction. 'It's a scene that's finally coming out into the open.'

'Not in Eden,' he rejected. 'If there's a case here and there, people will want it swept under the rug. It'll be bad for the newspaper. Bad for you.'

'But we can help these women.'

'Come on, they probably bring it on themselves.'

'That's not true!' Diane gazed at him in shock. 'Where's your compassion, Greg?'

'I don't want you running that article, Di.' His face tensed.

'Excuse me?' Was he trying to dictate her thinking?

'People are already seeing us as a couple.' He was terse. 'It wouldn't look good for me career-wise to have you pursue that subject.'

'You're worried that the *Guardian* and I will reflect badly on you?' she asked in quiet rage.

'We must think about my career. I have an image to maintain. That's important. I can't afford to –'

'I can't afford to continue this relationship,' she interrupted. 'Nobody's telling me how to think – or how to run my newspaper. I'll call a cab and wait outside. Goodnight, Greg!'

Diane paced as she reported her confrontation with Greg to Beth.

'I can't believe I was so blind!' she blazed. 'Greg didn't care about me. He was playing a game. I was a pawn on his chess board, to be manipulated at his will!'

'Honey, cool it. You didn't fall into his trap.'

'You should have seen him almost drooling when Hugh Jamison and Luke Cranston walked in with their wives. Because here was the kind of power he worships.'

'It's over. Stop fuming.' Beth chuckled. 'Save all that energy for something more productive.'

'We'll start right away on the abused women series.' Beth was right – why waste another minute even thinking about Greg? 'I'll check out magazines in the local library. You go to the Atlanta library and check out newspapers for the past eighteen months.' She suppressed a shudder. She didn't want to set foot in Atlanta if she could help it. 'We'll do an introductory piece, the way we talked about, asking for letters, then build from there.'

'Yes, boss lady,' Beth flipped. She was relieved, Diane deciphered, that work was taking precedence over moping.

The Monday before Thanksgiving was cold and grey with a threat of snow in the air. Diane had just arrived in the office when Gerry came in to deliver her Thanksgiving week column. It was a compulsion with Gerry to be ahead of her deadline, Diane realized.

'This cold snap will kill off my last roses of the year,' Gerry mourned when they'd exchanged greetings and she'd handed over the manila envelope that contained her latest effort. Her thirty roses bushes were the envy of Eden's other serious gardeners. 'Some years I've nursed them through right into December.'

'You'll still have roses for Thanksgiving day,' Diane predicted. 'You'll be taking bunches to the nursing home. Gerry, I was wondering,' she said on impulse, 'would you like to try doing some non-gardening articles for us? You know, pick a subject that you think would be interesting to local people . . .'

Gerry was suddenly radiant. 'You really think I could handle something else?'

'Of course, I do.' How sad that she was so insecure. How wonderful it would be to be able to say, 'I'm Kevin's daughter – your niece.'

'Let me think about it. I'm sure I'll come up with something.' Yet painful doubt undercoated Gerry's voice.

Diane hesitated a moment, then plunged in. 'You might want to work on a series we're planning now,' she said gently. 'It deals with the subject of abused women . . .' Her voice trailed off as she saw the anguish reflected on Gerry's face.

She watched helpless, berating herself for being callous, while tears filled Gerry's eyes and spilled over unheeded. She reached for a batch of tissues from the box in her desk drawer, handed them to Gerry.

'Does everybody in town know?' Gerry whispered.

'Nobody.' Diane rushed to comfort her. 'I didn't actually know,' she stammered. 'I remembered your dark glasses – and your sprained wrist the month before. Nobody knows,' she reiterated.

'The first time was six months after our wedding.' Gerry was fighting for poise. 'I left him and went home to my parents. My mother sent me right back. She said I couldn't disgrace the family with such an accusation. My mother's Catholic – to her divorce was out of the question.'

'You don't have to stay with him. You're a bright, beautiful woman – you can make a life for yourself.'

'I'm forty-three years old. I have no real skills. And my family would never forgive me if I walked out on Clark. Especially now, when his political career is beginning to take shape.' She paused for a long, laboured breath. 'Two years ago I told my mother I needed professional help – I couldn't deal with this any longer. She said it was my duty to the family to keep my "problem" to myself. I've been a prisoner too long, Diane. I don't know how to handle the rest of my life.'

'Scare him.' Diane clutched at this. 'He can't afford a scandal. Not in his position. And he needs your father's support,' she said bluntly. 'If he starts up again –' and they both knew he would – 'you threaten to call the police. Remind him it's against the law to batter his wife. Pick up a lamp or a piece of furniture and threaten him,' Diane pursued. 'Make him understand that if he wants to keep up the front of the "perfect marriage" he has to obey certain rules.'

Gerry's eyes mirrored panic. 'I don't know if I can do that.'

'You can do it,' Diane insisted. 'You came here to talk to us about doing a column, though I know what an effort it was. But it was important to you, and you did it.' She leant forward to cover one of Gerry's hands with hers. 'Be prepared. At the first sign of violence you go into your act. Stare him straight in the eyes and make him know you're serious. He can't afford to gamble.'

'All right . . .' Gerry's smile was shaky. 'I'll try. He's always tearing me down – he says I provoke him. But that's not true,' she said defiantly. 'But all these years I've never talked about it to anyone. Only to my mother that first time, when she sent me packing.'

'You can always come and stay with Beth and me,' Diane told her, and saw her astonishment and gratitude that a relative stranger would do this. But she wasn't a stranger. Gerry was Dad's sister, her aunt. 'But if you're willing to stay with him, you must make him understand he can't use you for a punching bag. Don't ever let him hit you again!'

* * *

Gerry knew from the moment Clark walked into the house this evening that he was in an ugly mood. She knew, also, that he wouldn't talk about it until Josie – their latest cook/housekeeper – left for the day. Apprehension was tightening the usual knot in the pit of her stomach. Diane's exhortation darted across her mind – a challenge she wasn't sure she could meet.

'I don't suppose there's any way we can avoid Thanksgiving dinner at your parents' house,' he said bitterly when Josie had served the main course and retreated to the kitchen. 'It's always such a bore with the four brats there.' Peggy's two daughters and Linda's son and daughter made appearances at Thanksgiving, Christmas, New Year's and Easter Sunday dinners.

'We're expected.' Josie was serving roast beef tonight, Clark's favourite. Maybe that would put him in a better frame of mind.

'The Old Man's moving ahead like a steamroller with the new research department.' He attacked a thick slab of roast beef with gusto – giving Gerry hope that he would overeat, have a couple of glasses of wine, and fall asleep on the sofa while they watched his choice of television fare.

'He's committed to it.' There was no wine glass at her place setting. At Clark's orders. So she found comfort in a glass or two of wine in the evening, she told herself in silent defiance. That didn't make her a lush. Mainly she had a couple of glasses before dinners at her parents' house. She needed it then. 'People in town are quite impressed.'

'I want to give a dinner party just before Christmas. For members of the City Council and their wives. And your father and mother, of course,' he added with a mocking smile.

'I'll make the arrangements.' Clark would complain afterwards. He always did, though she worked hard to make everything just right. Even Mother admitted her parties were successful, though she was a nervous wreck for days before each one.

She listened to Clark's litany of complaints about the day's activities. Then dinner was over, and she went out to the kitchen to talk to Josie about the menu for the following evening. When she went to join Clark in the den, she was relieved to find him sprawled in his favourite lounge chair, feet on the footstool. Asleep. She crossed to the TV, switched it off, and went upstairs to the master bedroom.

Welcoming the quiet solitude she kicked off her shoes and stretched out on the bed to think about her next column for the *Guardian*. The winter garden, she planned. Tell the readers how to prepare for next winter's garden as well as how to care for what was at hand.

Nobody in town knew that she was writing the column, even Clark. And now Diane was willing to let her try something more ambitious. She couldn't bring herself to write about abused women, but she might try an article about the wonderful spirits of some of the residents of the nursing home. Why must everything be downbeat? Better to talk about the *accomplishments* of people in their eighties and nineties.

Keeping watch for the sound of Clark's approach – though she suspected he would sleep for at least an hour, then watch another hour or two of television – she brought out a legal pad and began to make notes. Even though she wasn't getting paid, she was writing for a commercial newspaper. That made her a professional.

With her notes completed and stashed away, Gerry began to prepare for bed. When Clark came up, she'd pretend to be asleep. He rarely bothered to reach for her in bed. Sometimes she asked herself if he was having affairs with other women. But she dismissed these thoughts. Let him do what he liked – as long as he was discreet about it. It would be too humiliating if people here in town knew he was sleeping around, but that wasn't likely. The Councilman, the future Congressman, would want to avoid scandal.

She heard muted footsteps on the carpeted stairs and sighed. Clark was coming up earlier than she'd thought. She crossed to her dressing table, sat down, began the night ritual of brushing her hair. He'd been in a foul mood when he came home.

Was he feeling better now? From habit she tensed, fearful of another ugly encounter.

If he started up again, she'd do what Diane had advised.

The door to the master bedroom swung open. Clark walked inside. His expression told her his mood was still foul.

'The Old Man's a bastard,' he said contemptuously, striding to the bed. He reached under his pillow for the silk pajamas he fancied.

'What did Dad do now?' She fought to get her voice casual.

'I'm not on the Board of Directors for the new research department,' he spat at her. 'It was supposed to have been set up to help put me into office, but Hugh's running the show! And what did you mean – "What did Dad do now?"' he mimicked. 'I don't need your sarcasm.' He stood beside the bed, hurled his pajamas on the floor.

'I wasn't sarcastic,' she began, paused as he moved towards her. Remembering Diane's exhortations. She must be strong. 'Clark, don't touch me,' she warned.

'You goddamn little bitch! So bloody superior all the time!'

'Don't touch me!' Trembling but determined she reached for the lamp on her dressing table, raised it menacingly, fighting for control. 'You hit me again, Clark, and I'm calling the police!' Her eyes held his, defying him to take another step towards her. Let him not realize how frightened she was.

'You're nuts!' But, miraculously, he seemed frozen in place.

'You touch me once more, ever, and I'll call the police!' she repeated with greater strength. Diane was right – she could handle this. 'And I'm telling my father what you've done to me all these years!'

'You've flipped your lid,' he bellowed. But he was scared.

'I'll remain your wife,' she said, 'but you're never to touch me again. I'll play the devoted wife role in public – if you play by my rules.'

'You stupid little bitch . . .' He reached for his pajamas on the floor. 'I'll move my things into one of the guest rooms tomorrow. But if you make one wrong move, I'll kill you!'

Gerry stood immobile until Clark slammed the bedroom door shut behind him. She'd won, she thought with a mixture of disbelief and relief.

She put down the lamp, went to the phone, found Diane's home number in the phone book. Her face brightened when she heard Diane's voice on the phone.

'Di, I did what you said,' she whispered, though she knew that Clark couldn't hear her. 'I'll love you for ever. You've given me back my life.'

Chapter Twenty-One

When they launched the *Guardian*, Diane and Beth had told themselves that they would steer clear of state or national politics. They would focus on community affairs. But when presidential candidate Jimmy Carter was the winner in Iowa's precinct caucuses on 19 January of the new year – the first test for Democratic candidates – they knew they would come out for him.

'The *Herald* and the *Evening News* will butcher Carter,' Ron warned them at a Saturday evening at the Tucker house – with Jennie and Nicole enthralled at being allowed again at the dinner table with the grown-ups. 'The way they did when he ran for governor. Though according to yesterday's papers they don't expect him to win the Democratic nomination.'

'Nicole, let me cut up your chicken.' Elise was solicitous as her small daughter tried to manipulate knife and fork.

'No. I can do it.'

'I did mine,' Jennie pointed out triumphantly.

'I read in the *Herald* yesterday that Masters Memorial expects to have the research department in operation within a month,' Ron said. 'I see our new Councilman is now on the Board of Directors,' he added with sardonic humour.

Diane tensed while the others discussed the new research department, which was expected to lend stature to the hospital. According to the stories in the Masters newspapers, the Board of Directors was interviewing a string of young doctors dedicated to research in paediatrics. Had anybody contacted Cliff? Even as a resident he'd talked with such intensity about the need for more vaccines to protect against childhood diseases. She suffered recurrent guilt that she had abandoned her anonymous efforts to alert Cliff to the new opportunities, though he must surely be aware of them if he lived in Atlanta.

She was conscious of furtive glances from Beth. Beth knew this talk about the research department was unnerving her. How would she deal with the situation if Cliff should happen to be one of those chosen for the research team? He'd be coming here with his wife. Did they have children? Jennie's younger half-sister or half-brother, whom she could never know?

She was relieved when dinner was over except for coffee, which the adults would have in the living room. Beth was taking the two little girls off to Nicole's bedroom for a bedtime story, before they were put to bed for the night. This would be Jennie's first sleepover, Diane thought tenderly.

'Don't let them con you into more than one story,' Ron called after Beth while Diane and Elise headed for the kitchen for their coffee.

'Are you still interested in Dr Taylor's murder?' Elise asked Diane while she brought down the mugs from a cabinet.

'Of course . . .' Diane was instantly alert.

'Mom was telling me this afternoon that Mrs Taylor was complaining how the police have come up with nothing in all this time. It's how long? Two years?'

'It'll be three years in April.' She'd come back to Eden less than three months later. What had she accomplished? She had strong convictions – but nothing that pointed to the identity of the serial murderer who'd been stalking this town for over thirty years. So many small pieces that wouldn't quite fit together.

'I can see how frustrating it must be for her – to know that her husband's murderer is walking the streets free,' Elise commiserated. 'And she's such a nice woman, Mom says.'

'Maybe we could do a piece on the third anniversary of his death,' Diane said. 'Nothing that would bring the police down on our heads,' she added quickly. 'Not "Why isn't the murder solved?" but an *in memoriam* piece about how much he's missed and so on.' Of course, it would be a silent reminder that the police had another unsolved murder on the Eden records. 'It's a few weeks away – but perhaps I could call and ask Mrs Taylor's approval.'

She remembered how she'd approached Mrs Taylor about a front-page tribute to Dr Taylor in their first edition of the *Guardian*. At their initial meeting the widow seemed so grateful and co-operative, then she'd turned cold. But the *Guardian* hadn't been chastising the police about their not solving the case. She frowned, recalling the scurrilous attack by the *Herald* and the *Evening News* for their 'maligning the fine Eden police force'. She'd wait until late March, then call Mrs Taylor. Maybe now that she realized the police were doing nothing to solve her husband's murder she might drop some little clue that would lead to real answers.

Ten days later Diane ran into Norma at the supermarket. She was rushing into the store as Norma was hurrying out.

'Di, I haven't seen you in ages,' Norma bubbled. 'Look, why don't we have lunch tomorrow? I have so much to tell you.'

'Great . . .' Diane's mind charged into high gear. News about the research department? Was Cliff a candidate? She yearned to see him win a place on the team, yet dreaded the prospect of his moving to Eden. With his wife. 'Where? The diner across from the hospital?' Norma used to like the diner, and it was close.

'Perfect. Noon OK for you?' Norma was juggling bundles in her arms.

'That's fine. See you then.'

At errant intervals in the course of the evening and next morning Diane's mind replayed what Norma had said in their brief encounter. Of course, Norma knew she'd been seeing much of Cliff in those months she'd worked at the hospital. Did Norma's news concern Cliff?

Diane waited impatiently for the time to leave the office for her luncheon appointment with Norma. The weather was glorious as she headed for the diner. The crocuses were out already and the first daffodils pushing into bloom. Next month, April, Eden would be a wonderland, with the dogwood trees bursting into flower along every residential street. Even on Main Street dogwood rose from small patches of earth set into concrete and lent a charming air of informality.

She was glad she was early. The diner was a favourite in the area – already half the booths were occupied.

She waved from her window table as Norma sprinted into view. She hadn't seen much of Norma and Joe in the past few weeks, she realized guiltily. There was so little time for socializing.

Norma hurried into the diner, sat across from Diane.

'You're looking great,' Diane told her. There was a special radiance about her today.

'I'm exhausted.' Norma sighed, yet she seemed undisturbed. 'I just found out for sure three days ago. Di, I'm pregnant.'

'Norma, how wonderful!' Diane remembered how much she and Joe wanted a family, but had delayed because of finances.

'It was an accident,' she admitted. 'We still worry about the mortgage payments and the crazy inflation. But it's happened – and we're happy. We'll manage somehow. Oh, I haven't told Gladys or anybody at the hospital just yet. I suppose I'll have to soon. Anyhow, I plan on working as long as possible. When I can't – and after the baby is born – I'll run a typing service from the house. Hey, maybe I can do some freelance typing for the *Guardian*.'

'Let's work on that.' Having Norma on a freelance basis might be more practical than the part-time help they'd had thus far. 'I suppose Joe is out of his mind with joy?'

'He's so happy.' Norma's voice was soft. 'He vows he'll get a second job if necessary. He wants everything to be right for the baby.'

'How's Gladys these days? She was on the cool side towards me, the last two or three times I ran into her.'

'That set-to you had with the *Herald*,' Norma surmised. 'You know how she feels about the Masters family. About Lloyd Masters,' she amended. 'For years the hospital has been her life, and to Gladys the hospital is Lloyd Masters. Of course, you used to be her fair-haired child in the office . . .'

'Me?' Diane was startled.

'Sure. Didn't you ever notice? I think part of it was because Cliff Hendricks had such a thing for you. She was disappointed when you brushed him off.' Questions in Norma's eyes now.

'Cliff was very special.' Diane forced herself to smile. 'I was so lonely down here, and he was so sweet. But we were never really serious.' How could she lie this way?

'You should have seen how teed off she was when the *Guardian* lit into Lloyd Masters that way about their article on –'

'Norma we didn't light into him,' Diane broke in. 'It was the newspaper. We had to straighten out an undeserved slur.'

'Well, you know Gladys and Lloyd Masters. The man can do no wrong. And a lot of people in this town feel the same way.' But not Norma, Diane recalled. 'I remember six years ago when that paediatrics nurse brought complaints to the Hospital Board about him, she –'

'What kind of complaints?' Signals popped up in Diane's brain.

'It was sick,' Norma conceded. 'Everybody knew that.'

'What kind of complaints?' Diane prodded.

'Oh, she tried to say he was molesting the kids on the paediatrics floor – when he'd come in late at night to leave soft toys for some of them. Usually little girls. Everybody knew how he grieved about Alison's condition. You know, the nervous breakdown after she was gang-raped – and she never came out of it. And his only son committed suicide.'

Not suicide. Diane rebuked silently – he was murdered.

'What happened to the nurse?'

'She was fired. Gladys helped dig up evidence that showed her to be psychotic. Three residents testified to that. I doubt that she'll ever be a hospital nurse again. Of course, nobody had believed her.'

Diane's heart was pounding. Perhaps they should have believed that nurse. He'd sent all his children off to boarding school at the age of eight. Only Alison was kept at home. He adored Alison. Were all the murders committed to hide some ugly secret about Lloyd Masters and Alison? Could his wife – could Maureen Masters be the killer?

'No more stories tonight,' Diane said firmly, pulling the comforter up over Jennie's small shoulders as she and Jennie went through the nightly ritual of 'one more story'.

'All right.' Jennie sighed dramatically held up her arms for a good night hug and kiss.

'I love you.' Diane pulled her small daughter close.

'I love you, Mommie.'

Diane switched on the tiny night light and left the bedroom. She was impatient to talk with Beth about the part of the luncheon conversation with Norma that she had not reported earlier. The hint of perversion in Lloyd Masters. Was she allowing her long rage against her grandfather to colour her belief that the paediatrics nurse had not been psychotic? Beth would probably say she was jumping too fast.

Beth was watching a television newscast. She crossed to switch off the set when Diane came into the living room, then returned to the sofa.

'You've got something on your mind that you're bursting to talk about,' she said with an effort at humour, but her eyes were serious. 'I've known it since you came back from lunch.'

'Something weird that Norma told me.' Diane dropped into the club chair that flanked the sofa.

'Tell Mommie.'

Determined not to be melodramatic, Diane told Beth about the paediatrics nurse who'd made the charges, and how the matter had been handled at the hospital.

'You figure this ties in some way with the unsolved murders?' Beth appeared sceptical.

'Maybe the others knew this, too. They had to be got out of the way.' She took a deep breath. 'Perhaps I'm way off the track, but that could point to Maureen Masters.'

'So we have to find out where she was at the time of each of the murders.' Beth was contemplative. 'We check the society pages of the *Herald*. They never miss a trip of any of the Masters women.'

'Back to the public library. But I don't think it should be you or me,' Diane said bluntly. 'You know how gossip spreads around this town. I wouldn't want Lloyd Masters to learn that we're delving into back issues of his local newspapers. It was different before – they didn't know us.'

'Who could we ask to check it out for us?'

'Elise, but we don't tell her why,' she added, guilty at this necessary subterfuge. 'Just tell her it's important for us to know where Maureen Masters was on certain dates. Elise is a good friend. She'll do it.'

'Right. But, Di, this sounds kind of wild. Maureen Masters a serial murderer?'

'It sounds kind of wild to hear that Lloyd Masters, a supposed pillar of Eden society, was accused of molesting little girls.'

Beth hesitated. 'Norma didn't say anything about the research team being hired at the hospital, did she?'

'She doesn't know much about it. Only that a little-used wing is being set aside for the department, and that they'll be interviewing prospective team members soon. If – if Cliff's among the applicants, she'll be sure to tell me.'

'It's not likely he'll give up private practice to come back to do research in a small-town hospital.' A search of phone directories had told them he was in a group practice in exclusive Druid Hills. 'He's probably raking in money.'

'But Cliff didn't want to go into private practice,' Diane said passionately. 'He wanted to do research. Paediatrics research,' she emphasized. 'Which is what the Masters Memorial research department will be doing. Cliff *belongs* on that team. He trained here. Gladys said he was the brightest resident that ever went through the hospital. Maybe – maybe she recommended that he be considered.'

She was torn apart inside. She couldn't bear the prospect of Cliff's coming back to Eden – with his wife. Yet she ached to see him in the field that meant so much to him.

As Diane had anticipated, Elise accepted their research assignment, to be paid by the hour, without a question.

'I know this may sound weird to you, but it ties in with a possible story we may be doing.'

'Hey, I work for hire,' Elise joked. 'I do the job – I don't ask for a blueprint.'

At the end of a Saturday of research Elise reported her findings to Beth and Diane.

'On 8 April 1943 Maureen Masters – according to the society pages of the *Herald* – was at The Cloister on Sea Island Georgia.'

When Chris Robson was murdered.

'On 12 April 1950 she was in Paris – per the same source.'

When Dad was murdered.

'On 12 January 1957 she was at The Breakers in Palm Beach.'

That was the day Annie Williams was stabbed to death.

'And on 3 April 1973 she was in Paris.'

The day Dr Taylor was killed.

'Elise, you're wonderful,' Beth approved. Diane sat immobile in thought.

'That rules out Maureen Masters,' Diane conceded when she and Beth were alone. 'Where do we go from here?'

'Di, you always knew it would be rough. But the pieces are coming together. It'll happen,' she promised. 'Every little piece will fall into place.'

In the ornately furnished bedroom of their luxurious new apartment, Cliff and Sylvia were dressing for a Saturday evening dinner party at the Cartwright house.

'I'm giving serious thought to pulling out of the practice here to move back to Eden.' Cliff tried to sound matter of fact.

Hairbrush in hand, Sylvia swung away from her dressing

table mirror and stared at Cliff in shock. 'What the hell are you talking about? Why would you give up your practice here to move to some shitty small town?'

'Because I hate being in practice with Cartwright and the others,' he said grimly. 'At Masters Memorial I'd be part of a research team that could develop important vaccines. It's –'

'It's crazy!' she broke in. 'How did they come to contact you? How did they know where you were?'

'I send Gladys – the office manager of the hospital – a Christmas card every year. She recommended me along with several others. This is just an interview . . .' God, he hated these clashes with Sylvia! 'The competition will be tough. Not too many openings like this come along and –'

'I don't want to live in some small town!' she interrupted again. 'And what kind of money will they pay?' Her eyes were bright with triumph now. 'You can't afford to give up the money you're making with the group. We owe too much – the furniture, the two cars, our account at Saks –'

'The research team won't be earning the kind of money I've been seeing with the group,' he conceded wearily. 'Nowhere near it. But that doesn't matter. I'll be involved in work that has some meaning for me.'

'It *does* matter!' she shrieked. 'You can't afford to take small money! Even if they decide to offer you the job. I've worked too hard to make Cartwright like us – after all the times you've antagonized him.'

'Sylvia, do you want a divorce?' He'd known within weeks after their marriage that it was a horrible mistake. He was sure, too, that there had never been a suspected pregnancy. She wanted to marry a doctor – and he was the target. 'I won't object to fair alimony.'

'What kind of alimony could you afford if you take that research job? And no, I don't want a divorce. You'll get one over my dead body.' An irreverent thought passed through his mind: over her dead body he wouldn't need a divorce. 'I've worked hard to make a decent life for myself. You're stuck with me, Cliff. Forget about going for that interview at Masters Memorial. You're the handsome, soon-to-be-rich Dr Cliff Hendricks – the most popular member of the Cartwright Medical Center. And tonight when Dr Cartwright starts talking again about our buying a house in Druid Hills, you listen to him,' she ordered sweetly. 'Because I'll be so good, Cliffie, in a gorgeous new house of our own.'

Chapter Twenty-Two

Diane brooded endlessly about the nurse who had dared to try to press charges against Lloyd Masters. Of course, the hospital staff had rallied behind him, she thought with a mixture of frustration and contempt.

That happened six years ago – the nurse was long gone from Eden. Nobody knew where she was, Norma said; there was no way to interview her. At any rate they couldn't bring that up in the *Guardian*. It would be most of this town against the caring nurse who'd tried to stop him.

'Di, stop riding that bandwagon,' Beth reproached when they discussed this yet again a week later. 'She was probably a kook.'

'I think she was a very brave woman,' Diane said softly. Perhaps she was jumping to conclusions – but Lloyd Masters' relationship with Alison disturbed her. The only child he loved – the only child kept home. What went on in that house that nobody even guessed? Something furtive, sick?

'Let's hope she doesn't become another murder statistic,' Beth said after a pregnant pause. 'Another unsolved murder in Eden.'

Suddenly summer burst upon the town. Flowers were on lush display everywhere. Air conditioners began to hum. Residents began to water their lawns. Georgia was well ahead of New York in the seasons, Diane realized. Such deceptive serenity, such beauty here – but Eden had suffered three admittedly unsolved murders. And her father's made four. When would the murderer strike again?

On a glorious mid-May Sunday afternoon Diane, Jennie and

Beth prepared to go to a barbecue at Norma and Joe's house.

'Mommie, why can't I wear my party dress?' Jennie was wistful. 'We're going to a party, aren't we?'

'It's a barbecue,' Diane explained yet again. 'We don't wear party dresses. Beth and I are wearing our jeans.'

'All right.' Jennie sighed philosophically.

'I can't believe she'll be going into kindergarten in September. I feel so old,' Beth wailed.

'Don't let your mother hear you say that.'

Sometimes Diane worried about their limited social life. Not for herself – for Beth. They ought to join the synagogue, but each time they talked about this, they were waylaid by some issue that demanded all their attention.

Right now they were committed to Jimmy Carter's campaign for the Democratic nomination for president. No matter that they'd lost two advertisers who were staunch Republicans. Thank God, Diane thought yet again, that Mom and Uncle Erich had provided a healthy bankroll for the newspaper. They were just beginning to break even.

Arriving at Norma and Joe's modest, barnyard-red ranch house, they sniffed the pungent scent of charcoal burning on the barbecue. They admired the masses of pansies that lined the fieldstone path to the entrance.

'Hi!' Norma had heard them, was charging forward in greeting. 'How's my favourite little girl?' She leant forward to hug Jennie.

'I'm a big girl,' Jennie reproached. 'I'll be going to kindergarten soon.'

'Your roses are gorgeous.' Beth sniffed them.

'They owe a huge debt to "Gardening with Gina".' Norma gazed with candid curiosity from Beth to Diane. They'd been this route before.

'Gina's identity is her secret. But she's great, isn't she?'

Diane was pleased that Gerry seemed far less tense, more secure than in the past. She was even considering going public. 'I'm working my way up to it. I know my father will be furious.

But for the first time in my life I'm not catering to anybody. Only to me.'

'Who's hungry?' Joe demanded good-humouredly. 'I've got burgers all set to go.'

'Just smelling the charcoal makes us hungry,' Beth called back to him.

Involuntarily Diane remembered a barbecue here over five years ago, when one of Norma's friends – Gail, she recalled, who was in the midst of an ugly divorce now – had remarked on her resemblance to Gerry. Thank God, nobody else had picked up on that.

The women settled themselves on chairs on the patio while Jennie joined Joe at the barbecue. The afternoon was summer hot, but the heat was alleviated by a breeze from the Chattahoochee. Diane was conscious of a rare sense of tranquillity.

'How're you feeling?' she asked Norma.

'Tired. Tired all the time. But it's good,' Norma said softly, 'because I know it's part of being pregnant. We didn't want to admit it, but we were spooked by the calendar. The years were running by so fast – but fate took a hand.'

'Is it still a secret?' Beth asked. 'Or have you told Gladys?'

'I told her, and she was sweet about my staying on as long as I felt I could handle it. She pointed out that if I went into labour on the job, it would save me rushing to the hospital.'

'What's doing with the research department?' Beth probed, knowing, Diane understood, how *she* was dying to ask that. The *Herald* and the *Evening News* carried only vague progress reports.

'Oh, the Chief of Staff and the Board of Directors were interviewing all week.' Norma glowed now. 'Gladys was out of her mind that they took up her suggestion and contacted Cliff Hendricks. He came in for an interview on Tuesday.' Did Norma realize she was cold and trembling? 'Gladys says he's way out front among those who've been interviewed so far.' Norma hesitated. 'That won't bother you, will it, Di?' She was all at once uneasy.

'Oh, no . . .' Diane managed a light chuckle. 'Cliff and I saw a lot of each other way back when. That's all water under the bridge. But I'm glad he's in the running. He was so gung ho about research – particularly in paediatrics.'

Norma wavered a moment. 'Gladys says he's married now. He'd be giving up a very lucrative practice, but he's convinced the Board that this is what he wants to do with his life.'

'Norma, bring out the salad bowl,' Joe ordered. 'The burgers will be ready in another few minutes.'

Diane's mind was in chaos. She was happy for Cliff, terrified for herself. Cliff – and his wife – would be living here in Eden. She was bound to run into them eventually. At first, they'd be busy settling in. Cliff, always conscientious, would be too involved in his work to be socializing to any serious extent. He wouldn't read the *Guardian* – he wouldn't have time. She clutched at this knowledge. Besides, they hadn't seen each other since December 1970. That was another lifetime for both of them.

She was subconsciously aware that Norma was setting the table on the patio. Norma and Beth went into the house, returned with a huge salad bowl, paper plates, glasses for the pitcher of iced tea. Jennie was having a ball, Diane told herself, hearing Jennie's laughter as she cavorted with Joe. Cliff would have been such an adoring father.

Diane forced herself to join the conversation as they settled themselves at the table.

'Hey, the local betting is that Jimmy Carter will walk off with the nomination at the Democratic Convention in July. On the first ballot,' Joe chortled. He had crossed over from the Republican camp to become an enthusiastic Democrat.

'Yeah. Then comes Election Day in November.' Norma was grim.

'Don't be like that,' Beth chided. 'Most voters are so disillusioned with all the happenings in Washington. Watergate and the craziness with Nixon and his administration have convinced them we need a fresh voice in the White House.'

'An outsider – and that's Carter,' Diane pointed out. He was a state senator and a one-term governor. 'He's new to the national scene.'

'I was surprised to hear some people predict he'll even carry a chunk of the South,' Joe said. 'Wow, wouldn't it be great to see a Georgian in the White House? Half of Eden would run up to Washington for the inauguration.'

With a sigh of relief Cliff closed the door behind the moving crew. They'd been damn lucky to find a house on such short notice. He'd made the choice on his own – Sylvia had refused to come to Eden to look at what the broker had to offer.

'Our furniture is too big for these creepy little rooms,' Sylvia complained, glancing about the modest living room stacked now with pyramids of cartons.

'What doesn't fit we can store in the basement.' He reminded himself he'd vowed to avoid arguments with Sylvia. 'And it's a rental. We're not buying.'

'I'm starving,' she said flatly. 'Let's go out for lunch before we start opening up boxes.' She grunted in disgust. 'It'll take for ever to get everything put away. We'll be at it all week.'

His mother and father had offered to come down to help, but Cliff had insisted that wasn't necessary. They'd been shocked when he told them he was dropping the Druid Hills practice, but they'd understood. He felt a rush of love for them. He was living out the values they'd instilled in him. They tried to pretend they loved Sylvia – but he knew they were disappointed in his choice of a wife.

Unwarily he remembered how much they'd liked Diane, that one time they'd met her. Living here in Eden was going to be traumatic for a while. The town was full of ghosts. In truth, he'd been astonished when Sylvia refused a divorce. And disappointed. He'd put himself in thraldom for life. Sylvia would forever bitch about their not being wealthy, about how dull life was in a small town like this. Already she was voicing the old cliché, 'They pull in the sidewalks at 9 p.m.!' But she wouldn't relinquish being 'the doctor's wife'.

For a while he'd almost convinced himself they could be a family. With an intensity that startled him, he yearned for a child. But Sylvia was in no rush: 'We're young. It's time to enjoy life. Who needs to be tied down to kids? Later maybe . . .'

Diane cut out the article in the *Herald* that announced the arrival of the first two doctors on the Masters Memorial research team. She felt recurrent guilt that Jennie, on some jaunt with Elise and her small group, might pass Cliff on the street and never know that here was her father. She was ever tense at the possibility that one day Cliff and she would come face to face, and she must play out the script she'd written for herself.

People here in town accepted that she was divorced from a Vietnam veteran who'd given up all claims to their daughter. The three months' difference she'd set in Jennie's age was precious protection. If they should ever meet – and she dreaded this possibility – Cliff would be convinced Jennie couldn't be his child. Simple mathematics would tell him this.

But when Jennie started kindergarten in September, her real birth date would be on record. Diane had promised herself that they'd celebrate Jennie's birthday next week right on schedule. She and Beth had made a point up till now about being vague about actual birth dates, but now Jennie was old enough to question this. Still, nobody would run to Cliff and say, 'Jennie was born in mid-July.'

Each time she ventured on the street Diane asked herself if this would be the day she'd encounter Cliff. Norma reported she'd seen him at the hospital.

'It was Old Home Week for a few minutes there,' Norma blithely reported. 'And he's still Gladys's fair-haired boy.'

A week later Norma called to say she'd met Cliff's wife.

'She's the ambitious type,' Norma said. 'She probably loathes living in Eden – and hates it that Cliff is into research. She's not the type to yearn to see her husband win a Nobel Prize.

She's more interested in a seventeen-room mansion with an Olympic-size swimming pool and a matching summer house at St Simon's. Gladys hated her on sight.'

Diane commanded herself not to spend every waking hour thinking about Cliff. He hadn't the faintest notion that she was here in Eden. He was too busy even to think about it. She was relieved that he lived in a suburban area on the other side of town. Focus on the newspaper, she told herself. Keep too busy to think about Cliff. She couldn't afford not to focus on the newspaper; they were overspending the budget again because of their support for Jimmy Carter.

A day before Jennie's fifth birthday Jimmy Carter was nominated as the Democratic Party's candidate for the presidency, with Walter Mondale as the vice-presidential candidate. The *Herald* and the *Evening News* were running virulent attacks on the Democratic candidates. Still, Ron contended, there was a lot of anti-Washington feeling in Eden – as in much of the nation.

'Keep beating the drums for Carter,' he encouraged. 'The guy may just make it.'

For Jennie's birthday Diane had arranged with Elise to have a party at the Tucker apartment that afternoon, with Elise's small pre-school group, Jennie's friends. All four of the little girls were euphoric at the prospect of a party. Jennie insisted on consulting the other three about the birthday cake – '*chocolate*!' – and the ice-cream. Diane took Jennie with her to select paper plates, napkins, party favours. Hearing about the prospective party, Gerry had promised to supply flowers for the table and miniature corsages to accompany each place setting.

'Jennie knows now that her birthday is 15 July,' Diane said sombrely, 'not later, the way we said when we first came down here.'

'Nobody'll think anything about it. Don't get hyper, Di.'

Diane was distressed at being detained at the office until almost time for the party to start. She'd hoped to be there at least half an hour earlier.

'Cool it,' Beth soothed when the difficult advertiser had finally left and Diane gathered together the collection of party balloons. 'You'll be there in plenty of time.'

'They'll be watching the clock,' Diane worried, and suddenly smiled. 'They're so proud of being able to tell time.'

'Go,' Beth prodded. 'And remind Jennie we'll have our own little dinner party tonight.'

Diane pulled into the parking area behind the apartment complex simultaneously with Gerry.

'I'm awfully late,' Gerry apologized, emerging from her white Mercedes with a huge bouquet of summer flowers and a box lid containing the tiny corsages. 'Wouldn't you know I'd have a flat today?'

'It's OK, Gerry. Here, let me take the box.' She gazed in admiration at the tiny, exquisite, be-ribboned corsages. 'Oh, they'll flip when they see these!'

In the Tucker living room Elise was helping the little girls set the party table. In moments the room radiated a festive atmosphere.

'Gerry, stay for the party,' Diane urged on impulse. 'Maybe you'll tell them a story later. They love your story-telling hour at the library.'

'If you think they'd like that . . .' Gerry seemed on the point of retreating into shyness.

'Gerry, they'll love it!'

At shortly before five Diane and Gerry, in high spirits, left the party. The little girls had been drafted to help Elise with the clean-up.

'That was fun,' Gerry said. 'Thanks for asking me to stay.'

'Oh, while you're here, why don't we stop off at my apartment and let me give you my copy of *Ragtime*? You said you'd like to read it.'

'Great.'

Gerry was lonely, Diane thought. With all that family – all that money – she was lonely. But her husband had stopped using her as a whipping post. Thank God, she'd had the strength to stand her ground with him.

'The apartment is kind of messy,' Diane said, unlocking the door. 'Beth and I wait for the weekend to pull everything together.'

'I read somewhere that housekeeping these days is far less efficient than it was twenty years ago because so many women are out there working.' Gerry sighed. 'I feel so useless sometimes.'

'But you're not,' Diane protested gently. 'You do volunteer work. You're writing for the *Guardian* . . .'

'I'm so grateful that you let me.'

'The book's in my bedroom,' Diane told her. 'I'll just be a minute.'

Diane found the book beneath several others that were scheduled for her bedtime reading, returned to the living room, and stopped dead. Her throat was suddenly tight. Her heart pounding. She'd forgotten about Mom's photograph on the bookcase. Gerry was standing there, the photograph in one hand. Her face was drained of colour.

'Gerry . . .' So often she'd wanted to tell Gerry, yet she knew she shouldn't.

'Diane . . .' Gerry repeated the name as though drawing it from a distant past. 'You're Kevin's child. Kevin and Sophie's Diane.'

'So often I wanted to tell you,' Diane whispered. 'But I didn't want anybody to know. I was afraid –'

'I can't believe it.' Gerry's face grew luminous. 'Oh, Diane, how wonderful!' She held out her arms and Diane rushed into her embrace. 'I thought about Sophie and you through the years. You wouldn't remember, of course . . .' Her laughter was shaky. 'But twice when I was home from school I was allowed to baby-sit for you. Di, you were a precious baby – I loved you so much. I cried when Sophie ran off that way with you. First to lose Kevin that way, then the two of you.'

'There's so much you don't know.' Diane struggled for calm. 'Mom *had* to run off to New York. Your father was threatening to have her committed. He said she had lost her mind when my father died that way. But he knew where to find Mom and me. He knew Mom could only run home to her brother. He never once tried to contact Mom.' She paused. 'Mom told me so many times, "you were his only grandchild, and he never even held you in his arms." I don't know what he told you, Gerry, but he wanted no part of Mom and me.'

'Nor of me, really.' Gerry's eyes exuded the hurt of long years. 'All he ever loved was Alison. Of course, he was terribly upset when Kevin killed himself . . .' She paused. 'He considers it the family disgrace.'

'Dad didn't kill himself,' Diane said urgently. 'He was murdered. Your father wouldn't allow the police to search for his killer. Mom told me. She and Dad were so happy together. Dad had gone to the house that night to tell his father that he and Mom were going back to New York. They were so happy, Gerry. There was no reason for him to kill himself!'

'Is that why you came back here?' Gerry asked in sudden comprehension. 'To find out who killed Kevin?'

'On the twentieth anniversary of Dad's death, Mom jumped out a seventh-storey window.'

'Oh, my God . . .'

'She left me a letter and her journals. More than anything in this world she wanted to prove that Dad hadn't committed suicide, that they had shared a wonderful marriage. His father killed her – as much as if he'd stood there and pushed her out that window.'

'If there's ever anything I can do to help you prove that Kevin didn't kill himself, you know I will.' As though at the point of exhaustion Gerry dropped into the lounge chair.

'Please, don't tell anyone that I'm Lloyd Masters' granddaughter. Let it be our secret.' Why did that sound so melodramatic?

'It seems so terrible not to acknowledge you. You're my niece

– Jennie's my grandniece.' Her eyes glowed with wonder. 'I feel as though my life is suddenly enriched.'

'I've tried so hard to dig into the past, to find some lead that would point to Dad's murderer. Not just for Mom,' Diane conceded. 'I need to know, too.'

'It was twenty-six years ago,' Gerry reminded tenderly. 'The chances are slight.'

'I'll keep looking.' This was not the time to burden Gerry with her suspicions. 'But I'm so glad you know.' Tears filled her eyes, spilled over. 'But no one else, please. No one else.'

Chapter Twenty-Three

Cliff fussed with his tie. This was the third time in his life he'd been forced to wear a dinner jacket. He hadn't been happy about it the other two times either. But Lloyd Masters had decided to give a formal dinner party on the Monday of this Labour Day weekend to welcome Masters Memorial's new research team. Why go through with this shit? They'd been on the job two months – they felt like old-timers already.

'Zip me, Cliff . . .' Sylvia offered her back to him. 'I can't reach it without breaking an arm.'

He pulled up the zipper. 'Are you sure you ought to wear something like this?' If the neckline was any lower, she'd spill right out of it, he thought – doubtful about the tastefulness of her hot-pink and black dinner dress that she boasted was a 'knock-off' of a Saint-Laurent original. A big-deal French designer, he gathered.

'It's terribly smart.' She bristled. 'Not that I'd expect you to know that.'

'Sylvia, I saw the bill from Saks,' he said grimly. 'We can't afford those prices.'

'If you expect me to live in this flea-bag of a town, at least let me have the pleasure of a decent dress when we're invited out. I've never been so bored in all my life. I was thinking I might get a job –'

'At the hospital?' he asked in alarm. The hospital was his cherished escape hatch.

'God, no.' She flinched in distaste. 'There's a woman who just opened a shop in town. She sells customized jewellery. It might be fun. You're never around. Two or three nights a week you're stuck at the hospital. You spend half the weekend there.'

'That's the research scene.' Cliff checked his watch. 'We should be leaving in a few minutes.'

'What's this guy Masters like?' Sylvia paused before the cheval mirror, lifted a hand to smooth the sleek blonde hair that fell to her shoulders.

'If he was an actor, he'd probably play a retired judge or a wealthy patriarch – which he is,' Cliff told her. 'He exudes power and loves it.'

'You don't like him,' Sylvia challenged.

'I didn't say that,' Cliff hedged. 'But I spent over three years as a resident at Masters Memorial – he saw me hundreds of times because he has a way of prowling about the hospital at odd hours – but when he met me last month, he had no recall of me.'

'He controls the purse-strings at the hospital?' Sylvia reached for her small twenties-style mesh evening bag.

'That's what I hear. He's the great philanthropist.' Cliff's smile was mocking; he'd always felt a coldness in Lloyd Masters that didn't fit his image.

'Let him be a greater philanthropist to people who work for him,' Sylvia flipped, her eyes resentful. 'We're living on peanuts.'

'Hardly that.'

'Nowhere near what you were drawing with the Druid Hills group,' she shot back. 'You were crazy not to fight for more money here.'

'You don't fight with these people. They lay out the deal. You accept or reject. OK, let's get moving.'

The Masters house was brilliantly lit as they drove up the long circular driveway. Cliff noted the old-model Valiant that belonged to Len Weinstein parked below, along with a white Mercedes and a red Jaguar. Sylvia would be pleased. She said it was gauche to be the first to arrive at a party.

A maid opened the door, led Cliff and Sylvia to a living room that was almost as large as their entire house. Lloyd Masters strode forward to greet them with a gracious smile, a courtly bow for Sylvia. He relished this role, Cliff thought, yet felt an odd detachment in him – as though they were all players in a performance he was staging. But he remembered Len's cautionary words: 'So Lloyd Masters turns you off – don't ever let on. That guy pulls all the strings at the hospital.'

'Let me introduce you to part of my family.' Masters led them to a cluster of people at the far corner of the room. At one side Len was in earnest conversation with a man Cliff recognized as a local judge.

Cliff also noticed Gerry and Clark Watson. They didn't remember him from that night in the emergency room.

'How're they treating you at the hospital?' Hugh Jamison asked, after general introductions had been made. A houseman circulating now with a tray of champagne-filled glasses. Jamison was on the Board of Directors, had sat in on the interviews, Cliff recalled.

'Fine,' Cliff assured him. 'I'm impressed by the equipment. All top of the line. Of course, I'm partial to Masters Memorial – I served my residency there.' Why was he trying so hard to be ingratiating? But at least Jamison remembered him.

A few moments later Terence Crane, the third doctor on their research team, arrived with his wife, along with a white-haired, rather grim-faced woman who had come alone. More introductions were made. Cliff felt a rush of sympathy when he realized the older woman was Dr Taylor's widow. He'd read about Taylor's murder in the Atlanta papers. He remembered him from his resident days.

Sylvia was making a point of showing her admiration for Lloyd Masters, Cliff noted. She figured what had charmed Cartwright would be effective here. He was aware, too, of the annoyed glances Masters kept aiming at the entrance to the living room. Then a tall, aloof woman in a dramatic black chiffon dinner dress appeared.

Instantly Cliff knew this was their hostess. He sensed a whiff of disapproval as Maureen was introduced to Sylvia. The cleavage, he guessed with faint amusement – and the hot-pink of Sylvia's dress. Still, Sylvia was garnering covert, and not so covert, glances of approval from the men present. Not an unusual occurrence.

'Where are Luke and Peggy?' Cliff heard Maureen demand of her husband. Her impatience obvious.

'Here they are now. And the photographer from the paper . . .'

So the dinner was to be the setting for photographs to grace the society pages of the *Herald* and the *Evening News*. Realizing this, Sylvia was euphoric. Eden might be a small town, but she was moving up to a new social level. In a bitter moment she'd confided that her family had always lived in the 'shittiest house on the block', even though the neighbourhood was decent. Her mother and father – both long dead – had been fall-down drunks.

When the photographer had completed his assignment, Maureen Masters ordered her guests into the dining room. The enormous dining table was set for eighteen. Everybody here chosen for a specific reason, Cliff surmised. He suspected that Gerry Watson wasn't entirely happy at being here, though her husband, seated next to Sylvia, seemed to be enjoying the occasion. Gerry Watson was a beautiful woman – who, somehow, reminded him of Diane.

At the dinner table Lloyd Masters began a laudatory monologue about 'my dedicated research team'. He talked with pride about the recognized – though minor – accomplishments of Dr Crane, by far the senior member of the team. The old man was praying they'd come up with something solid, Cliff interpreted, and he'd jump in to take credit. Kevin Masters Memorial Hospital was ostensibly a memorial to his son; it was more a monument to Lloyd Masters himself.

Cliff remembered Gladys's loyalty to Masters. Much of Eden felt the same way. Yet he suspected that whatever Lloyd Masters did for Eden, he did with ulterior motives. Terry Crane had warned Len and him right off that it was important to play politics here: 'That's the road to more funding – and funding is our life blood. Play the game, and we'll do well.'

Then dinner conversation took on a political note. No doubt here about whom the Masters family supported in the coming election. Cliff exchanged a brief glance with Len – the 'bleeding heart liberal from New York' – who was making an effort to hide his rejection of what was being said at the table.

The food was superb. The conversation, guided by Lloyd Masters, was hardly scintillating. Then, when the houseman and maid had served the luscious peach shortcake and were pouring coffee for the guests, Lloyd Masters tapped on his water goblet for attention and rose to his feet.

'I've had a discussion with the Board of Directors of our new research department,' he announced with relish. 'And we've agreed that it's to be known from now on as the Dr Desmond Taylor Research Department. I'm sure he would like that, Zoe.'

'He'd like it if the police department tracked down his murderer,' she said with unexpected acerbity. 'I think it's outrageous that they've just swept his murder under the rug.'

'Zoe, don't talk like that about our police department,' he scolded gently. But Cliff saw the rage in his eyes. 'You know they've done everything they possibly could. It was a tragic loss to all of us, Zoe. Desmond was my close friend for over thirty years.'

As part of her morning routine, Diane settled at her office desk to read the *Herald* shortly after her arrival.

'That dinner party Gerry was dreading is spread all over the society pages,' she reported to Beth. Then all at once she was cold with shock. 'Cliff was at the party. Here's a photo of him with his wife.' For two months she'd walked around town with dread, fearful of encountering Cliff, even while she yearned to see him. She avoided driving past the hospital. She avoided the area where she knew he lived. Even if he should see a copy of the *Guardian*, it was unlikely he'd notice her name on the masthead, she recurrently tried to reassure herself.

'Let me see.' Beth leapt from her chair to lean over the newspaper gripped in Diane's hands, stared in silence for a moment. 'If that dress was cut any lower, her navel would be on display.'

'Norma said she used to be a nurse.' Diane fought for composure. 'She met Cliff at the hospital in Atlanta where he was treated after the accident.'

'Not exactly his type.'

'Who's to know what's his type?' It was crazy for her to be upset this way.

'Look at this!' Beth pointed to a paragraph far down on the page. 'The research department is to be named for Dr Taylor. Of course, they don't mention his murder – or that it's never been solved.'

'Doesn't that bother his wife?' Diane spied Zoe Taylor's name beneath one of the photographs. 'Doesn't she ever ask herself why this town has seen three acknowledged unsolved murders?' She remembered her mother's neverending anguish that her father's killer walked the streets unpunished.

'It happens that the police can't track down murderers. Mrs Taylor can accept that.'

'I can't!' Fresh rage rippled through Diane. 'This lovely serene town, with such ugly secrets hidden in its shadows.'

Later in the morning Gerry arrived with her garden column copy.

'Big party at the family house last night,' Beth joshed.

'I hate those parties,' Gerry said candidly.

But Diane knew it was part of a tacit deal between Clark and her to play the scene. Gerry couldn't divorce him. Her mother – the devoted Catholic when it fitted her mood – would have been outraged. And Gerry had no funds of her own. She was afraid she couldn't support herself in the outside world. If the *Guardian* ever really took off, Diane thought recklessly, they'd have a place for Gerry on their staff.

'Mrs Taylor must have been pleased that the research department is to be named for her husband.' For once, Diane thought derisively, Lloyd Masters was bypassing his own family.

'She wasn't wildly responsive,' Gerry said after a moment. Diane exchanged a swift, surprised glance with Beth. 'She's still upset that the police have never caught Dr Taylor's killer.'

'I understand they didn't make much of an effort.' Why had Mrs Taylor turned cold to her when they'd run the memorial piece on Dr Taylor? Had Lloyd Masters told her to steer clear of the *Guardian*? Perhaps she'd still hoped then that the police would come up with suspects – and a conviction.

'I was thinking about an article for the paper.' Gerry's voice brought her back to the moment. 'Actually three articles. A profile on each of the three doctors on the research department team.'

'Gerry, you'd lose your cover,' Beth pointed out.

'I may be ready for that.' Gerry's eyes were defiant. 'Do you think the *Guardian*'s readers would like background material about the research team?'

'I think it would be great.' But Diane's heart was pounding. Cliff would surely read the article when it was published, even if he'd never read the paper before. Would he see her name on the masthead?

She must face it: she couldn't hide for ever.

Cliff was self-conscious about meeting Gerry Watson for the interview for a little weekly called the *Guardian*. He was astonished that she was working with a newspaper other than the two dailies owned by her father; in a tiny way in competition with him. She'd already interviewed Len. The *Guardian*'s photographer had come to the hospital to photograph him, Len said.

'A sharp gal,' Len approved. 'She comes from New York. I wanted to ask her out for dinner or a movie, but with our nutty work schedule, I chickened out.'

'You don't call them gals,' Cliff reproached, echoing his mother. 'Where've you been the last ten years? You call them women.'

'Maybe I'll track her down and give her a buzz when it looks as though we'll have a few evenings clear.' Len's face lighted. 'My social life needs some real uplifting.'

As pre-arranged, Cliff met Gerry Watson for lunch at the diner across from the hospital. She'd suggested they make it very early or very late to avoid the crowds. He'd settled for two o'clock. At ten minutes to two, still wearing his white lab jacket, he left the hospital and hurried across the street. Walking into the diner, he spied her immediately. She was waiting for him in a rear booth, where they'd be able to talk with privacy.

Again, he asked himself if the situation with her husband had changed. It had shaken him up, back in his residency days, to realize that a gently bred, intelligent woman like Gerry Watson could be a battered wife. They had seen a fair amount of abused women in the emergency room – though usually the women were from poor backgrounds – and all covered for their men.

Len told him about a doctor on staff during his residency who had beat up his wife about once a month. 'I tried to talk to her once when she came in alone with a cut that required seven stitches. You know what she said? "I provoke him."'

'Hi.' Gerry greeted him with a warm smile, yet he felt a shyness in her that was appealing.

'Have you been waiting long?' He directed a guilty glance at his watch.

'No. I just arrived.'

A waitress approached. They ordered.

'Do you mind if I tape this?' Gerry drew a small tape recorder from a tote beside her.

'Not at all.' He was uneasy about being taped but ashamed to admit this.

The questions Gerry put to him were about what he had expected. Len had briefed him. Only when she asked him about his wife did he grow tense. He couldn't tell her his marriage was a ghastly mistake; that his wife wouldn't let him off the hook because he was expected to be her ticket to a life of privilege.

'We'd like to run a photograph with the article,' Gerry told him while she switched off the tape recorder and returned it to her tote. 'Would it be all right if we send our staff photographer over to the hospital? At a time convenient to you, of course.'

'No problem.' He liked Gerry Watson, though he thought that her sisters and her mother were icebergs.

'She'll call you,' Gerry said. 'Her name is Beth Bertonelli. Oh, would it be better to buzz you at home in the evening?'

'That might save her some chasing around.' Cliff reached into a pocket for a scrap of paper and pen, scribbled his home phone number down for her. 'If I'm not there – and my hours can sometimes be crazy – have her leave her number and I'll get back to her.'

'You might like to see the newspaper.' Gerry reached into her tote again. 'We focus mainly on community affairs, though we are going all out for Jimmy Carter.' Her eyes met his with a hint of conspiratorial laughter. They both knew her father's newspapers were waging a fierce campaign for Gerald Ford.

'Thanks for everything,' he said gently, and shoved the newspaper into the pocket of his jacket.

With his usual haste Cliff returned to the hospital. Not until past 10 p.m. did he and Len agree to call it a day.

'For a single guy this town is the pits,' Len complained, then his face brightened. 'I'm giving that photographer from the *Guardian* a call tomorrow. You know, "How did the photos come out?" And then I'll suggest dinner Saturday night. She's a New Yorker – we're *simpatico*.'

Cliff chuckled sympathetically. 'Good luck.'

'Good night – see you tomorrow.' Len took off.

Removing his lab jacket Cliff realized the folded over copy of the *Guardian* was in one pocket. He hung up the jacket, took out the newspaper and scanned the first page. Now he turned to the inside. The 'New Arrivals' column held his attention for a moment. The town was growing – but it would never rival Atlanta, for which he was grateful. He liked the small-town flavour of Eden.

His eyes moved unsuspectingly to the masthead, clung to

what he saw there. He was cold with shock. His throat tightened. 'Co-Publishers: Diane Phillips and Beth Bertonelli.'

Be realistic, he ordered himself. It was another Diane Phillips. But that possibility was immediately eradicated. Diane's friend in New York had been called Beth. It was Beth who was to go with her to the hospital for the abortion. The abortion she hadn't wanted.

He stood immobile, struggling for calm, digesting what he had just discovered. *Diane was here in Eden*. But he wasn't free to go to her, to plead with her to forgive him. He was tied for ever to a wife who'd never release him.

Chapter Twenty-Four

Cliff paced about his special corner in the lab, made a pretense of checking on experiments in work. At brief intervals his eyes darted to the clock. Beth Bertonelli was due at any moment to take his photo for the *Guardian* article. Sara, the department's receptionist, would summon him when she arrived. It had been arranged for them to use the smaller conference room.

The phone rang. He lunged to pick it up.

'Hendricks.'

'The photographer's here,' Sara told him. 'Come make like a movie star.'

'I'll be right there.' Diane had to know he was here. She'd authorized the article. Beth must know about Diane and him – she was Diane's best friend. Gerry Watson had suggested and arranged for the articles, he gathered. Diane hadn't tried to sidetrack them. Was it her way of letting him know they could exist in the same town as though nothing had ever happened between them?

He hurried out of the lab and down the hall to the reception area. His mind was in chaos. How was he to handle this situation? Pretend there'd never been anything serious between Diane and him? They'd planned to be married when he finished his residency. Beth knew about that. She knew about the abortion.

'Hi.' He managed to sound casual as Beth turned from the window at the sound of his approach. 'I'm Cliff Hendricks.'

'Beth Bertonelli.' Her smile was polite, inscrutable. 'I gather you've set up a place for our shooting.'

'Yeah. A conference room right down the hall here.'

He led the way, forcing himself to make polite conversation about the weather. Inside the conference room she opened her camera bag, brought out her camera, squinted at the floor-to-ceiling expanse of glass.

'We won't need lights.'

For the next fifteen minutes she focused on positioning him, took several shots, tried another angle, still another. At last, with the roll of film used up, she called the session finished.

'Beth, can we talk a minute,' he said compulsively.

'Sure . . .' But her eyes were wary.

'I can't believe there are two Diane Phillipses with friends named Beth.' He forced a smile, took a deep breath. 'Your partner is the same Diane Phillips who worked here at the hospital about six years ago?' His heart was pounding now. He was conscious of a knot in his stomach.

'Yes.' She was nervous, anxious to break away.

'We – we knew each other then.' God, he sounded like an idiot. 'How has Di been these last years?'

'She's fine now. She married a few months after she left here. A Vietnam veteran she'd known in college.'

Beth was avoiding eye contact. She thought he was a bastard, Cliff told himself.

'They have a darling little girl. Jennie will soon be five.'

His mind was jolted to fast computation. She'd gotten pregnant again just months after the abortion. Jennie – her little girl – should have been theirs.

'The marriage was a mistake. They got a divorce when Jennie was a baby. Di took back her single name.'

Diane must know he was married. How could he ever make her understand how it had happened? But what difference would it make? She hated him. The way she'd run off had made that clear. Sylvia had a stranglehold on him – she'd never agree to a divorce.

'Tell Di I wish her all the best. She's very special . . .' His

267

voice was husky. 'I – I hope we'll run into each other one of these days.'

'I'll tell her.' Beth zipped her camera case shut, gave him a farewell smile and took off.

Enmeshed in an aura of disbelief, Diane listened to Beth's report of her encounter with Cliff.

'Cliff's not angry at you – he's angry at himself,' Beth told her. 'He's still in love with you. He's a tormented man.'

'But he married a blonde nurse named Sylvia,' she reminded Beth. So what if Cliff loved her? It was too late for them.

'I don't know how she hooked him, but I'll bet it was with wild manipulations. Norma says she's working part time at Some Place Special.' Diane stared blankly at Beth. 'That fancy new gift shop in town.' One of their advertisers. 'The one that'll make up earrings and necklaces to match an outfit. Pricey for this town. I don't think it'll last long.'

'Tell me again what Cliff said about me,' Diane probed, knowing this was childish. What did it matter?

'He said, "I wish her all the best. She's very special." Then he said he hoped he'd see you around one day.'

'There'd be no point in that.' Diane was suddenly apprehensive. 'And there's no way he'll ever know that he's Jennie's father. I won't let that happen.'

'You're getting paranoid. Even if he knew, he wouldn't try to take custody of Jennie. No court in this country would let that happen.'

Normally autumn was Diane's favourite season – both in New York and in Eden. In the autumn the oppressive summer heat at last dropped. This year she was scarcely aware of the change of season. Repeatedly she reran in her mind the report of Beth's meeting with Cliff. He wasn't angry with her. He still loved her. But their timing was still all wrong. There were tormented moments when she considered closing down the *Guardian*, running back to New York. Yet perversely she couldn't bring herself to leave Eden – Cliff was here. And her father's murder still remained unsolved.

Jennie had started kindergarten and was enthralled with her schoolgirl status. Gerry had 'come out of the closet' and her garden column and articles offered Gerry Watson as her byline. If her father objected, Gerry ignored it. Beth was going out regularly with Len Weinstein. Each time Beth brought home new gossip about Sylvia. Diane scolded her for repeating this – yet she absorbed it with agonized hunger.

'Len says Cliff practically lives at the hospital. He hates to go home. And you know how gossip flies around this town. Their maid told somebody else's maid that Cliff and Sylvia are fighting all the time.'

Diane told herself that Cliff's marriage, his wife, was of no concern of hers. From the owner of Some Place Special, who came in every week to make some minor changes in her ad, she knew Sylvia continued to work there part time. The owner seemed pleased with her.

'Sylvia brings in the men who're looking for gifts for their wives. They like her to advise them.' Nancy, the gift shop owner, chuckled. 'And they just love looking down that cleavage she always offers.'

A few days before Beth's birthday Diane wandered over to inspect the windows – denying to herself that she was overwhelmed with curiosity about the woman Cliff had married. She lingered in ambivalence, then walked inside. This was insane, she reproached herself, her face hot with guilt.

Nancy came forward with a welcoming smile. The blonde in the tight skirt and the silk blouse with one too many buttons opened at the neck was Sylvia. Diane recognized her from the photograph in the *Herald*.

'I'm looking for a birthday gift for Beth,' Diane explained to Nancy. That was Cliff's wife? The last woman in the world she would have expected him to marry. 'Something in silver . . .' She tried not to stare in Sylvia's direction. 'Beth loves silver.'

*   *   *

Election day arrived. Many Georgians were ecstatic when Jimmy Carter won the presidency. The *Herald* and the *Evening News* lamented this in colourful prose, predicted galloping inflation coupled with recession. The Masters papers insisted that while the country might have gone for Carter – and he had won by a narrow margin – it was understood that Eden had voted overwhelmingly for Ford.

With the approach of Thanksgiving Elise and Ron invited Diane, Jennie and Beth to the mid-afternoon holiday dinner at their apartment. Lou and Sally Tucker would be there, too.

'What shall I bring?' Diane asked.

'Bring yourselves,' Elise said. 'I'm making the turkey and the side dishes, Mom's bringing a pumpkin pie and a chocolate cake. Nicole doesn't like pumpkin pie, but she adores chocolate cake.'

'I'll bring the cranberry sauce,' Diane decided. 'I'll let Jennie help me make it. She'll love that.'

Diane awoke early on Thanksgiving morning – the temperature low for Eden – and lay in bed while heat rose in the radiators. In a little while it would be warm. Her eyes turned to Jennie, sleeping soundly in the other twin bed. Her mind darted backwards through the years to Thanksgivings in New York with her mother and her uncle. For her mother holidays had been bittersweet occasions as she recalled the holidays she'd spent with Dad, when they'd been a family.

Diane left her bed to pull up the blanket Jennie had just kicked aside. She crossed to the window, gazed out at the grey morning through a chink in the drapes. Would Cliff be going to his parents' home this morning?

His parents had been so sweet that Thanksgiving Cliff had taken her home with him. They were warm, loving – they would have been such wonderful grandparents. That Thanksgiving six years ago she and Cliff had been so sure where their lives were heading. Looking back, she raged inwardly, it was so easy to see the mistakes that had been made. Always for Cliff and her the timing had been wrong.

'Mommie –' Jennie called out with an aura of heady anticipation in her voice – 'when will we start making the cranberry sauce?'

Cliff prowled impatiently about the small, overheated living room. Sylvia was never satisfied unless the house was a tropical jungle.

'Sylvia, we'll be late,' he called down the hall to the master bedroom.

'There'll be nobody on the road this morning.' Her voice was petulant. She'd wanted to have Thanksgiving dinner in the one restaurant in town that was open today. Without his parents. 'We'll make good time.'

She'd be sugary sweet to Mom and Dad when they first arrived at the house, Cliff guessed, but in two hours she'd be restless, watching the clock, looking for some excuse to cut out early. Mom and Dad would pretend not to notice. They were always uncomfortable, unsure of themselves, in Sylvia's presence.

He remembered the Thanksgiving six years ago when he'd taken Di home with him. He and Di had pretended they were just casual friends from the hospital, but they knew Di was special to him. They'd waited eagerly in the weeks ahead for some word, some indication that he and Di were serious. But too soon it was all over between them. Nothing in his life had gone right since then – except the job at Masters Memorial.

Gerry sat in silence beside Clark while they drove to the Masters house for Thanksgiving dinner. At intervals he made a sarcastic remark. He hated the holiday dinners with the four children in the family present – noisy and fighting among themselves, vying for adult attention. How beautiful it would have been, Gerry thought, to spend the holiday with Di and Jennie! So quickly they'd become precious to her – her secret family.

'Luke will be sullen because I'm on the City Council and the Old Man is plotting for a seat in Congress for me – with no

271

political plans for him,' Clark predicted, momentarily smug.

Could Dad push him into a seat in Congress? She wouldn't go to Washington with him.

'Hugh will be pissed because the Old Man still hasn't appointed him publisher.'

'You've moved beyond the newspaper,' Gerry reminded him. He'd been sleeping in the guest room since that night she'd put him on warning. But several times lately he'd come home with the scent of a sultry perfume about him, stray blonde hairs on his jacket. It would be so humiliating if people here in town discovered he was having an affair. But if he was, she reminded herself in a flurry of rebellion, she'd have grounds for divorce.

'Oh God, the mob's already here.' Clark groaned as he pulled up into the driveway behind cars belonging to his in-laws. 'The zoo's in session.'

Gerry and Clark joined the gathering clan in the living room. Gerry lingered to chat with her nieces and nephew rather than joining her sisters. Clark was right in complaining they were terribly spoilt, but only in material things. They had seen more of nursemaids and counsellors at summer camp through the years than they had of their parents. To a stranger, she thought bitterly, they would appear the ideal family, three generations gathering together for Thanksgiving dinner. Logs burning in the fireplace. Aromas of turkey roasting in the oven permeating the house. Admittedly a family touched by tragedy, she conceded – but in the eyes of most townspeople that lent them a special aura.

For one heated moment her eyes clashed with those of her father, listening with an air of boredom to an argument between Luke and Hugh. Then his eyes swung away. She'd anticipated an angry dressing-down from her father when he discovered she was working for the *Guardian*. It hadn't happened. He was too involved with his determination to move Clark from City Councilman to Congressman to have time for her.

*　　*　　*

Only days after Thanksgiving Eden began its preparation to welcome the Christmas season. The traditional red and green lights were strung at frequent intervals across Main Street. Christmas trees were being set up. Some shopkeepers were already decorating store windows. With 1977 approaching Diane was painfully conscious of the passage of time. She hoped – though she suspected this was futile – that Mrs Taylor would at last go public with demands that the police make a stronger effort to track down her husband's killer.

On a cold grey morning, when residents were guessing that snow, rare in Eden, might be falling by afternoon, Diane opened up the office alone. Beth was driving over to Atlanta in pursuit of a new account. She and Beth were both encouraged by an increase in advertisers in the last three weeks, which more than compensated for their loss in the heat of the pre-election campaigns. At last they were being accepted as a permanent feature in Eden.

Diane settled at her desk to work on the layout for the next issue. In the corner of her mind she debated about trying to talk with Zoe Taylor about their running an article on her distress that Dr Taylor's murderer had not been apprehended. Beth would be against it; they'd be asking for another attack by the *Herald*. Yet such a feature could be the launch pad to unearth the other unsolved murders. All this time in Eden and she'd accomplished *nothing*.

She glanced up to see a man standing indecisively outside the door looking in. All at once she was cold with shock. *It was Cliff.* As though aware that he had captured her attention, he reached for the knob, pulled the door open, walked inside and towards the counter.

In a haze of disbelief she rose from her desk, moved towards the front of the store. Her heart was hammering. It was though the years had melted away. She remembered their months together, the joy of being with him. For Mom there had been one love in her life. For her there would be only Cliff.

'Diane . . .' His voice was a caress. 'I know I shouldn't have come. I have no right . . .' His eyes seemed to devour the sight of her. 'But I couldn't go on this way, knowing you were in town. I had to see you.'

'It's been a long time.' This was insane. He was married – he wasn't free to come to her.

'Beth told me about your marriage, your divorce. Your little girl.'

'Jennie's wonderful.' Oh, he would love her! But that couldn't ever be.

'I've made some terrible mistakes. Crazy ones.' He shook his head in self-reproach.

'We all make mistakes,' she whispered, yearning to alleviate the hurt, the desperation she sensed in him.

'I want all the best for you, Di. I had to come and tell you that myself.'

'I was happy for you when I heard you had been chosen to join the research team at Masters Memorial. I knew how much it would mean to you.' How could she stand here this way and carry on a conversation with Cliff?

'I tried so hard to find you. I called every Phillips in New York. Have you any idea how many there are?'

'We had an unlisted phone,' Diane explained. This is unreal.

'I know I shouldn't be saying this.' He paused, took a deep breath. 'I've asked Sylvia over and over again for a divorce. She swears she'll never let it happen. But if I could just once in a while drop by here and see you for a few minutes, it would mean so much to me.'

'Here at the office,' she stipulated after a moment. How could she deny herself this? 'I – I think that would be all right.'

'I'll always love you, Di.' His eyes clung to her face for a moment, then he turned and walked towards the door.

He reached for the knob – and something snapped in her mind.

'Cliff . . .'

'Yes?' He spun round to face her.

'There was no marriage for me. No divorce.'

'Your daughter?' The question was a strangled gasp.

'*Our* daughter, Cliff.' How could she be telling him this? But Cliff would never do anything to hurt Jennie or her – she *knew* that.

'Di!' His eyes radiated a joyous shock, a soaring tenderness.

'She was our baby. I couldn't give her up.' Her face was luminous. Let Cliff know he had a child. It would help him to survive his stormy, captive marriage. 'But nobody must know,' she exhorted. 'Nobody!'

'Nobody,' he promised, eager to reassure her, struggling to absorb this revelation with a blend of joy and wonder. 'Do you have photographs?' A wistfulness shone from him. 'Could I see them?'

'I have snapshots in my wallet.'

She returned to her desk, fumbled in a drawer for her purse, brought out her wallet. As though afraid to trespass, Cliff waited at the counter.

'She looks just like you,' Diane told him and handed her wallet across the counter. 'Like her grandmother on your side.'

'I can't believe it . . .' He shook his head. 'I can't believe it. It's wonderful.'

This was insane, Diane chastised herself. She had done what she had promised herself would never happen. She had no will in Cliff's presence.

'Would you like to see Jennie?' Involuntarily the words escaped her.

'Di, it would be the most wonderful moment in my life.'

'Saturday,' she decided. 'Beth and I will bring her into the office with us. Come in to pick up a copy of the *Guardian*. But Cliff, she mustn't know. She must never know.'

Chapter Twenty-Five

Close to noon Beth returned from Atlanta. Hounded by self-recriminations Diane reported her encounter with Cliff.

'I know it was crazy, Beth, but I couldn't stop myself.' She shook her head in disbelief. 'I'd sworn all along that Cliff would never know about Jennie. Why did I fall apart that way?'

'You'll have to draw lines,' Beth warned, disturbed by this turn of events. 'And it'll be rough, now that you've opened the door.'

'I know Cliff would never do anything to harm Jennie. He stood there – and I had this compulsion to tell him. It – it just spilled out.'

'Len says Cliff's so unhappy – though he loves the work he's doing. I understand his wife just drives him up the wall.'

'What's with you and Len?' Diane made a determined effort to move into less painful territory. 'You're seeing a lot of him these days.'

'Almost any night he gets away from the hospital at a decent hour. Which actually isn't too often.' But Beth's conversation, Diane thought tenderly, was peppered with comments by Len.

'I suspect it's getting serious,' Diane teased.

'I think he's serious. If he is – and I *am* –' Beth confessed – 'can you imagine my mother? I can just hear her talking about "my son-in-law, the doctor". But hey, let's stop jumping the gun. This could all be in my head.' But her eyes told Diane she didn't believe that at all.

'You'll be here with me on Saturday,' Diane pointed out.

Normally, they took turns coming in on Saturday mornings. 'Don't leave me alone with Cliff.'

'Jennie will be with you,' Beth reminded. 'But I'll be there, too,' she promised.

'My head is in such an uproar – like a food processor gone berserk.' She managed a shaky laugh. 'I keep asking myself – have I made a horrible mistake?' It had been so agonizing these last months – knowing Cliff was in town, yearning to see him.

'Play it by ear. You know you can't get involved with Cliff again. But who's to be hurt if you see each other now and then? In the right surroundings,' Beth emphasized. 'Not alone.'

'We both know that, Mommie.' Diane's smile was tender. 'I'll be good.' But already she was counting the days till Saturday – when she'd see Cliff again.

Still, doubts tugged at her. What if Cliff, in an unguarded moment, said something to his wife about Jennie? She shouldn't have told him. Yet, perversely, she was impatient to bring him together with Jennie, to see the joy and wonder and love that was sure to shine from his eyes.

In a sheer black 'barely there' bra and matching bikini panties, Sylvia sat at the edge of the queen-size bed – tense with rage as she talked on the phone with Cliff.

'What do you mean, you can't make Nancy's cocktail party?' she shrieked. 'I told her we'd be there!'

'I can't get away. We're having a conference in half an hour. It'll probably go on until eight or nine. You go to the party alone.'

'I don't want to go alone! I told Nancy I'd be coming with you. Nancy wants men there. She's trying to add a little glamour to this town.'

'I'm sorry,' Cliff said tiredly.

'You'll be sorrier,' she warned with syrupy sweetness. 'You know when you make me mad I just go on another shopping spree.'

'Sylvia, stop it! Don't force me to call in your charge cards.'

'Don't you dare threaten me! I'm warning you, Cliff –' She paused as Betty Lou, who came in to clean and cook four days a week, appeared in the doorway with the freshly pressed cocktail dress Sylvia had planned to wear to Nancy's cocktail party. 'Just lay it across the bed, Betty Lou. And you can leave now – we'll be eating out tonight.'

'Yes, ma'am.' Betty Lou glowed affectionately. In Betty Lou's eyes, she was like a movie star, Sylvia understood. Betty Lou's daughter was running around town in her discarded Saks' clothes.

'Sylvia?' Cliff's voice brought her back to the phone.

'I'm not going to the party,' she told him. 'And don't expect dinner when you come home. I told Betty Lou we'd be eating out after the cocktail party. Pick up Chinese or something for yourself.'

Off the phone Sylvia sat hunched at the edge of the bed, seething with supposed hurts. Cliff was such a bastard! Why had he dragged her to this awful town? Why had he given up that gorgeous practice? Then a smile lifted the corners of her mouth.

She'd call Nancy and make some excuse about not coming to the party. Nancy wouldn't care if she didn't show – it was male guests Nancy wanted. She glanced at the clock on her night table. Clark would still be at the office. She'd buzz him and suggest they go out to a motel and play house.

She called Clark on his private line – he'd told her always to do that.

'How are you, sugar?' she purred when he picked up. If he could see her this minute – in black bra and bikini – he'd be popping out of his pants.

'I'd be lots happier if we were together doing what we like best.' That hoarseness in his voice told her he was already doing it in his mind. God, he was a rabbit most of the time, she thought impatiently, but she meant to teach him better.

'I'm free,' she drawled. 'Shall I meet you at the usual place?'

'I'm running short of time,' he apologized and paused. 'Look, 'why don't I pick you up and we'll run over to the house?'

'What house?' She was alarmed. Sometimes he got too reckless.

'Not mine,' he soothed. 'I've got the keys to the Old Man's house. You know, for emergencies when nobody's there. He's in Montgomery for two days. Maureen's up in New York for a week on a shopping spree. The servants are on their winter vacation. I'll pick you up in twenty minutes. OK?'

'Yeah, OK.' She churned with anticipation. She hadn't been inside the Masters house except for that dinner party not long after she and Cliff had moved to town. A lowly research doctor and his wife didn't move in the same circles as the great Lloyd Masters and his wife. It would be a hoot to do it in their house. 'In twenty minutes, sugar.'

Wouldn't it be something if Clark decided to divorce that dumb wife of his? He was talking about running for Congress soon. Wow, it could be a real ball to be a congressman's wife! That would be moving up in the world.

She rushed into action. Wear the cocktail dress with the customized earrings Nancy had made for her. She pulled on the dress, which clung to every curvaceous inch of her, reached into a drawer for sheer black pantyhose. She was humming under her breath by the time she headed downstairs to wait for Clark. Who needed Nancy's shitty cocktail party with a bunch of horny women floating around?

Sylvia watched from the foyer for Clark's car to roll into the driveway. He'd want to make a fast getaway, she assumed – neighbours could be so nosy. At least, this time of year it got dark early. There he was! She hurried from the foyer, locked the front door, ran to the car – the door already open in welcome.

'Christmas is coming early this year,' Clark jibed, taking one hand from the wheel to fondle her breast beneath her open coat.

'Got a present for me?' Her smile was provocative.

'We've got a present for each other. In the main guest room of Lloyd Masters' mansion,' he drawled.

Yeah, she told herself, he found that amusing, too.

At the Masters house Sylvia waited while Clark pulled out his keys, unlocked the front door. With a flourish he gestured her inside. In the darkened house he carefully locked the door, took her by the hand and led her across the wide foyer to the stairs, switching on the wall sconces, which Maureen Masters boasted had come from an Italian palace.

'We'll sign ourselves in the "presidential suite",' he said mockingly, 'where my father-in-law puts up his important guests from around the country.'

The guest room was at the end of the corridor, before a flight of stairs that led to the attic. Wow, this was a huge house! Someday she'd own a place like this, give fabulous parties. Maybe in a suburb of Washington, she told herself, giddy at the prospect – when she was the wife of Congressman Clark Watson.

Clark opened the ornate door of the favoured guest room, reached inside for the wall switch. Instantly soft illumination bathed the spacious room.

'Get out of your clothes,' Clark ordered, pulling off his jacket.

'I'll help you first,' she murmured. This time she'd take charge; let Clark finally understand that she was something special.

'OK.' He was amused. 'Help me.' But while she unbuttoned his shirt, his hands were already at the waist of his slacks. He was always in such a rush – but not tonight, she promised herself.

He stood naked before her – broad-shouldered, hairy-chested, and with stomach flab that shrieked of too much liquor and overrich food.

'All right, time for action . . .' He leant amorously towards her.

'Lie down.' Her eyes were full of promise as she shoved him onto the king-size bed. 'And enjoy,' she mocked, reaching to pull the sexy black and magenta cocktail dress above her head.

She tossed it to the floor, posed before him in her black bra and sheer black pantyhose.

'Let's get this show on the road!' One of his favourite expressions, she thought with amusement. But tonight she was the director.

With provocative deliberation – breasts spilling over her bra – she leant forward to peel away her pantyhose and tossed them on the floor, noting that she'd thrown them beneath the bed's valance.

'Syl, you're not starring on a runway.'

'I'll be there.' She walked to flip off the wall switch. 'It's more romantic in the dark,' she anticipated his objection. 'I like it that way.'

In the total darkness of the room she made her way to the bed, lifted herself above him, heard his grunt of welcome as they met. Then all at once she froze.

'*Is somebody in the house?*'

'Who could be here?' His hands reached to fondle her breasts while he lifted his hips in impatience. 'Come on, show me how hot you are!'

Now she abandoned herself to passion. Here she was queen! Clark would remember tonight. He'd want reruns.

And then all at once she felt cold steel at her back. *A knife? Scissors?*

'Oh my God!' she screamed in a high, thin wail. 'No! No!'

Chapter Twenty-Six

'Mommie, I don't want to wear a cap,' Jennie rebelled as Diane came forward with cap and mittens.

'It's cold and blustery out,' Diane soothed, pulling on the colourful ski cap. 'You'll be glad you're wearing it.'

'But the sun's out, Mom –'

'It's winter,' Diane said firmly, attaching mittens to the sleeve of Jennie's jacket. This was a scene they went through regularly. She straightened up at the sound of the doorbell. 'That's Ron with Nicole. It's time to leave for school. Let's go, baby.'

'I'm not a baby.' Jennie's routine reply. But she held up her face for a goodbye kiss.

Diane trailed into the kitchen, where Beth was pouring coffee for them. They'd have breakfast later at the office, their daily extravagance. Tomorrow morning, Diane reminded herself with a recurrent blend of anticipation and apprehension, Cliff would come down to the office to see Jennie. She'd been counting the days till she saw him again, yet she was fearful of having made a wrong move.

She switched on the small radio on the counter and the tail end of a recorded programme greeted them. Then the news-caster came on.

'Local residents will be shocked to learn that murder struck Eden early yesterday –'

'Oh God!' Diane gasped, simultaneous with the newscaster's completion of his sentence.

'– evening. The body of the wife of a recently arrived doctor in town – Dr Clifford Hendricks – was discovered at dawn along the Chattahoochee River by a pair of hunters. She'd been brutally stabbed. Dr Hendricks is being questioned by the police regarding the murder of his wife. We'll bring you news bulletins as we receive them. In the Lakewood section of –'

Diane leaned over to switch off the radio, dizzy with shock.

'What could have happened?' Beth stared at Diane in disbelief.

'Cliff couldn't have had anything to do with it!'

'Look, it's natural for them to question him.' Beth was trying to be conciliatory. 'He's the husband of the victim.'

'How can we find out more about what's happening?' This wasn't like the other murders, Diane reasoned in a corner of her mind. Those other times there had been no suspects. But Cliff wasn't a suspect. *Was* he?

'Let me try to call Len. He goes to the lab early.' Beth rose to her feet. 'I'll call on the living room phone, you pick up the extension in here.'

Diane clung to the extension while Beth dialled. Len wasn't at the lab yet, she thought in despair while the phone continued to ring at the other end. Then the ringing stopped. Len's voice came to them.

'Good morning, Weinstein.'

'Len, what's happened?' Beth demanded. 'We just heard the news on the radio.'

'I don't know much more than you heard,' Len said. 'I understand the police woke up Cliff to tell them they'd found Sylvia's body. He'd gone to sleep around 1 a.m., he said. He'd thought Sylvia was out at some party –'

'The news report said the police were questioning Cliff,' Diane broke in. 'Is he a *suspect*?'

'It's natural for them to question Cliff.' Len managed to sound calm, but Diane sensed his anxiety.

'Is he being charged?' Diane demanded.

'He's just being questioned,' Len repeated and hesitated. 'Lloyd Masters has an attorney standing by with him.'

'Why Lloyd Masters?' Again, Lloyd Masters was tied into a

murder in Eden. Where were the pieces that kept eluding her?

'Cliff called me from the police station to let me know he couldn't be at the hospital for the meeting that had been rescheduled for this morning. I did what everybody does when there's a crisis at the hospital. I called Lloyd Masters. He said he'd have an attorney over within an hour.'

'Cliff shouldn't be represented by a local attorney,' Diane said instantly, knowing this sounded irrational. 'Have Cliff's parents been notified?'

'I'm sure they have,' Len soothed. 'I'll try to get permission to see him later. I'll get back to you.'

He rang off and Diane stood motionless by the phone. Beth returned to the kitchen.

'We'd better leave for the office,' she said gently.

'Let's take the radio.' How was this murder linked to the others? Instinct – or was it fragile hope? – told Diane it was. She searched her mind for answers.

'They'll question Cliff, then let him go. He'll call you.' Beth was determinedly optimistic. 'This isn't another of the serial murders.'

'Isn't it?' Diane challenged. 'All right, maybe I'm reaching. But this is the wife of a doctor on the staff of Masters Memorial Hospital. There *is* a connection.'

Diane and Beth drove to the office. Immediately Diane plugged in the radio, turned it on, the sound muted but audible enough to alert them to a bulletin. Not until shortly after noon did the radio station come forth with any news.

'Dr Cliff Hendricks is being held for the grand jury. The district attorney expects an indictment for the murder of his wife.'

Two minutes later Diane was on the phone to Len, guessing that he was accomplishing little in the lab today.

'Len, why are they holding Cliff?' She had to keep cool. She couldn't help Cliff if she fell apart.

'Cliff has no alibi for the time Sylvia was murdered.' Len sounded uneasy. 'Our conference last evening was cancelled.

He went home. He was alone at the house. He told the police Sylvia had gone to a cocktail party – but she never arrived there.'

'Who's representing him?'

'Some lawyer named Gregory Lewis,' Len told her. 'I understand he's handling some deal for Masters right now.'

'Greg's a real estate lawyer. He knows little about criminal law! He hates it!' Greg would be useless as an attorney for Cliff.

'Do you know him?' Len sounded surprised.

'I did at one time.' Did Lloyd Masters want the murder pinned on Cliff? 'Cliff needs a sharp criminal lawyer – somebody from outside of Eden.' She searched her mind for answers. 'I'm calling his parents in Atlanta.' Len couldn't understand why she was so emotionally involved. Later he'd know. 'I'll explain about Greg.' She didn't dare try to see Cliff. She mustn't introduce the suspicion of another woman in his life. That would only make things worse for him.

'Let me have the phone, Di.' Beth reached to take it from her. 'Len, if you talk to Cliff again, tell him the *Guardian* will be fighting to clear him. We know he's innocent.'

Battling self-consciousness – there was no time for that now, she told herself – Diane located the phone number for Cliff's parents' home. No one responded. All right, try the shop.

Diane was faintly breathless when someone at the shop responded. 'May I speak to Mr or Mrs Hendricks, please?'

'Mrs Hendricks is out of town.' Here in Eden, Diane guessed. 'I'll try to get Mr Hendricks to the phone . . .' The woman at the other end sounded distraught. 'Who shall I say is calling, please?'

'Diane Phillips. I – I'm a friend of Cliff's.'

'Oh.' The woman was suddenly alert. 'One moment, please.'

A moment later Bob Hendricks was on the line.

'Hello, Diane,' he said gently. She hadn't expected him to remember her.

'Mr Hendricks, I felt I had to call you. I understand an attorney named Gregory Lewis has been brought in by the hospital to represent Cliff. I think it's important he be removed from the case. He's a real estate lawyer – he knows nothing about criminal law.' And the prosecutor expected the grand jury to indict Cliff.

'I'll take care of that.' Mr Hendricks was grim. 'And thank you for alerting us, Diane.'

Her voice dropped to a whisper: 'Cliff's going to be cleared – I know he isn't guilty.'

The radio remained on in the *Guardian*'s office but Diane and Beth learnt no new details. Late in the afternoon Beth went out to pick up a copy of the *Evening News* at the newsstand two blocks south. Diane was at the door, waiting impatiently for her to return.

'It's all across the front page, of course,' Beth said wryly, handing over the newspaper. 'Nothing much new. She was fully clothed except for pantyhose – and one earring was missing. They think she was killed with a pair of scissors.'

'And Cliff has no alibi for the time she was killed.' Diane's eyes clung to this statement in the *Evening News*. Cliff had told the police that a conference scheduled in the research department had been cancelled for the evening. He'd gone home, remained there all evening. Alone.

'They're making a lot of the fact that he didn't call to report Sylvia missing,' Beth said. 'He was asleep – he didn't *know* she hadn't returned from Nancy's party.' She hesitated, radiating inner debate. 'The police know the relationship between Cliff and Sylvia was not good. A neighbour admitted to hearing noisy battles and –'

'That's not a motive for murder,' Diane interrupted. 'Lots of husbands and wives fight!' She fought for poise. 'Let's look at the situation logically. Sylvia never arrived at Nancy's party. So where did she go?'

'The district attorney alleges that when Cliff's conference was cancelled, he came home, fought with Sylvia – and killed her.' Beth sighed. 'It looks bad for him.'

'Then what the *Guardian* has to do is to prove she was

murdered by somebody else – a serial killer.' Diane was struggling for calm. 'Chris Robson died in 1943, before Cliff was born. Annie Williams died in 1957 – Cliff was a little boy then. He wasn't in Eden when Dr Taylor was killed. And now the serial killer has struck again.'

'Di, how do we *prove* that?' Beth protested gently.

Diane's mind charged into action. 'We'll reopen the other murders that haven't been solved. Chris Robson, Annie Williams, Dr Taylor. Prod people to come up with fresh information. Make them realize what's happened in this town!'

'Sylvia's murder isn't like the others. This time they have a suspect. I know Cliff isn't guilty,' Beth added before Diane could protest. 'But the police will never connect this with the other murders. And they see no link between each of those.'

'We have to flush the other murders out into the open, ask a lot of questions. So the police will scream we're maligning them. The *Herald* and the *Evening News* will tear us apart. *We have to prove that Sylvia was murdered by a serial killer.*'

'We'll run out of steam fast.' Beth was worried.

'No, we won't. Because we're going to go back and search every corner. No holds barred now.' Diane had refrained from talking to Mrs Robson, the mother of Chris, because of what Elvira had said. Mrs Taylor had been reluctant to talk – but just a little while ago she'd complained that not enough had been done to find her husband's killer. She'd possibly be more co-operative now. 'We'll interview Chris's mother and Mrs Taylor.' Annie Williams' family had moved away – nobody knew where. 'This is Cliff's life at stake!'

At 5.30, as they were preparing to leave the office, Len called.

'Why don't I pick up Chinese and bring it over to your place in a little while?' he said when Diane picked up the phone. 'You and Beth won't be in the mood to cook tonight.'

'That would be nice,' Diane told him gratefully. Had he seen Cliff again? Did he have more news?

On Friday nights Jennie and Nicole had sleep-overs at each other's apartments. This was Jennie's night to sleep over at

Nicole's. Ron would bring her home in time for breakfast tomorrow morning. With Jennie's bag packed for this small adventure Diane walked her over to the Tucker apartment, kissed her good night and talked briefly with Elise and Ron about the news of Sylvia's murder.

People knew that Cliff had been questioned, but still they were fearful. If he was innocent, a murderer remained on the loose.

'God, it's like Dr Taylor all over again,' Ron said sombrely. 'What is there about this town?'

'We have a serial murderer on the loose,' Diane said bluntly. 'Someone who kills every few years.'

Returning to the apartment, Diane found Len there. With the radio on for any possible news, he and Beth were transferring food from paper cartons to serving bowls.

'Len's discovered a great Chinese restaurant,' Beth told her. 'The China Garden.'

Tears blurred Diane's vision as her mind rushed back through the years. 'Cliff and I used to go there.' She saw the astonishment on Len's face. 'Cliff and I knew each other when he was a resident at Masters Memorial and I worked in the office there. It seems a million years ago . . .'

'He never said a word.' Len gazed from Diane to Beth, sensing there was more than Diane had revealed.

'We broke up – it was a crazy misunderstanding.' She fumbled for words. 'I went back home to New York . . .'

Len realized this was not the time to ask questions. He settled down to report what he knew. Using the lab as an excuse, he'd managed to see Cliff just before he'd come over to see Beth and Diane.

'Cliff said his father dumped the lawyer Lloyd Masters had hired for him. Some big-time criminal lawyer from Atlanta is scheduled to take over. He realizes he needs somebody on the ball.' Len was uneasy. 'The district attorney's been checking around town for word about his relationship with Sylvia. It was known their marriage was rocky.' Len shook his head in frustration. 'The maid was hysterical, I gather, when she found out what had happened. She went to the police and gave a statement about how Sylvia was upset because he'd threatened her. Not to kill her,' Len said impatiently. 'Cliff told her on the phone that evening that he'd cut off her charge cards if she didn't stop running up horrendous bills. The maid heard her yell, "Don't you threaten me, Cliff."'

'What are people saying at the hospital?' Diane asked.

'Nobody believes Cliff could do it.' He hesitated. 'Unless, somebody said, he just flipped out because she was such a bitch.'

Chapter Twenty-Seven

After a night of intermittent, troubled sleep, Diane came awake with reluctance. Her bedroom door was closed. She never closed the door. In sudden alarm she pulled herself into a semi-sitting position. Then the reassuring sounds of early Saturday morning TV cartoons reached her. Jennie was home. The aroma of freshly perking coffee filtered into the room.

She thrust aside the covers, slid her feet into slippers and left the bedroom.

'Hi, baby . . .' Diane crossed to hug her small daughter, sitting tailor-fashion on the floor. 'Not so close to the television.' An automatic reproach. Why did they all think they had to climb into the screen?

'Beth made me banana fritters,' Jennie said complacently without removing her gaze from the current cartoon.

'Were they good?' Diane shot a grateful glance towards Beth, bringing a mug of coffee into the dining area.

'Super.'

'Coffee?' Beth asked.

'I'll get it.' Diane headed into the kitchenette.

'I'll go into the office this morning.' Beth repeated her previous evening's offer. 'You work here at home till Jennie has to leave with Nicole for their birthday party.' After Len's departure, they'd roughly laid out the front page of the *Guardian*'s next issue, which had to be in the hands of the printer by 5 p.m. on Monday. The headline: 'SERIAL MURDERER LOOSE IN EDEN'.

'I'll go over all the print-outs from the microfilm machines,'

Diane said. The spoils of years of research. 'I'll call Mrs Taylor at a respectable hour –' she glanced at the clock. It was just minutes past eight o'clock. Too early – 'and ask her to see me.'

'She was cold last time,' Beth warned.

'Gerry said she's bitter now. The police haven't come up with one lead on Dr Taylor's murder. I'll use that as a wedge.' She turned to the kitchen radio, silent for now. 'Any news?'

'The coroner reported there was no indication of rape.'

Diane was startled. 'If Cliff's a suspect, why would that come up?'

'I gather his new lawyer asked because Sylvia's pantyhose were missing. I suppose he was hoping to point suspicion away from Cliff. The newscaster mentioned again the one earring that was missing. One of those custom deals Nancy makes up at Some Place Special. Clips-ons,' Beth added. 'You know how many women lose clip-ons.'

Diane brought her mug to the table, sat down. Jennie was still engrossed in the TV cartoon. This was the morning Cliff was to have seen her.

'I'd better get moving. Have breakfast, Di,' Beth urged. 'You'll need your strength. We have a rough time ahead of us.'

Diane waited until ten o'clock to call Zoe Taylor. Her heart pounding, she geared herself for what must be said. Her voice sounded strange, she thought, while she recited her prepared message.

'But what has this new murder to do with my husband's death?' Mrs Taylor asked guardedly.

'I suspect we're seeing the work of a serial murderer. If I could sit down and talk with you about this . . .'

'When would you like to come over?' An undercurrent of excitement in Zoe Taylor's voice now.

'As soon as possible.' Diane gripped the phone with aching intensity. Mrs Taylor wouldn't be cold this time.

Mrs Taylor was silent for a moment. 'This afternoon? About two?'

'That'll be fine.' Diane breathed a sigh of relief.

With the TV as a welcome baby-sitter Diane brought files into the living room, pored over their contents, pausing now and then to scribble on a legal pad points to emphasize when she met Mrs Taylor. She warned herself there was a chance that Mrs Taylor would run to Lloyd Masters with her accusation of a serial murderer that somehow involved him. She must make it clear she knew he wasn't the murderer – just the catalyst that seemed to bring on the killings. Still, she knew there was danger in antagonizing her grandfather. She was sure he played by his own rules.

The hours dragged until it was time for her interview with Mrs Taylor. She dawdled with Jennie over lunch, then dressed her for the afternoon's birthday party. Elise had volunteered to take the two little girls to the party and to drop Diane at the office.

In the car, Diane listened, only half-hearing, to Elise's report on the senior Tuckers' determination now to finance her opening a modest day care centre in town. Her mind focused on the approaching interview with Mrs Taylor. She breathed a sigh of relief when Elise pulled up at the office.

Diane hurried inside. 'Did you talk with Len?' she asked Beth.

'Yeah. He called a few minutes ago. He spoke with Cliff's parents this morning. They're terribly upset, but pleased with the way the new lawyer has jumped in. He tried for bail but that didn't work out.'

Diane shuddered. 'It makes me sick to think of Cliff in a jail cell.'

'Go talk to Mrs Taylor,' Beth ordered compassionately.

Mrs Taylor lived in a stately colonial house in the most exclusive section of Eden – two blocks east of the Masters house. A wing of the house had been Dr Taylor's office. Now the drapes were drawn, the sign removed.

A maid admitted Diane, led her to the living room. The furniture was tasteful and expensive. Dr Taylor had obviously enjoyed a lucrative practice – but then he'd been practicing in

Eden for over thirty years. When Mom and Dad lived here, Diane realized with a tightening in her throat. Had Mrs Taylor known Mom and Dad?

'Please come sit down, Miss Phillips.' Mrs Taylor's formality indicated a wariness. 'Would you like tea or coffee?'

'Either would be fine,' Diane said, all at once uncomfortable at being here.

'Please, don't cater to me.' Mrs Taylor was annoyed. 'You must have a preference.'

'Tea,' Diane said, and managed a shaky smile. 'I limit coffee to mornings and traumatic occasions.'

'Of which life has many.' Mrs Taylor turned to the maid, hovering at the door. 'Carrie, we'll have tea, please.'

'I know what I have to say may seem bizarre,' Diane began, 'but please hear me out.'

Mrs Taylor listened, her face impassive, while Diane explained her conviction that a serial killer had been operating in Eden at wide intervals over the past thirty-three years. She resurrected the still unsolved murders of Chris Robson and Annie Williams – and insisted Cliff had not murdered his wife.

'This will be another unsolved murder unless we track down the killer.' She hesitated, reading disbelief in Mrs Taylor's eyes. 'Don't you think it's bizarre that all these murders go unsolved?'

'Bizarre, yes. But what makes you believe a serial killer has been responsible?'

'All of the victims were in some fashion connected to Lloyd Masters,' Diane explained. 'Chris Robson was his daughter's classmate. Annie Williams was a maid in his house. Your husband was his friend and family doctor, and Sylvia Hendricks was the wife of a doctor at Masters Memorial. Lloyd Masters is not the killer,' she acknowledged hastily. 'He's the link.'

'But I don't understand.' Mrs Taylor was shaken. 'How can I help you?'

'I'd like to go over with you everything you can recall about the day your husband died.' Diane's voice was gentle. She knew the pain this would recreate in Mrs Taylor.

Mrs Taylor sat immobile, struggling to recall for a few moments. 'It was like any other day. Desmond made early hospital rounds right after breakfast, as usual. He came back here to his office for his appointments – between 10 a.m. and noon and again between one and four. He took a nap before dinner – which he always did – woke up and read the evening newspaper. After dinner he made a house call. He was one of those dedicated doctors who still made housecalls.' She was battling against tears now.

'A neighbour told me how wonderful he was about housecalls.' How awful of her to put Mrs Taylor thought this, Diane chastised herself. Yet Mrs Taylor wanted nothing so much as to see her husband's murderer brought to trial.

'He made his housecall, went to the hospital to look in on a patient. When he hadn't come home by midnight, I was anxious. I called the hospital. He was always so thoughtful. If he knew he'd be away far into the night, he'd have somebody call me. They said he'd left before 9 p.m. I was upset. I called the police. They found his car on the river road.' Her voice broke. 'His body was close by.'

'What specifically did the police do?' Diane probed.

'They did nothing!' A vein throbbed at Mrs Taylor's temple. 'Nothing! Oh, they talked to people at the hospital,' she conceded contemptuously. 'They questioned his housecall patient and the family. Nobody knew anything. They told me they'd questioned a vagrant. He had an alibi.'

'May I see Dr Taylor's office?' Diane asked.

'Of course.' Mrs Taylor glanced up as the maid arrived with the tea tray. 'Just put it down, Carrie. I'll pour. We'll have our tea first,' she told Diane.

While they sipped their tea, Mrs Taylor reminisced about her life with Dr Taylor. They'd had no children, but his nieces and nephews and hers had helped fill that void. Theirs had been a good marriage, Diane understood.

'Desmond and Lloyd Masters were friends for many years,' Mrs Taylor said. 'He had great sympathy for Lloyd – the trials that family went through with their son and their daughter. But why would somebody kill him because of his closeness to Lloyd?'

'That's what we're trying to find out, Mrs Taylor.'

'Let me show you his office.' Mrs Taylor rose to her feet. 'I haven't changed a thing since that day. I can't bring myself to go in there. Once a week Carrie goes in and cleans.'

At the office door, Mrs Taylor hesitated, then opened it. Winter sunlight managed to filter through the drapes at the windows of the reception room. Diane visualized the pleasant reception room filled with waiting patients.

'The door on the left ...' Mrs Taylor pointed to the area beyond. 'I'll show you Desmond's office.'

The office was a small, carpeted room furnished with a large leather-topped desk, three chairs, and a pair of lamps. Feeling herself an intruder, yet knowing she must search for whatever tiny lead might be here, Diane walked into the room. She focused on the desk calendar, reading the list of patients who had been seen by Dr Taylor that final day of his life. And then her eyes settled on a memo pad at one side of the desk.

Excitement spiralled in her as she reached to pick up the memo pad. Initials were scrawled across the small page: L. M.

'Did you see this?'

'I haven't been in here since Desmond died,' Mrs Taylor reminded, moving forward to inspect the page. She stared blankly for an instant. 'What does it mean?'

'Dr Taylor must have seen or talked with Lloyd Masters some time in the course of that day.'

'But what does that mean?' Mrs Taylor repeated, bewildered.

'Every victim of an unsolved murder in Eden in the past thirty-three years was in some way involved with Lloyd Masters,' Diane reiterated. 'Something in Lloyd Masters' life motivated these murders.' Diane paused, all at once feeling exhausted. 'Until we can figure out what that is, we're nowhere.'

Diane drove back to the office, frustrated, yet feeling herself at the edge of a breakthrough. She told Beth about the memo pad bearing Lloyd Masters' initials.

'There's still that missing piece.' Beth sighed.

'I need to talk to Chris Robson's mother,' Diane said. 'Maybe she'll supply that.'

'You said Elvira told you she was getting on in years and frail,' Beth cautioned.

'I have to try. Where's the phone book?'

Diane dialled Mrs Robson's phone number, still listed under the name of her late husband. She waited impatiently for a response. On the tenth ring she hung up.

'She's not there.'

'So you'll try her later,' Beth shrugged this off.

Not until Sunday morning was Diane able to reach Mrs Robson on the phone. She explained that the *Guardian* was preparing an in-depth story about the unsolved murders in Eden – going back to the murder of Chris Robson. She paused at the sound of Mrs Robson's strangled gasp.

'Why must you bring up all that horror again?' Mrs Robson whispered in anguish.

'Because we hope to push the police into some action now. We suspect these murders are all the work of one killer. May I come over and talk to you about this?'

'I – I don't know what I can do,' Mrs Robson said after a leaden pause. 'But yes, I'll talk with you if you like. Not tomorrow,' she said. 'I'm going to Atlanta on a day trip with my Senior Citizens' group. But Tuesday morning if you like.'

'Tuesday will be fine,' Diane agreed, fretting in silence at this delay. 'Around ten o'clock?'

'Ten o'clock,' Mrs Robson agreed, yet Diane sensed that already she regretted this decision.

'Perhaps it's just as well you won't be seeing her until Tuesday,' Beth consoled Diane. 'We've got a hell of a lot of work to do between now and 5 p.m. tomorrow.'

Lloyd Masters looked up in annoyance as Clark burst into his office without being announced – without even a knock – and closed the door behind him.

'Clark, you're losing control of yourself.' Didn't the bastard understand they could carry this off only if he stayed cool?

'That fucking newspaper – you know, that weekly giveaway . . .' Clark swallowed hard, struggling for composure.

'What about it?'

'The word's running around town. The publisher went to Zoe Taylor with a story about a serial killer being on the loose here. The *Guardian*'s claiming Cliff Hendricks didn't kill his wife, the serial killer did. It'll be spread all over the front of their next edition.'

'Oh no, it won't!' Lloyd rose menacingly behind his desk. 'Because you're going over to Comstock Printing and you're telling Doug McIntyre he's refusing to print the *Guardian* any longer. Starting today.'

'What makes you think he'll go along with that?' Clark was dubious.

'Damn it, Clark, I own that building. Tell him he dumps the *Guardian* right now – or when his lease comes up for renewal in five months, the rent will be doubled.'

'Can we get away with that?' Clark's air of panic was receding.

'We can do it. That's commercial property. There's no kind of control in effect. You get over there and you tell him there'll be no edition of the *Guardian* out on Thursday.'

'That'll take care of one week's newspaper,' Clark admitted, but he was still uneasy.

'Before the *Guardian* can get its act together, the Eden police will have a case against Cliff Hendricks that will be airtight. We'll find a witness who saw him dump his wife's body on the river bank on Friday night. Work it out with Luke. That'll puncture their balloon.'

The Christmas lights were already bathing Main Street in warm colour when Diane – lugging a huge portfolio – hurried from the car and into the *Guardian*'s storefront space.

'You won't believe what's happened!' Pale and breathless,

Diane rushed towards Beth's desk. 'Doug McIntyre has dumped us. He said he won't be able to handle the paper any longer. Starting today,' she added grimly, dropping the portfolio on the desk.

'Lloyd Masters!' Beth was unnerved. 'I was afraid of something like this when we started with the serial killer story. But how did he find out?'

'Mrs Taylor must have said something to somebody – not thinking, I suppose, that it'd get around town so fast.' Diane sat down in sudden exhaustion.

'Where'll we find a printer who'll get the paper out by Thursday noon?'

'In Atlanta or Marietta or maybe in Columbus.' Diane's face was etched in determination. 'For a price we'll have the printing done! We start making calls first thing tomorrow morning. Make it clear that money is no object. What we want is delivery on time.'

'You have an appointment with Mrs Robson tomorrow morning,' Beth reminded.

'You make calls to printers. I'll keep the appointment, then rush back to the office. The next edition of the *Guardian* has to come out on schedule. The district attorney has to know that voices are raised on Cliff's behalf in this town.' She paused. 'Oh God, I wish I could go to see him!'

Tuesday morning was dank and cold. Diane drove slowly, going over in her mind the directions Ron had given her because she was unfamiliar with this part of town. It was an area of run-down houses, ill-kept grounds. Here it was, a modest, white clapboard, set on a tiny but neat plot, a narrow flagstone walk leading up to the entrance.

She sat in the car, recalling what Elvira had told her about Chris Robson. His father had suffered a massive stroke three days after his death. His mother – who'd married right out of high school – had had to go out to work to support them. Mr Robson died twelve years ago. Mrs Robson had retired in 1973.

Lloyd Masters had sent a cheque to Anne Robson every month from the time of Ray's stroke until he died.

Diane left the car and walked up to the house. Mrs Robson, a small, slender woman with short white hair, her face devoid of cosmetics except for a dusting of powder, was at the door. With an air of wistful excitement, she led Diane into a small, impeccably neat living room. Diane saw the collection of photographs that lined the mantelpiece: Chris, from babyhood to his high school days.

'I was shocked to hear about the death of Mrs Hendricks,' Mrs Robson said, 'but I thought the police were sure her husband had killed her.'

'Mrs Robson, Cliff is innocent. His wife was another victim of a serial killer here in Eden. There have been three unsolved murders in Eden. Your son, a woman named Annie Williams, and Dr Taylor.' She mustn't talk about Dad. That would come later. 'Annie Williams worked for Lloyd Masters. Dr Taylor was the Masters family doctor – and Chris was a classmate of Alison Masters.' Her heart began to pound as she saw Anne Robson's sudden agitation. She clutched at this. 'Mrs Robson, tell me about Chris and Alison Masters.'

'I swore I'd never tell,' she whispered, clasping her hands in tormented recall. 'It seemed the right thing. Why cause Alison more grief?'

'You could be saving Cliff's life.' Diane leant forward urgently. 'What weren't you supposed to tell anyone?'

'It was so awful. Chris and Alison were going together – the way high school kids do. He borrowed his father's car so he could drive them to a movie. It was during the war – gas was rationed. But it was his birthday, so his father said he could take the car. They were on the road when a bunch of hoodlums blocked their way. They raped Alison and killed my boy.' She closed her eyes as though to deny recall.

'Mrs Robson, please go on . . .'

'Alison walked to a phone booth at a gas station half a mile down the road and called her father. She was out of her mind already but still knew enough to call him. He picked her up and went to the car. Chris was dead. He notified the police. They agreed to say nothing about Alison's being raped. It was clear she was in no mental state to identify either the ones who raped her or the one who fired the gun that killed Chris. Nobody was allowed to question Alison – Dr Taylor said it would be useless. And Mr Masters wanted to protect her. Nobody was to know about the rape, though it did get around town. She never went back to school. She's never left the house since that night. There's always been a nurse to keep her sedated.'

'I'm sorry to have to put you through this,' Diane said softly.

Why hadn't her grandfather allowed the police to question Alison? Perhaps it would have been useless, but shouldn't the effort have been made?

'It was wrong of me to talk like this,' Mrs Robson chastised herself. 'Mr Masters has been so good to us through the years. But hearing about this latest murder brought it all back so sharply. I want so much to know before I die,' she said with a sudden surge of strength, 'that whoever killed my boy will pay for it.'

Gerry sat in silence beside Clark as he drove. She was conscious of how little they talked since the night she had threatened to call the police if he hit her again. Just as well, she told herself – considering he'd been in such a foul mood for the past three days.

'God, I'm sick of these family dinners,' Clark grumbled as he turned into the driveway of the Masterses' house. 'Why does there have to be a dinner party every time your mother returns from some place?'

'They don't enthral me either,' Gerry said, eliciting a fast glance of surprise from him. Until now she'd always pretended she looked forward to family gatherings.

'All your mother and sisters ever talk about are clothes and their next pit stop,' Clark drawled contemptuously. 'And your father's so pissed at Carter's election he's talking about not going to Washington for the inauguration. I was supposed to go with him and your mother. I need some Washington exposure.'

'He'll change his mind.' Clark hadn't expected her to go, she noted with relief. She loathed playing the devoted wife. How had Mother endured it all these years?

Walking into the house, Gerry geared herself for a dull evening. Though tonight, she surmised, there'd be much talk about Sylvia Hendricks' murder. The whole town talked of nothing else. She couldn't believe that Cliff Hendricks was guilty. Diane and Beth were convinced he couldn't be.

In the living room her two brothers-in-law were deep in Georgia political conversation with her father. Clark strode across the room to join them.

'Gerry, you should run down to Palm Beach and get some tan,' her mother said after a perfunctory exchange of greetings. 'You're always so pale.'

'Mother, tell us what you bought in New York,' Linda ordered. 'Mostly resort clothes?'

Gerry stood by in strained patience while the other three women discussed the merits of Bill Blass, Yves Saint-Laurent, and Oscar de la Renta. Gerry was relieved when they were ordered to the dinner table. Food would be a diversion.

'No talk about the murder at the dinner table,' Lloyd Masters ordered when Peggy launched into an avid report about Sylvia Hendricks' missing pantyhose. 'Her husband's a member of the hospital research team, so I instructed Hugh to hire him a lawyer. At hospital expense,' he emphasized. 'But he fired the man, hired somebody else. It's his problem now. He's probably guilty as hell.'

'But isn't it strange that she was dressed for a cocktail party, but her –'

'Nothing morbid at the table,' Maureen stopped her. 'Lloyd, what's this Clark tells me about your not going to Washington for the inauguration? I was looking forward to it.'

'God, they're making such a show of it!' Lloyd grunted in

disgust. 'A special train out of Atlanta.' He exchanged supercilious glances with Clark. 'If we go, it'll be on the company plane.'

As usual, the men retired to the library for coffee and cigars. The women were served their coffee in the living room. Gerry sneaked covert glances at her watch. Thank God, Dad usually called the evening over at ten o'clock sharp.

'Oh, damn –' She frowned at the broken nail on her right index finger. 'I broke a nail,' she interrupted the trio involved in trashing Rosalyn Carter for her taste in clothes. 'All the way down. I'll run up to one of the guest rooms for some nail scissors and a Bandaid.'

Grateful for an escape even at the price of a broken nail, Gerry went upstairs to the guest room her father liked to call 'the presidential suite'. There was bound to be a manicure set there. She hurried inside, crossed to the dressing table and found all she needed. As she turned to leave she noticed a huge dark stain on the beige carpet. As though somebody had spilled a bottle of ink or paint, she thought curiously. Her mother hadn't been in here since she got back or she would have noticed it.

All at once a small, bright object – half-hidden beneath the bed – captured her attention. She reached to pick it up, inspected the circlet of magenta taffeta and black lace. It was an earring, she saw – designed to match a dinner gown or a cocktail dress. Sylvia Hendricks had been wearing a magenta taffeta and black lace cocktail dress when her body was found.

On impulse Gerry dropped to her knees, lifted the valance and looked under the bed. For an anguished moment she stared at a pair of sheer black pantyhose.

Sylvia Hendricks' earring. Sylvia Hendricks' black pantyhose. In her father's house.

Chapter Twenty-Eight

Gerry emerged from the shower, reached for a lush lilac bath towel. She'd hoped for some relief from the tension that created pain between her shoulder blades, but the ache remained. She'd slept little last night – in constant battle with her conscience. The earring she'd found in her parents' guest room last night lay hidden in a tray in her jewellery chest.

How could she implicate her father? Was there some weird explanation for what she'd discovered in that room – something that had nothing to do with Sylvia Hendricks' murder? Yet how could she allow Cliff Hendricks to be tried for a crime she couldn't believe he'd committed

She flinched in recall of that moment she'd identified the earring and then – for no logical reason – stopped to glance beneath the bed. She felt sick again, visualizing the pair of black pantyhose there. She remembered the huge blob of ink on the beige carpet – meant to conceal a bloodstain?

Wrapped in the towel she went into her bedroom to dress. From the floor below came the raucous sound of the vacuum cleaner. As though this was just another day. If she told the police about the earring, about the pantyhose that had been swept under the bed, she'd be exposing her family to disgrace. Not just her father – her mother, her sisters and their husbands, her nieces and nephew. But who else could have been in that bedroom with Sylvia Hendricks except Dad?

Then with a cataclysmic impact an answer leapt into her mind. *Clark had a key to the house.* Clark had come home reeking of sultry perfume, with stray blonde hairs on his jacket.

Sylvia Hendricks was a blonde. Had Clark brought her to the house because he knew no one would be there – and killed her in a moment of rage?

How could she deal with this? What was she to do?

Three hours of frenzied phone calling this morning had elicited a firm willing to take on the printing of this week's *Guardian* despite the tight deadline. They'd run around the clock, deliver by noon on Thursday. Beth was preparing to drive to Atlanta with the mock-up when Len walked into the storefront.

'I'm on my lunch break,' he said. 'I brought coffee and turkey sandwiches for the three of us. Is that OK?'

'Great.' Diane forced a smile.

'Have I got time to eat?' Beth was doubtful.

'You'll be there fifteen minutes later,' Diane said. 'Eat.' She turned to Len with wistful hope. 'Anything new from Cliff's attorney?'

Len focused on opening his coffee container. 'Nothing good.'

'What do you mean?' Diane exchanged an anxious glance with Beth.

'He got word that the police have some witness.' Len sighed. 'Somebody's out to pin this on Cliff, no question about that. The witness said he saw Cliff dump Sylvia's body on the river bank. He wrote down the licence number –'

'This happened Friday night!' Beth exploded. 'Now he comes forward?'

'He told the police he was nervous about getting involved, then his conscience got the better of him and he came forward.'

'It's a lie,' Diane whispered. 'Lloyd Masters set this up!'

'We'll have a hell of time proving it,' Len warned. 'But the attorney's out working on it already.'

Gerry stood by the window and watched twilight creep in. She'd remained secluded in her bedroom for much of the day, torn between conflicting directions of mind and heart. Early in the afternoon she'd dismissed Josie for the day. When Clark came home from the office, she'd confront him with what she knew. Had he or her father killed Sylvia Hendricks?

In the fading daylight she saw a red Jaguar turn into the driveway and pull to a stop. Clark emerged and strode towards the door. Talk to Clark now. Demand the truth from him. She couldn't run away any longer.

She was at the head of the stairs when the phone rang. She went back to her bedroom to pick it up.

'Hello?'

'Has Clark come home yet?' her father asked brusquely.

'He just came in. Hold on.' She went into the hall. Clark was in the foyer now. 'Clark, Dad wants to talk to you.'

'I'll take it in the den.'

Gerry returned to the phone. She heard Clark's voice.

'What's up, Lloyd?'

'Get your ass over here. We need to talk!'

Gerry returned to the window, watched while Clark climbed behind the wheel of his car and drove away. What did Dad and Clark have to talk about that was so urgent? She thought again about the earring hidden in her jewellery chest, the black pantyhose that lay forgotten beneath the bed. Why was she waiting to confront Clark? How could she be silent about what she knew when Cliff Hendricks' life was at stake?

Her hands trembling, she reached for the phone and dialled Diane's number. Let Diane be home while she had the courage to speak about the unspeakable . . .

Diane heard the phone begin to ring as she put the key in the lock of the apartment door, heard Jennie and Beth debating in the kitchen over the merits of spaghetti versus tuna noodle casserole for dinner and seeming in no rush to answer the phone.

'Damn!' Diane was clumsy in her anxiety. *Don't stop ringing.* There, the key turned over; the door was open. She charged to the phone as Beth headed in the same direction.

'Hello?'

'Diane, could you come over to the house?' Gerry asked

urgently. 'I need to show you something. I – I don't know how to deal with it . . .'

'I'll be right over,' Diane said.

'What's up?' Beth reacted to the alarm in her voice.

'I don't know – but I will in a few minutes.'

Clark hadn't started up with physical violence again, had he? Diane churned with anxiety as she collected her coat and, car keys. She'd warned Gerry to call the police if he laid a finger on her again, but Gerry had worried about the family's reaction to this. To the devil with the family! It was Gerry's safety that was important.

Night had closed in about the town by the time Diane arrived at Gerry's house. She hurried through the damp cold to the door.

Gerry was waiting for her in the foyer.

'Are you all right?' Diane asked anxiously.

'I'm all right, but I must show you something. It's upstairs in my room.'

In her bedroom Gerry strode across the floor to her jewellery chest, reached into a drawer, pulled out a small object. Diane waited – breathless.

'Look at this.' Gerry's voice was taut. 'Could this be Sylvia Hendricks' missing earring?'

Diane gazed in shock at the magenta taffeta and black lace covered disc – the description in the police report flashing across her mind.

'It's Sylvia's.' Diane was giddy with excitement. 'Where did you find it?'

Gerry took a deep breath. 'It was on the floor of the guest bedroom at my father's house.' With one swift movement she returned it to the jewellery chest, as though it were a poisonous insect capable of biting. 'How can I tell the police I found this in a guest room in my father's house? And under the bed,' she whispered, 'I saw a pair of black nylon pantyhose.'

'Gerry, you have to tell them!'

'It might not be my father.' Gerry fought to continue. 'It could have been Clark. My father or my husband.' She shook her head with an air of disbelief. 'This is a nightmare . . .'

'It's a nightmare for Cliff,' Diane said gently. But this would clear him. *If* Gerry would talk to the police.

'Cliff's such a fine man, I know – no matter who was being held – I should clear him. My mind tells me that, but how can I bring such disgrace to my family?'

Diane deliberated a moment. 'Gerry, I want to tell you something nobody in this town knows. Only Beth – and Cliff. I knew him six years ago, here in Eden. We were very much in love.'

'Oh, Di . . .' Gerry radiated compassion.

'We planned on being married when he finished his residency. We didn't plan on my getting pregnant –'

'Cliff is Jennie's father?'

'I was supposed to go back to New York for an abortion. It was the wrong time for us to have a child. But I wanted her so much. I broke off with Cliff, allowed him to think I'd had the abortion. It was just the wrong time for us to be married. Gerry, it's Jennie's father being wrongly accused of murder.'

'I have to face my father and Clark with what I know.' Gerry's voice was anguished but determined. 'Will you go with me?'

'Of course I'll go with you. But leave the earring here,' Diane cautioned, and saw instant comprehension in Gerry's eyes.

With a mutual sense of urgency Diane and Gerry hurried from the house.

'I'll drive,' Diane said. 'Let's take my car.'

Diane geared herself for the imminent invasion of her grandfather's house. A house where her father had spent much of his life, when he wasn't away at boarding school or summer camps. A house where her mother had suffered endless indignities.

'You're coming in with me?' Gerry asked when Diane pulled up before the Masters house. Wind was whistling through the trees.

'I'll be with you, Gerry.' This would be an explosive confrontation.

The front door was unlocked. They walked inside, heard two men arguing loudly.

'They're in the library,' Gerry said. Diane followed her across the foyer and down the hall.

'Damn it, Clark, how could you make such a fucking mess of this?' Lloyd Masters shouted. 'You're supposed to be so sharp!'

'How could I know the man's wife would tell the D A he was an alcoholic liar? That he was out cold that night?'

'It's your business to know! That's what I pay you for!'

'Look, this is your problem, not mine!' Now Clark was defiant.

'Don't you –' Lloyd stopped dead at the sight of Gerry and Diane at the entrance to the library. 'What are you doing here, Gerry?' His eyes settled on Diane. 'And what's *she* doing here?'

'This is Diane,' Gerry told him quietly. 'Kevin's daughter.'

Why had she said that, Diane asked herself in shock.

'She has a right to be with me.'

Lloyd's face was drained of colour. 'I don't believe it!' he blustered, and turned on Diane. 'And even if you are, don't think you can come down here and get money out of me! I –'

'I don't want your money!' Diane lashed back. 'I wouldn't touch it. You're an evil man. I came to Eden to find out why you lied about my father's murder.'

'Kevin killed himself. Dr Taylor testified to his deep depression. He –'

'You know that's a lie!' Diane broke in. 'For thirty-three years you've been lying for the serial killer who's haunted Eden. Why? Who are you protecting?'

'I don't think a serial killer murdered Sylvia Hendricks,' Gerry picked up with perilous calm, commanding her father's attention. 'After dinner last night I broke a fingernail. I went up to your "presidential guest room" for a Bandaid. On the floor, peeking out from under the bed, I found Sylvia Hendricks' missing earring. I –'

'Where is it?' Clark exchanged a startled glance with his father-in-law.

'Where it's safe. And under the bed I saw a pair of black pantyhose. Sylvia Hendricks was murdered in that room.' Gerry's eyes swept from her husband to her father. 'By one of you!'

'It wasn't like that,' Clark sputtered. 'She –'

'Shut up, Clark!' Lloyd ordered, his eyes moving over the heads of the two women. 'I'll be right back . . .' He was striding to the door.

What had diverted him, Diane asked herself.

'I didn't kill her,' Clark said while Lloyd disappeared down the hall. They heard heavy footsteps heading up the stairs. 'I'm not taking the blame for something I didn't do!'

'Dad killed her?' Gerry asked in an agonized whisper.

'No!' Clark dismissed this impatiently. 'It was your crazy sister. Her nurse was in a drunken stupor. Alison sneaked downstairs. You know she does that sometimes, usually when she's out of cigarettes. She came into the room. It was dark. We didn't know she was there. She plunged a pair of scissors into Sylvia's back. *Alison* killed her!'

All at once their attention was diverted by loud voices somewhere in the house.

'I told you, Alison! Never smoke near the drapes. Look what you almost did!'

'I remember, Daddy! It all came back to me! I saw them in bed, and I remembered! *You killed Chris!* You didn't want me to do it with him. Only with you! You always said it was our secret –'

'Alison, what the hell are you doing?' Lloyd Masters' voice was harsh with alarm. 'Put down that kerosene lamp! You'll burn down the house!'

'I remember everything now! How I was so mad at Kevin because he was fighting with you that I took the gun from your desk drawer, and I shot him. I killed Annie because you were mad at her for something. I killed Dr Taylor because I was tired of all those needles in my arms! I didn't remember then about Chris. Not till I saw *them* in bed – like you and me, Daddy. Why did you have to kill Chris?'

'I smell smoke!' Diane punctured the stunned silence of the three in the library. She raced from the library to the hall, saw smoke already seeping from an upper floor, started up the stairs.

'Clark, call 911!' Gerry yelled, trailing Diane.

At the top of the stairs they halted. Flames, darting from the third-floor room that had long been Alison's sanctuary, were forming a barrier. They heard Alison's hysterical sobbing, Lloyd Masters' agonized efforts to calm her.

'We have to get them out of there.' Gerry rushed to mount the second flight of stairs. Diane drew her back as intense heat surged towards them.

'We can't get through!'

'They'll die!' Gerry started forward again, then retreated.

'The fire trucks will be here in minutes.' Clark called to them from down below. 'Come on down! We have to get out of the house!'

They stood before the house in the dank December cold while flames darted through the windows, fed by the rising wind. Knowing there was no way to save the two imprisoned in that third-floor room. Doubting that they wanted to be saved. Disbelieving, stunned by Alison's disclosures. Gerry clung to Diane's hand. The two women were sickened by what they'd heard, what was happening.

Oh yes, Diane thought in anguish, pieces were falling into place now. The father who loved only his oldest daughter. The man who crept into a paediatrics ward late at night, alone and unobserved. The caring nurse who had been banished to hide his sordid secret. The wife who was seldom home – running from reality.

'The fire trucks are here.' Clark heard the sirens that heralded their approach. By now, flames were shooting through the third-floor windows, embracing the overhang of the roof. No chance that Alison and Lloyd Masters could be brought out alive. 'Look, nobody heard what Alison said! We don't know what happened up there! It would ruin the family!'

'We heard,' Diane defied him, knowing Gerry would confirm this. 'Cliff Hendricks is not going to be convicted for a murder he didn't commit.'

*   *   *

It was close to midnight – the temperature at a record low – when Diane and Gerry walked with the younger of the two detectives to his waiting car. The house garishly surrounded by yards of yellow tape that marked it as a crime scene. One fire truck remained on the scene as a precautionary measure. Dishevelled and shaken, Clark was climbing into another car with the other detective.

Earlier Clark had summoned his personal attorney on his car phone. The call finished, he'd approached Gerry and Diane with grim determination.

'Let's keep our stories straight – for the least possible damage.'

'We'll tell the truth,' Gerry had said. 'There's no other way.'

Diane knew the anguish Gerry felt at the death of her father and sister. But the truth must come out. Clark understood it was safer to confess to adultery than to be involved in Sylvia's murder – though he would be indicted for obstructing justice. Still, with some manipulation and a sharp lawyer he might come off with a suspended sentence and probation. And Gerry had grounds for divorce. Her mother couldn't stop her now.

'It'll be warm in the car in a few minutes,' the detective said with an air of apology as he pulled away from the kerb. 'The heat comes up fast.'

'We're all right,' Gerry said quietly.

At the police station Diane and Gerry gave their statements. They were aware that Clark and his attorney were closeted in another room. Some of the Masters mystique remained, Diane thought as the detective arranged for a police officer to drive Gerry and her back to the house to pick up her car.

'Would you rather be dropped off at your house first?' Diane asked. A return to her house would inflict fresh pain for Gerry. Then I'll pick up my car.'

'Could I stay with you tonight?' Gerry's eyes a mute plea.

'Of course.' Diane reached to take Gerry's hand in hers for a moment.

'Oh God! Peggy and Linda don't know! Mother doesn't

know!' Maureen Masters was on one of her trips to New York. 'I'll tell Peggy and Linda tonight. I'll call my mother in the morning.'

'I must phone Cliff's parents.' Diane's face aglow. 'They'll be so relieved that Cliff will be cleared.' Technically, she understood, Cliff would not be instantly vindicated. There were channels to go through. But she must let his mother and father know what had happened.

At the apartment, Beth waited up in obvious anxiety.

'Cliff's going to be cleared,' Diane told Beth. 'I must call his parents.'

'At this hour?' Beth was doubtful.

'Beth, it's great news. Let them know.'

'And I'll call Len.' Her face was bright with love. 'He'll be so relieved.'

Only Jennie slept well this night, Diane thought when the three women abandoned a pretense of sleeping and gathered in the dining area for coffee. It was a few minutes before 7 a.m. Residents would be picking up their morning papers at their doors or tuning in on the morning news. They'd be stunned by the sordid revelations that radio and television newscasters would give them.

'I'll wait till nine to call my mother.' Gerry closed her eyes a moment. 'Peggy and Linda said that I should be the one to tell her. Luke will handle funeral arrangements.'

Diane understood there would be no fine memorial service for Lloyd Masters and his oldest daughter, just a quiet, private burial away from the accusing eyes of the shocked community.

'Would you like us to go with you to the funeral?' Beth asked gently. The charred bodies must first be released by the police department.

'Would you?' Gerry's eyes moved gratefully from Beth to Diane.

'We'll be with you,' Diane promised.

'The others will remain in town only long enough for the will to be read,' Gerry surmised. She managed a faint smile. 'But I'll be here. You're my real family.'

This morning, Diane resolved, Jennie would not attend her kindergarten class. In two or three hours, she hoped, with all the necessary formalities out of the way, Cliff would walk out of the police station. Jennie would go with her and Beth to the office. Instinct told her Cliff would come to her there. He knew he had a date to meet his daughter.

'I dread going back into my house, but it has to be done.' Gerry's voice brought her back to the moment. 'What's the old platitude about life going on?'

'We'll drop you off on our way to the office,' Beth told her.

'I'll call my mother then.' Gerry paused in inner debate. 'This isn't the time to talk about such things, but I want you both to know. My father's will divides his estate between my mother and my sisters and me. I mean to use my inheritance to join with you in establishing a daily newspaper here in Eden. Oh, I know Luke and Hugh will sell off the *Herald* and the *Evening News* and they'll continue to run – but our newspaper will be the voice of the community.' Her eyes moved from Diane to Beth. 'That's what you two want, isn't it?'

'That's what we want.' Tears welled in Diane's eyes. This would be Dad and Mom's memorial – a newspaper dedicated to their ideals.

'It's terrible to say it at a time like this, but I feel reborn.' Gerry's eyes reflected a blend of pain and hope. 'I know where I'm going with my life.'

At shortly before nine Beth pulled up before Gerry's house. In time, Diane guessed, Gerry would sell and move into a place not tainted by the past.

'We'll talk later.' Gerry leant forward to kiss Jennie, managed a smile for the other two, and left the car. She walked to the stairs that led to the house she'd shared with Clark, but which her father had contrived to deed in her name.

Now Beth drove towards the office. Diane sat in silence while Beth carried on a lively conversation with Jennie – who couldn't know that her whole life was about to change. Jennie had lost a great-grandfather and a great-aunt – but she was about to welcome her father.

Diane focused on how to make Jennie understand that her father was alive. Jennie knew only that she was about to receive a surprise.

'Mommie, what?' she pleaded yet again while the two women settled in the office. 'What?'

'It's a big surprise,' Beth reminded. 'You'll just have to wait for it to happen.'

Shortly after nine, Diane saw Cliff approaching the storefront entrance. She rushed forward to meet him. They clung together for a few moments in rapturous reunion.

'Jennie, there's your surprise,' Diane heard Beth say softly. 'That's your daddy.'

Cliff released Diane. His face luminous, he walked with deliberate slowness towards Jennie – knowing this was a traumatic moment for her. She mustn't be frightened. He dropped to his haunches, held out his arms in a tentative gesture of affection. But she must make the next move.

'Are you really, really my daddy?' she asked after a moment.

'You bet I am.'

'Can I tell Nicole?' She lifted her face to Diane. 'Mommie, can I tell Nicole?'

'Of course, you can tell her, darling.'

'Daddy, Daddy!' Jennie hurled herself into his arms.

Somewhere a young nurse who had tried to right a terrible wrong would know that she had been vindicated. Chris Robson's mother would know her son's murder had been avenged. Zoe Taylor would know her husband's murder had been avenged. And Diane had fulfilled her mother's last wish.

A family that had almost died in the Holocaust was alive and would flourish.